CATALYST

Catalyst

L.A. Rae

Catalyst

Cover art by Jade Merien

ISBN (Paperback): 979-8-9863633-0-1

For Momma.

Your unconditional love and support is everything

In Loving Memory of Vixey. 2010-2022

PROLOGUE
SAYING GOODBYE

"Take me for a ride Lykos, just one last run. I want to feel the wind in my face."

My mother's words were the most precious thing in the world, now that any one might be her last. The lilting voice shook, rattling with the raspy shutters of lungs plagued with sickness. Hazel eyes that had dulled these past months, now shone oddly with life. Acceptance had settled over her weeks before, neatly folding away the worries of the world for someone else to discover.

She swore she had fulfilled her purpose and that Nemesis would be waiting for her. She said the Goddess had guided her to me when I was an infant. That the Gods had lost their sway over humans and disappeared as a result didn't seem to matter. She claimed they were still watching and because she was devout, Nemesis still spoke to her when she could. I never could decide if I believed or not. Though perhaps I, above all others, should have.

Now that I was grown, my mother said she couldn't keep me here any longer. I'd argued, but she had merely smiled and wrapped me in a hug. She knew as well as I did that I would never leave her alone. Weeks later she got sick; that had been a month ago.

There was nothing that could prepare me for this day, which she claimed was her last.

Nothing.

My chest felt tight, tears had threatened to break free all morning, but I had to be strong. I'd do anything for my mother, even if the smile she gave me broke my heart. She was ready, but I would never be. There was nothing I could do but try to make her last day everything she desired of it.

Her slim hand shook as she held it out to me, rising from bed onto limbs that had once been strong and bold, but had now withered away. The gray strands of hair framing my mother's face were just as wild as I'd always remembered them. The hue reminded me that she had seen far more years than most, though her face didn't look a year past fifty. There had never been color to her hair, not for all my twenty-eight years. She claimed it was a blessing from Nemesis, though she would never explain exactly what that meant.

"Alright, Momma, one last run."

I could only whisper the words, too scared anything louder would break under the pressure and reveal just how scared I was to see this day through. So much was welling up within, sending my mind spinning with everything I should say. When my mouth opened, she smiled up at me and I couldn't speak. Love poured over me as she smiled. There was no fear in her eyes, and no worry wrinkles at the corners of her lips and eyes.

She looked happy and excited.

All the words I wanted to say died on my lips, tears welling up as my jaw clenched and chewed in an attempt to contain my emotions. The world disappeared as I closed my eyes. A lifetime of memories were displayed in the darkness, imprints of her, that I feared would one day fade. A cool hand pressed against the heat of my cheeks, a mother's loving caress.

"Do not be sad my little fox. My adventure ends today, but yours is only just beginning. The answers you seek are out there, beckoning." The words grew sharp edges and stabbed me in the heart, a sob escaping my lips even as she stood and held me close. Even at her body's frailest, her spirit remained the strongest force I'd ever witnessed. Fingers cupped my chin, forcing it up so that I had to open my eyes and look at her. All the words in the world would fall short of that inescapable typhoon of love. Once again my lips parted, but no words fell out as my throat closed off, the air seeming void of oxygen. A nod would have to suffice.

Our home was not large, but we had built it ourselves when the villager's tolerance of my shifting was depleted. A cute baby kitsune was easy to accept, but a beast the size of a horse was not. Fear drove us to the edge, but their love for my mother kept them tolerant of our presence. My life was peaceful and mostly happy, but with every year I grew more restless as the persistent and strange dreams became clearer.

As I helped her out of her bed and into our open living area, it was very obvious how frail she had become. The once thick frame of her build had withered away, wiry muscle now in the place of a warrior's bulk. She stood proudly, but I could feel the shake in her step.

I moved into the living room of our cozy two bedroom cabin. My mother waited, leaning on the wooden kitchen table as I let the magic within take over. As the first waves rippled through me, I focused on the details of our cabin to help me breathe through it. Long ago I had built the table and carved out its body for shelves. It was the only thing that separated the open living space from the kitchen. The walls that separated our rooms were also wood, but the outer walls were made of stone. The thatched roof, as well as the floor and walls, were all held together with sunbaked river clay. The color was like rust, its warm hue reminding me of a sunrise peeking between mountains with how it lay between the stones.

Pride beamed from my mother, a mesmerized look always on her face when she witnessed my shape shifting. There was always pain with the shift but compared to the emotional havoc my heart was suffering, it was nothing more than an ant bite.

My joints shifted with a sickening 'pop' as the bones were displaced, lengthened and then realigned. The muscles tore and regrew, an inferno of heat streaking across their surface. My arms and legs lengthened along with my fingers. It felt like knives had been slid through my fingertips as the nails fell off and claws burst through. Calluses from years of hard work turned into sensitive and sandpaper-like paw pads.

The face was always the most disorienting as my ears grew into large triangles that twisted and flinched at every small sound. Next my muzzle lengthened, the fox nose absorbing fifty times the amount of scents a human might, causing me to sneeze. The change in my eyes caused a dizzy sensation that threw me off balance, everything blurring and then refocusing with sharper detail, my stomach roiling in response.

Shock took care of the pain at that point, numbing me enough that I was only aware of the tailbone for the way it off set my balance. All at once it grew and split, skin erupting forth to cover it while vibrant red fur exploded from the follicles. As the magic swirled and settled the hue shifted, black stain settling at the tips of the tails, ears and legs.

There I stood, a huge fox with nine tails in the middle of our cabin, watching as the woman I loved more than anyone in the world beamed at me. She had been the only person who had never faltered or flinched. She was my rock, but soon she'd leave me to float down the river of life alone.

Lowering myself to the floor I waited patiently as she carefully pulled herself up onto my back. Arching two tails up like a skunk, I wrapped the lengths securely around her before I rose to my feet, her legs no longer able to squeeze my sides enough to hold on. Her slight weight broke my heart as I barely registered the pressure of her upon my back. She would leave this plane whole and herself, but she was far from the wild yearling she'd been a year ago. It would be selfish to try and keep her longer just to save myself from heartbreak.

Resolute was as close to okay as I could get, but I would try to embrace the day if only for her sake. Ducking to make sure we both cleared the doorway, I set off into the morning.

The woods around our home were as familiar to me as the back of my hand. The years spent wandering the paths and foraging would serve me long into the future, but these rides, usually with my mother upon a horse instead of my back, were the most treasured days.

The deep sadness ahead would overwhelm me if I let it, so I shook my head as I trotted down our lane towards the shaded trails. This memory, these last few hours together, they had to be happy. I would not get a redo.

Spring had come and the world around us was laced with color, so I headed towards the places I knew she loved the most. At our usual spot she gripped a bundle of my fur tight to let me know she was ready. Lithe limbs, made for running fast and leaping high, set forth in motion, racing down the trails. The earth was soft beneath my feet making the run easy and smooth. A whooping of pure happiness, followed by whole hearted laughter, caused my ears to twist backwards, a panting smile pulling at my canid lips.

Running had always pushed away my thoughts and allowed my mind to breathe and clear. Today was no different. My heart was heavy but my feet were light and the sound of laughter every time I cleared a half-fallen tree made my soul full. These would be the memories that would get me through the days ahead.

We ran around the entire town's border, slowing to an easy walk so that a field of wildflowers could be properly appreciated. At least that was what I told myself; it had nothing to do with wanting to prolong the inevitable. The wildflowers made us sneeze, but I breathed in deep and felt her do the same. I didn't dare to look back at her, I wasn't strong enough. Instead, I trotted to where the river broke off and a small stream fell from a tall rock formation. It was the closest thing to a waterfall I'd ever seen. The old ruins hidden behind the water had once been a place of worship, but the earth had reclaimed it.

Musical laughter filled the air as I darted in and out of it, yapping my own laughter until I happened to catch our reflection in the water. She used the stilling water to look too, and I saw the soft puffy pinkness of her eyelids; a sign of the silent tears she had been shedding the whole time. The knife in my heart ripped through over and over again, but she simply smiled and laid a hand against my neck.

There was no way to ease this wound. We didn't laugh again.

The walk home was slow, my claws dragging the earth until I stood looking down at our home from the top of a small hill. My feet felt like lead, and I found myself unable to take another step towards a future without my momma in it. She knew, as she always did.

"Do not change. I only want you to listen." She tapped my shoulder, our cue for when she wanted me to lay down. I curled my tails against my sides, hugging myself in a failed attempt to keep my emotions in check.

I feared the words to come, sure that they would be the ones that stuck with me. Panic began to rise, the look she gave me too reminiscent of all the other goodbyes I'd faced. Flexing my paws into the earth to try and ground me, I bid my heart to still and my nerves to calm. They didn't - but oh how I tried.

"You have to follow the call inside you Lykos. I have cherished every day we have shared together, but you have stayed here - for me - long enough. Find your reason to live. The dreams will guide you, but the magic within already knows where you need to be. Let this be the last day that you ignore it. There is a life behind you to cherish and one ahead to seize." Her voice rattled, quivering with emotion. My own bubbled within me, making my chest hurt as I tried to breathe normally.

"Nemesis beckons, she will escort me into peace just as she will guide you to your future. Be true to yourself my little fox and everything will be okay. Do not be afraid. I know this will hurt, but I will always be with you, my child. You are never alone." She paused and took a long breath, her gaze filled with love as she waited until I met her gaze.

"I love you more than I have loved anything else in this world. Nemesis asked me to raise you, but the love I felt for you was instant. You have been my reason to live, now let me be your reason to keep going."

Foxes are peculiar creatures, our noises unique in their chattering and whimpering way. To a stranger who didn't know better my sounds would have been simple fox talk, nothing strange beyond the giant creature they belonged to. My blessed mother, however, knew the truth. She leaned forward and hugged my neck as I cried, the sobs uncontained though the tears would not shed in a human way.

They didn't stop when we finally made it home and I shifted back, though they were silent now. I helped her back in bed, the life already leaving her face. My voice was a stranger to me as I whispered beside her ear, sharing one last embrace that I didn't want to relinquish.

"I love you momma. It's okay, I'm not ready, but I know you are. I promise I will do as you say. I'll find a way and I'll follow the magic."

As I finally sat back she smiled, but it wasn't at me. Looking at a shadow in the corner of her room she said only two words, her last. "You came."

Time escaped me as I sat on that bed laying over my mother's hand and crying into the sheets. Then, all at once, as if she had wiped them away and said 'No more', they stopped and no matter how much I tried to get them to come, to offer some relief to the tidal wave of sorrow within, they didn't.

My chest hurt, the muscles in my stomach ached and my body was stiff from staying in the same position for what must have been hours. The tears had left salty streaks down my cheeks and my sore and tired eyes blurred from the abuse. My mind and body fell numb, but there was no relief in it.

Duty drove my movements, her body had to be burned so her soul could be completely released from this realm. If

Nemesis truly had come for her, I could not make her suffer in waiting.

"Take good care of her…" The words were whispered, but I could have sworn the shadows shifted in response. Perhaps it was just the moisture in my eyes and the exhaustion in my soul. Just a trick of the soft candlelight.

The pyre wood had been cut earlier in the week, for she had insisted she was ready and so I must be too. I stacked the wood without thought, intermittently padding the layers with hay, then I layered a lush mix of hay and wildflowers on top. Every bit of my body was shaking, but I numbly moved through the ceremonial words, my alto voice raised in a song that should have been joined by our fellows, but it had only ever truly been the two of us.

"Death may take you from this world and into the next, but memories of you will be eternal in the hearts of those who love you. Let the Gods be kind and guide your way, now there is no more suffering and no more pain. We bid goodbye until we meet again." My words trembled, squeaking out as my throat closed with emotion.

She lay there, beautiful and serene atop the pyre, but as I stood holding the torch, my legs would not allow me to move forward. The sun's progress, which I had watched like a hawk all day, was forgotten now, even as it slipped behind the trees. Embers flicked onto my skin and small blisters rose. Still, I stood frozen, lost to the world in this moment and unable to return.

Something warm touched my arm and made my cold skin jump, my entire body jarring along with it. A sympathetic face met my bewildered gaze. Mira, the baker's daughter from the village, stood at my side. We had been friends long ago, until her mother forbade it. Behind her a few others had also come, placing small bits upon the pyre to send along with her to the afterworld. They all kept a far distance from me.

"She sent a letter to me by way of the healer." She said nothing more than that, simply took the torch from my hand. My grip was so loose it almost fell to the earth as she guided my fingers away. With two strides and a quick glance back at me, she set light to my entire world.

My tears had run dry, so I simply stood there in silence, all the words I hadn't said lost to the winds now. Something inside told me she knew them all anyways. When the pyre had finally burned to ash, my nose and lungs burned from the smoke, but I refused to move even an inch. Darkness settled upon the earth and a clear sky allowed the moon and stars to shine brightly above.

Mira was still there, holding my hand as if she'd never let go twelve years prior, disappearing as if she'd never existed to begin with. The realization made me uncomfortable, but the slight squeeze she gave was the only thing holding me to the earth. Her words brought me back to reality.

"You can't stay here Lykos. The King has posted a reward for a magical creature who hides in a human form. Most of the villagers want nothing to do with the King, or loved your mother enough to say nothing, but..."

"But the others know well what I am and think the Mad King will actually reward them? Funny that they won't breathe my name or match my eyes, but they have no problem selling me to the highest bidder."

Her words hurt, despite my lack of love for the villagers. Afterall, this was my home - or at least it was the only place I knew. They may have shunned what I was, but they did not mind benefiting from it. Who did they think kept the predators at bay and the butcher stocked? The betrayal stung, even if it wasn't surprising.

She sighed softly, her lips pulled down in a frown. "I saw the butcher's son ride out the night the healer told us of your Mother's fate. He is still foolish and bitter enough to take the chance."

"Good thing I didn't plan on sticking around then." Nonchalance was my intention, but even my own ears heard the bitterness on my tongue. Hopefully it was just enough to hide the stream of fear threading through my body. Thankfully no one would look close enough to notice the shaking in my hands.

There were so many stories about the cruelty of the King and his monstrous followers. If the Gods had still walked amongst us, he'd have surely been a favorite of Zeus who had once embodied depravity and cruelty.

The thought of being caged was horrid all on its own, but to be handed over to the King? I'd probably end up as a throw rug on the throne room floor. There could be no worse fate to follow my mother's death.

"What will you do now? Where will you go?" She looked at me with furrowed brows, her lips turned down. It was the same way she'd looked at me when the villagers had cursed me out of the village.

A sigh fell raggedly from my lips, my chest tight and the emotion within raging like a hurricane. The question itself terrified me, but more than that I feared letting my mother down, so I answered the only way I could.

"Above all else I'll stay away from those who would cage me. I have to figure out what these dreams mean. I could never leave her to seek the answers. Now... I just hope I can find faith in something, the way she did."

The woman who had been my entire life, my one source of unconditional love, was gone. The ache in my chest threatened to choke me as I said one last, silent, goodbye. Turning from the embers, I grasped the memory of my mother's last smile and held it close to my heart. For her I would seek the answers. For her, I would live and try to find happiness again. Perhaps I'd even find a home where I was accepted. What would that even look like?

CHAPTER ONE
THE SOUND OF WATER

*D*rip. *Phedoup. Drip. Phedoup. Drip.*

The sound of water dripping was slowly but surely driving me mad. Endless days imprisoned in a lifeless cell started as dull and quickly grew to be unbearable with that incessant dripping. Counting how many drops fell became futile. I either became drowsy and slipped off into the chaos of my dreams or became so triggered that I thrashed about and made as much noise as I could to drown out the echo. Always, the sound slowly crept back into my realm of hearing and again the cycle would continue. The puddle on the chilled stone grew slowly, as if my sanity had become liquid and crept out of me to gather at the farthest end of the room. The moisture also added to the hard cold, causing it to seep in through the pores and chill the soul. The hard shivers that sometimes struck locked my muscles so that all I could do was whimper and shiver.

It was both amazing and terrifying what the mind could do with a repeating sound. One might hear it a number of ways, often in conflict with itself - being both soft and loud or sharp and nearly silent. Infuriatingly, the culprit was out of reach of both brute strength and cunning, though the first week I had been imprisoned I gave both a valiant effort. The leak lay hidden behind a crack in the ceiling of the cell, surely some leaky tub somewhere being ignored. The sound was a constant companion and one of the few things that separated my dreams from bleak reality.

Glancing across the span of my cell there lacked any sort of bedding beyond a litter of hay in one corner and a pile of soiled and worn blankets in the opposite. I might have moved the hay to provide a softer sleeping area, or to stop the water droplets, if it were not for a lack of latrine. As it were, the only thing that made the area bearable between cleanings was that the musty old hay covered most of the scent of excrement.

In the basement level of whatever building I had been sequestered in, the lighting was poor, even for me. Everything felt sticky with humidity and gross. The stench of the place was never fully hidden from my keen nose, making it even more miserable. Breathing in the muggy air made my lungs cry out in protest, my magic the only explanation for a lack of illness in them.

Each day was not much different from the last. The dripping of water upon the floor of the cell echoed off the walls until my mind felt ready to burst. Right about the point when my hands were buried in the mess of my long brunette locks, head pressed against the cold floor, the guards would rush in.

Their presence was always preceded by a stampede of heavy footfalls. Although not large in stature, the five men walked as if laden with iron. Every time, the horrid screech of the metal latch against its prison screamed through one ear and out the other. The noise always caused my teeth to grind together, the pressure in my clenched jaws sending shocks of pain up to my temples and into my eyes.

As was usual, a familiar stench followed them into my room. I had hardly been fed well enough for the fear that they smelled of, but quite a few remembered past injuries. Although most remained wary, a couple still felt sore enough to pay me back for their wounded pride whenever opportunity presented itself. The memories of fists and boots made my body flinch when they tried to grab me. I kept my eyes closed against reality for I knew this play well enough to see it even behind my closed lids. They surrounded me, grumbling to themselves and trying hard to find a clean spot on me to grab.

My flesh had purpled and turned a sickly yellow green, the soreness never gone but temporarily forgotten until their hands grabbed and pulled without giving pause. My legs worked to lift me from the earth, the muscles screaming from disuse and hesitant to commit to an action. Pain was an old friend who had long overstayed its welcome.

As I stood and tried to walk, something hard struck the back of my knees. My legs folded and the cold floor met me with a hard embrace. I laid there waiting, sputtering on the sour air until they jerked me up. The momentum of their pull aided them in slamming me against the unforgiving stone walls. My body screamed and cried out, but it was an endless struggle trying to guess what action they desired from me. I frantically tried to meet them in the middle, only to catch a knee in the gut. The force of it made me retch, though nothing came up.

With each encounter my healing grew steadily slower. There was no rhythm or rhyme that I might follow so that the brutality lessened. There was so little fight left in my sore and exhausted body that they hauled me down the hallways with ease. All I could do was try and learn as much as I could every chance they gave me and find a way to escape. Thankfully, they were once again too busy keeping their balance to notice my study of the passageways.

In the far corner stray rays of sunshine danced across the floor causing dust particles to twirl in the light. Where there was sunlight, there were windows, so that must be the stairway up. Each time we passed it I struggled just enough for them to pause so I could grasp anything that might help me escape. Today's gain was the sound of footsteps on old wooden planks - stairs for sure. The way they creaked made my ears hurt, knowing there would be too little grace left in me to avoid the sound. Still, a sliver of hope coiled in my soul; there wouldn't be guards stationed by noisy stairs.

The guard dragging me by my left shoulder yanked me forward, making my footing slip on the worn floor.

"Walk you damnable beast." His annoyed grunt preceded a second jerk.

Unable to get my feet back beneath me, my knees beat a horrid rhythm upon the ground as they banged against the floor. The purple of bruised flesh would appear quickly and stay for days. The ache would eventually disappear, but only because worse would replace it. Such was my life now. Such would it remain until I died or escaped. I couldn't let the former happen. There were far too many questions I needed answered and I had made a promise that I did not plan to break.

"Goddess help." The words had been spoken ironically to myself for years, but now they were mumbled earnestly.

The window of survival was quickly closing on me and I could feel the walls beginning to collapse. I didn't have much time, or hope, left.

Deep breaths were too painful, so I took short ones that made me cringe. The smell of sweat and urine was so potent, I could practically taste it. Paired with the rough jostling of being dragged, I was quickly overwhelmed with nausea. Still, I tried to focus on my surroundings, there had to be something that would help me escape, some small thing.

I counted the doors as I passed them: three on the left, two on the right. Nothing had changed from the last time I'd been brought this way, but I swore the shadows looked different, deeper somehow. Perhaps I'd missed a lantern that had run dry.

The last room's door swung open with an abrupt cry from the bloated wood and rusted hinges. The sound made me jump out of my own skin, nerves shot. The wall of heat that hit me as I was dragged forth might have been a comfort, had a thick waft of smoke not followed. The normally chill room was filled with the unseen oil smoke from lanterns that hung every five feet, fully opened so that light poured out to reach every inch of the barren room.

There was a single chair that I could just make out before my senses became completely overloaded amidst this new form of torture. My vision blurred as the light overwhelmed my sensitive pupils, and just as soon as they pulled me forward and plopped me into the center of the room, my nose began to tickle and a fit of sneezing overcame me. Rope pulled taut at my ankles and then wrists. The tiny hairs dug themselves beneath the flesh, a few breaking off beneath it to fester later.

Each jolting sneeze sent pain through my bruised body and jerked it against my bonds. Tears fell from my eyes as they tried to cleanse the smoke away but succeeded only in keeping my sight obscured. I could not grasp onto anything as everything overloaded into a skull splitting migraine. The sound of my pulse quickening resounded in my ears even as I fought to keep my breathing even. Panicking wouldn't help me, I just had to stay calm.

Just as soon as I caught my breath another sneezing fit began until the panic welled up and spilled over. Quick breaths repeated despite my effort to slow them. The quick influx of air made my head spin as the oxygen decreased. The room twisted and turned, bile rising to burn my throat.

"No, no, no." The muttered words sounded like they came from someone else, though I knew they passed my lips. I couldn't breathe, I couldn't see, the world was dissolving around me, no images, just pain and fear as my human mind shut down and animal instinct took over.

"Oh man, she's freaking out pretty bad this time." I couldn't tell where the guard's voice was coming from. The sliver of control I'd had was gone. My breathing increased. I was trapped. I would die here in this shitty little room. No one would know. I teetered in place, held fast and breathing like a frightened rabbit. A shadow slid over me. Was that a cool hand against my forehead? The memory of my mother's touch caressed my mind just before a burst of light behind my closed lids made me shriek with pain.

It was too much. The world disappeared

My name carried on the winds, soft and sing song like a child's rhyme.

"Lyyyyyy- kooooossss"

That voice. I had heard it before, but only ever in my dreams. A warm sensation filled my chest, my stomach tightening as a bundle of nerves made butterflies flutter within. My legs ran forward, the world dark around me, but something pulled me in the direction I had to go.

"Where are you?" There was no reply, so I kept searching, the dark sky above offering no help as the moon and stars remained hidden.

"Please, come find me." The voice sounded worried, but it came from nowhere, my keen ears unable to place it. The world slipped by as I ran and ran, unseeing but knowing I was headed right by the pull within.

I had to get there. I had to find her. Her? Who was she? Why did she call to me? The sky suddenly broke and the world lit up as a strike of lightning crashed to the earth. Just ahead a silhouette stood, facing away from me. Just as I reached out an arm to grasp her shoulder, another strike lit up the world, electricity jolting through me as it hit.

The stinging outline of fingers across my face jerked my head and brought the world back into focus. Gasping at the shock of it, the world and my predicament caught back up to my mind. What a cowardly and meek little beast I'd become, so frightened by a smokey room that I passed out. Yet while away I had almost reached the nameless woman who haunted my dreams. The pull, which had become more frantic the longer I stood still, was a constant reminder of my mother's last words and the only thing keeping me going.

A second slap etched another handprint across my jaw. Unnecessary, but it did draw the world in a sharper light once my brain stopped rattling in my skull. The pain was loud and a blanket of desperation still held me tight as I tried to make heads and tails of the room. Everything shifted and blurred. My hands shook, muscles twitching as my lips trembled, though the cause was no singular thing.

A familiar pattern in the distance drew my focus, allowing my overwhelmed senses to dial in on the repeating sound. The tapping of high polished boots on stone rang out, every tap like a brass instrument being hammered beside my head. Nausea roiled and the taste of bile rose in the back of my throat. My flesh burned from bruises and heat, while my lungs breathed fire into my nose and mouth. Still, the sound of those taps forced me to ignore the way my body screamed like a banshee. Worse would soon follow.

A sneer pulled my lips back from my teeth before I could think better and stop myself. My cracked lips bled, the metallic taste familiar and the small bit of moisture relished. A growl vibrated low, its presence felt through my entire body. The sound barely reached my lips, but pure loathing etched itself into every sound wave.

My defiance lasted only a moment before the smoke tried to chase my lungs from my body once more in the form of a coughing fit. Weak. Too weak to even pull myself from the empty numbness that was rising from my feet and traveling up my body. How I would get out of this in one piece was beyond me.

The smell of rich cologne added to the horrendous blend of smells as the steps paused at the doorway. A hearty laugh preceded the man who caused this suffering.
Fucking bastard.

The words rang so loud in my mind I had to reassure myself they hadn't passed my dry and broken lips. My tongue graced them tentatively as if the words would have left a taste behind just as foul as its subject. Nothing. Perhaps I had some self-control after all, or maybe it was my own small dose of madness.

The door finally swung open with the same cries of protest as before, and inside the doorframe stood the gaudy Mad King. Robes of bright orange trimmed in green with yellow birds embroidered down the middle clashed in such a way that made my eyes squint. The light danced across the silky materials and my blurred vision swayed, my stomach once again churning.

The very air around him set my skin crawling, the glint in his eyes sending my hair upright. The sensation was a blaring warning, everything about my dual nature screaming there was something wrong. It was like smelling soiled meat amongst what appeared to be a perfectly healthy slab; the eyes were blind to flaws on the surface, but the gut knew better.

It might have been that there was always a bit of magic around him, though it was never attached directly to his scent. Instead, it was like a fog that gathered around but never quite touched, despite the lingering moisture on one's skin. The idea of it puzzled me, but any time I contemplated the idea I found that I could not grasp the feeling again. That was even more worrisome, only powerful magic could erase its own footprint.

Mother said the King had been an average enough man to start, but as soon as the crown had rested upon his head madness had seized him. His rule had left his people in fear, their wealth stolen out from under them so that they barely made it through the winters. The people had been so weakened that they could barely manage to fight back against the cruelties he allowed his imported guards to commit. Those in the castle's shadow kept their heads down and their noses as clean as possible for fear of hanging or beheading.

The King did not keep prisoners, she had said. Yet here I sat, a prisoner all the same. Which cruel Fate had veered me off my path? Perhaps I'd find one and let her know what I thought about it, if I ever managed to glimpse freedom again.

As my mind tried to clear and focus, the Mad King caught my gaze, his lips pulling toward his ears. I prepared for the inevitable even as I struggled to breathe evenly.

"What will it be today, Lykos?" His smile was cruel, madness all that lurked in his features. Casually he leaned forward, hands in his silken pockets. He had all the finery of a King, with the posture of a childhood bully.

A small cough shifted into a scoff at his pretense of choice. Alto notes came out broken and dry, but I'd not yet lost all my spirit.

"Oh, you know, just the usual. You will ask me questions and when you don't like the answers, I'll be dragged away bloody and bruised."

"Very well then." He flourished a hand and the shuffling of the guards started toward me.

The groan of wood from a step preceded a burst of pain against my left side. The pain radiated. Just as shock might have numbed it, a second strike landed in the same place, a fresh eruption of fire spreading beneath my skin. Groans were all that escaped me, though I wanted to snarl and curse and flail.

Shock from the trauma of the first two punches numbed me for a moment, but it wouldn't last. Just as I caught my breath from the stress, the wood shifted again, this time from my other side. The first guard pulled his punches to save his hands, but the other had once been a blacksmith and his punch would have every bit of his weight behind it. Bound as I was, I tried but failed to lean away from it. I felt it in all its entirety.

His weight moved through his arm, the impact sending me flying sideways. My chair was caught by the first guard, allowing none of the impact to disperse to the earth below. My keen ears honed onto the awful sound of ribs cracking, followed by a yelp of pain that burned my throat as I tried to scream. There had been a time I'd considered myself tough. Now, I didn't even know what the word meant.

My pain caused my attackers to laugh, at least so long as I was bound. Let my pain amuse them; they couldn't deny the fear that tainted their sweat when they were left alone with me. I had the memory of their fear and that alone would keep me from breaking completely. If only they knew the real monster I could be, if only I had strength enough to show them all. Sure, I was weak right now, but only because they'd used magic to catch me. Even as a human, they'd have had a much tougher fight if it had ever been fair.

"Change and all this stops." The King's voice split through the grunts of the men who hovered, poised and ready to hit me. He did a good job at hiding his nerves, but his urgency had slipped through with the latest interrogations. He was getting desperate.

"Empty promises in exchange for miracles? That's fair." My lungs rattled and wheezed, but I managed the words just above a whisper.

Knuckles skid across the surface of my face with a force my grandmother could have improved upon. The copper taste of my own blood tainted the tip of my tongue as my lips split again, the soft flesh pressed hard against a sharp canine tooth. The third brute who'd hit me grinned in satisfaction, but I ignored his false sense of pride. He was a boy playing at being a man, scared of his King just as much as any commoner. He'd pissed himself during my first interrogation and learned the importance of securing my bindings. A laugh sputtered out at the memory.

"So glad you think this is funny, I'd hate it if you weren't enjoying yourself." The King's smile was sickening.

He walked forward but I didn't even have the energy to react as I desperately tried to ignore the pain radiating from my body. Every smokey breath burned my esophagus, the cracked ribs making it difficult for my lungs to expand smoothly. The pain and warmth of the room caused sweat to bead and run down my brow. The salty drops stung, but they helped clear my vision enough to focus on my torturer.

A sudden pressure at my jaw tilted my head up as the King's unkempt nails dug into my cheeks, the pressure making my mouth gape. There was no explaining the strength in his frail form aside from that taint of magic. It had slowly increased with every encounter, or at least it felt that way as day by day I became weaker.

The stench of old magic, mixed with the King's breath, made my nose wrinkle with disgust. In his free hand he held a small vial, its cork held between his rotting teeth. The taste in the air around it was distinctive, yet inescapably nondescript. I had little choice but to swallow the foul liquid as his grip threatened to break my jaw at any sign of resistance.

"Now you damned beast, if you won't change then you will tell me why and no lie shall cross that damned tongue of yours!"

My magic stirred and hummed, hope springing forth for a split second, only to fall the next. The sensation started out exhilarating and comforting, then twisted as the liquid seemed to grow thorns, my body immediately trying to reject what felt like acid sliding down my throat. There was limited magic left in this world, so I cringed to think how old and potentially deadly the concoction must be. That my magic reacted so fervently was proof enough that it was a genuine potion, but if it had intent of its own was yet to be seen. Magic always knew magic, it was one of the best and worst things about being a magical creature.

"Why won't you shift into a fox?!" He stepped back only far enough that he could look into my eyes. His body was nothing more than a blur as my eyes continued to water, tear trails marking my cheeks even more heavily as the pain of breathing continued my torture.

Bile tried to rise as a lie rose on my tongue and I was forced to choke back my smartass reply. A truth potion. Rumors had always said they still existed, but none had ever been recovered successfully. Had I the mind, I might have wondered how many had died for this one. The sting of the magic left me no chance to ask.

His sneer was victorious as I gagged but I'd be damned to the Underworld before I let this puppet win so easily. Magic always had loopholes; there was a finesse in every ounce of it. He had played with magic, was influenced by it - but I was a part of it. Of that at least, I was certain.

"I can't." Exhaling in relief, I immediately regretted the action, forcing a glare in order to hide a wince of pain. There was no lie, so no fire to follow the words. I was too weak to shift, even though I wanted to with every fiber of my being.

The King's face contorted and fell even as I braced for a strike that didn't come. He cursed as he stared at me, his face twisting in confusion, then horror. I tried desperately not to let the snicker in my throat rise. The pain wouldn't be worth it. He then began muttering to himself, panic skewing his tone much higher than its normal range.

"Perhaps it needs time to work. No, no, she is too weak to have done that. Surely, she is hiding something. What if she doesn't know? What if we were wrong?"

His body jerked back as if flinching from a strike, hands half-way rising in defense before he seemed to catch himself. It was as if he were having a debate with someone, though he spoke only to himself. When his mumbling finally ceased, he addressed me once more.

"Where then is your partner sleeping? Surely, she will call forth the beast inside you!"

He was inches from my face now, his foul breath heavy and hot, fury turning his skin a deep scarlet that made his bloodshot eyes look even more crazed than usual. He was desperate and I was increasingly confused. Unable to think of anything witty or roundabout to say, I simply reacted.

"I don't know what you are talking about." Every word burned in my throat, but no bile rose, as if the potion itself was unsure if the words were truth or a lie.

Confusion swarmed my mind even as blood beaded up on my face, his frustration having exploded across my face. The long unkempt fingernails tore a line across my forehead and cheek. The slap stung but compared to my brutalized sides it was a mosquito bite. Thankfully, I couldn't breathe well enough to remark on it and so likely spared myself more injury.

This was not the first time he had alluded to me having some sort of partner out there waiting. The idea that I was considered too dumb to make it this far alone, or in need of someone to come to my rescue, did not sit well. The latter made me furious, but in my weakened condition, there was little argument I could use to heal my wounded pride. A rescuer was starting to sound pretty damn good right about now. That truth only annoyed me further.

"How does your magic awaken what is in others? The legends have recorded it! Every time you resurface, magic returns. Now, tell me how!" His words were sharp, spittle flecking across my face in his anger. The image of a rabid dog frothing at the mouth was not far from what my distorted vision saw before me. No matter how he phrased his questions I still had no viable answer for him, in spite of my precarious situation, my patience waned, and my words slipped out unfiltered.

"What legends? Resurface? How deep does that madness go? I have no clue what you are talking about. How could legends speak of me if I'm living and breathing right now?!?"

There was no pause, the next question came without an answer, his anxiety apparent in the way he began to pace and flail his arms.

"What are you looking for?"

"The answer to my dreams." My honest reply was a whisper, the truth tearing me apart. The answer had plagued me time and time again after waking from dreams that felt like memories but were scattered like leaves upon the breeze.

Always, I felt pulled by the magic in my core toward some unnamable thing. Nothing could ever quiet the tugging and anything or anyone that might tie me to a place only made it throb with more ferocity. There was no escaping it until I tracked it down, wherever that might be, whatever it was. I had yearned to leave, to find its source and live every day a little different from the last. Mother had known it, but neither of us could bear the parting to find it. Now nothing held me back but this cage.

"What dreams?" he spat, his pace pausing for just a moment.

The potion would do its job, but I could at least be as vague as possible.

"The ones I've had since I was little."

He scoffed. "A child's fantasy. Useless. Why would a girl from such a small village be heading east? Who do you serve!?!"

Here the words 'no one' rose along with bile and I could not understand where the lie was. I had pledged to no one, though my mother had been a devotee to Nemesis and by proxy her mother Nyx. I coughed at the taste rising on my tongue and thankfully my lack of response was not noted, panic and fury now pouring out from the King.

He continued to pace, nearly at a jog now. The nervous energy rose and spread to the two men standing at my sides. They leaned forward, muscles twitching - ready to deliver more punches at the smallest of signs; anything to keep his wrath and madness off of them.

The Mad King continued to mumble to himself, arguing with the air it seemed. The scent of magic made me nervous of whomever aided him, but also gave me relief. He held no true magic of his own, which meant there was a real possibility he wouldn't be able to catch me a second time. In the least, the banter between himself and this invisible force allowed me a moment to breathe.

"Why do you seek the Amazons?"

The sudden shift of subject puzzled me, but I knew better than to tempt fate further, especially with my healing abilities waning. That I would eventually end up with them had crossed my mind more than once, but I had hardly even found a direction to follow before I was captured, so why did he assume that was where I was headed?

My response died before it could pass my lips as the magic bit and stung my tongue. I coughed, unsure how the words 'I wasn't' were a lie. I had not been headed to the Amazon lands, at least not yet. They were perhaps the most kindred spirits I would find, but my goal had always been to find the cause of my dreams and the incessant pulling of my magic.

A kick to the middle of my thigh caused a grunt to issue forth, the hit catching right between my muscles; a reward for my delay. The hits to my head and the stuffy room created a fog in my mind that was becoming too thick to navigate quickly. The King's pacing increased and a fist slammed into my stomach. Coughing, I tried to catch my breath and keep the bile down, even as I mumbled the only response I could think of.

"I was headed east but I wasn't looking for the Amazons." He didn't notice the wince from my tongue stinging.

Apparently I should have been though.

"Useless bitch. Throw her back in her cell." His words were practically a scream, the high pitch like lightning in my skull.

"Told you." The words were too soft for any beyond the guards who man-handled me to hear. It was my attempt at defiance, though a pitiful one.

The Mad King continued mumbling to himself, the jumbled words just barely audible as he walked away.

"I don't think she is it. We should just kill her. The scroll said. No, of course I'm not. Very well. Yes, I'll try the other thing. "

"Dunno why some mangy fox is worth all this trouble anyways." The guards were chatting away, though those were the only words I could grab. Their rough motions caused the world to spin as hands pulled me backwards, then hauled me up. Shortly after, everything was absorbed by darkness. My mind slipped away, sweet oblivion welcoming me into her arms.

I dreamt again of chasing something far away, desperately being beckoned forth even as I was forced to stand stagnant.

CHAPTER TWO
POKING THE HORNET'S NEST

Jolting in place, I woke with a start as my heart pounded in my ears and my vision cleared just enough to see Leola. The King's daughter was sitting on the floor beside me, waiting for me to wake. Her presence calmed me in one breath and filled me with dread in the next. She was not nearly as volatile as her father, but there was always an uneasy sensation of standing on the precipice of danger with her. Her temper tantrums were not as physically brutal, but the consequences of sending her into one were still bad.

At least it wasn't the guards coming back for another round.

For a brief moment the taste of freedom had danced upon my tongue as I ran through the grasslands of my dream, headed towards mountains in the far distance. I could almost taste the fresh air that had lifted my tangled locks into the air, but Leola's presence grounded me quickly. The sensation slipped through my fingers like water, right alongside my hope. She looked mildly annoyed at first, brows dipping towards her nose, but she quickly twisted her face into something more pleasant.

Leola, like the beatings and the sound of the dripping water, was one of the few constants that somewhat marked the passage of time. She visited once or twice in a week, I guessed, usually coinciding with the interrogations, which provided a long enough absence for the cell to be cleaned. She was what most would call a bright young woman, though her passions easily bordered obsession from the way she described them to me. There was no doubt that during my imprisonment I had become her most recent - perhaps at the beckoning of her father. I did not bemoan it, but I did not trust it either.

Anyone who had come near me viewed me now as a possession of the King's and so tried to hurt or ignore me. I found it ironic that men and women who were just as caged as I was, only without the bars, would have no sympathy. The sound of a familiar voice and steady conversation was perhaps the only thing which anchored me to life after such a long period of isolation and torture. That and a promise to my mother. Surely I'd have already lost my mind by now if it weren't for both.

She was keenly aware of the edge she held over me, often using it as leverage. It made me wonder if the sweet woman who occasionally peeked through was merely a mask or a glimpse of who she might have been if life had treated her to a better father. There wasn't much to be done for it, she held no distaste for the life she lived that I could see.

A sigh fell from my lips, regret instantaneous as my ribs protested sharply. Leola 'tsked' at me, the tone dismissive in a way that annoyed me to no end. Her belief that I should at least *try* to appease the King was an issue of debate on many a better day. What she expected from me was still a mystery, but I tried to appease her with a soft nod, too exhausted to make a retort. That she'd entered the room without waking me was far more concerning. I should have woken up the moment the door screeched, if she'd wanted to, she could have killed me then and there.

Instead, she cleaned my wounds with hands that were soft and supple from having never known a hard day's labor. The urge to lean into them was hard to resist, but the few times I had before the look in her eyes had sent my hair bristling. The burn of the alcohol she used hardly registered amongst the other ailments overloading my senses; the newest being a throbbing at the back of my skull. That alone was reason enough to accept when the bottle of liquor was pressed to my split lips. The warm liquid burned, but the soothing warmth that spread through my chest afterwards was worth every drop of liquid fire. There was none left when the bottle was pulled away, my head spinning lightly from the rush of it. Leola smirked knowingly, like a cat who had cornered the mouse. She continued her administration, taking long strips of cloth and wrapping it around my chest to help stabilize my torso.

She spoke the entire time she bandaged me. The notes were usually a bit too high pitched for my tastes, but today I was particularly displeased with her shrillness as my skull split from within. She spoke of only the most trivial things, her entitlement obvious, and her words were always careful to exclude anything that could be useful.

"I've got a new horse coming. Father says a man on the outskirts acquired it from the Centaurs, and he bought it off him so the beast would have a decent life."

Bought seemed generous since there was no doubt that the man's compensation had been to keep his life. No one would sell a Centaur bred horse unless they had no choice. Long ago the Centaurs helped nurse Poseidon's favorite mare back to health and in return he blessed their herds with intelligence and beauty. Many tried to breed horses purchased from the Centaurs, but they only ever resulted in average foals.

I might have rolled my eyes if the movement wouldn't have hurt. The only decent thing that beast could hope for now was to go unnoticed long enough for someone to smuggle it back out. There was a time I might have asked about the horse and allowed her to enjoy bragging, but this round of questioning had hit far harder than anticipated, so I said nothing.

"It amazes me that you can take such beatings and still live...I suppose that is why Father is so certain of what you are. Why don't you just change for him? Or for me? He'd believe me if I told him. If it's something you prefer to only do for a woman. They say shapeshifting can be very intimate."

The growl that tried to escape me died before it left my lips, the attempt proving to be a huge mistake. The air my lungs released twisted into a series of pitiful noises I didn't recognize. Tears welled up in my eyes. Everything ached and the broken ribs would take too much energy to heal immediately. Breathing hurt in a way that made even the soft whimpers an accomplishment. The attempt to sigh in exasperation, as a compromise to silence, cost a heavy price.

"Why do you even care?" The words barely made it off my lips.

"Why do you not want me to?" She tilted her head, but I couldn't trust the concern in her furrowed brows. She reminded me of a cat, waiting until you turned away before pouncing. I didn't trust her any further than I could throw her.

Pity crossed Leola's features as she took my silence as an answer and continued doctoring me up. There was little I hated more than that pitying look that was barely shy of disgust, but in my current state I'd take it over a tantrum. After wrapping my torso and cleaning most of the blood and tear stains from my face, she helped me to the pile of shredded blankets upon the floor in the corner. A den of sorts they had said. The insult accompanied a lack of proper cot for their belief that this would encourage the beast from within.

Idiots, all of them.

"Even if I could. Why would he want me?" It wasn't the first time I'd asked, though each time I got a different answer.

"If you are so curious, perhaps you should just do what he asks and find out for yourself." Her words held an odd tone, almost like she wanted to laugh but was holding back, like a child trying to fib.

"As if I could in this state." My words were muttered, but she heard them.

"The world has changed Lykos. The old Gods have faded from even our continent. Stories from other lands say new Gods have arisen. I would become the Goddess our people need before bowing to another's claim. All it'd take is a small spark to bring magic back into the world. You could be that spark."

None of it made sense. Yes, the Gods had faded, but it was our own doing. When the Fates were brought down, mankind took hold of their own destiny. The belief that Gods and Goddesses were all powerful faded away and with it, so did their power. The immortals lost their ties to Earth and were no longer able to cross from Olympus. Now magic was rarely seen, but when it was, it could be traced back to bloodlines that had long ago been blessed.

That I was a magical creature was indeed rare, but just as Centaurs still existed, so must other creatures born from the Gods. They just stayed hidden so they were not hunted and caged. Not unlike the situation I now found myself in.

"You two have read too many Bard's tales. No one except children of the Gods were ever able to become such."

She smirked, as if she knew something I didn't. I might have asked, but something told me that I'd be walking into a trap.

Too late for that you idiot.

My consciousness finally slipped away from me, Leola's knowing grin the last thing I remembered.

Curled carefully upon the floor, my eyes remained closed as I tried to fall into the flashes of comfort found in my dreams, which plagued me all the harder for my lack of movement. A woman was always there in the darkness, lovingly picking me up from the shadows and pushing me onward or beckoning me to her. There were moments of such loving devotion mixed between horrid scenes of bloodshed. What did they mean? Why were they so familiar? Whose love engulfed me like the ocean in those brief moments?

I had to know.

Something called to me and I could not escape it, so I must escape here.

Unfortunately Leola was my only hope, aside from some miracle. She smelled of horses, so I must have been out for a while; presumably long enough for her to leave for a ride and return.

"I won't live much longer...not like this." I cracked my eyelids open, the words spoken as if to myself.

Glancing sideways, I looked at the woman who sat before me, her moods unpredictable on the best of days.

Leola's hazel eyes grew wide, her teeth chewing the short ends of her fingernails. Her blonde locks fell in ringlets to her shoulders, hiding her face momentarily as she averted her gaze. There was a wariness in the way her eyes shifted to and fro, as if a debate were happening. I had been trying for months to get her to help - even to join me and get out from beneath her father's thumb.

Perhaps a bit of life out in the wilds or amongst the common people would give her a better sense of how the real world worked. She had thus far balked every time. Today, however, she looked more intently at the wraps. The wide strips hid ribs which were black and blue as I labored to breathe, wincing when the reflex pulled too deep.

She nodded, though I didn't know if it was an answer or a nervous habit. There was no commitment in the motion, barely a full action in and of itself. One might mistake it for the slight dip one's head does when counting out something in the distance. There was no energy left in me to hate her or her delusions. The things she and her father spoke of made no sense to me, but it didn't need to. They stood between me and everything I could ever want.

Carefully, my hand stretched forward, my weight shifting just a hair as my fingers wrapped gently around her wrist. Squeezing lightly, for there was no strength in me to actually be forceful, I guided her fingers away from her mouth.

Her brows tilted in a fretful manner for only a moment, then something switched. She smiled brightly as her entire demeanor turned around, much in the manner her father had the second he took the crown.

"I will get you some fresh soup and some healing herbs, that will help you along!"

A wisp of strangled air fell from my lips but I nodded agreeably, instantly regretting both actions as the motion made my head light. She bolted up and out, locking my cell behind her just as diligently as ever. The sound of that blasted slip of metal falling into place would forever be a bane to my existence.

Rolling onto my back I let my vision remain unfocused as I tried to tap into the underlying layer of my being. I just needed to focus upon it enough to stir my magic. The threads were there; silent rivers of power and mystery without tangible structure. If only I could grasp them. Try as I might, I wavered, my focus drawn away by the blasted dripping of water upon the hard stone floor.

Tears fell down my cheeks unbidden. The heat of them dissolved into a cold chill as the temperatures dropped with every passing day, leaving me cold with nothing for company but my own thoughts. How far into the season were we? Had it been weeks? Months? It had been warm when they caught me. Was the cold early or had time passed me by?

There had been no lie. I would not survive winter in this stone prison if I managed to even scrape through Fall. They wanted me to change, but I couldn't have even if I'd wanted to. The onslaughts had been too frequent in the beginning and now I was too weak to do much more than keep myself alive. Even if I managed to escape, the odds of me surviving the trek to the Amazon's land were low.

What a sad state I was in. Thank the Goddess that my mother was no longer here to worry after me. I only hoped she could not see me from the Underworld. Perhaps Nemesis would shield her gaze if she could. Afterall, the Underworld was part of her domain.

I wonder if we will suffer there now, as punishment for our rebellion. Suppose I've at least gotten in some practice if we do.

In the beginning I had often wondered if I could bring myself to try and manipulate Leola with affection. The guards had whispered often enough that Leola fancied me, but as I spent more time with her, I believed there was little truth to it. She wished to possess me just as her father did, perhaps even more so. She had frequently hinted that I might help her achieve greatness, so perhaps this idea of Godly-hood was what she'd meant.

There had been stories written of those corrupted by magic that was not their own. The same hint of madness lingered upon her skin that had tainted every breath of the Mad King. It was a subtle influence that could not be readily acknowledged as natural or imposed, but it was there. It tickled my nose in the same manner as peppercorns and its presence always made the two of them more cruel.

It would explain the strangeness of her scent, as well as her stark mood changes.

Even if Leola truly did fancy me, I could not reciprocate it. Sure, I could have tried to seduce her, to barter my freedom with affection, but what good was a life cursed with a rotten beginning? Trading one prison for another would get me no closer to what called out to me.

My soul did not stir for her, nor had it any other being in the manner of which the bards sang. Instead it tangled with my magic and yearned for something ever in the distance. Sure, there had been a pretty girl or two who had turned my head and taught me all the ways one could express fondness, but it was not love.

The price for my gift seemed to be an eternity of solitude and if this captivity continued, a short life. The latter had certainly been the subject of wagers amongst the rotating guardsmen. They didn't even try to muffle their bets and if I could, I'd have certainly taken a piece of them for myself. The wound they struck upon my pride was a deep one.

What a pitiful beast I was now. Far fallen was I from the majestic kitsune that had roamed the forests, wild and free of all but that silent pulling. If only I'd stayed home, I might not be in this poor set of circumstances. Such a cruel reward for chasing shadows and daydreams.

Some time later - for I had no sense of the passing of time except for the occasional murmured words of the servants in the hall - Leola diligently returned. The door to my cell clamored loudly, jolting me from an uneasy sleep. The young woman beamed proudly and I tried to mirror her lightness but I couldn't muster up the energy to produce more than a soft sort of moan as I tried to sit myself up. She drew in a tight breath and huffed it out even as her hands took their telltale place upon her hips, a sure sign of a potential tantrum.

"You could at least pretend to be grateful."

Wincing, I mustered up enough focus and strength to sit myself up. Leaning heavily on an elbow, I curled my legs underneath me, desperately trying to keep my torso straight. The stance of her body was like a wild cat poised to lash out, her imagined tail whipping out in annoyance. Had there been any patience left in me I might have smiled and made nice. Unfortunately, I had run right out of patience, letting it flow through my piss and soak into the straw set aside for the purpose of defecation. This game of house was wearing on my already tired soul and I had nothing left to give but sass.

"I appreciate all the kindness you have shown me Leola, your *friendship* has made the difference on many a day, but I am a prisoner. I was forcefully taken, imprisoned and have been tortured repeatedly. When you do something to help my freedom, then I will happily show you all the multitudes of gratitude you desire. I'll even half-ass hobble out a dance of happiness. Right now, this is all I can give you."

I braced for rebuttal or violence, knowing I was too tired and weak to defend myself, but all that met me was stunned silence. That, perhaps, was worse than verbal rage or physical retaliation. Those things I knew, those things I understood. The simmering that met my eyes like heat was a bit more unsettling because I didn't know what it was preceding. The hairs upon the back of my neck bristled even as the muscles along my back tensed, the reaction painful but completely instinctual.

Leola stared down at me, fury sparking in her eyes as her hands clenched into fists. There was silence, except that ever steady dripping. Somewhere in the space between us the sound crept like a living, breathing, thing. It was likely the only thing that could have managed to stop whatever onslaught brewed beneath her surface. The sound edged forward and tugged like a child on its mother's skirts, the silence amplifying its constant nagging.

Leola turned to look at the culprit, her fury seemingly broken for its distracting resonance. Confusion furrowed her brows, water droplets clearing her vision of its burning fires. Her fists unclenched and a sadness moved across her face as her head followed a drop from the ceiling to the puddle below. Without a word she turned and left, leaving the food and herbal tea behind.

My words may have been cold, but so was the floor I slept on. Confused but too tired and hurt to process it, I laid back down and as the pain shot through my body, the world darkened and my mind slipped away.

Time passed excruciatingly slowly. No longer was there any pattern to when I was fed or my cell cleaned, though thankfully the interrogations had ceased. The smell of piss and shit became unbearable more than once, so I knew it had been weeks and not days. Still, time was a slippery thing and now I had no way to measure it at all. Days passed, weeks, perhaps even a month before Leola finally returned.

The cell door randomly opened one day and revealed Leola holding a meal. Her eyes were bright, though the pupils seemed a bit wide even for the dull lighting of the cell's interior. There was no real way to pinpoint what it was, but something felt a bit off. Her smile was just as charming as ever, if a bit wider. The warmth was surely falsified through willpower and determination, but nonetheless effective. A spark of recognition sent my tense muscles back to relaxing, the comfort of a familiar face needing to do little coaxing for my mind to ignore the oddities which accompanied it.

In that moment, as my body relaxed and a burst of excitement warmed my veins, a realization hit me hard: I had missed her companionship. Somewhere along the road I'd become extremely reliant upon it.

A quiet voice blared a warning in the back of my mind, causing me to shake my head in an attempt to absolve the buzzing. Still, the nagging would not dissipate.

A rose is beautiful but still has thorns.

The voice in my head might have been my own, but I wasn't sure. Were my dreams bleeding into my days?

When the door had shut behind her she set my poor excuse for food on the floor and bounced over to me.

"I've had the most brilliant idea!!" Her voice filled the room with a high pitched shout that hurt my sensitive ears.

Dread of what would come out of her pretty mouth mixed with a desperate prayer that she would not stop speaking. My own mind had nearly driven me mad without stimuli.

"What idea is that, Leola?" Surprise filled me as my dry lips formed words for the first time in days. The tone was dry and wispy, but finally heard by another. There had been bouts in which I profusely filled the cell with my voice followed by days of self-imposed silence that sent me falling into the darkest reaches of myself. It was during that period the dreams bled into the day and grew more volatile. Was that madness?

"We could be wed! Think about it, Lykos! My father could hardly argue against it. Together we could wake the magic in me and you'd be free of this cell! I'd ascend with you at my side. It's the perfect solution."

The air went out of me. The shining light in her eyes showed no signs of a manic play at humor, but surely it was a joke. The muscles in my jaw grew slack, the gape apparent to me only for the threat it posed to allow saliva to slide out.

"What?"

The scent of my own sweat and piss mingled with the ever sweet fragrance of whatever oils she had bathed with and my stomach turned. Even that stark difference in station could do nothing to make the sound of her proposition appealing. I'd rather swim in my own piss and go crazy from the sound of water dripping than be the pet of a spoiled Princess. Especially one with delusions of Godhood.

Dressing up a chain as a leash would not fool me.

She had her hands spread wide in anticipation of some great celebration and all I could do was sit there balking and slack jawed. How could she even fathom that this was an acceptable offer? The proposition was insane by all measures which I would trust.

There was no point in even trying to figure out what she meant. I'd tried over and over but it never made sense.

Waking magic? That simply wasn't how it worked. These delusions had gone too far. None but the Gods could do that and none had walked this plane in centuries. We cast them aside and that was that; if you weren't born with it, you weren't getting it.

The breath I drew and held was all I could manage to try and hold my temper. Was this why I had been left alone for who knew how long? So that the threat of what refusal meant might linger above my head just as the deep gray thunder clouds gathered before letting loose their monsoon? The irritation buzzing in the back of my skull said 'yes'.

My attempt to calm my temper and coax my patience forth failed in epic proportions as the breath I took exhaled into outrage. There was no filtering of the words, no softening of the blow. Weeks alone had made me far less hospitable than they might have expected. Humans might be more reasonable when caged and cornered, but animals were not.

"Are. You. Fucking. Kidding. Me? The perfect solution for who? Everyone except me!" My words were shouted, the moisture leaving my throat and creating raw lines that burned. I didn't care. My outrage was too extreme to bother with quenching my thirst first, surely the hoarseness would only emphasize my words.

She stepped back and put her hands on her hips indignantly, the silken material that gathered beneath her hands proof of the distance between us.

The threat of a tantrum was unmoving as fire coursed through my veins. The tingle of magic in my fingertips created a warm sensation I ignored, despite how satisfying it would have been to show her what kind of creature she was really dealing with. If I had not been caged and crippled they would not have stood a chance. Her safety relied upon me being kept weak, as did her confidence and pride.

Marriage would offer no salvation for me, only a pretty mask to hide the ugly truth.

"Even if I were capable of that kind of love, do you honestly think I would choose another form of imprisonment? I can't help your father with whatever insane idea he's got stuck in his head. Or you for that matter. I will not live on a leash Leola and if you cared for me at all, as you pretend to do, you would never ask me to!"

There had never been a soul who had dismissed the word impulsive when describing me. I was often quick to react instead of approaching a situation with intent and sly craft, despite my foxy other half. Mother had warned me it would be what brought trouble to my doorstep numerous times.

Really though, who could possibly blame me this time?

No regret filled me as the words left my lips, even as I clearly saw the potential chaos my impulsive words might cause. Much like one stone might tip and cause others to fall away from a wall, this one choice too might make such a ripple of destruction. What else could I do, as stuck as I was behind stone walls and metal doors. I was too weak to shift, let alone break free.

Surely if ever there was a time to lash out it was now, might as well see where the stones landed once they fell.

Tears streamed down Leola's face but that weird glint in her eye seemed to jump forth on the backs of the salty drops. There was rarely anything genuine in her tears aside from anger, though both gutted me just a hair. Whether out of pity or preparation was debatable.

Cold swept over me, shadows flickering across the wall as time seemed to freeze for a moment. A silent prayer was all I had left; the King would surely kill me now.

"Nemesis help me, I've set fire to my own pyre. If you have any mercy left, I could use some."

Leola bent down and picked up the bowl of now cold mush while letting loose an ear piercing scream. The contents splattered everywhere as the solid wood made contact with my face. A sudden sharp sting near my cheekbone preceded the clatter of its fall. In her fury she screamed once again, this time potential words created amidst the noise before she fled.

"You're dead!" She turned on heel and practically ran out, slamming the door behind her.

The door didn't open back up, but I had listened to the sound of that lock falling into place for longer than I could track. This time it hadn't slid home.

My heart blared in my eardrums, hope skyrocketing so hard that my head became too light to rise. Gingerly my limbs shuffled me forward upon hands and knees, muscles straining from the disuse of captivity. As I stared at the door, disbelief consumed me until I almost forgot to breathe. The deep intake that finally forced itself into my lungs expelled the fog, my body lurching forward to the door.

One of the blankets that had been scattered in a fit of crazed delirium, onset by the blasted dripping, had slid under the door as it had shut. The cloth had not been thick enough to stop the door from closing, but with any luck perhaps it had offset it just enough for the lock to miss completely. Crouching behind the door I listened for what seemed like an eternity, though it was no more than a few moments.

Silence.

Praying to the Mother of all things, I pulled on the door. The sound made me want to cry as the door moaned and slid open. There would be no second chances here. No mercy. The only option was to make it out or die trying.

Leola had likely made a scene and I'd pay for her bruised ego sooner rather than later, meaning my window to run would be very slim.

My broken ribs had mended, but the cost had been letting all the other bruises and cuts remain. It would hurt the whole way, but I would at least be well enough to move at more than a shuffle. Whatever Goddess had granted me this small bit of luck would surely have my gratitude the second I had a free moment to give it.

With limbs that shook from exhaustion and malnutrition, I half crouched and pressed myself against the wall, creeping forward at what felt like a snail's pace. My adrenaline caused my blood to pump rapidly, giving me the energy I needed but also making my vision blur as I became light headed from the increased blood flow. The scattered oil lamps hanging high on the walls swirled and danced for a moment before focusing enough for my feet to once again know up from down.

Halfway down the hallway things started to balance out as my senses grasped more clearly at the stimuli surrounding me. All the pacing in the world could never equate to the feeling of moving forward with intent. My body buzzed with the thrill of it, making me feel as if it was a beacon about to get me caught at any moment.

The hallways were musty and the air was thick and muddled making it easy to tell which turns would take me back to the spot of sunlight I had glimpsed. I could have shouted with joy for how sweet even this stale air was compared to a cell that smelled of me in every gross sense of the word. I could feel myself being overloaded, though I tried not to focus too hard on any one stimuli. The task was made harder for my desperate desire to soak it all in.

Weakness was a stench I would be glad to rid myself of, but it was not one I could wash away overnight. Instead, I let my fear help push me forward. I couldn't lose this chance for freedom.

Peering around the corner, I watched as at the end of the hall the guards rounded a corner, headed away from me. The world shifted unnaturally even as I kept a hand against the cold walls to try and ground myself. Anxiety and hope filled my chest in equal parts as I took my chance and bolted.

Fingertips and toes held my balance as I ran the hallways crouched low, using both hands and feet to pull and push myself forward. If anyone glimpsed me perhaps they might take me for a weird and gangly dog. Either way, it eased my equilibrium and helped to stabilize my vision. As I ran down the one hallway I'd never been drug down, the pitter patter of my bare feet on stone disappeared, replaced with the creak of abused boards.

The smell of fresh air led me to the stairwell and I crawled up the steep steps. There weren't any sounds above or behind, only the beating of my racing heart in my ears threatening to blow the drums and leave streaks of blood in their wake. Step by step I felt every bruise and every aching muscle but beneath the pain was a thrill of the chase. How long had it been since I'd raced the rabbits in the woods? My soul ached for the feel of grass beneath my feet. Clinging to the promise of nature beyond these stone walls I let my callused fingers slide across rough wooden planks, ever rising.

I slipped onto the next floor trying my best to stay in the shadows. The scent was not much better here, but there were windows. The moon shone outside, its silver light scattered through a few panes whose dark stain had faded or peeled. The rough score of the stone hinted that this building was not one well cared for, likely used for servants and prisoners of the special, non-public, sort.

There was moisture on the cold floor, wood still instead of stone and no rug to be found. The silver light did little to disillusion the poor shape of the hallways. Broken glass lay pushed aside where storms had knocked the panels about too roughly and discolored squares marred the walls where paintings had once hung.

A strong breeze whispered down the hall, tainted with must but far cleaner than anything I had smelled in ages. Sniffing the air flowing beneath the doors, I moved forward carefully, finding most rooms occupied, though all seemed well asleep or distracted.

Heavy moans behind one door caused my face to go hot and sent me carelessly rushing around the next curve of what I now was certain to be a tower from the shape of the hallways. Pressing myself against the cold stone wall, I turned to find a wide eyed boy looking at me. He said nothing as I pressed a finger to my lips in a quiet plea. The Goddess seemed to hear and answer for a moment.

Then the moment ended.

The sound of a yell caused a jolt through my muscles. Practically falling over myself, I looked back the way I had come. The voice was far off, no one in sight, but the sound of alarm was unquestionable. Fear filled my core as I looked down the hallway, searching for a way out. The little boy pointed down the way I'd been heading, even as he slipped into his own room, the sound of a lock latching into place following.

Better a bystander than accomplice.

The reverberations of footfalls on the old creaky stairs rose behind me. I couldn't risk moving slowly. I dropped down to the ground and ran, hands and feet extending like a beast, the distribution of weight allowing a quieter stride. I quickly rounded the next turn and dove into the first unlocked room I found, shutting and locking the door behind me.

A squeak behind me made me want to curse. Peering around into the shadows I spotted a servant girl who looked far less confident than the boy. She was barely a scrap of a thing, bright blue eyes stark against alabaster skin flushed pink. She couldn't have been more than seventeen and the world had already dealt her a rough hand, as was evident in the bruises along her arms and across one cheek. Her eyes were wide with surprise and her trembling lip spoke of fear.

Whether it was fear of me or what would come to her if they found me there I could not say.

"Shhh! Do not speak and I will not harm you." My words were firm but whispered. Desperately I hoped she too might have a silent pact to simply not get involved. From the look that crossed her face and the deep breath she took I knew that would not be the case.

The girl yelped as I leapt up from my crouch and lunged. Her face contorted to produce what would have inevitably been my doom, the high pitch of youth sharper than a whistle. I clamped my hand over her mouth just in time to muffle the noise.

"I'm sorry about this, but I cannot die here." She wiggled, squirmed and fought with both legs and arms. She bit into my fingers, but there was no pain that I had felt that could move me away from survival. She was strong, but I was desperate. My arm wrapped around her throat, cutting off the airway and preventing her jaw from opening. As soon as she went limp I released her back to her bed, making sure that she breathed, even if it was a bit faint. I would not kill an innocent but I'd be damned if one killed me.

Crouching behind the door I pressed my ear against the wood and heard the shouts that shouldn't have come so soon, but were inevitable.

"The building is locked down! Search the rooms! I don't care WHO is occupying them!"

Cursing under my breath I narrowed my eyes and tried to make sense of the mess that was this girl's room. A sigh of relief slipped from my lips as I spotted a small slit in the wall. The window was covered in heavy wooden slats to keep out the cold air, but the nails were poorly driven - probably done by the child herself with scraps scavenged from the yard. Climbing onto a desk that wobbled horribly, I reached up and snatched the boards off with shaking hands. The first came easily, the second I had to throw my body weight behind. The pull sent me crashing backwards as the unbalanced table gave way, a croak of pain creeping out with a huff of air that was forced from my lungs.

"Did you hear that?" I heard the yell as I lay splayed against the hard floor, my head thankfully cushioned by the pooling of the girl's bed sheet upon the ground.

The voice didn't sound too close but the hallways carried the sound and bounced it back easily enough that I couldn't be certain. There was very little time to think. Even less time to pray. No choice but to move.

Luck had it there was a shirt on the floor. It didn't fit well, but it would work. Slipping it over my head I scrambled up and out of the glassless window without any heed to where I might be landing on the other side.

Cold, fresh air filled my lungs and just as quickly left them as I managed to roll through my landing and smack flat down onto my back for the second time. Wincing from pain, I quietly thanked the heavens above for the thick layer of hay beneath me and the long sleeves of the shirt I'd just stolen. The earth was hard but the hay saved my bones and the shirt may well prevent freezing. I might have taken a moment and cried from the joy of fresh air and earth beneath me, if the sound of boots smacking stone wasn't gradually increasing. If I was lucky there would be time again to enjoy the simple pleasures of life. Now was not it.

The goat pen I had landed in abutted the short tower, casting deep shadows that protected me from immediately being spotted. The beasts eyed me cautiously from the other side of the corral, angrily bleating at me for waking them. Their noise would draw too much attention.

I rolled to my side and crouched in the shadow of the lean-to, gasping.

"Holy shit that hurt."

My body burned, muscles that hadn't been used were getting a crash course in mobility. The night air and clear sky allowed my senses to expand. As my breathing slowed I scanned the area I'd landed and pinpointed my goal.

The tall trees on the other side of the courtyard were exactly where I needed to be. I winced to think about trying to climb the stone wall that backed the woods. The sound of more guards arriving meant I didn't get the luxury of finding an alternative. The only option left was to make a dash and try to leap the wall - or damn well die trying. The latter seemed the more likely scenario, but at least I'd die free.

Clumsily, I slipped between the goat fence, glad to be rid of their bleats. I snatched a thin coat and saddle bag from the horse stall next to the pen. I could only send a prayer to the Goddess that there was something useful in the bag's contents, as I couldn't afford the time to check. Thankfully the gelding was an old one, his face grayed out and covered with scars that proved he'd earned his retirement. He hardly flinched when I neared, his nose velvet soft against my hand. The contact grounded my soul, pulling it back from the dark recesses of confinement. Kissing him softly on the snout, I disappeared just as quickly as I'd popped up.

There was a time when I could have measured the distance and guessed as to where the guards were, but even as they made a ruckus searching, I couldn't manage it. My vision was less blurred but sounds seemed chaotic, as if I should have been able to twist my ears as well in this form as the other. Frustrated but too desperate to sulk or wait, I took a deep breath, counted to three and then ran.

Halfway across the courtyard, the ground turned from clay to stone beneath my feet, the change in terrain causing me to stumble. My eyes had been too busy scanning for guards to pay it any heed. It wasn't much of a pause, but it was enough to reassure watching eyes I was not simply a stray dog; they were far more graceful. They spotted me. As I recovered my footing, their rough voices shouted for me to stop. Desperately searching the ground for traction and enough grace to keep me steady, I continued. The whoosh of an arrow flying past made me run faster, but it also forced me to dodge blindly, causing my path to collide with a guard's.

Roughly scrapping the earth with my hands, I kept my balance just enough to dodge his grasp. His sword, however, was another story. The blade was drawn and as I spun to get away from him I felt its sharp edge slice through the scrap of cloth covering my right thigh. There was no time to react to the pain before a punch from a different guard landed against my face and spun me back to the man with the short sword. A yelp escaped my lips as the blade slid across my side this time.

"RUN!" My mind screamed.

I ducked onto all fours, the next swing flying above my head. Kicking hard off the earth I dove away, rolling twice before gripping the earth with hands and feet once more and shoving myself toward the wall. Their feet followed me even as another arrow cut a line across my shoulder. I might have cried from pain or joy, the noise from my throat unrecognizable even to myself. The unmistakable flutter of hope ran through me as I spotted a crate and altered my course. Adrenaline was all I had and it was all I would need with the aid of that extra three feet. My other form could have cleared it easily, but there were barely any reserves left of my magic; these clumsy human legs would have to do the job.

The cold stone beneath my feet disappeared as the coiled muscles in my legs sprang out and pushed my body skyward. There was not much left to give, but all that was shot through my limbs. I'd only get one chance. Solid wood met the soles of my feet as they curled against the edge of the crate to propel me further. Scrambling to pull myself over the rough stone, cuts and scrapes were added in number to my body, even as my nails broke and ripped.

Strenuously hauling myself atop the wall I allowed gravity to aid the rest.

"This isn't going to feel good."

The words slipped from my lips just as I glimpsed over the other side. Too late to change my mind. Rolling over the other edge, I prayed to channel my inner cat and land safely on my feet.

The earth met my feet with a hard pulse of pain shooting up my skeleton. Thank the Goddess, nothing broke as I fell forward into a roll that carried me into cover. Crawling through the bramble and underbrush I struggled my way further into the woods. The deep earthy scents were as familiar to me as my own hands, the tickle of the dead grass a warm embrace after what felt like years without touch. Finally, I was back home amongst nature.

A few minutes to catch my breath was all I could afford. There was no time to relish it fully, though my body ached for rest. Hoisting the saddle bag to a spot that was not wounded, I gathered myself back up to move. They wouldn't stop, so I must not either. I ran for my life and the promise I had to fulfill.

The night had taken my trail and hidden it. Fall had littered the forest floor with an amass of leaves that shifted and flowed in the wind, covering my tracks just as quickly as I had made them. The wind howled like the raging ocean, its current moving through spindly and bare tree branches, devouring all other sound. A soft haze of fog settled onto the forest floor, creating ghosts and ghouls that would just as easily catch the eye as anything else moving in the woods.

The weather grew colder and colder as night drew deeper into its hour. What had been a mild fall chill was now completely cold, creating tangible puffs as air escaped from my warm lungs. The rocky terrain was laid out in such a way that one reached higher elevations without even realizing it, making the cold seem crueler than before without reason.

With no idea how far of a trek I was in for, there was very little choice but to keep moving. The dull pull of magic I could not name thrummed just a little louder with every step I took. It was as if it sang from the joy of my movement, even as it had clawed at my mind when I had sat idle. The path I was now set upon carried me East, ever toward the Amazon territory. The irony that I was now going exactly where the Mad King had thought was not lost on me. On a better night I'd have laughed, but tonight I could only curse, as much as commend, my stupidity and recklessness for getting me here.

Walking was enough of a challenge before, and now there was a deep gash on my side with flesh that had begun to pucker in a way I did not trust. It was still seeping blood, the torn bit of shirt I'd pressed to it only slowing it down a bit. The slice on my thigh was, thankfully, shallow, but if it got infected it would kill me more quickly than the cold.

Like an annoying child I repeated the same words in my head over and over.

"I have to keep moving."

Soon enough the trees began thinning, spread out amongst loose rocks and large outcroppings that had been chiseled at by the forces of nature. The haunting slivers of wood stood tall and proud, bending their frames to ebb and flow with the wind's moods. The rocky trails blended in upon themselves, their depths considerably deceitful. One moment the steps looked wide and steep, then -just as a footstep was measured- the illusion broke, jarring my bones as impact was made far sooner than I'd anticipated.

The higher I climbed the sharper the cold bit my lungs, even as the scattering of fall leaves offered moisture to the air. The ground became considerably more dangerous, causing my pace to slow as I struggled to pull myself up steep banks and over slick rocks. The only comfort in my struggle was knowing that the men who were undoubtedly following me now would have to face the same or find a longer way around. If they were foolish enough to bring their horses, they would definitely lose what distance they had gained here.

I took as few breaks as possible, unable to risk taking the time to hunt for sustenance, though I had lucked out and found some pressed trail bars and a canteen for water in the saddlebag I'd stolen. The raging growl of my stomach did not cease upon receipt of the meager offerings, but the nauseating empty sensation I felt had faded. A few fresh puddles amongst the rocks had provided enough hydration to keep my tongue wet, but little more.

Time, as it ever did these months past, blurred together in an immeasurable stretch. Blisters rose and broke upon my feet even as they slid on rocks that tore my flesh like a sharp knife. Everywhere I tread I left clear evidence of my struggle behind in scarlet streaks. The trails became slicker from the rain that passed ahead, causing me to tumble far more times than my pride would admit. Too soon my body felt drained of its reserves and just as battered as before.

Pausing long enough to wrap my wounds in wet dead leaves, I dug into the rain soft earth between two giant boulders. The red clay which held them firm when hardened from heat, would suffice in staunching the bleeding. It stung like a hornet when the clay pressed into the wounds, but it ceased any bleeding. Infection might fester, but I still had a few days before that would matter. All I could do was push forward harder and hope that I was close enough to make it. The clay at least would make sure the bleeding didn't deplete me before the guards caught up. Surely the exhaustion would take me before either of those, but I wouldn't help it along.

How long had I been running? Running being a very generous word for my staggering pace, but who could say how long or far I'd come at this point. Day passed into night several times, though the storm clouds cast out the sunlight so that there was hardly any difference between the two. Could it have possibly been a week? I couldn't be sure, though logically my mind said there was no way I'd have made it that long.

Trudging forward so slowly made me painfully aware of every bruise and cut that littered my body, the coolness of fall stealing every ounce of body heat I produced. The sun tried to creep past the clouds, but even when the light spilled out before me, the cold chill of the mountains tore away any warmth. The pines had begun to scatter their needles even as the varying species of leaf bearing trees had begun their changing of color and shedding. Vibrant reds and oranges lit up the sky like fire with bright yellow flashes mixed in. The fallen leaves created a reflection of it on the earth, their hues stark against the greens of their non-shedding cousins. The world spun a beautiful web of color that mesmerized my eyes and made me yearn for the same blazing hues of my fur coat.

It was in that moment when I had paused to take in the awe of color around me that I saw it in the distance: smoke billowing out behind me. It was too close for comfort though far enough to assure that their hounds had not yet picked my trail back up. The wet earth would muddle my scent just as it had distorted the impressions left in mud and clay.

Once the dogs found my scent again there would be no hope. Their masters surely knew I was slowing and just like dogs sent to run the deer to exhaustion, I would be prey to the whims of men just as relentless.

Every twig snapping underfoot set my nerves on end, the anxiety building to the point a squirrel bounding in the trees had my hands shaking like the fall leaves and my body leaping out of its own skin enclosure. The throbbing of my heartbeat marked a pace steadier and far more speedy than my steps. There was no distance great enough until I found the river.

There was nothing left to do but keep moving, yet even that effort was debated as my body yearned for rest. Sleep had begun to come far too deeply and quickly for me to risk laying down or sitting too long.

Perhaps I should just stop and let sleep take me.

The idea was not altogether unappealing, the odds were high in favor of my dying before they drug me back to the Mad King anyways. That at least was some comfort.

The idea of sleep and rest consumed my mind to the point that I lost focus on the earth beneath me. My body betrayed me and I lurched forward. A yelp fell from my lips as the slick earth reached up to embrace me, my arms too weak to catch my body and soften the impact. The winded breath I'd had was gone. I coughed, only to feel what must have been a dozen new injuries amassing my body as a singular jolt of pain. The exact source was indiscernible, but surely the gash at my side seared the worse as the clay cracked and it pulled open.

I couldn't even muster the energy to cry. There I lay for a long moment, my gaze taking in the red and orange leaves scattered across the forest floor, their glowing hues a fire against the mountain's smoky mist. The musty smell of decay hit my nostrils as I finally managed a deep breath, the warmth of it creating a puff in front of my face. A smile formed in my mind although there was no pull from the muscles controlling my lips. Such a simple joy in life, the amusement of creating visible puffs of air in the cold, yet I could not even express it properly.

As good a place as any to die I suppose.

The morbid thought was not without its own sense of beauty. Eventually a sunset array of leaves would cover my prone form and just as the leaves do, I would return to the earth.

Hell of a lot worse ways to go.

That, however, would be far too easy and my life was not that convenient. With a deep breath and a puff of air I attempted to heave myself up onto my arms. The lean muscles shook and I collapsed, sending my face right back into the pile of dead leaves. Wishing to weep from the audacity of it all, I stubbornly tried again. This time the world disappeared from beneath me when the muscles gave out.

There was nothing but silence and darkness as my consciousness stirred. The memory of trying to rise came slowly so that I couldn't make heads or tails of where I was. Confused, I tried to clear my blurry vision unsuccessfully, the dark splotches simply deepening until I closed my eyes and lost myself to the darkness again.

The sound of voices stirred my mind back to reality. The notes seemed almost like a growl at first, until solid words formed and fear gave my heart a kick start. The undeniable tone of commands meant that the King's guards had caught up to me. My pulse quickened as my shallow breaths drew the panic in deeper. Fear ripped into my soul and my brain filled me to the brim with energy I shouldn't have had as it pumped adrenaline out.

MOVE!

My body screamed, my brain trying to produce action without immediate success. Hours had surely passed as I'd lain on the earth, the wind kicking loose leaves from their branches, gathering them to bury my body in a sea of warm hues. A bud of hope blossomed in my chest at the thought that they might simply walk right past me, completely unaware of my presence if I could only stay still. The blossomed bud withered into a dry husk and disintegrated the second the baying cry of a dog who'd found a scent rose into the wind.

FUCKING MOVE LYKOS!!!

A voice I might have known as my own, on a better day, screamed inside my mind. The mind splitting rattle of it lit a match beneath me and somehow I found the strength to pull myself up to make a mad dash forward.

The bellow of the scent hound filled my ears as I tore through the brush, my already destroyed clothing shredding even more as I pushed forward with the last bit of reserves my body would be capable of. The voices of the men called out behind me in surprise and anger. Something was off, but I was too consumed with making my body move to understand any of it.

Twice, dead branches snagged my feet trying to pull me once more to the earth beneath. The sharp bark of live trees tore my hands as I caught myself on the young saplings around me long enough to launch myself forward again. For all that I had contemplated giving up since my escape, in this moment there were no doubts that, more than anything, I wanted to live and to be free. My heart was broken and my will had been twisted but I was still alive, still breathing, and miraculously still moving.

The magic in my soul had sputtered out all it could and seemed to have thrown just enough into my system for this one last dash. The sound of a river caught in my ears and a sudden burst of hope struck me just as a whistle preceded a fresh jolt of pain that split my back open to a blast of heat.

The impact threw me forward but my legs refused to buckle this time. Instead, they locked up. A shadow neared, though I didn't dare cast my eyes back to see whom it belonged, then almost as if I'd been shoved, my legs finally gave way. The momentum sent me over the lip of a rock, causing me to stumble over the edge into the rushing depths of the Tula River. The freezing waters numbed my entire body so that the pain disappeared, but left my limbs useless. The water choked me as the current drug me far beneath the tumultuous surface.

The irony of it all flowed over me just as the icy waters had. I had finally reached the amazon lands, only to die on the border.

My body had been pushed well past the point of its expiration, yet the magic within had propelled me even further, just for me to drown or die of hypothermia. The same calm moment of acceptance as I had before, when I had watched my breath freeze in the air beneath the falling Autumn leaves, filled me now. Death was a kindness in its own way. The pain would stop, there would be no more chains, no more deceit, no sadness or anger.

The river curved into a sharp point that broke on a batch of rocks then pushed up onto a shoreline. The tangle of rocks grabbed my limbs and forced my direction even as the current pushed me back to the surface and then up the edge of the shoreline. There was hardly any weight left to me, but what I had was enough to hold me to the sand. An attempt to laugh turned into a harsh sputtering as I tried to draw air into my burning lungs only to choke on the cold water still in my mouth. Weakness prevented me from clearing it completely. The coughing stopped but I could not speak. I saw the men with their dogs, cursing along the cliff line. I couldn't help but feel triumphant, despite my situation.

Take that you bastards! You failed.

They would have to return home empty handed or risk war with the Amazons. With that last spiteful bit of satisfaction, I closed my eyes. I could let the cold take my pain, and let my body finally rest. That odd sense of peace consumed me as warmth blossomed in my soul, my mind calmed completely for the first time in years.

I failed to get my revenge, but perhaps this was an even more satisfying end. Let the Mother take me back. I longed for a place to truly call home and her arms were the safest place I could think of to find. The image of wings pulling me in close to someone's bosom filled my soul with heat, even as my body froze on the sandy shore of the riverbed. The tiny pebbles that dug into my flesh were left unnoticed as my mind dove into the warm feeling of an embrace. The world went dark as the wings spread and sheltered me, then a bright light drew close. This was it. I was going home.

CHAPTER THREE
THE OPPOSITE OF DYING

My senses awoke with a tingling and prickling that left my mind confused. I found myself feeling heavy, but hadn't they always said death was like being released? Shouldn't I feel like I was floating? As I realized that there was very real pressure against my body and weight to what must be my limbs, my head buzzed with another sensation. There was murmuring somewhere, the sound muffled at first and slowly becoming more discernible.

There was concern in the first tone, followed by an angrier note that made my hair want to bristle in defense. I thought I heard words but the world was still too fuzzy. I failed to quite grasp that somehow I was still alive, even though there was undeniable evidence in every sensation that poked my mind into wakefulness.

The darkness that surrounded me was not a lack of light, but an inability to open my eyelids. The stretched canvas of skin became an artwork of dots and lines, remembered shapes presented as light in the absence of it. Slowly my mind caught up with itself though what it found was not in the least bit pleasant. Panic struck me like an iron pan to the face and was quickly followed by all the pain blockers of my unconsciousness dissolving like cane sugar on the tongue. My dry lips cracked and bled the instant they parted as I let out a cry of pain. What I had thought would be a loud yell came out as barely a squeak, my body completely spent and then some.

The voices suddenly went quiet and then returned, this time clearer, a confirmation that I had in fact managed to produce sound. The extra warmth near my body disappeared alongside the extra pressure, only to return quickly after.

"She's awake! Goddess help her! The medicine shouldn't be wearing off this quickly!"

The voice was pleasant, a soft soprano filled with kindness and concern. The sincerity in it made me pause, not that I really could do much more than lay there and try to breathe anyways. How the hell was I still alive? I couldn't fathom it, but the pain searing through my body like lightning trapped between clouds was proof enough that I hadn't reached the afterlife. Despite myself another whimper of pain fell past my lips.

"Shhh Shhhh, you're safe now, rest. Rest." She slipped something past my lips, the tangy flavor reminding me of the fruits often traded for as special treats in my village. My eyes still refused to open but it didn't matter. As if her words were a spell cast over me, I felt myself give into the oblivion of unconsciousness once more.

The world felt heavy and dazed. A dream or a memory, I was never sure which one. The edges always seemed tattered and faded, like I was on the verge of understanding but couldn't quite grasp the whole picture. Colors were too vibrant one moment then dull and muddled the next. Like oil from cooked meat when it spread across water's surface, the world shifted and turned, ripples of color followed by gray shades that turned again to hues that didn't quite fit properly. One moment I watched the world pass from the eyes of a human, the next the Kitsune within took in the world. Then there were weird moments in between when I saw everything with both and grew nauseous from it.

The smell of sweet bread tickled my nose as I lifted my head toward the sky. This time it was my fox's snout that tilted up, the nostrils at the end flaring tentatively, perceiving more in that sweet scent than any human could. The black fur of my forelegs flashed ahead of me as I followed the scent at a prancy trot. The earth beneath my paw pads gave way in smooth flicks of ankles, nails scraping gently to produce a soothing 'schhuuuut' sound.

Following the trail without any measure of time, my eyes got lost in the array of green leaves and brown branches. Full summer foliage created a heavy canopy, casting long lines of sunshine in chaotic patterns and patches. Lost in the tangle of dancing light I became aware of a presence watching from above. The sweet bread scent, filled with cinnamon and hints of sugar, settled heavy at the base of a tree. Reaching up its length I stretched as far as I could, my foxy form extending to a low branch with ease. I easily matched the sand horses in size; they were known for their speed and spirit, nowhere near as large as the farm horses back home.

As I searched the tree branches above, a delicate peal of laughter floated down to me from a high branch. I searched the dancing light and shadows but could not find the owner, even when I released my branch and tried to find a better angle. Around the tree base I danced until finally the laughter taunted me again from another tree a few feet away, though its branches had not stirred nor had the leaves whispered their upset at being rattled.

Intrigued, I continued to follow in the same manner I had trailed the scent, until the laughter moved so quickly that I had to run to try and keep up. The prancy trot turned into a fully extended lope, but even that pace threatened to leave me in the shadow of my prey. Gathering myself I pushed and pulled with my feet, limbs extending until they might pop from their sockets before they met the earth only to leave it just as quickly. The branches of my tail intertwined to become a single entity, acting as a propeller and keeping my balance without the drag that occurred when it was splayed out in multitude.

I ran blindly, eyes cast up with no worry to where I was headed, merely the raw determination and certainty that I had to find the owner of that sweet and familiar voice. As I continued to run the laughter suddenly turned into a sharp shriek of fear. In that same moment I realized I was no longer running, but now stood perfectly still in a clearing, the scent of sweetbread gone like it hadn't existed at all, my breathing as calm as if I had just awoke from a pleasant sleep. Turning my gaze across the grassy clearing I caught slight movement on the opposite end. I crept forward toward a form crouched on the ground. The shadowy body hunched over so that I couldn't make out anything other than the blue-black cloak that covered it.

Reaching out to grab the form's shoulder I was forced to leap back when it suddenly jerked around. I stared into cerulean blue eyes that matched my own, except red had seeped in around the edges. Blood covered the vague form's face, the features somehow indiscernible despite how clearly I saw the eyes and blood. Fanged teeth snarled back at me and as I noticed the heart in its hands, it lunged. Tripping backwards the shadows of the forest engulfed me, their hands grasping my fur and pulling me back.

My body jerked awake with a hard start that lifted me off the ground, the impact from landing pushing the air from my lungs. Sweat clung to my face and the back of my neck. The strands of hair that had become saturated itched and made me feel as if I were being strangled. Panic sent me lurching forward, but I was pushed back down, a hand holding me in place as someone kept softly murmuring things I didn't immediately recognize as actual words.

I quickly realized that the haunting images were no more than a fever dream. Taking a deep breath, I blinked the blur from my vision, thankful that my eyelids chose to lift this time around. The night sky looked down upon me, the moon high and only half full, dozens of stars winking flirtatiously at unreachable distances. There were no clouds and so no rain. Unfortunately, that also meant any heat the sun had been kind enough to bestow would simply dissipate the second it sank beyond the horizon.

I turned my gaze to take in the surroundings beyond the naked trees that obscured the full painting of the night sky above me. The motion was not an easy one, the battering the river gave me had not been kind to my skull. With only a mild wince, I managed to turn to see that a makeshift camp surrounded me. I'd been laid into an alcove of rock surrounded by thick pines. Straw had been gathered to offer a bit of padding against the hard stone beneath me, the scent of sap registering only after my mind tied the images all together- a sure sign I'd taken a blow or two to the head.

A small fire danced just near enough for the heat to reach my skin but far enough off that the wafting smoke didn't choke me. There were rocks stacked around it to protect it from the wind, as well as to provide a surface with which to cook upon. Even as I blinked to try and focus on the details, the scent of egg wafted on the curtails of burning wood, causing my mouth to water with hunger.

The woman who had held me in place was still crouched beside me. She said nothing, merely let me take in my surroundings, undoubtedly recognizing the wide eyed look of surprise and panic scrawled across my face. In those moments of awe at still being alive, absorbing details of the world around me I had practically forgotten she was there. When I finally focused back on her, I jerked back a bit in surprise. She offered an amused smile but didn't laugh.

She had kind green eyes with hair that was light blonde and cropped short so that little spikes pointed outward messily. The look was one I'd seen on the youths in summer, but the weathered texture to her skin warned she wasn't as young as she appeared. She wore a winter cloak that looked to have been made from rabbit furs or some other fluffy creature. The original scent was long gone so I couldn't decipher exactly what it was.

There were three other women who sat on the other side of the fire similarly dressed. Their eyes watched me curiously while a fourth stood off to the side. The outlier's eyes were a bit more hard and wary, her dark hair falling in unruly waves past her shoulders. That was all I could really make out with the weariness clinging to me as it did. I did however notice the tribal tattoos on the women. Although I had no idea what their meanings were, it was a sure sign that I had done it. I had made it across the river into the Amazon lands, and somehow still lived enough to bask in the frigid cold of victory.

I turned my head back to look at the woman who was taking it upon herself to nurse me back to health. I tried to sit up a bit, but the wound at my side sent a jolt of pain that was answered with another at my back and echoed in a dozen other places - like a choir blessed with poor timing. I cringed and gave up the effort, managing to hold on to consciousness for my defeat.

"A- ar." My words thrust out their arms and barricaded themselves in my throat, causing me to cough. Lips as parched as a desert split immediately, casting copper upon my tastebuds. The blonde woman quickly brought a mug of water up to my lips and helped me to drink. The water hit my stomach hard but my throat was desperately dry and the liquid brought instant relief. My voice was raspy, but I tried once again to voice my question.

"Are you Amazons? I made it?" I had to be sure, even with the evidence right in front of me, simple and plain enough a toddler might have looked at me as if I were an idiot for asking. Still, I needed to hear those simple words - confirmation that I wasn't just delirious or trapped in some unique and vivid purgatory.

She tilted her head curiously and gave a slight smile, questions dancing behind her eyes though she seemed to bite most of them back. "Yes, sister, you are safe in the boundaries of the Vouno' tribe lands. Now that you are conscious however, I must ask why it is you have come and why you have sustained such extensive injuries doing so. Who did this to you?"

I sighed, the action not without pain. How could I put it into words, all that had happened, so that they might understand it without revealing too much. How might I even manage to form that many words with what felt like a desert in my mouth. I had been assured the Amazons would protect any who dwelled in their territory, but I couldn't trust anyone - not until I truly knew their intent. I was not exactly what one might call normal and although Amazons were open minded, they were still human and humans always feared what they didn't understand. There was too much at risk and I had fought too hard to get here to ruin it with pure honesty - at least when it came to exactly what I was.

"The Mad King wished me enslaved, or perhaps worse than that. I still don't know what that insane brute fully intended. I simply managed to get away and came here."

The woman laughed at my blasé explanation. With a hand holding her chin, she cocked her brow and tilted her head in a manner that expressed exactly what she said. "Something tells me 'simple' is hardly the word for it. Though a better explanation can wait until you are properly recovered."

I sighed again. None of it was a lie, but there was a great deal more between the gaps than I thought I had words for; even when I didn't feel as if I'd been in a losing battle against an avalanche. I couldn't afford to tell them too much, especially while vulnerable. There were things even I didn't understand, so how could I ever ask another to? Raising a shaky hand to my eyes I pressed against the ache just behind them, pleased that those muscles at least still listened properly. Exhaustion threatened to take me under if given just a brief relief from the pain of my wounds. If only sleep was an escape from the mental circles I was running as well. I knew better than to hope for a night without dreams.

When I reopened my eyes the stern face of the woman standing across the fire caught my gaze and refused to let it go. I swallowed hard even as I felt my body bristle. It felt as if she were looking through me trying to delve straight into my soul. It was an alpha stance if ever I'd seen one, though to be fair I could not relate to it. The pack mentality did not run dominantly within me, but I could be a social beast when the need arose.

She nodded slightly but I could tell that she was not convinced I was worth the efforts of nursing back to health. Thankfully, she didn't bother prodding me for information when her alto voice rose to address me from across the fire.

"A day's rest and then you either give us a believable explanation, or we will toss you back across the river." She turned and walked away.

I let out the small breath I had been holding and the woman beside me giggled lightly. The sound was nothing like the menacing notes of crazy that had hidden in Leola's laughter. These giggles were pure light and they felt like fresh air tasted. Perhaps that was just the magic of healers - everything about them seemed to soothe you.

"Don't worry, she's not as hard as she likes to let on. Sleep now, we need you well rested and healing before we can take you home. It's okay, you are safe and this will help you sleep."

That word, 'home' caught me off guard and I met her eyes sharply as she spoke it. She gave me nothing more than a knowing smile as she handed me another mug of water that tasted slightly off. Then there was nothing but the darkness and peace of a dreamless sleep.

The next day I was in and out of sleep. By the time Xalia demanded a proper explanation the sun had begun to set. Serah gave her a glare that held no heat, but the warrior pretended not to notice.

"Start from the beginning. How and why were you taken prisoner?"

A groan slipped past my lips as I looked up at the sky, the subtle blending of red and orange far more interesting than a trip back down the road I had only barely gotten off of.

"Sheer stupidity I'm afraid. They had a ground trap dug and I ran right into it trying to get to an injured fox they'd tied on the other side of it." Remembering the poor beast sent a chill down my spine, its beautiful orange coat stained red, its throat slit open, and the broken leg that had caused it to scream dangling from the hands of the man who had taken its life. He'd been the first guard, of many, I'd taken a bite out of. If it hadn't been for those enchanted bindings I'd have sliced his throat in turn.

"What did they charge you with?" Serah asked with earnestness, her eyes curious.

"Existing, apparently. The King thought I could give him answers I could not, even with a truth potion." The two watched me carefully, though to be fair I had no intentions of flat out lying to them. I owed them my life and although I remained wary, there was no reason not to trust them with at least the simplest version of my truth.

Xalia narrowed her brows for a second then gave a small sigh.

"Not the first one I've heard of being grabbed for something similar, though you are the only one to come back from it. How did you escape?"

"Sheer dumb luck. Leola, the King's daughter, thought she could do what her father couldn't but when I made her particularly angry she got sloppy and left a door unlatched. The rest you know. I ran and by some miracle made it to the river."

As the words passed my lips my mind became extremely clear on that matter. The pieces all locked together into the perfect portrait of Leola, a knife behind her back and a sweet smile on her face. There had been no true friendship, all of it had been manipulation to get to something they thought I had. Every touch came when I had needed gentleness the most. There had been so much conditioning to make Leola appeal to me in every way possible, a fool would have seen through it with ease. Yet I had been so battered and broken, that if it hadn't been for the humming pull and the dreams, I might have succumbed completely in the end, just for relief.

"Lykos, are you alright?" Xalia was leaning towards me, almost seeming to care. Serah grabbed her by the arm.

"Alright enough questions for now! I'm hungry and dinner won't make itself."

With a wink Serah took Xalia off, leaving me to my thoughts, which quicker than anything faded into more sleep.

Serah, my self-appointed caretaker, was a sweet young woman who was training to be a healer. She claimed to merely be a novice, but I was fairly certain she was being humble. There was almost always a smile on her face, the aura about her warm and welcoming. There was no part of me that doubted her sincerity, her kindness was given by choice not naivety. Her constant concern for the world around her was evident in the sweet way she approached even the wild flowers that stood in her way; always trying to crush as little as possible beneath her feet.

Serah's good nature manifested in her ability to talk about any and everything. Her talkative nature meant she was more than happy to fill my conscious hours with her knowledge of all things; the first and foremost being just how lucky I was to be alive.

"We were coming back from a meeting with one of the villages that runs along the southern border when we heard the barks of the boar dogs." She made a face as she paused, sadness there but also anger.

"It's a true shame what the poor beasts go through. They are hardly ever treated with an ounce of kindness when used by the King's men. Those nasty brutes are just as cruel as the slavers they were purchased from."

"They definitely don't hold their punches, that's for sure." A laugh fell from my lips as Serah looked at me with wide eyes. "It was them or me, suppose it was an easy choice."

She frowned at that.

"Artemis must have blessed your journey, the rain that followed behind you saved your life just as much as we did."

Had the water not washed away my scent, it would not have merely been the baying scent hounds I'd heard but also the vicious snarls of the boar dogs. As it were, they hadn't risked losing control of the beasts without a proper scent to follow. Yet I couldn't account for it, surely it had rained ahead of me, not behind? Had I somehow cut across the storm without even knowing? There was no way they should have lost me so quickly, but there was also no use in debating it and looking a gift horse in the mouth.

Miracle I even made it that far at all. Perhaps Artemis did throw me a bone.

The Gods and Goddesses had long ago fallen out of favor, only the Amazons openly prayed and honored their Goddess any more. Yet always my mother had believed they still walked amongst us, observing even if they didn't interfere.

Since it was strictly forbidden for outsiders to hunt in Amazon territory, they had detoured to make sure that the group had not trespassed and that was when they stumbled upon me. As she rehashed the discovery of me along their shore, barely alive, her face grew a bit concerned and confused for a moment. It was barely a pause, but I wondered what she was choosing to leave out.

"They didn't try to come get me?"

Serah's lips curled into a delicate smile, pride in her eyes as she looked over to where Xalia stood.

"Oh they thought about it, but Xalia has perfect aim and made it very clear they wouldn't return if they crossed."

There was such fondness in the look, a tinge of jealousy slid into my gut. It was not that I desired Serah or Xalia. No, I simply longed for that depth of affection. There always lacked that level of connection with any woman I thought myself fond of. The pull inside me always over-powering any crush I managed to develop. As a result, loneliness had been a steady companion, no matter how crowded the room.

"Perhaps one day, when she doesn't look like she will try to kill me if I speak to her, I'll swallow my pride and thank her for that."

Serah's lips curled into a smirk, shaking her head lightly as she motioned for me to sit up so that she could check my wounds.

"Maybe if you swallow that pride sooner, she will stop looking at you like that."

"Probably, but let's not get ahead of ourselves. After all, I've had enough miracles granted in the last few days that one more might seem greedy."

She crooked a brow at me, then burst out in giggles that made me grin with satisfaction.

"Oh good, my sense of humor is still intact. Wasn't sure it had survived the drowning."

Serah shook her head and looked like she was going to slap my arm but thought better of it.

"This is going to be a fun trip home." Her grin lit up her face and it was easy to see how even someone as hard as Xalia could fall for the spritely woman. There had been no lack of looks from the warrior to the healer when she thought no one was watching.

"You really are healing amazingly fast, Lykos. I do not know how you managed to survive all these wounds, especially with how dark your clothes were stained."

As today proved no different than the last dozen, I merely nodded my agreement as I laughed.

"My mother always said I was touched by Goddess' and that Nemesis herself looked after me. She would never tell me what made her so certain beyond my healing, but she remained ever loyal to Nyx and her daughter even after our village shunned us for it."

In truth there were no lies in my words, though it was not my mother's belief in the Goddesses that had shunned us. No, they would tolerate our presence, but only if the cursed fox stayed out. My mother prayed and we obliged; the next day we left to live on the outskirts. However, my mother was not without her own brand of spite. We could survive without their aid, but by running the prey animals off their traps we forced them to rely upon us for anything larger than a squirrel. Our game had amused my mother even up to her last day on earth, when she swore Nemesis came for her personally, smiling at the shadows as if she spoke with an old friend.

"I wouldn't be surprised if there is truth to that. Nothing else explains it."

Lost in memory, Serah's words drew me back and when I focused on the world I found Xalia staring at me. Her eyes were narrowed but not in a challenging way, almost as if she were trying to pinpoint something familiar that she couldn't quite name. I quirked a brow at her but she merely walked off.

Serah assured me that Xalia was merely skeptical of outsiders but I couldn't stop worrying that she saw more than I was comfortable with. It wasn't often people could sense magic, but the few who did usually lived in the wilds closer to nature, just as the Amazons did. Thankfully, Serah's spunky personality quickly pulled me back to more pleasant thoughts, especially when she cleared me for movement.

"Well, I can't explain it but you look great, considering what you have been through. As long as you don't push too hard, I'd say it's safe for us to get you moving."

"I'm happy to wager it's safer to get me moving than keeping me idle at this point. Besides, I'm fairly certain Xalia will murder me in my sleep if we don't start moving soon."

Serah rolled her eyes but laughed all the while, throwing a roll of bandages at me as she stood up to start breaking camp.

"So dramatic you are! If she kills you it's going to be while you're wide awake, much more satisfying that way." Shock rippled through me, but her laughter assured me of her humor, even if it was in an unexpected form.

I was shooed away when I tried to help Serah and cohesively ignored by Xalia and the other Amazons when I asked how I could help. At first I thought they might think me completely useless, until I caught Serah giving a hard eye to one of the women who had been walking my way with a pack that needed to be tied to the horses. She promptly turned and did it herself. Sighing, I accepted my role as a burden for the time being, not wishing to have any more skepticism attached to my health than there already was.

Standing out of the way I worked on stretching my sore muscles. The wraps around my feet cushioned the deep bruises, the slices having healed while I slept. Dark marks still tarnished my skin where the worst injuries had occurred, but I'd recovered enough energy for my magic to stir again, healing the internal wounds first. Only someone who had seen me as I was fresh out the river would be able to tell how remarkable my recovery was. Although my body healed physically, my emotional and mental state was questionable at best.

The tea Serah had given me over the past few days had given me peaceful sleep, but could do nothing to dull the stirring of my magic as we set off towards their village. My fox had been quieted for necessity, then was out of reach for mere lack of energy left to give, but now amongst the wilds I could feel her stirring. That other part of me would soon be attainable once more. To think of shifting brought a surge of excitement that almost drowned out the nervous apprehension of whatever it was calling to me.

Packed and ready, we set a slow and steady pace. The horses were anxious to get a move on, but quieted under the hands of their skilled riders. I rode behind Serah when my legs became too tired, my body still depleted of energy.

The terrain was much as it had been on the other side of the river. The rock face had been carved out over centuries by wind and rain so that the trail looked impossibly steep until you approached it and realized it was just an illusion. The stone looked like a wall until you had climbed and looked down. The edges were smoothed out so that the depth of one outcropping against another was indiscernible by the human gaze.

The trail curved back and forth, masking travelers from the prying eyes of those below once they had reached halfway up. It was at that point that the trail narrowed, hidden behind boulders that had long ago fallen. Tree roots held them steady as the spindly giants grew tall enough that they had to bend with the wind. The trees did not seem to thin on this side of the river and there were more firs here that refused to lose their needles.

The terrain was easy enough for the horses to climb, but only if you knew which paths to take. Serah often had to point me in the right direction when we led. The fall leaves were constantly shuffled by the icy mountain breeze, hiding the trails beneath their foliage. It was the wind and tightness of my chest as I tried to breathe that eventually alerted me to the changes in elevation.

During a pause the youngest of the group, Clara, stood beside me as I gazed up at the tall trees bowing to the wind. Her smile was shy, but her lips were full and her eyes bright with excitement and awe. She had made a point to try and converse whenever she thought Xalia and Serah were not looking. I couldn't bring myself to take the elder Amazon's caution personally; I could see in the way Clara eyed my recovering muscles that they merely hoped to keep the young woman from making a fool of herself. The youthful Amazon would grow to be a beautiful woman, but she was barely old enough to be rutting around another woman's bed, let alone a stranger ten years her elder.

"They say that long ago the Gods promised this side of the river protection no matter what season. That is why our trails hide themselves, rocks cluster where we need them to, and our trees do not grow their spring foliage until the river becomes too full to pass."

I indulged her as one would a younger sibling and nothing more, happy to learn as much about her culture as possible before I was face to face with the Queen.

"Do you believe that?" I finally asked her as she finished her once over of me from the corner of her eye, not even ashamed to have been caught in the act.

Foolhardy that one.

"I dunno. It's been true as long as my family has lived here. Stories have to get their truth from somewhere don't they?"

"Perhaps the better question is did they promise that protection when the Amazons lived here or someone else? Then at what price did that bargain come? The Gods never give without expecting something in return."

I watched as her brows furrowed in contemplation, trying to remember her history lessons now that she was presented with something they might be relevant to. One of her friends had pity on her and came to drag her away as we set back off. I smirked to myself as she cast a look back to me, expecting some immature explosion of words that would be meant to convince me she knew the answer.

"I'm going to have to think and get back to you...."

I nodded and waved her off.

When we had traveled far enough into the Amazon lands for the younger scouts to go alone without worry, Xalia sent them ahead to inform the Queen of our impending arrival. Clara waved enthusiastically, promising she would ask her teachers about the inquiry I'd presented her with. With the absence of the younger Amazons, I found myself with two polar opposites of personality and an increasing desire to be capable of moving quicker as Xalia's focus became a bit more concentrated.

The next morning I stirred from sleep earlier than my companions anticipated. Their hushed voices were not quite low enough for my keen hearing to miss, though they had taken extra precautions by moving to the opposite side of the camp, barely within reach of the fire's heat. I was hardly surprised to find myself at the center of their argument, though the tones being used were far less mild than I'd witnessed thus far. We were two days out from their home and although I understood Xalia's concern I was also quite annoyed by the way she spoke. It was Serah's admission that first caught my attention, though not what kept it.

"I'll admit her healing is beyond what it should be, but that's no reason to shun the poor woman! You are being more than distrusting Xalia, you are being downright RUDE! We have seen plenty of women who were born gifted in some way."

She huffed angrily, her face turned away from me so that I could not see the expression that made Xalia's eyebrows tilt off kilter.

"This is our *home* Serah! Our family! There is a difference between women we have grown up with and strangers found half-dead. You have a big heart, but it's going to get you hurt one day..."

Thick with passion, I could hear the slight quiver at the edge of Xalia's voice, the firelight grabbing her features and casting them in shadow so that I could not make out the finer details. Serah's voice held no reservations, just as strong and bold as she ever was soft and kind.

"She deserves a chance. Who knows what she has been through."

There was a long pause filled with all the unspoken words between the two friends. Afraid to breathe in case they overheard, I held my breath as I waited for the conversation to continue.

"She is scared, injured and one woman...give her a chance to at least prove herself before you condemn her to whatever fate she is fleeing!"

In that moment it dawned on me that Xalia could possibly have some kind of effect on my future. It wasn't a settling notion considering how much she distrusted me. I could have been open and honest, but there was so much they wouldn't understand. I had sensed Xalia's judgment the second she'd laid eyes on me; no quarter given. At that moment I could not recall if I had given her reason to suspect any kind of ill intent, but I was reassured of my own actions by the ally I found in Serah. She was a sweet woman but by no means naive. I wouldn't try to sway Xalia's opinion of me, let her think what she wanted, I would be hard pressed to need approval from anyone aside from myself. Besides, she'd likely see right through an act.

I was healing quickly enough to be able to hold my own within a few days, after that I could make my own way if need be. The question was did I really want to? The answer was no. I didn't want to be alone anymore. Above surviving I had only two goals: To find whatever pulled my magical leash, and to find a home in more than just a physical sense.

I would need to win them over, though I wasn't sure how. That I would try to extend a bit more kindness towards Serah was certain. I was poor with words most of the time, but I could at least try to convey my appreciation for her faith in my worthiness. I wasn't entirely sure I deserved her care or kindness, but I wasn't about to do her the disservice of turning it away or taking it for granted.

Tired of listening to my fate being discussed like a horse at auction, I made a show of pretending to have just woken up. Stretching so that they would disperse without knowing any different, I added a large yawn that wasn't altogether false once it was started.

Xalia gave a roll of her eyes and stomped off, but Serah offered a bright smile that shone in her eyes.

"Good morning! I hope we didn't wake you."

Her gaze held a silent question and I couldn't help but smirk. Her smile wavered for only a split second before she gave a shrug and a wink.

"Don't you worry, she will come around."

"I think you have an overly optimistic opinion on that matter."

My words were rewarded with a playful swat to the head. Somehow I had found myself a friend.

"OR maybe you are merely too pessimistic! She is just worried. She has seen many things she will never speak of. It makes her skeptical and stubborn, but she is as loyal a friend as one could ever ask for."

She gave a telling sigh that made me arch an eyebrow and wiggle it.

"Sounds like someone is crushing hard!"

She again swatted at me, both of us laughing lightly, causing the grumpy Xalia to comment loudly that the horses would not saddle themselves. We only laughed harder and once Serah had examined my wounds to make sure I had not torn the stitches and the healing flesh was no longer puckered or raw, we made our way over to the horse we had been alternating between.

The black steed that Xalia was saddling whickered at me and I smiled fondly in response. His legs were all marked with white stockings and there was a white snippet on his nose that looked like a scar. Catching the beast's nose in my hands I planted a kiss on the soft velvet before letting him lick the salt from my sweaty palms. I casually walked up to Serah and playfully swiped the now slobber covered appendages on her arm, causing her to squeal and chase me around her spotted mare. Used to our antics, the mare merely snorted and smacked me with her tail as I used her rump to keep balance while skidding around her.

"I'm pretty sure this kind of activity goes against my healer's orders!" I taunted from across the back of the mare with a winded laugh.

"Then you shouldn't have wiped slobber on her!" She darted forward again.

I would have missed the expression on Xalia's face if my peripheral vision hadn't been so keen, but the adoration was clear as her gaze followed the healer's form disappearing behind her steed. The look was quickly covered with a scowl, however, when Serah nearly collided into me as she ducked beneath her mare and cut me off. Serah steadied us then finally punched me in the arm. As I laughed and walked to the other side Xalia grumbled something at her that I didn't quite catch but it caused Serah to pause and shortly after pout. Whatever was between them, it seemed a delicate thing that had not yet been said by either, though anyone with eyes could see it.

Not wishing to hold us up any longer and the mood properly spoiled by Xalia's comment, I cinched up the mare's saddle and clamored up. Then, just to spite the woman for ruining the mood, I offered Serah to ride along behind me. It wouldn't be the first time we had sat double together, so she took my proffered arm and sat behind me with a sad glance to Xalia as the taller woman stuck her heels to the black beast and moved ahead. The rest of the day quickly slipped into the normal rhythm of travel, silence enveloping us as we simply strove to stay warm atop our mounts.

The next day marked our last bit of travel. We had risen high in the mountains only to plateau off and dip down again. The wilds that sprung up were spared the heavier storms by the taller cliffs that spread out alongside the valley. This allowed the trees to stand tall and grow far thicker than I'd have ever imagined in the mountains.

Perhaps these lands are protected by the Gods.

The thought arose from the memory of what the young Amazon, Clara had said. These lands were certainly designed to be protective and easily defensible. The valley served as a funnel for any who might try to reach the Amazon village. It was not an expansive shot of land, but it served its purpose. As much as we had traveled downhill to reach it we now climbed up its backside to get to their home.

The sound of a waterfall marked the first posted scout. A thick barreled tree rose from a split boulder, lumbering tall with limbs threatening to go bare. The waterfall alongside it spilled down from a crevice high above in the cliffside. The sound was used to hide the shifting of the woman high in the treetop, but I could always sense the eyes of a predator. I turned to look at the woman who hid amongst the trees and let a smirk pull at my lips when I found her face wide with surprise. Serah waved as we went past, then snickered into my back.

"You're gonna fit in just fine."

Even Xalia spared a moment to cast her gaze back and nod approvingly.

When we finally arrived I was surprised to find that the village itself wasn't nearly as fortified as I had imagined it would be. There were no high fences or visible offensive measures. The high mountain created a solid and safe barrier to the rear of the village while huts lined the far left and seemed to be the center of life amongst the Amazons. I guessed that these were probably where the basic work took place, the sound of a blacksmith's hammer coming from somewhere in that area. The far right had rows of trees that had long ago been planted close together, just gapped enough for a person to slip between but too narrow for a horse to pass.

As we had traveled Serah told me this was how they kept their horses from roaming without having to hobble the beasts before the fences had been built. The trees were first planted so that they would act as a buffer so that the grass seed would be able to stick this high up on the mountain. It was a hardy sort of seed they'd harvested from small native patches. They had originally found the grasses by following the wild goats. The barrier went all the way around the pasture with only one entrance wide enough to get a double brace of horses through.

I was amazed that they had the forethought and patience to look after the future generations, knowing that the trees would take years to do their jobs, but trusting that one day it would pay off. Just as they had done with the trees they had also worked the mountainside to their favor. The Amazons had long ago carved tunnels that led to hot springs and from there channeled the warm air into large communal rooms where everyone could warm themselves in winter. I would not yet get to see the latter, but Serah had assured me on the trip that I would get a full tour and free access to a hot mineral bath once I'd met with the Queen.

I was impressed when Serah told me all of these things, but seeing it all in person made me nervous. It was more than I could have ever hoped for and yet it was not yet truly in my grasp. Whether or not I was allowed to stay past my meeting with the Queen was up to the council. I had asked after their leader and her council women, trying to gauge how best to present myself, but predictably the Amazons were unwilling to give anything away other than their ruler and council women were all well respected and loved. The reassuring smile I'd received from Serah did little to comfort me now.

We dismounted the horses and tied them to posts near what appeared to be a lookout perch. The trough of water was full and clean and fresh hay had been dropped into the nets hanging from a hook between the two posts.

"Take care of the horses for me, will you Clara?"

Xalia's words drew my attention to the young Amazon who had bounded up with eyes lit up like it was a celebratory day. Her smile was filled with all the naivety of youth as she nodded enthusiastically at Xalia. The stern Amazon did not roll her eyes as I might have, but instead gave the duty off to her as if it were indeed an honor she had earned. It was the long sigh and grimace she shared with Serah after that reassured me I had not missed anything there. The over eager young woman was certainly enthusiastic but had also likely spent the whole day before we arrived gossiping like a fool. Her eagerness was nothing new apparently.

I took a deep breath as we walked toward a large hut positioned a bit further off from the rest, my eyes focusing on my footsteps so that I wouldn't notice the eyes of all the women around me. None stared for long, soft curiosity the only thing I could pinpoint from my averted gaze. When we finally approached the hut, Serah left me to stand next to Xalia while she disappeared behind the door and announced our arrival to the Queen. Muffled voices exchanged pleasantries but the wood doors were thick to fight the cold and made their words little more than whispered sounds without meaning. A few moments later Serah emerged.

"They are ready for you. Don't worry, they've already had breakfast!" She winked and slapped my forearm as I rolled my eyes and gave her a couple of clearly faked laughs.

"Serah the comedy bard everyone!" I sneered but she merely stuck out her tongue as Xalia tried to hide her amusement with an eye roll.

"Don't keep them waiting Lykos - go in." Her alto notes were not cold but instead merely practical. I had seen her cut up a few times with Serah but other than that she was stiff and serious pretty much all the time. Leave it to Xalia to kill the light mood. I didn't bother responding, instead I merely opened the door and slipped inside.

The hut was a lot more open than it appeared from the outside. A fire was built up at the far side of the room, a bit of oil giving the smoke a pleasant scent that I couldn't quite pinpoint but was something similar to lavender. The heat did nothing to help my nerves and I found myself quickly starting to sweat. I had been given a spare cloak and the thick deerskin seemed to shrink around me as the eyes of all the women within watched me like hawks. I took a deep breath and stepped forward as the woman at the head of the table beckoned me forward with her hand, her face giving away nothing other than a few tell-tale signs of seasons past. Despite her weathered features there was no hint of gray in her dark blonde hair. Her hazel eyes were equally just as sharp, though they sparkled with untold wisdom.

Beside her sat a woman who had obviously earned her place at the table, several scars marred her otherwise handsome face. I thought her to be younger than the rest of the women, but not by much. Her eyes were hard but not in a way that made me uncomfortable, instead it left the impression that she had seen much in her years and probably deserved my respect. The woman beside her sat particularly close, her hands folded on top of the table as if she had all the time and patience in the world. She was the only one to offer me a smile as I caught her gaze.

On the opposite side of the table an old woman with stark white hair watched me with sky blue eyes that left my soul feeling bare. I tried to keep her gaze but found that everything in me screamed to deflect. I averted my gaze away with a respectful dip of my head even as her scent trickled across to me. The smell of magic weaved into her essence so strongly it amazed me no one else seemed to notice. The stir of it caused me to wince as it tickled my nose to the point I thought I might sneeze.

The woman beside her was tall and lanky with the look of a scholar, her fingers smudged with ink that had left a streak across her nose and cheek where she'd rubbed her face. I took this all in within only a few moments, but it was long enough to prompt the Queen to speak and immediately draw my attention back to her commanding presence.

"Why have you come to Amazon lands?"

Her voice gave nothing away but she tilted her head ever so slightly as if she were curious to see what I would say, even though there was no doubt she had already been told.

"I had no other choice." I let my voice carry softly, nothing abrasive in its tone nor anything particularly exciting. Perhaps if the truth sounded as dull as possible there wouldn't be as many follow-up inquiries.

She quirked her brow at my response, giving the distinct impression that she would not be swayed from prying. Her hands drew up to her chin and supported her head as she leaned forward, reminding me of a curious cat waiting for her prey to run so the hunt would be more exciting.

"So then, had you another choice where might you be?"

A sigh escaped my lips before I could catch myself even as I swiped a hand across my eyes, exhaustion bearing down on me even though my body was well on its way to recovering.

"I would be far from these lands Queen, far from the reaches of the Mad King and his cruelty.... I mean no offense, a life with the Amazons sounds like a dream I could hardly conjure in my sleep, but I would not put others at risk for a grudge held against me. I doubt he will give up on capturing me."

The queen glanced towards the elder woman who smelled of magic, a smirk suddenly pulling at her weathered features. I didn't quite understand what was happening, but the Queen nodded as if she had already known where my thoughts might lead.

"What is it that draws the King's mad eye to you so certainly? Surely you must have wronged him in some way?"

The bait was set, the trap lingering somewhere just beyond where I could not see it. There was a deep wisdom flowing through the room and even as I waded into its depths, I could not fathom its extent. A lie would be known just as easily as it had been with the truth potion just weeks prior. I had no desire to withhold information from the women who might give me aid, but I also had no desire to be hunted like the animal I was either. There upon the edge of truth and lie I balanced, ever staying within the gray edges that might conceal and protect, casting my line out with the tide to see how far I might swim before drowning.

"The only wrong I seem to have done to him is existing in a manner to which he was not satisfied. He and his daughter seek magic, they believe they can become Gods somehow. He demanded of me things I could not oblige and even when under a truth potion, my answers only angered him more."

Glancing around the table I purposely avoided the magic scented elder and instead perused the expressions of the rest of the council. None felt the need to shield their reactions as they all seemed in agreement that my words held truth.

"Well, she is not wrong, though she skirts around the whole of it. I doubt even she is aware of what draws her to our lands." The older woman addressed the Queen while placing a weathered hand upon her arm.

"Your wisdom is heard, Rhea. Perhaps trust and a little bit of faith on our end is where we should start."

The old woman finally caught my gaze as I turned my head to listen to her speak, her lips curling into a bright smile that creased her wrinkled face further. My body froze in place as she refused to divert her eyes. Her gaze felt as if it peeled back layers until she could caress my soul.

There were whispers in the air around her. It was something too high for human ears and yet practically visible to any eye that might seek it out. There were colors to it all if one knew which spectrum to look through. Her magic reached out to caress my own, the sensation mimicking the soft stroke of fur along my spine. The motion was innately intimate yet I felt no intrusion, merely a sense of calm.

Magic knew magic so there was no doubt that at least one of the council women knew exactly why the Mad King might seek me out. What remained to be seen was what she did with that knowledge.

"Perhaps he will come, perhaps not... "

The Queen nodded permission to the scarred Amazon, who now spoke. Her voice was gravely but I found that it wasn't unpleasant in the least.

"My Scouts have reported to me that while you were unconscious the men chasing you attempted to cross the river to retrieve your body. Dead or alive."

I could feel fear contort my face as I listened to her words but she held up a hand to calm me as she continued. A sense of dread filled me and restricted my lungs, the expression on my face likely one that would have embarrassed me to see in a mirror. The soft stroking of magic continued, keeping my body from bolting when the fear of a trap might have overwhelmed me.

"We are not so cut off from the world that we do not know what is going on beyond our borders. They were refused passage across the river, as you know, but not because they were told you were alive. As far as the guards know you died on the banks of our river and we gave you a proper burial. Serah and Xalia made sure to build the funeral pyre where they could see it burn."

Relief flooded my entire body allowing my lungs to expand in a flurry that caused me to gasp for air. The women closest to me garnered laughter from it, though there was no cruelty in their amusement at my relief. Instead the sound was fringed with understanding, as if they had all been in my shoes and needed to laugh off the nervous shadow of a memory.

"Mother help me, you might have led with that bit of information." The words were out before I could curb them, my arm out to brace myself against the wooden table between them. Nerves had caused my hands to begin shaking, something I doubt the Queen missed.

The Queen laughed though I sensed she caught the sour lilt to my tongue. In truth I was far more hurt that Serah had not told me rather than the Queen waiting to do so.

"We might have done a lot of things, be glad testing your reactions was the worst of it." The scholarly woman looked at me sideways as she spoke, her voice bland as she stated the words matter-of-factly, no sort of inflection given to the words that hinted at any dual meaning.

"So then, if your only disinterest in joining our tribe was fear of bringing us trouble, I believe that to be resolved for now. When you are considered healthy enough by our healer you will be given two options; leave our lands, or pass our tasks in order to join our ranks. Serah has vouched for you and I trust her judgment, however we will each meet with you between now and then to determine if we agree with her assessment. For now, you need to see the healer."

I wanted to know exactly what she knew, what they had heard about the Mad King's actions, but a quick scan of the room made it very clear that I had been dismissed. They were kind, their smiles genuine, but there was a quiet pause that lingered in their actions. My head had begun to swirl and the room faded out of focus as my senses became overwhelmed by the fragranced oil burning. When I finally focused, the Queen gave me a smile. Something about it said she knew more than she was saying.

Much like a dog that let the fox be blamed for a dead chicken.

I gave a half bow, not truly knowing what I was doing. When I rose I found the almost cloudy blue eyes of Rhea watching me. There was something severely unnerving as she met my gaze and refused to blink. A shudder ran along my spine as if she had looked right through me, passing like a spirit and taking a tiny bit of me with her. I made haste to leave, hoping that my exit was polite enough to pass.

I couldn't really complain about the outcome, if nothing else I had time to heal and figure out what my next move would be. I had only let myself hope that I would make it to these lands, the idea that I might be allowed to stay had never crossed my mind. There would be time enough to absorb the entirety of the meeting and all the events preceding it. That singular truth bore with it the truest extent of relief I had felt in years.

"Come with me, you need to see the healer." Xalia's tone left no room for argument.

Given my only other option was to wander around aimlessly searching for it myself, I gave no argument and merely fell into step alongside her. As she weaved in and out of the huts, my gaze wandered as I tried to commit as much information as possible to memory. There were very few differences at first glance, the huts varied in size but otherwise the materials were all the same. The mountains provided an innumerable amount of stones to work with and so large stones were stacked and held together by a unique clay mixture I had not seen before. The roofs were similarly constructed, except with much thinner and flatter rocks, likely chiseled off for that specific purpose.

"Why stone roofs instead of straw like most villages?" My voice was low, my ignorance understandable, but not something I wanted to parade around.

Xalia paused in her stride to allow me a moment to take in the hut we were passing, pointing to the roof as she offered an answer.

"Although our winters have not been as bad the last few years, we can see heavy snows. Stone roofs withstand the weight of it and take less damage in blizzards. A stray fire will only scorch stone, where straw feeds it."

"Suppose it's no real hassle to find building materials either." I ran a hand along the side of the building and found it smooth, the winds undoubtedly having worn the rough edges down over the years, dissipating any raised seam that might have once been.

"Exactly. Where we built into the mountain itself provided the material for our exterior buildings, which eliminates the need to haul it elsewhere." She smiled proudly and I could not fault her for it. The Amazons were even more impressive in person than they had been in stories.

As we continued walking only a few lingering gazes followed us, their expressions seeming more curious than surprised. Considering the excitement surrounding the young scouts, it was easy to assume that most had heard about my arrival already. Scouts were trained to report what they found and the young ones were always exceedingly good at spreading it like wildfire.

Although the huts were not distinguished by any form of sign, flag, or unique coloring, I knew the healer's hut as soon as we headed toward it. It stood at an angle so that those entering the camp could only see the front and a small piece of the side. This gave the illusion that it was of little importance, when it was probably the largest of all the buildings. Likely it had started as one building which kept being extended with additional rooms to meet the needs of a growing populace. There was a bench built along its side, presumably a place for non-emergencies to wait, which effectively drew the eye away from the disjointed mark where more stone had been added later; the color of the clay was slightly off there. The smell of herbs and oils clung to the air around the hut as potted plants swayed in the crevices of windows absorbing sunlight.

Serah suddenly appeared in the doorframe and offered Xalia a bright smile as she held the door open for us to enter. Despite my hopes, she did not stay afterwards, instead she merely gave me a playful wink and trotted off towards the scout tower where we had left the horses. Xalia watched her go and I couldn't help but smirk when she turned to find me watching her. She rolled her eyes but shut her mouth mid-motion.

A middle aged woman came from the back of the hut and crooked a brow as she caught sight of us. The energy around her was filled with hints of magic though not nearly what I had felt around the councilwoman. This was far different, softer. This was a woman who was subtly touched and held in favor by one of the Gods. Undoubtedly she had been gifted a talent which aided in healing.

Her voice was light and airy, barely more than a loud whisper as she spoke.

"Ah so you must be the one Serah spoke of, yes? Lykos was it?"

I nodded, a slight smile curling the edges of my lips as she pronounced it the way my mom always had, as if the 'k' in it were capitalized. I'd never really had a preference on it one way or another but the familiarity warmed me.

"Yes Kyri'a that is correct."

Her eyes brightened as I spoke, their gold hue only adding to the essence of fire that lit her hair in deep auburn.

"Oh and manners alongside a proper speech! Bless the Goddess for that! The way our neighbors educate their girls is lacking I'm sure you know...Alright let's have a look at you then! Off with you Xalia I'm sure the girl would appreciate privacy after being watched like a hawk."

Her words were still soft but I was surprised to hear no room for argument in the lilt of her voice. I smirked, giving Xalia a halfhearted salute even as the hard warrior spared a warning glare my way before stepping outside again. The woman chuckled as she watched me.

"Don't you worry, once she warms up to you that one there is as loyal as a sheepdog to its flock."

Grinning, as I pictured the latest litter of puppies the sheep farmer's daughter had shown me before I had left, I moved over to where the healer was waiting for me.

"So everyone says. I can't say I actually care whether she does or not so long as she doesn't try to get me into any trouble."

"Aye, I can see why you'd want to avoid that! Seems to me you find enough trouble on your own eh?"

I shrugged, then pulled the deerskin cloak from my shoulders with a grunt; a few particular muscles were still quite angry with me for the stress and strain riding had put them through. Once that was done I undid the laces on my injured side and let the deerskin vest flop open. It would be enough to allow the healer to pull the material up and back to see the wounds beneath. I had not yet acquired a spare linen shirt but since I was not busty the vest worked well enough.

Her hands were soft and warm but I flinched at her touch simply out of reflex. There had been a time once when I had made myself insensitive to the tickles of my playmates by playing with my ribcage. Now, I leapt back like a shook rabbit. Oh how far down the rabbit hole I had fallen. Even a lover's embrace had often sent my skin crawling before it could be coaxed to relax and enjoy the sensations. Perhaps it was merely the fox in me, always aware of the hunters on my tail.

The healer did not comment as she worked, peeling back the bandages that had been stuck to me by the means of diluted sap. It pulled at the skin but was hardly a burden. After a minute or so prodding the edges she nodded, satisfied at the state of the wound at my side and then examined where the arrow had pierced my back. I had already healed more than usual, but since she didn't see my original state I'd hoped perhaps she might not notice. The woman proved far more knowledgeable than I had given her credit for, though Serah might have had something to do with that as well.

"You must be touched by the Goddess, sure as I'm standing here you're healing twice as fast as you should."

I offered her a kind smile and nodded, she would undoubtedly report back to the council, so I stuck with my original defense.

"My momma would always say the same, since I healed fast even as a child. I think it merely that wounds look far worse when they are on someone my size and complexion - blood is far more noticeable on fair skin."

The healer looked me over and simply nodded. I supposed it must have sounded reasonable to her, though her eyes seemed to go somewhere else for a moment before returning to my lithe and rather short frame.

"You will need to do better about stretching these muscles. Start small but do it daily, otherwise they will heal short and ache all through winter. Some archery practice will strengthen your shoulders and back again. I imagine proper meals will do the rest of the work."

She handed me a jar with a salve in it, a smile on her lips as if she knew me better than she did.

"Just because the wounds heal on the surface doesn't mean they are healed beneath. This salve will soothe the worst of the aches, but don't push yourself harder than your body can take. If you need to find me, I'm usually here, otherwise just ask around, I'm Gwenn."

I sniffed the salve and regretted it instantly as the heavy scent of spearmint burned my nostrils. The healer laughed as I made a face, shooing me out the door as soon as I had gotten my clothes straight.

Xalia arched her brow as I stepped out still forcefully blowing out my nose to try to get the tingle out. I held up the salve and she raised her hand in defense.

"Shit works wonders and smells great on the skin but damn is it strong in the jar."

A sneeze crept up and finally relieved the tickle in my nose though it had caused my eyes to water. Once I'd collected myself Xalia motioned for me to follow her again. Without any familiarity of the area I was left with little choice, so I followed her like a lost puppy.

She was indulgent and filled the air with explanations as to the function of every hut we passed as she gave me a quick tour of the village. Her manner was not entirely unfriendly, but it was apparent that she was not comfortable with the quickness that had been my acceptance into the fold. I could feel her tension, bunched beneath the skin like a fox waiting for the perfect moment to leap. It was something that would need to be resolved quickly, especially if I decided to stay, but for now I let her be uncomfortable so long as it didn't afford me any trouble.

She finally showed me to a small hut that would be my home through the duration of my stay. She asked if I had any questions, but I couldn't bring myself to prolong her company. With a nod she warned me not to cause trouble and to ask if help was needed; the village was small enough that everyone had been informed of my arrival and would point me in the right direction. I wasn't completely sure if that was comforting or terrifying.

Exhaustion still clung heavily to my body so when I laid down to test the bed, I didn't make it off until late into the afternoon when a soft tapping finally roused me from sleep.

When I finally stumbled to the door and opened it I found Serah beaming at me. Her arms were filled with bread rolls and dried meat as well as a basket of fruits. Her spikey blonde hair had been slicked flat from a bath, green eyes bright with excitement that was infectious.

"When you didn't appear for supper, well I figured you were avoiding everyone. Looks like you were just catching up on sleep instead!"

Holding open the door I ushered her in, closing it behind and taking the basket from her as soon as I could. The hut was minimally furnished but had everything one might need, including a square table in the kitchen area. There were only two internal walls, which formed an 'L' in order to separate the bed area from the rest. The open floor plan allowed for the small space to feel bigger and easy customization. I found it simple but cozy, like a den of sorts.

Setting the basket upon the table I searched the cabinets along the wall for cutlery and successfully found two clay plates while I was at it. Serah smiled at my success and distributed the meal equally; not even bothering to ask if she was welcome to join me, instead acting as if she had done this a dozen times. Perhaps she had, she certainly had a way of slipping into the fray without anyone feeling put out for it.

That I might have found a true friend in Serah caused me to smile as we sat across from each other, eating as she rambled on about this and that. Never once did she push or prod for more information, she merely shared her day with me pausing on occasion to eat. The one sided conversation was enjoyable and quickly I found my mind lulled to inattention.

"You should go by there tomorrow."

I had zoned out too far while she spoke and it took a second to piece together what she'd been saying moments before. Something about a woman named Onya. She shook her head and smirked at what was surely a lost look on my face.

"She is in charge of handling the horses, I think you'd enjoy her company."

I nodded silently, afraid if I spoke too much somehow all the things I wasn't saying would be written across my face. She took it in stride and simply offered a smile as she cleaned up the food, left the dishes in a stack for me to clean, and moved to the door.

"Thank you Serah, truly." Finally I managed to form a complete thought and push it to my lips. As if emphasizing that a day of sleep had not been enough, a yawn pulled at my jaw as I covered my mouth.

She laughed.

"Alright alright, get some more sleep you brute! I'll be back tomorrow night to hear all about your first day. Yes, I'll bring food, but then you gotta go socialize and get your own." She popped out of the hut with a wave before I could protest.

The bed I slept in was far from luxurious but since the alternative was the hard ground, it was comparable to a cloud. I awoke the next morning and stretched with the satisfaction of a full day's true rest. There was nothing quite like sleeping without the stress and worry of being attacked and killed in the night. It was a strange thing when it finally hit me the night before as I had lain in bed, full, warm, and comfortable. I was free. There was no reason for anyone to think I was alive. The sensation hit again as I rolled out of bed, nowhere to be and the freedom to go anywhere.

Although I felt a twinge of guilt for those who I had known, the overwhelming sense of relief quickly dissipated the rest. I smiled broadly and caught myself off guard when I suddenly laughed and couldn't stop.

I'm free.

The words turned over and over and I could hardly believe they were real. It filled me with energy and after tearing through a leftover roll of bread I decided to follow

Serah's suggestion and explore the village. The first place on my list was the stables.

Friendly smiles and waves greeted me as I walked along the packed clay path towards the stables. I offered nods and half smiles in greeting, my desire not to be stopped and pegged with questions seemingly answered. There was a bustle as the women made preparations for winter. The fall chill was still pleasant, but there was a threat of much worse always on the horizon. Thankfully, that was still a month away according to Serah.

The sun shone brightly as I stepped through the line of close grown trees, slipping through the shadows to the other side with ease. Pausing to let the sunshine envelope me, I closed my eyes and focused on the way the heated beams created a pleasant hum of warmth across my flesh. The cold mountain air tasted of frozen streams, trees that had already begun to lose their foliage and the heavier notes of dust and hay. A smile turned my lips as the smell of horses floated toward me and drew me back to where I was. No place ever felt like home the way a horse stable did.

Looking out over the fields, I found myself impressed with the size of their herd. The village had close to a hundred women currently living there, being the smallest of the Amazon tribes for its place amongst the mountains and there were nearly half that amount of horses. Fifty might seem like a low number in theory, but considering their home it was impressive they sustained them through the winter months.

I watched as the horses in the section closest to me grazed without so much as lifting their heads at my presence. They were obviously older, some showing their age in the way the fur around their eyes had faded, or the way their backs swayed. As I walked along the grassy slope it was easy to see many sported scars that had long since stopped growing hair. I guessed this must have been the retired horses, all too old to care to try and squeeze through the tree barrier that served as a fence and too seasoned to mind that my scent held something a little extra.

Further across the open expanse I noticed that there were indeed fenced areas such as pastures and training grounds, but the stables themselves were built partly into the side of the mountain just as the village was. There were plenty of people moving about their business, though none seemed too bothered when they spotted someone out amongst the fields. Everyone here had a place and job, so there was far more to be concerned with than someone who decided to take a break among the horses.

Careful not to spook the younger horses in the next field over, I ducked between the fence and started down the primary trail to the stables. The yearlings across the path trotted the fence line curiously until they caught wind of my scent and bolted with kicks and bucks that were clumsy from their youth.

As I approached a few of the women eyed me. They tilted their heads as if trying to figure out if they knew me or not, but I was quickly saved from any suspicious questioning when a voice called out my name.

"Lykos I presume?"

The voice was soft and yet confident despite the slight question tinged to the sentence. The soprano notes had an accent that was different from the rest of the Amazons I had encountered. She had a lilt that lengthened the words but not unpleasantly so. The woman who claimed ownership was just as unique.

Where most of the women were of a natural mahogany complexion, Onya's skin held a slightly redder tinge to it, her hair was smooth, long, and the mixed browns of tree rings and bark. Her eyes were what really set her apart. Bright green eyes practically glowed in the shadows of the barn where she stood, her white teeth showing as she offered a smile that I couldn't help but return. She was stunning, and although no taller than I was, her demeanor made her seem so. Her piercing gaze met my own without any caution, though when they found the blaze of my cerulean gaze she seemed to almost pause in thought.

"You would be right in doing so. Serah thought I might find myself something useful to do here, or at least be amused long enough not to find trouble."

At that she smirked and nodded, taking a moment to clearly look me up and down, not without a hum of appreciation.

"Although I do not trust Serah's motives, I do need some help."

I cocked my head in question but she merely gave me a wink and waved me over to follow her. I wasn't sure where she was going to lead me, but at this point I had nothing better to do than follow her. She took a path down the center of the stables, stalls of varying sizes lining both sides, the smell of hay and horse apples becoming a potent combination as a few Amazons worked on cleaning out the empty ones.

"Do you have any experience with horses Lykos?"

Onya's voice was sweet in the air, something familiar there that I could not name. The accent perhaps, though I couldn't recall meeting anyone with it before. I tried not to let my mind wander and worry over it for now.

"I do. I used to help break the yearlings my mother raised and rode my own gelding quite often."

My response was quiet, modest, and I hoped satisfied Onya's curiosity.

"Great! I have a fresh crop of imports from the Centaurs. We give them time to adjust of course but it's been a few months now and they have been left idle far too long. I'm afraid with the skirmishes and other disturbances brewing at our borders so often, it's left me quite shorthanded. Would you be interested?"

I couldn't figure out the weird sense of apprehension that filled my gut, but I also knew that I would go crazy if I sat idle. With a smile I nodded my head and she beamed back at me, her bright eyes full of warmth. From there she introduced me to the batch of new recruits, a beautiful array of colors amongst them; something the Centaurs were known for in their horse stock. Paints of all kinds of variations and colors met my eyes as she whistled and five spunky horses came toward the fence at a full gallop from across their field.

Apprehensive, I stepped back from the fence and soon appreciated my own forethought as their still clumsy movements sprayed dirt and grass into the air as three of the five miscalculated and almost crashed into the wooden planks. Onya simply laughed at their antics.

"Lively bunch this lot! They are all just as intelligent as rumored, imbued with the magic of the Centaur lands, so feel free to address them directly, they will respond. Isn't that right Bella?"

She spoke to a soft looking young mare whose deep brown eyes stood starkly out against the white of her piebald face, a few large spots of white were also thrown across the canvas of her otherwise red coat. The young mare tossed her head in an obvious show of 'yes'. There was something that filled the air around them that I recognized faintly, similar to Serah's but more intimate. I couldn't place it though, it was something like an old memory, almost déjà vu but only in scent. Had I ever encountered such a beast before? I was certain I had not, yet the same flicker of familiarity at Onya's accent occurred with these beasts.

Walking back up to the bunch I stretched out a hand with my palm flat and facing skyward. The young beast closest to me was a beauty and curiously extended his neck so that he could reach out to touch me. His mostly white face was marred with a patch of red at his right eye, and the side of his lip, his intelligent brown eyes catching my own as his nostrils flared tentatively at my hand. The texture of his muzzle was something to behold, softer than velvet or silk, still lacking the roughness age would bring it. He blew on my hand, tickling my fingers as a voice buzzed through my mind very much opposite of my own inner monologue. The shock caused my body to jolt in place, though I tried not to show surprise anywhere else.

"You are not what you seem are you?"

The intelligence in his eyes gave me no reason to doubt what I was hearing, but it was obvious to me that Onya did not have the same pleasure I was experiencing. A smirk flitted across her face as she watched me jump in surprise, but I saw it only from my peripherals as I maintained eye contact with the horse in front of me.

"How on earth are you speaking to me?"

His voice was sweet, still young and playful though wise beyond his years. *"I would suspect that it's magic. You are filled to the brim with it, more so even than we are. It'll be a pleasure working with you."*

I smiled in amazement, struck dumb so that I could only nod in response. He simply whickered what rolled in my mind as ironic laughter and took off across the field once more, the rest following him and leaving me alone with Onya.

After an encounter like that, how could I not agree to the work? Onya was excited to have me along and spent most of the day with me, showing me around and introducing me to several of the other horse handlers; all of whom were very friendly but also quite busy and so kept moving forward with their tasks rather than lingering. The latter made me feel much more at ease for the lack of attention.

Onya was more than content to drift into comfortable bouts of silence as well, which afforded her quite a few points in my book. She often would stop and just breathe in the air and I found myself smiling alongside her as we made our way. My wounds had not yet healed enough for me to help much, but where I could I gave a hand.

"I promise I'm much less useless when I haven't been sliced and shot recently."

My words came unabated as I stood watching her toss bales of hay into a stack, advising when it was off center but unable to do much more. Her laughter was charming even as she huffed with the effort.

"I promise to give you enough work later to make up for standing around watching me bust my ass."

"At least it's a nice one." The tease fell from my lips before I could curb it and thankfully it was met with nothing more than hearty laughter.

"Hell it ought to be with as many squats as I've gotta do around here! Stick around and maybe yours will turn out half *ass* nice."

The words rolled off her tongue and she winked for emphasis but I was already snickering, the humor striking me in a way that I hadn't enjoyed in a while. The snicker soon became an ongoing giggle that turned contagious as we both stood there holding our sides laughing.

When we finally went our separate ways that afternoon, I was thoroughly exhausted but equally exhilarated at the potential that life seemed to have stretched out before me. Perhaps things really would be different now. I truly was free.

Serah came by to eat supper with me but made it clear that I would not be afforded the convenience of her kindness the next day. We laughed over the obvious antisocial tendencies she could see me trying to embrace and she assured me that she would quickly nip them in the rear, as well as myself, should I try to prove difficult. With all her kindness, how could I possibly resist her friendship? Ignoring the shit eating and self-satisfied grin that held her face up for the next hour, I shared my day with her.

When I began to yawn, we said our goodnights. I assured her that I would make sure I was cleaned up in time to join her at the meal hut the next afternoon.

After spending another day with Onya at the stables, I made sure to rinse the worst of the dust off in a trough before heading with her to the food lodge. She and the other horse handlers quickly caught me up on how the process worked and the rules set in place to keep the workload fair. It was simple enough; if you couldn't cook, you took a turn washing up. The only ones who were excluded from the rotation were the Scouts, who kept patrol, and the horse handlers. The logic was that these two parties were always out in the weather and constantly doing physical labor and in doing so earned their way.

"Though, if you want to get on the cooks' good side and earn a few extra sweets, bring 'em fresh ingredients in winter." One of the stable hands whose name I had yet to catch whispered as she passed me a roll lathered in honey, licking her fingers clean afterward.

"Or get their fires ready in the mornings. The morning cook is an older lady whose bones ache, so she hates a cold kitchen." This came from Onya as she directed me toward a table filled with familiar faces.

Serah smirked as she saw me walk over with Onya. Her brow raised when I got closer, but I said nothing, instead bumping into her playfully as I sat down. She chuckled when it caused her to hit Xalia's elbow, knocking the roll from her hand and back onto the plate. Onya sat across from me while the other two stable hands filed in beside me.

The conversation while we ate was sporadic and of no importance either way, but when another Amazon's figure sauntered over, everyone's attention seemed to be caught.

"I told you it'd take less than a week." Serah giggled the words to Xalia who merely shook her head, though I did see her lip curl into a slight smirk before she shrugged it off. Serah's exuberance as she'd leaned over resulted in Xalia dropping a spoonful of food back to her plate. The sweet healer didn't even care to look abashed and once again I found myself pondering their relationship as Xalia remained unphased and patient, as if it were a normal occurrence.

I looked up to find that the new woman's dark brown eyes were taking me in thoroughly enough to be considered rude and I felt my hackles raise in defiance to the challenge in her gaze. She offered a saucy smile and wink in response, her voice rolling off her lips in a way that made me think of honey dripping off the comb.

"I don't believe we have had the pleasure of meeting just yet, I'm Camilla."

She extended a hand and with a sigh to replace the eye roll I felt like producing, I set my hand in hers. She drew it up to her lips and planted a delicate kiss there, to which I responded by giving her hand a tight clench that made her yelp lightly - an action that brought a triumphant grin to Onya's face. Camilla was, unfortunately, not to be so easily deflected. She merely took her hand back and sat down beside Onya, unperturbed.

"Lykos was it? I must say all the talk has done you no justice! Those eyes of yours are quite more enchanting than the ocean they have been compared to."

I smirked and turned my eyes pointedly to Onya, though I kept Camilla in my peripherals to catch her reactions.

"Strange, I know we washed, yet all of a sudden I smell a fresh load of horse shit."

I felt a bit of pride when I heard Xalia's laughter at my far left, though she did her best to choke it back on her food. Onya was far less cordial, slapping the table and grinning from ear to ear as she laughed, the sound quite pleasant. Camilla for all that I could take from her, was, if nothing else, quite a looker and a very good sport. She held her hands up in defeat and finally relaxed her pose instead of leering forward.

"Alright alright, can't blame a gal for trying." She answered laughingly, pushing aside the two short braids that hung loose from the batch of hair that was pulled back into a bun. When the teasing started from all sides, she waved it off with a flourish of her hand.

Something about her made me sure this would not be her last attempt. If I was to be frank, Onya had a much better chance at drawing my interest, but just as it had always been, my attraction was half-hearted. The thought of either woman only made the thrumming pull I had been feeling since childhood, and following for the past year, beat louder. There had been a time I'd lain with women in hopes that it would drown the pull, but only the opposite ever occurred. The few times I had tried to court a girl, something had always gone amiss.

The rest of the evening was filled with chatter and laughter that warmed my soul but also pulled my eyelids down. I finally had to excuse myself for fear I might fall face down into the table. There was much to be said for good company, but it was still tiresome business.

Serah proved to be a loyal friend, making sure to check in on me throughout the weeks to come and always offering a comforting smile. Had I a sister, I'd have hoped she would be like the spunky young healer. Xalia's indifference cracked here and there but Serah seemed not to notice, or at least didn't acknowledge, the warrior's jealousy. I might have reassured the woman it was strictly platonic, but it amused me far too much to watch her make an ass of herself instead. Afterall, everyone could see the way Serah looked at Xalia just as well as I could.

The topic of her own feelings managed to come up one afternoon when she brought Onya and myself lunch during a milder day. An impromptu picnic was set up while the horses we had been working with enjoyed a bit of grazing. It was Onya who spoke up, far less hesitant to push sensitive subjects than I was.

"So have you and Xalia figured things out yet? Or are you both still dancing around what is blatantly obvious to the rest of us?"

I watched Serah's face turn a deep red as she tried not to choke on the water she had been sipping. I laughed and shook my head but waited silently alongside Onya, who I noticed leaned my way with a sly smirk before looking pointedly at Serah.

"Way to slide into a conversation gracefully. You almost killed me, Onya!"

Serah shook her head, the spikey locks of her hair swaying in the wind so that a wayward strand split her eye so that she looked like she had a scar.

"Nonsense! Now spill!"

I elbowed Onya in the ribs and pointed at the water that had sprayed onto Serah's shirt.

"Don't you see her shirt? She already did! "

Giggles were shared at Serah's expense until she sighed deeply, and we silenced in order to hear her gentle voice.

"Every time I try to bridge the conversation to it, she shuts down or suddenly has to leave. I do not get it. She can run straight into danger without a second thought, but when it comes to admitting our feelings, she balks and runs like a spooked deer!"

The frustration was there, and it was clear that waiting was beginning to take its toll on Serah. Her eyes had begun to water, and she took a deep breath to control herself. To her credit, Onya looked quite regretful for having asked, though she reached forward and squeezed Serah's knee, offering her an encouraging smile.

"I'm so sorry Serah, I thought for sure things had worked themselves out after seeing the way she was watching you last night."

I cocked my head in question at Onya, who shook her head and shoved me playfully.

"If you had come out with me, you'd know."

I rolled my eyes and shrugged my shoulders. I didn't regret my decision to stay behind and help the cooks clean up; it had earned me a full loaf of cinnamon bread and a small jar of strawberry jam. That the Queen had stopped by for something and seen me being useful didn't hurt either. Still, I was curious as to whatever it was that had transpired.

"I thought it finally might as well. When we finished the dance, she kissed me and it was like everything I'd ever wanted had finally fallen into place…But when I offered for us to go somewhere more private she ran away again…some bullshit excuse about being on duty."

Onya reached out again and gave Serah's hand a squeeze, no words falling from her lips. I was fairly certain that was because Onya had never had to deal with such complexities in a relationship. One of the stable hands had said that the woman had never dated within the tribe. There were whispers that she had a secret lover somewhere, but anytime she was teased about such things she merely winked and said it wouldn't be a secret if she told.

Although I knew that Xalia had, in fact, been on duty last night, I was also aware that she was held in high regard amongst the women and so wouldn't have been questioned for taking leave. I had watched the way Xalia's confidence only wavered around Serah when she realized people were watching them and I could smell the nervousness on her when Serah neared. There was a way she tapped her fingers against her legs that screamed familiarity. Anxiety could be hidden easily if those around you didn't know the signs.

"She's probably afraid she isn't good enough."

Both heads turned to look at me as if I had spoken some foreign language. As a rule I had never really contributed to these types of conversations, though I did listen. Their surprise didn't discount my words and after a few moments Serah took them seriously.

"What do you mean? She's perfect in every way possible!"

Shrugging my shoulders I leaned away from her and toward Onya, my free hand pulling a piece of hay that had been caught on my shirt and popping it into my mouth to chew.

"It's no secret that you two are vastly different people. Serah, you are one of the warmest souls I've encountered and I daresay everyone would agree that you are the best of us."

At this Onya silently nodded agreement and Serah's eyes teared up at the statement, though she let me continue.

"So for someone like Xalia to accept that she is good enough and deserves you...Well, that takes time and probably a bit of a push. She loves you, she just has to accept that she's allowed to and what anyone else might think doesn't matter as long as she's who you want."

They looked at me like they didn't know who I was. Well they could join the club, I didn't know where the scrap of wisdom came from either. I sat up and opened my arms just in time to catch Serah as she flung herself at me, the momentum causing me to fall backwards. Bewildered, I held her while Onya giggled at us until Serah finally sat back and wiped tears from her face, her smile once again lighting her up.

"Thank you."

I felt the heat of a blush rise as she kissed me on the cheek. Once she was back in her own spot, the conversation was turned to lighter things and we finished our meal. When Serah packed it all up and headed back to her tasks for the day I found myself under the scrutiny of the horse trainer.

"What?"

She smirked, hand on her hip as she looked me up and down. "You are full of surprises is all. Perhaps there really is more to you than good looks and a steady hand?"

"Oh, so you admit I look good eh?" Onya rolled her eyes even as she kicked a stray horse apple at me, the hay ridden poop falling apart against my pant leg.

I might have been insulted but she laughed and gave me a slap to the arm as she walked past me. The rest of the afternoon was spent on chores that kept me warm in the growing cold, but didn't take away from the bliss of my cozy hut and bed. When I finally laid down for the night I couldn't help the smile that stuck to my face.

Maybe I could really find a place for myself here. What if this place could be everything my mother had hoped for me? A home with friends that were just as good as family. Could that be what the magic was pulling me towards? For the first time in a long time I fell asleep with hope in my heart and a smile on my face.

CHAPTER FOUR
DELUSIONS AND GOAT PATHS

A week or two later I had my second meeting with the council. They had all visited me at least once since I had arrived, mostly just to see if I was settling in well. I had been rather amused when the scholarly councilwoman had ventured down to the stable to find me, her distaste for the smell of horse flesh evident in her sneer. None had lingered, though I was sure they had been getting reports from various sources on my coming and going. They had all been friendly, but it didn't make it any less intimidating to be meeting them all at once again.

Xalia came to find me, her dark hair tied back so that her features seemed more sharp but no less attractive. I found her to have softened a bit toward me ever since my talk with Serah. I didn't know why, but I wasn't at all put out by it.

"Don't be nervous. Everyone can see that you fit in here and are making yourself useful. You will be fine."

I cocked a brow at her but couldn't help but smile in appreciation. She just shook her head in response, eyes rolling as if she regretted saying anything nice.

"Hurry on before you end up late. This was literally the *last* place anyone thought to look for you and the Queen has requested you early."

I nodded, though if she had asked Onya she'd have easily been able to tell Xalia where I went to get away. Prince's paddock was empty since he had been let out to pasture, but I often waited for him by the gate or hid in the fresh wood shavings of his stall. Fairly certain he had avoided me on purpose, I left an apple as an apology for being moody the day before and rose to my feet. Dusting off the worst of the sawdust as I ran, I made my way towards the center of the Amazon village.

I offered a soft rapt across the door before opening it. When I entered the hut, Gwenn was among the council women and smiled warmly. Her inclusion immediately set me on edge, her reluctance to clear me for duty was evident, however she couldn't argue with the fact that somehow I had completely healed. Although the faces around me were kind, an old fear tugged at my pant leg, begging me to cut and run now before it was too late. The Queen looked up from her paperwork and motioned me to take a seat, which I did hesitantly.

"We have been discussing it at length and have agreed; you have exhibited every quality we look for in an Amazon. Due to this, your request to stay on as an Amazon has been approved. We will assign an Amazon to accompany you and will give you a day's notice before you set off to complete your initiation task. If you complete it you will be a guest no longer, instead you will be a member of our family."

I felt a wave of nervousness fall away as excitement rode its curtails and swallowed me up. I grinned and nodded, unable to gather words appropriate enough for the moment. I tried to speak but the words fell silent, tears threatening to well up as the truth settled across my shoulders. I could have a real home; one where no one knew what I was enough to hate me for it. The blue eyed elder laughed as she watched me struggle again to find the words to thank them.

"Don't worry lass, speechless is as big of a response as words and says it all.

There was a rustle of leathery wings above me, the leaves swaying in the slight breeze causing my keen ears to lose track of their movements. My heart leapt forward in chaotic bounds as I spun on my heels, unsure of what tracked me but filled to the brim with anticipation. The sounds of the forest began to cry out in protest at the intruder, birds squalling in fear as the small prey beasts fled, all but ignoring my presence as they darted past, giving me a wide berth but seeming more fearful of what they could not see. In the trees I

heard again the sound of wings, followed by what I could almost swear was soft laughter.

The earth tangled at my feet, the wilderness too seemed to grow frenzied, vines snaking out as the undergrowth burst forth with life and tried desperately to strangle each other with their pleas to rise further and faster. The tangles of thorns and ropey spindles tried eagerly to grasp my legs, panic rising to fill my chest in response. I couldn't be too late. For a moment I couldn't understand what it was I was going to be too late for and paused just long enough for the foliage to snare my left leg, sending me careening forward. Face first into the earth I fell, too soft.

As my eyes fluttered open I found myself in a clearing of overturned earth, soft to the touch but smelling not of earth but death. The scent hit me like a wall, causing my stomach to flip as a familiar sense of dread drove panic through my core. Frenzied I began to tear through the earth, tears rolling down my face as I got nowhere, the earth filling in with every scoop out until it was no longer just rich earth that I was trying to shovel out, but instead something far more moist. Moving my body to the side a light fell upon the substance beneath me, revealing shimmering crimson that seeped up through the ground until I was scooping handfuls of the warm liquid. Still frenzied I didn't even flinch as the blood continued to bubble up and began to splatter across the front of my body. With each attempt to remove it the blood grew warmer until the heat began to scold my exposed skin and I screamed in pain, a blinding light suddenly bursting through my body.

With a hard jolt and a desperate gasp I sucked in a deep breath. Sweat rested upon my brow and dripped into my now open mouth. Heat radiated from my body despite the cold air surrounding me, my blanket now discarded at my feet. I looked around and could find nothing wrong, but Camilla watched me carefully from across the still burning fire. Her eyes were calculating but not cold, her bright brown eyes framed by long almost black locks that were usually tied back in braids.

"Need me to come keep you warm and chase away the nightmares?"

Her flirty voice was just as charming as it was annoying, causing my scowl to shift into a smirk that flickered across my lips as my breathing slowly calmed. Disoriented as I was, I tried to play off the surge of emotions that followed me into wakefulness.

"What makes you think you aren't the subject of my nightmares?"

The taunt was a bit more gruff than I'd intended but she took it in stride as usual, though she caught me off guard when she grew serious.

"Because it wasn't my name you were mumbling before you started to twitch and screamed."

The pressure of my hands against my eyes did little to hide my stress, however it did buy me time to shake off my confusion. The sigh of exasperation that fell from my lips surely solidified the fact I had no clue I'd spoken a name or even screamed. What was I too late for? The feeling of desperation seeped into my pores and carried a chill down my spine, the blood curdling scream suddenly catching up to me, the name on my lips ringing as clear as daylight. I said nothing in regards to that, shrugging it off as a random nightmare. Surely there was nothing uncommon about saying a Goddess' name in one's sleep.

"I'm sorry if I woke you".

She shook her head and offered me a smile.

"I couldn't sleep, so don't fret."

Lying back down with my blanket pulled up, I tried to figure out the meaning behind these ever persistent nightmares and the eerie feeling that I was being beckoned toward something- or perhaps warned away? I was no closer to understanding them, or what had drawn me here to begin with. The dreams now plagued me just as the Mad King once had, but at least he had been tangible. I had searched the trails endlessly and gotten no closer to whatever taunted me.

Perhaps it was simply nerves, after all this was my first true task set by the council women. I desperately wanted to belong here and make a home with these amazing women. Serah had assured me if I failed I'd be given another opportunity to prove myself, but I didn't like the idea of failing my first go.

Camilla offered a smile that was just a smidge less provocative as she spoke, her voice always a warm rumble of playfulness tinged with sincerity.

"Don't worry Lykos, you will do just fine, I'm here to make sure of it."

I rolled my eyes and turned my back on her, not wishing to show just how much these dreams had begun to rattle me. That she had heard me was bad enough, best to play it off and try to catch some more sleep.

When morning finally broke, I rose to relieve myself and found the cool mountain air as refreshing as it was chilling. Goosebumps ran up my arms as I pulled my cloak close around me, wishing I had been allowed to go this venture alone. Of course it made no sense for me to go unaccompanied since the Amazons knew their own land like the back of their hands. When I returned Camilla had already broken camp and waited for me by the horses. I smiled at the young stallion who had become one of my closest and dearest of friends, though the first few weeks had been one hell of a wild ride figuring out our unique dynamic. His voice in my head had become something like a warm tickle; the sensation was an intrusion, but a welcome one.

Good morning my lady.

"Good morning Prince"

The beautiful paint lowered his head so that I could reach him more easily, quiet expectation in the gesture. Shaking my head I rubbed the fur around his ears, making sure to give the insides a good scratch before scrubbing his face softly and getting a wash of hair all over my cloak as payment. Wiping my hands across my clothes to shake the loose hair off, I stepped back enough for him to lift his head. Planting a kiss on his jaw I moved to his shoulder and checked the position of the saddle and tightened the girth so I could mount. Playfully he swished his tail just as I stepped up into the stirrup, the long length catching me full in the face with a satisfied *snap*. Sputtering I held back a growl, reaching forward in the saddle to flick his ear. Prince's laughter was evident in his soft nickering.

"Brat!" I spat, though there was no fire behind the words. That earned me another smack with his tail, this time across my ass since I was still leaning forward over his neck. Camilla laughed as she watched our antics, my face scrunched up as I rubbed my butt, though I conceded the victory to him with a pat to his neck.

"Alright you two, let's head out or we won't have enough daylight to get where we need to go." Camilla led the way on a completely average chestnut gelding, though to see her dote upon him would convince you he was the best in the barn.

A full day and another few hours of the following brought us to the point where I would leave my companions and trek on foot. The task I had been given was not a particularly hard one in theory, though I dared not scoff at its simplicity as it had been presented as a serious task to be respected. The stores of herbs that had been used to help me heal were to be replaced, along with a particularly rare flower which only grew in one place on the mountain. The herbs were simple enough to gather, but the flower was another matter.

There was a small alcove amongst the high mountain rocks where the plant would grow every other year. Its petals, flowers, and even thorns could be used for a number of ailments - many of which appeared during winter, therefore increasing its value. The plant only bloomed in the late fall, making now the most optimal time to harvest it. The amazons saw it as a sign of good fortune, since the timing was perfect, but lacked the heightened senses to smell the snow storm pushing in from the east.

Lucky me.

Swinging from the saddle I stretched my legs out before giving Prince a kiss on the soft flesh of his muzzle, enjoying the grassy scent that mixed with dust around his nose. His usual twinge of magic caused my nostrils to flare as a tickle inevitably changed into a sneeze. Camilla gave me a confident smile and a wave before taking Prince's reins from me. She would head out to a scout hut and run her patrol shift before coming back to collect me. If I hadn't come off the trail by then she'd come find me, assuming something had gone amiss. I scoffed at the idea and turned to make my way up the barely discernible goat path forged in the slope of a cliff.

Three hours into the climb I was beginning to hate life with a fiery passion that started in my feet and rose to spew venom from my lips in the form of curses. The fire shooting up my calves and across my thighs set my speed as it forced me to pause long enough to let the sensation of stabbing knives fade. My breath created little puffs of mist before my face as I panted heavily, the thin and icy air burning my lungs. I wasn't by any means out of shape, but there was definitely something to say for the difference one's terrain and elevation made.

The rocks were loose and slick with ice from the morning dew which had now frozen as the temperatures continued to drop. The sky had stayed a miserable overcast of gray clouds that were strewn in that soft way that hinted at snowflakes. The lack of sunlight made it even harder to spot the shimmer of ice and more than once I skidded far too close to the edge for comfort. The air smelled of the brewing storm that couldn't be more than a few days off, assuming the wind didn't pick up. I prayed to the Goddess that it would wait long enough for me to get to a warm hut to ride it out.

What had to be several hours later, the sweat beneath my cloak was almost enough to make me part it and let in a breeze. Thankfully, I was wise enough to know it'd freeze and have me in worse shape than I'd started, though the strain in my muscles almost convinced me there would be enough heat to melt it.

So the pattern continued until I plotted along only partially conscious of my actions, the ebb and flow of getting too hot and then too cold lulling me into a tide void of time. The curses flew from my mouth every time a cramp caused my feet to stumble, forcing my hands to catch myself upon the rocks, the soft flesh splitting open even with the protection of gloves.

More than once I wished my fox had not hidden herself deep within my soul, no longer pacing the shallow depths of my skin. I'd gone too long without shifting and my magic had been burned through. The connection to my shift had begun to recover with my health, but I feared how long it'd take to fully pull her back to me. There had been a necessity in locking her away, but I mourned the repercussions. Oh how I missed my other shape with its four legs, sure footing and thick winter fur coat.

The spiraling trail had been large enough to allow one person to walk with space but as I came to a fork I'd been told to veer left at, I realized why this was considered a worthy task. Rocks had fallen from higher up the mountain and peppered the trail until it was barely wide enough for the adolescent goats whose toes could find footholds in the tiniest of grooves. There were no handholds aside from sharp juttings of rock that would just as soon slice you open as help balance. The path would hold, but it would also take much more than sweat and tears to get to the other side.

There was no way of approach which would prove better than the other so I took a moment to gather myself. Months locked in a prison cell had not afforded me the opportunity for climbing so my legs and feet were already unbearably sore. The muscles screamed protest even as they begrudgingly fell back on memory. After taking a few minutes to garner the distance, I settled on waiting to move forward. There was little sunlight left and no way to know how long the treacherous path would take me. Choosing to err on the side of caution, I moved off towards the main trail again and used what sunlight remained to set a camp.

I set myself up in the crevice of the main trail, its curvaceous path providing a natural wind block that would allow me to build a small fire. I quickly went about gathering what brittlebush I could as kindling and a couple of wet logs that had fallen upon the path. Thankfully I had thought ahead well enough to pack flint and strips of leather soaked in burning oil. The oil was a unique blend that allowed the strips to burn longer and hotter; it wouldn't do for anything long term but it could ignite wet wood and boil water quickly.

As I lay curled as near as I could to my small fire I tried to block out the persistent pull that ever ached inside my core. It seemed ridiculous that this sensation could possibly be the flower I sought, but with every step towards the damn thing I felt the pull tugging ever harder. Perhaps it was merely the call of some source of magic. It would make sense that such a hard flower to grow in this region would only do so by aid of some small magical source seeping into the earth. That had to be it, yet even as the words passed across my mind I knew them to be false. The jolts of pain that had begun to tickle my fingertips and send numbness down my legs was far from some benevolent magic spring. Exhaustion finally took me as the sun slipped far below the ridges, but there was no relief in sleep as the strange dreams became even more vivid.

I felt the stirring within my soul. A burst of bright colors, illuminating even the darkest and deepest of shadows; music made into light that harmonized perfectly with the decadent thrumming of life that coursed through my veins. Every nerve ending lit up like the stars in the sky, a buzz of electricity sending jolts through my core until I was nothing more than a blinding burst of energy.

The smells of nature surrounded me: deep caverns with heavy must, the salty swirl of the ocean, soft whorls of fragrance from fields of wild flowers and the fresh chill of mountain air. All of it reached out to touch, caressing softly, remodeling my body from the inside out. I could not feel it anymore, but I was very much aware of my bones shifting and changing, everything occurring within the blink of an eye as I ran and leapt onto the earth -lengthening, stretching, strengthening, muscles and tendons bunching and extending while the soft shifting colors of my hair spread and burst out as long fur. Claws, fangs, ears, and finally a tail that split into nine long lengths appeared as the change took hold. This was a form I had longed to embrace but was forced to suppress.

As I landed I took in a deep breath filled to the brim with tantalizing scents. My ears shuffled atop my head, pivoting around to catch even the slightest of sounds. It had been too long. I stretched my long limbs and relished the feel of power just under my skin. The earth between my toes was like a connection to Gaia herself. I stretched my length low as my rear raised up, my tails flaring out behind me like a fan. An appreciative 'hmmm' bringing me back to reality as the adrenaline of the change continued to flitter through my veins. I turned my bright blue eyes back to catch the satisfied smirk of a woman I could almost make out in the depths of shadow.

I turned towards her, taking in her admiration and feeling myself glow with pride at her approval, though I wasn't exactly sure why. Afterall, I wasn't sure I knew this woman. Still I couldn't help but keep eye contact as her violet gaze locked onto my own, the shadows seeming to be a part of her, clinging desperately as she stepped from their grasp, calling and crying out for her to return.

I felt my heart skip a beat, her chiseled features absolutely breathtaking set against the backdrop of her raven black hair. The light filtering through the forest canopy caught her in a silver sheen that highlighted the blue glow of its hue. She reached a hand out to me and my newfound height made it easy for my muzzle to meet it. The action seemed as natural as breathing. I took a long whiff of her scent and felt my body burn with a fire that ignited deep and low in my core. She slid her hand up across my head and between my ears then ran it along my back, all the while keeping her eyes on mine.

"Just as soft as ever my beautiful Vixen."

Her voice was practically a purr, the soft alto of it a pleasant rumble in the air. Where I was more fox than human I swore this woman was more a feline than anything else. The familiarity set my nerves on edge as the image warped and she suddenly cried out in pain, as if something had reached out and struck her in the heart. It disappeared just as quickly as it had occurred and my vision swirled as she turned toward me, her hands stained red with blood. I jolted wide awake, the same name as before on my tongue.

Panting with fear and panic I bolted straight up in my makeshift bed, the extra blankets I had wrapped around myself falling away so that the cold slammed into my body like a wall. Gasping I gathered them back to me, wrapping myself as tightly as I could while my body shivered with shock and cold. Such heartache and pain as I had never known poured through my soul, leaking out of my eyes and staining my face. There were no words to describe or understand the sensations that overwhelmed me. The images scattered in the wind just as quickly as I tried to grab at them. The pull in my core felt like a burning flame as it jolted and then settled back into its usual background pull.

"What the fuck is happening to me?"

My words were lost with the breeze but with my head in my hands I tried to grasp the invisible strings dangling just out of reach. My own ignorance annoyed me and angrily I kicked the remnants of my long burnt out fire. Glancing to the sky I measured the moon's pacing across its dark blue floor, the stars glittering from gaps in the scattered clouds. Hours had at least passed while I dreamt, rather than mere minutes.

"Dreams. Phsh. More like nightmares...Nightmares that feel like memories..."

A shudder ran along my spine as the memory of blood brought back a sliver of that gut-wrenching pain. All I could do was wipe my face as my emotions finally calmed with the ebbing away of the images. I had to get myself moving. There was no sunlight to raise the temperature, but I doubted even the sun's rays would penetrate the chill in my blood now. Movement was my only option and with my legs at least a bit rested, the challenging path before me seemed a bit less daunting; especially if it helped chase away the nightmares.

Packing up my belongings and thanking the heavens for my improved night vision, I set off up the goat path that was hardly a path at all. The first hour was slow but steady and as the sun rose in the distance I was able to speed up my progress. It wasn't until around noon that I finally felt the ground leveling off as the fire in my calves, thighs and ass cooled. The pull within had grown from a soft thrumming of an unsteady beat to a nauseating throbbing much akin to a headache, which pulsed in perfect rhythm with my heart.

Pausing so that I could catch my breath, I spotted a movement at the edge of my vision. Lifting my head enough to cast my gaze across the flat area, my breath caught and a sigh of relief passed my lips as I spotted my quarry. There on the far side of the plateau stood a small batch of the flower I sought. Blue petals danced on the wind, their edges dotted with white splotches that held no symmetry. Their long green stems with slim leaves and deep red thorns contrasted sharply against the light gray backdrop of the rocks that they grew between.

The hope of sweet relief from the pain that caused my body to ache, the deafening roar of my heartbeat in my ears, and the numbing cold that seemed to reach into my bones, made me careless. Without regard to what surprises the terrain might hold, I darted forward and reached out to caress the closest flower. The moment my fingers touched its petals my vision dissipated in a momentary blast of light as the pain climaxed and what felt like a bolt of lightning shot through my skull and seemingly through the earth, which crumbled beneath me, leaving behind a quick sensation of falling followed by complete darkness.

The familiar sensation of waking without knowing what had happened confirmed my blackout and hurt my pride. Dirt fell against my face as I shifted just enough to get an idea of how my body lay, the movement causing a sudden emptiness that overwhelmed my senses until I could not tell what was up or down. The sharp pains of a crash landing ached my bones but the throbbing of my head had dissipated in a way that made me light headed.

Checking my extremities I found nothing broken. The numerous lacerations across my body now told a tale of my struggles against both the mountain path and whatever hole I'd landed in. Stifling a cough, I carefully moved the debris from my body before standing and dusting off. The soft pats were enough for me to quickly decide I'd just stay dirty, the number of bruises on my body growing by the second. Tearing a strip of my undershirt I carefully wrapped one particularly rough cut running down my forearm, the blood seeping through for only a moment before the pressure was able to staunch it's flow.

Testing my body I took a deep breath, succeeding with only a slight fit of coughing. There was certainly an ache, but nothing that felt severe. So why then had the thrumming pull of magic gone silent? It was as if the instrument had suddenly broken and could no longer carry its tune. That in itself drew panic into my mind far more so than the scent of my own blood and the taste of copper on my lips.

Bright sunlight poured in from high above me, causing ripples of dust particles to glitter in the air. As my gaze fluttered across the hole above, I realized what had crumbled were clay blocks and wood. Whatever I had been treading across was human made. My weight, ever slight as it might have been, was enough to trigger the collapse. Only a small section had fallen through while the rest of the roof remained intact. Perhaps there was something here that would explain it all; the dreams, the pull, why the Mad King wanted me.

"First things first Lykos, make sure you can actually get out of this hole before you explore it."

Turning in place, the scent of mildew assaulted my nose, the air stale and now filled with dust and debris. The room was a large one, the floor made of smooth rock, perhaps even carved from the mountain's own surface and lacquered with some kind of cured sap stain to preserve it. It was beautiful in its own way. When the sunlight hit the ground it sparkled, the light reflecting off minerals within and scattering across the room, allowing my eyes to adjust well to the dimness beyond the hole. There were columns carved from the mountain's body throughout the space, supporting the high ceiling. I scanned the roof and could just make out the roots of a plant that had somehow weaved itself through the wood planks. As I followed it back to its source, I was led to my hole.

"Of course I step on the one spot that the damn plants have penetrated."

Sighing I stretched my limbs out and rolled my shoulders to try and ease some of the stiffness out of my body. Once I was satisfied that my body truly was whole, I circled the area I had fallen through, hoping I might find an angle where things looked more in my favor.

There wasn't one.

"I'm never going to hear the end of this." Swiping my hands over my eyes in exasperation, I focused instead on the expanse of my would-be tomb.

Towards the far end a beautiful mural had been painted. Like the floor, it had once been protected, though the images were not so well defined where the glossy coat had been slowly chipped away. I traced my fingers over the image of two maidens astride beautiful horses; the blonde sat upon a black steed, the raven haired woman upon a palomino whose hair matched her companion's shade. The forest was lush around them and the sky was painted so that the stars were easily seen above. On the adjacent wall the mural continued, showing a great palace where two figures, who must have been a God and Goddess, seemed to speak in conspiracy, though the paint here had worn too much for me to make out which names to place on them. Just behind that the Fates stood faceless, their hands spinning and weaving the webs of life.

A familiarity overcame me as I traced over the patterns hidden in the paint. Something in me recognized the images as if I'd seen them before when they had been fresh and filled with life. Perhaps it was something that had been recreated elsewhere. So much of my younger years were a blip, I could hardly hold onto much. Then, of course, were the dreams which had blurred into my waking days so much that I had often thought them opposite - the dreams memories and the memories dreams. It made my mind a bit muddled.

Letting my hand fall back to my side, I continued to examine the rest of the room. There were no windows and no doors, making it seem as if it had been built and then sealed like a tomb. The oddness of it all was only increased when a peculiar shadow in the last corner caught my attention. Moving closer I let my eyes adjust to the deeper shadows until everything appeared as sharp as if light had shone. A growl instinctively fell from my lips as I leapt back in surprise. It took a moment for my mind to register what I was seeing.

A humanoid figure sat perched atop a large slab of beautiful marble. The platform allowed the creature to lean out as if she were about to lurch forward and snatch any unwelcome trespasser. The features of what was certainly a womanly figure were smooth, keen craftsmanship having gone into the seamless lines and smooth detail of her bodice. She was perched with her legs bent, the muscles of her calves pronounced, as were her thighs and stomach. Wings were set out from the back, stretching in a threatening posture that made the frown of her lips menacing.

The only scrap of clothing that had been carved upon her body was just enough to cover her particulars. The strip of cloth twisted around her body and curved down to the marble slat, offsetting the wings and balancing the structure.

The artist was something special for the smooth curves were uncanny, no blemish upon any surface of the creature. There were no sharp edges aside from the lengthened points protruding from the tips of the wings and the teeth jutting out from behind thick lips. Taking in the details, I found myself enthralled with the depths of the statue. Her expression was one of pain and anger.

Somewhere in me a soft thrumming echoed the same pulling beat that had called to me.

Shaking my head to draw myself away from the statue I kicked the base of it and gave a frustrated shout. Surely the mystery of my magical pull was not just some craftsmanship in the mountain. There was no way it could be so simple, or so stupid, my entire life had revolved around it.

"Well this is just fucking great!" My shout bounced back at me, loud and frustrated.

There were no doors, no windows, and no obvious way that someone might have escaped after creating this beautiful room. Instead, they had to have locked themself away. Perhaps the rubble that now lay in a pile hid a collection of bones from whoever had come before me. After what felt like an hour or more of searching the small room to no avail, I collapsed back onto the ground where I had started, trying hard to contain myself.

"This cannot be real. Everything I've gone through chasing this damn magical tug and what does it end up being? A useless statue that some magical crafter buried in the mountain!" My grumble sounded bitter even to my own ears. Tears of frustration streaked my cheeks, their salty trails freezing on my face. How could this be it? I couldn't even begin to swallow the amount of disappointment rising within me.

I settled myself in a spot of sunshine, the wind had not yet figured a way to twist its way down into the room and so the warmth was not immediately snatched away. Still painfully sore from the climb and the fresh wounds, I curled myself up to rest before repeating my attempt to sort out the unique predicament I found myself in. With no way to escape what could easily become my tomb, I reassured myself Camilla would eventually come looking for me.

Even if I were to pull the magic from within, the heights were too great and it had been too long; that other piece of me no longer rustled just beneath my flesh. The beast that had once rampaged, seeking its freedom from within, remained silent and still. The thought tore at something within my heart. So much had been lost beyond my freedom these last few years and for it to be all for nothing - I couldn't bear to think about it right now. There was no comfort in the hard earth, but the journey and fall had exhausted me. Sleep took me quickly, saving me from my mental spiral of disappointment and heartache.

A subconscious apprehension stirred me awake. Confusion filled me, my mind slow to process my surroundings until I heard something from the far corner. After a few minutes the sound of claws scraping rock resonated around the room, causing me to jolt into an upright position, eyes widening as I searched the shadows. Adrenaline ran through my body, my pulse throbbing in my ears.

"What in the Underworld?" I had checked every corner, I should have been alone.

The shadows shifted and shuttered as the shuffling of leathery wings echoed high into the room's ceiling. The sound was familiar, an echo of haunted dreams. Blinking I tried to focus my blurred, sleep heavy vision for just long enough to see into the dark depths of the furthest corner. There was mockery in the soft shuffling that seemed to come from everywhere and nowhere at all.

Suddenly, as if someone had wafted it in my direction, a heavy dose of magic tickled my nose. The familiar scent hit my gut like a tree limb. My breath hitched in my chest and I lurched to my feet as I finally made out the sharp lines of the statue and found haunting and familiar violet eyes staring back at me. Frozen in place, the hair on my neck and arms rose with apprehension. I was caught in the stare of a predator, the growl rising from my throat matched by her slightly deeper one.

I stood, muscles tight and ready to react, though there was a slight quiver to them. The scent of magic rolled off her like an addictive perfume, lingering in the air and mixing with strands of something familiar and intoxicating. There was no tearing my eyes from the challenging stare of this ancient predator. Her lips curled into an almost cruel smile as she stalked towards me. She moved on all fours at first, slowly rising and approaching as one might a frightened pup. Her voice came out like a purr, saturated with charm and silky smooth.

"I had wondered how long you would leave me waiting, Lykos. Seems the Fates have been slow to show their cards this hand." Her melodious tone was like a beautiful knife whose glistening edge distracted from the piercing sharpness that could easily cut deep. Despite that, there was such a deep affection in the way my name rolled off her tongue that I almost believed she must have been an old friend.

Confusion filled my already clouded mind, my name upon her lips pulling a heat into my core that felt like a stirring of the fox long in slumber. The tickle of magic reminded me that this could all just be some sort of manipulation and I shook my head as if I could physically shake it off. As I found her gaze again the haze started to dissipate, the caress of magic withdrawing and allowing a clearer mind.

The truth threatened to drown me in images that had long planted foreign sensations into my body and mind. Had I not seen those same eyes in my dreams just as surely as that damnable pull of magic tugged me in any direction she moved?

Panic began to rise from the background of my mind as my name upon her lips truly settled into my consciousness, registering like a thorn that had festered for days before being noticed. She knew me.

"How? How do you know me?" The words slipped off my lips as barely a whisper.

Wide eyed, I stared as the creature before me moved ever closer. Her movements were both surreal and terrifying, laced with such beauty. She came close enough to touch and her hand cut through the rays of sunlight, the once granite form seeming to shimmer beneath the light.

"You and I have quite a long history. I've known you my entire, expansive, life Lykos. We are connected in ways that will not readily make sense."

Fingers inches from my face, reality caught back up to me. Faster than lightning I snapped at her hand, a snarl of warning rumbling from deep in my chest as she yelped in surprise. The creature before me then burst into laughter as she pulled her fingers back to her, checking that they were unscathed.

That melodious voice echoed in the cavernous room as she continued to laugh, her vibrant eyes dancing with amusement even as I glared as ferociously as I could.

"Some things may yet change in this world, my beautiful Vixen, but so many other things never do."

"I'm not *your* anything, and what is that even supposed to mean? "

Venom fell from my lips as her amusement annoyed me, confusion pushing my frustration to even higher levels, fueling my temper. What in Hades' name had I crashed into? How did she know me? Could she really be the woman from my dreams? If so, why was I drawn to her? What brought me here? A soft throbbing in my skull was my only answer.

Fear made my lip quiver. What would the answers mean?

"Stick around and perhaps you will sort it out. Though, from the looks of it, not much of a choice at this point." She gestured to the hole above me, her tone sobered and dry.

Annoyed and prideful I snorted and turned from her. It was the absolute dumbest thing you could do to a predator, but there was rebellion in the action. Showing off my vulnerable side was meant to emphasize her insignificance, that I didn't see her as a real threat. As I stood there though, her presence felt like a balm, soothing nerves that had forever been on edge. For all the questions she evoked, my anxiety didn't spike and that nagging pull had finally calmed.

Even as I felt the shift of air as she moved forward and to my side, there was no more bristling than before; no sirens blared in my mind alerting me to danger. Her presence felt like a mere extension of my own, a figment of my imagination that had always been there unacknowledged until now. Cocking my brow I almost reached out to touch her, to affirm she was real, but she spoke and broke me away from the temptation.

"Quite the jump, even from four legs..." Her eyes searched my face knowingly, "Shame you can't fly."

She nonchalantly stretched her wings, blotting out the sunlight for a moment before letting them fold back into neat stacks against her back. Her voice was even, seeming sincere in the casual way she stated the obvious, but there was a glint in her eyes that held nothing but mischief. A frustrated sneer pulled my face at her triumph.

"Asshole." I muttered softly, irritated that she held the upper hand.

Then that subtle bell in my mind rang politely to inform me of something amiss - four legs she had said. Vixen, she'd called me. She not only knew who I was, she knew *what* I was. How was any of that possible?

Dreams aren't real. They can't be.

The thought did nothing to convince me as I looked upon the creature beside me.

"Who and *what* are you?! How is any of this possible?"

The rudeness of my question occurred to me after the sharp tone of my words reverberated back at me, my voice louder than usual and sounding distressed. She seemed merely amused at my conflictions, staying only an arm's length away; very clearly unafraid of any threat I might pose.

With an exaggerated sigh and the most dramatic of displays she obliged my inquiry. She spread her leathery wings wide, their texture absorbing every ounce of light that dared to touch them, and in a sweeping motion she crossed her legs as if to curtsey but bowed low, her long onyx locks cascading to cover her face. She managed to peer out from beneath them but didn't rise until after she had spoken.

"What I am is a gargoyle though it is not what I have always been. Who I am you will surely remember with time, though I imagine it is a name you seek, to which I can readily supply you; I am Nyx."

Her wondrous introduction was admittedly charming, though on a less spectacular figure I'd have found the whole display quite abhorrent and ridiculous. The puzzle pieces clicked together and an image and name clashed loudly in my mind. A blast of heat spread across my entire body as nightmares that felt like memories came to the forefront of my mind followed by a name that had been screamed for.

"N-Nyx?" There was a trembling to my lip that I could not stand but could not help. She crooked an eyebrow and a smirk fell across her features.

"Yes, named after my grandmother. Nyxia Medusesis officially, but I've always kept it simple. Since the Gods are pretty much restricted to their own plane now, it's a lot less confusing."

Her tone was one of curiosity and hope. Her body leaned in slightly as if she searched for clues on a map for where this would lead. I stumbled backwards, tripping over a large rock and falling back onto the pile of rubble, a cloud of dust and what I barely registered as snow puffing up around me. She made to step forward but hesitated and merely looked at me curiously.

As I stared at her image all I could see was blood and all I could hear was a scream that had torn from my throat in anguish over it. It was one thing for her to know me, some magical gift could explain that - but for me to know her? No coincidence could explain that.

The nightmare had felt real but I had dismissed it as a mere dream. The magic within truly had been pulling me towards this place. Here, where the image of my dreamscape stalker now stood; tall and proud and.. . . concerned? Her own tenderness spoke volumes of familiarity yet there was no logical explanation to be had. Was I hallucinating? Had the magic in me finally told me to fuck off and literally grew legs to leave me behind since I could not let it out to run free?

Panic began to encompass my body as my mind spiraled into an endless realm of possibilities, each one becoming more ludicrous than the next. Sunlight dappled my skin but the warm sensation could not puncture a hole in the chaotic bubble I swam. A warm hand however, apparently could.

Focusing again on my surroundings I registered the hand around my wrist. Nyx crouched beside me, her eyes glistening with concern, mouth parted to reveal sharp fangs stained pink at their tips. A pair of scars matching their position cut the smooth texture of her bottom lip into segments. For a moment I was lost in their details.

She was speaking but it took a second for my mind to catch up.

"Breathe Lykos, breathe. It's going to be okay."

"Are you real though? I've seen you in dreams. Bleeding. Dying...How can that be? How do you know who I am? We can't know each other from dreams, surely. You feel so familiar."

Nyx smiled gently, though the slant of her brows seemed sad. The violet hue was mesmerizing and haunting all at once, adding to the eeriness of her expressions.

"Well, I had hoped that perhaps you might dream a bit more sweetly this time around, but alas, trauma tends to win out."

"I don't understand."

"I know Vixen, I will explain some of it but first let's just take a minute to get you calmed and perhaps out of the snow." She pointed up at the sky for emphasis. The hole above us had become snow cloud gray and flakes were beginning to fall down through the empty space in flurries, the stray sun rays now gone. The snow storm had picked up speed or I had been out far longer than I'd thought.

Nyx reached out a hand and after a moment's hesitation, I took the proffered arm to help regain my footing. The warmth of her skin was not at all what I'd have imagined after having seen her sitting as a statue, cold as ice. Letting my fingertips brush along the inside of her forearm, I gently took her wrist, turning her arm so that I could watch the dull light dance across her skin, which still held an almost shimmery quality. That it was a bit of an intimate motion dawned on me shortly after and caused me to quickly drop it once more. The ease which I felt with her, and how easily I fell into it was incredibly disturbing. It felt like whiplash, dream and reality pulling me in opposite directions.

She seemed mildly disappointed as the corners of her lips subtly turned down, but she said nothing, merely moved over to where her slab of marble still sat. Curious as to what she was doing I followed. Intrigue was more palatable than the discomfort of confusion. She slipped her hand into a crevice where her foot had sat before, straining only for a moment before the slab gave and lifted. When she shifted I could see a small compartment revealed. She pulled out a leather bag which had seen better days and whose design was nothing that I had ever encountered.

"It's amazing how well things survive when they are hidden away from the elements and cured with a bit of magic." She gave a half-hearted smile and, from the bag, pulled out a cloak. The material was nothing I could name, but she set it aside so that she could search an inside pocket. She smiled as she pulled a necklace out, glancing up to me for only a moment before she slid it back, shielding its design from me.

"Ah, here we are." She grabbed a vial from the depths of the bag and uncorked it. The scent that flowed from it was sweet and lightly fragranced with lavender. Magic tainted the air as she held it out to me.

"What is that?" The words fell from my lips with a colder edge than intended.

"Just take a deep whiff, it'll keep your head clear and calm. Trust me, you're going to need it, none of what I'm about to tell you is easy to swallow."

Giving her a skeptical brow raise, I took the vial and lifted it to my nose, the scent pleasant and the magic nonabrasive. Unlike the truth potion, this was magic with no intent to harm; healing magic at its most simplistic. There were no demands, mere suggestions and my own magic welcomed it, allowing it to creep in and relax the deepest parts of me that had coiled tight.

She smiled her approval and accepted the vial back, corking it and putting it into the bag. After she settled herself on the marble slab, I sat down with my back against the nearest pillar, legs pulled in to conserve warmth as the temperatures continued to drop. Snow was now collecting on the pile of rubble in the middle of the room.

"Things will become clearer now that we have met. Our magic is...linked, in a way that is unique."

"So what I saw, it was just some crazy dream because our magic was interacting?"

She cringed at my words, perhaps trying to figure them out, her own words were a bit stilted, as if she were trying to remember the right ones.

"Yes and no. Forgive me if I pause, it has been a very long time since this language was dominant and your accent is a bit heavier now."

"That doesn't make any sense, it's literally the only language spoken on Aio'nios."

That sent a bit of shock across her face, eyes wide and brows raised. She finally nodded, accepting the information.

"I have been asleep for quite a while it seems. Who claims these lands for their own now?" Her fingers rose to massage her temples, as if she were expecting an impending headache.

"The Vouno' Amazons, but don't change the subject. What do you mean yes and no?" My words were sharp and earned a glare which almost made me want to crawl back into the shadows. Her violet eyes softened after a moment, a sigh of exhaustion emphasizing her own lack of patience.

"That is a relief at least."

Impatiently I waited, my eyes taking in the more delicate details of her face as I let the silence linger with expectancy.

"Yes our magic reacts to one another, just as most magic will, but no it wasn't just some crazy dream. It was a memory, a very old one."

She pushed back her long black locks, letting them fall back between her folded wings. There was a sense that much was being left out, but I honestly didn't even know how to start an attempt to sort it out. Instead I took in her visage as a distraction. As a statue her chest and clothes had been the same hue, but now I could see the wrap was actually stained. As I let my eyes linger there I realized the hue wasn't a brown dye but instead long dried blood. Confusion must have contorted my face for she followed my line of sight and looked down at the wide strips.

"Don't worry, it wasn't mine this time. Even if it was, I heal when I sleep."

There was something about the way she said sleep that made me think she wasn't talking about closing her eyes for a night. That I might have seen her in memories was a wild thought, yet didn't my own existence stand as proof that magic was wild and unpredictable? Pressing my palms to my eyes I tried to blot out the world for a moment. When that didn't work, my vision merely changing to splotches of varying light shades, I resorted to my default maneuver - ignoring it until it made sense.

"So how did you become a gargoyle then? Must be pretty old considering this place hasn't seen the light of day in probably ages."

She smiled at the sudden change of topic, relief causing her shoulders to relax, her eyes less severe as she looked at me. "My mom turned me into one, at my own request of course. It's surely still rude to ask a lady her age, so I'll leave that a mystery."

"Wouldn't that be Nemesis, if your grandmother was Nyx? I've never heard of her having that kind of power." Of course I'd never heard of Nyx having a daughter and didn't know how said daughter could still be alive, either.

"Nemesis is my momma, yes. You would be surprised to know her range of power, but she is not the one that gifted me this. My other mother, Medusa, did."

My mouth opened and shut one, twice, three times before I could truly garner a response to that. This beautiful creature before me was not only the daughter of Nemesis but also Medusa? Medusa was the one creature who even now caused fear to chill the blood of any man who heard her name. My own mother had loved and adored Nyx and Nemesis both, but none dared speak of Medusa and her snakes without tossing salt over their shoulders for superstitious belief that she'd come and eat them alive.

The Nyx in front of me laughed aloud, the sound the most beautiful cadence I had ever heard. My heart skipped a beat as her entire face lit up with genuine amusement, bright violet eyes sparked with a tenderness that I felt a brief pull of jealousy for. She caught her breath and grinned.

"By your face I'd say her legacy has not been forgotten! Oh I know she will be pleased if she doesn't already know. She always preferred to be left to her own devices. That was what caused her and momma to go their separate ways you know! Momma was always intervening, drawn to humans like flies to rotting fruit and all mom wanted was to live their lives in happy bliss away from it all."

That opened a floodgate of questions that I knew would be rude to ask of a stranger, yet as I sat there staring at this gargoyle I felt like I was seeing an old friend again. The sensation was the topping of this shit cake that I had found. It only confused me more, but I couldn't bring myself to resent the ease in which we settled into each other's atmosphere. Surely if she'd wanted to harm me she would have already and there was nothing threatening in any movement she made.

"That is...definitely something I would like to hear more about, but I'd like to get out of this hole in the ground before the blizzard following this snow flurry really traps us." I took a breath and paused as my pride pummeled my insides, fighting against what I would say next. Oh how I hated to admit defeat, but we both knew there would be no way I could get out of this box on my own.

She rose to her feet, amusement in the curl of her lips as she rested her hands on her hips expectantly. Oh she was a bitch and she knew it. Swallowing my pride hard, I mumbled the last of my words. "Could you help me out?"

She grinned like a cat that had caught a particularly fat mouse, her fangs showing as a growling laugh fell from her lips.

"Of course I could and if you ask very sweetly I will." She emphasized her statement by spreading her wings wide, their leathery texture causing a rustle in the air.

"Can I trust you?" This was all too much, I couldn't be stuck here on top of it all.

"Yes, but you don't have to. Simply trust yourself." Her words were simple and soft.

I deepened my glare even as I rose to my feet, refusing to give the appearance of groveling as I puffed out my chest and said slightly louder, "Please Nyx, will you fly me out of here so I don't freeze and starve to death."

She giggled and it took all my control not to smile at the sound.

Nothing made sense, except that it all did. Hadn't I followed the magic and dreams here? Wasn't she exactly what I'd been looking for? The missing piece of the puzzle. Might as well trust that if nothing else.

I quickly regretted my decision.

Nyx rather efficiently and literally swept me off my feet in a blur of movement. One chiseled arm slid around my back just as she used the other to buckle my knees. Instinctually I grasped her around the neck and the smirk she wore made me want to snarl. Her body was soft and I felt my face warm when my body recognized the fullness of her chest pressed against my own. Just as she may have noticed she set off with a running leap, taking me with her as her large wings pushed the air away from us, launching us up into the opening. With a soft thud her feet hit the ground and we were out. She immediately released me, looking a bit winded and flushed.

Two seconds later the woman came crashing down on top of me, burying me under her sparse weight, the flurries of snow dancing around us unheeded. Groaning as I struggled to get out from under her I finally pushed her off, exasperation flowing from me in the form of a heavy sigh. Baffled at the sudden predicament I found myself in, I leaned over to check her breathing. Her breath was warm and steady against my hand and the soft scent of cinnamon tickled my nose as her hair was ruffled by the wind. Could this day get any weirder?

Taking care to be ready to jump back if she lashed out, I tried to jostle her awake. She hissed in response, causing me to jerk back. When I tried again she finally cracked her eyes open.

"What the hell was that?" I crooked my brow expectantly.

Nyx groaned and took several deep breaths before she pushed herself into a sitting position, her arms visibly shaking beneath her. After a few moments she pulled her wings towards herself and at first I thought she was going to simply fold them against her back, but with a yelp of pain she folded them in on themselves and then back beneath her skin. Twin streaks of blood slid down her back, soaking into her wrap.

"I apologize. I forgot how quickly the blood will rush when you haven't eaten in a couple of centuries. I may need a bit of help staying steady, but I can walk.... Just don't let me do that again until I've had a proper meal.

The last thing I needed was to be held responsible for this woman any longer than necessary, but I couldn't just leave her there to die in the cold air, especially after she'd just helped me escape a would-be tomb. Not to mention everything else.

"Take me with you, if you would. I have nowhere else to go and the Amazons have sworn to always hold a place for me."

She sounded exhausted so I merely nodded and did not press the matter further. Part of the Amazon code was to help those in need, so really I had no other choice. That I felt an odd desire to keep her close on a more personal level was something I wasn't ready to contemplate, let alone accept. There was certainly a better time and place to figure it out, best to just jar that shit up and push it to the back of the shelf for now.

Nyx had grabbed both of our bags, so I took a moment to procure a couple flowers, since I had not been able to grab any upon my descent into the abyss. Careful to preserve the plants the best I could, I added Nyx's bag to my own before adjusting it onto my back. Offering her my hands I watched as she tentatively reached out to take them.

The daylight no longer glittered across her skin, making me wonder if she had truly ever been stone to begin with, despite what I had seen with my own eyes. Her grasp was delicate, fragile almost, as I pulled and she returned the effort to get her lithe frame off the earth. She was average height, so a good head taller than myself, but I had plenty of hidden strength within and so I easily supported her weight. Despite that, she leaned only slightly into me, just enough to keep her shaky balance so she could walk, as she had promised.

"I'm stronger than I look, so let me help you. If anything this will make me look even better in front of the Amazon council."

A hint of light sparkled in her eyes as I mentioned the Amazons and her lips curled into a soft, fond smile. "Thank goodness this is still their land. I always worry what I will awaken to…or rather if I'm early or late to the bloodshed. I do prefer early, it makes things much easier to adapt to."

Her words were spoken as if the subject was nothing more than talk of the weather. What was worse was that I felt no stir of alarm from it. My senses were not in the least prickled to danger, even as those sharp fangs glistened in my peripherals, her delicate touch hiding the strength behind those defined muscles. Her presence had settled into my orb of existence as if it had always been there. The throbbing pull of magic had calmed and although I felt a stir beneath my skin, it was not an unpleasant one. Indeed, it was one I had missed sorely over the past year.

As I guided us back down the narrow path I had come up from, our bodies shuffling along sideways, I felt the urge to fill the silence between us, missing the lilt of her voice amidst the pounding of the wind and snow.

"How long do you usually *sleep* for?" I thought the question was reasonable.

She sighed as if I was some petulant child she'd told the story to a hundred times over again. I glared.

She shook her head, but if there was an apology on her lips she didn't express it. Instead she merely answered my question.

"The gaps vary. It can be a few years or centuries, but in turn I can be awake for just as long. When I solidify my magic calls out until there is an answer, then I awake once more."

Continuing to move along, our pace slow but steady despite the difficulty added by the wind and snow, I tried to fathom a creature that awoke for centuries only to sleep for just as long. What a lonely life it must have been. Unfamiliar with what a gargoyle was beyond the obvious implications, I asked the next logical question.

"What exactly do you eat?"

She leaned in on me a bit more, her steps staggering over a particularly rocky patch of trail, our height difference extremely apparent in that moment, though I was secretly glad for the forced closeness. Every time she touched my skin the heat in my body warmed me from the inside out.

"Food, same as you. Or blood, whichever is easier."

Her nonchalant tone bothered me more than her reply, though that wasn't even for the proper sort of reason. Her sudden disinterest in the conversation caused me to worry that she might be far worse off than a bit of lightheadedness. Trying to engage her, I figured it wouldn't hurt to tease her, perhaps liven her up a bit to help get her evened back out.

"You might have mentioned that a bit earlier.... You know, before I hefted you down a trail and let you lean over me with my neck exposed like a free entree'."

I got the exact result I had hoped for, and more. Her laugh was musical and her violet eyes glinted with mischief even as she gripped my waist to balance as she stepped over some loose rocks.

"Oh my dear Vixen, you don't do yourself justice. You would most assuredly be nothing less than a decadent dessert!"

Rolling my eyes even as I shook my head in disbelief, I couldn't help but laugh. A blood sucker with a flirtatious streak; no wonder she liked the Amazons. The compliment made me blush but my face was already red from the cold and wind, so it hid just how much I enjoyed the attention, though I turned my head away just in case.

She smirked, nudging me gently as she gave me a serious sidelong glance.

"I would never drink from you without permission."

I scoffed. I was as much of a predator as she was, did she really expect me to believe that? Reading the doubt on my face she gave me a grin.

"Don't worry, your mind can be skeptical, but your soul knows the truth. It'll catch up soon enough."

"Whatever."

I leaned forward against the ever increasing wind gusts, letting the conversation die as the snow began to get thick enough to obscure our vision.

When we finally made it back around to my previous campsite the snow was too thick to keep going, but thankfully the crevice I had chosen had an overhang which prevented most of the snow from falling there. Only the particularly wild gusts were able to cut through the channels to douse us in snowflakes.

"There should be a break between this storm and the next. We can get to the outpost then, it's not far once we get off this wretched goat path."

Nyx's purple eyes watched me as I set up camp, their hue unsettling and yet so striking that I found myself fighting not to turn and look into them. When I finally settled myself upon my makeshift bedspread and pulled out my reserve food, I let my gaze meet her own. My breath hitched, her wild eyes ensnaring me in a look that was far more intimate than our association would ever warrant.

There was no looking away once I'd locked on.

My cheeks grew hot as a blush crept across me, the warmth traveling down my extremities and settling deep in my core, the magic within stirring, riled up by the exhilaration that spiked. The look in her eyes spoke of desire and so much more. There was something there that I could not quite grasp the meaning of. Nyx suddenly blinked rapidly as if startled and her face pulled back into a neutral expression, embarrassment filling her voice as she spoke.

"I apologize. You are pure magic to look upon. I'm afraid I lost myself, it has been a long time since I laid eyes on such beauty."

Although usually quick of wit and sharp of tongue, I found myself speechless and quite at a loss. This wasn't just an idle flirt. I had been called a great many things, beautiful was occasionally amongst them, but her words were far more honest and raw. Something unimaginable lay in the depths of her words, like the greatest of artists, weaving a hidden image into what seemed so ordinary at first glance. My mind was clueless and yet inside the fox stirred when she looked at me like that; like I was water and she had been parched in the desert for days.

"I'm sorry, but I really don't understand any of this."

She nodded and brushed a hand across her face, a smear of red reminding me that she had been bleeding not too long ago. Not knowing what to do, but suddenly unable to stay idle in front of her, I stood up and gestured to her.

"Let me clean your wounds, then we can eat and get some rest. Perhaps things will be...clearer then." Even as I said the words I wasn't quite certain if I meant the snow or the information I had received.

She shrugged, eyes drooping tiredly, lips pursed in pain, though whether it was physical or not, I was uncertain. There was no point in asking what hurt, the way she glanced away from me assured me that it was unlikely she'd say. There were so many holes and so much information that I was lacking, yet the undeniable truth was that something unseen had been drawing me to her and hadn't yet ceased.

Taking some bandages and a salve from my bag I settled myself behind Nyx, dropping a pressed bar of dried fruits and nuts into her lap as I did so. She didn't say anything but began eating it with the energy of a stubborn child who couldn't leave the table until her least favorite food was finished.

The sun was still up, though with the still flurrying clouds it gave a dull cast of light. Even so I could easily see two huge scars running parallel to her spine, interrupted only once by the wide strip of cloth keeping her chest covered. Wetting a clean cloth with a bit of water left in my pouch, I reached out to wash away most of the grime. She shivered when my fingertips touched her, but otherwise became still as stone, her skin just as smooth as a polished river rock when my hands brushed against it.

"Touch of stardust." My lips pulled into a smile as I traced a scattering of freckles. Nyx's chest filled and released in a slow sigh at my words.

There were no wounds to apply the salve, undoubtedly a perk of the magic running potent through her veins, but I rubbed a thin layer down the long scars just to be on the safe side. The numbing properties of the cream would head off any discomfort she might have in the muscles underlying. A profound sense of desire stilled my hands for a long moment, the warmth of her flesh a temptation I longed to indulge in. Barely resisting the urge to run my hands along the defined muscles of her shoulders, I pushed myself back to my feet, returning the salve to its place in my pack before settling back down on my makeshift bed.

There might have been an opportunity to speak more upon all the things which now ran circles in my mind but comprehension seemed out of reach as the tumultuous rushing of thoughts overwhelmed me. Without a word I curled myself into a ball, rudely flipping myself so that my back was turned to her, preventing any conversation she might have attempted. Any other time sleep might have eluded me, but tonight it was snared almost as soon as my eyes had closed.

The sky twisted and turned, a shroud of thick fog mixing with billowing swirls of smoke. The combination threatened to choke out life, but there was none left in the village. The setting sun had spewed a noxious orange tinge across the sky that made the heavens look like a sickly fire spirit, dancing its last dance. Upon the ground, everything burned. Heat hit my flesh but there was nothing of worry or remorse coursing through me. The ground lay soaked with gore and littered with the bodies of hundreds of soldiers, all bearing a symbol I didn't recognize. Casting my gaze down I realized my body was splattered with dirt and blood, the scent assuring me that none of it was mine. I felt a wicked grin etch into my face as a musical voice flitted across my hearing.

"I think I broke a nail"

Nyx's figure approached from a side path, her skin shimmering with what I thought might be sweat. As she came closer I saw that she was completely covered in blood. Her violet eyes were more alive than the flames that reached ever higher amongst the fast burning huts. Her inky mane was a wild mess that framed her sharp features, muscles twitching as adrenaline continued to course through her, blood lust changing into something else as her gaze took me in from head to toe and back up again. Elongated fangs slipped past her full lips as she smiled, her wings were fully expanded and the sword she held fell to the earth with a clatter as she quickly removed the space between us.

Strong hands gripped my lower back and ass, the possessive feel sparking even more heat into my body as she slammed ours together. A soft squelch registered faintly as blood and sweat lubricated our forms, the bit of armored clothing we had equally ruined. I reached my hands up to cradle her face, heart threatening to beat out of my chest as I gazed into those eyes. Something registered that I had seen this before, that insanely annoying sensation that although I knew this was but a dream, it was too real - more like a memory played back in live action. The movements were my own yet not.

I pulled her face towards me, her wings blocking out the chaos around us as I drew her lips against mine. The heavy scent of smoke was not enough to prevent the slight prickling of cinnamon to make it to my sensitive nose, causing me to smile against her full lips. A sigh passed her lips to tickle my face as she leaned back slightly. Her face suddenly pulled down into a frown as her eyes cut past me just before a sharp pain ripped through my stomach. The screeching sound escaping her lungs chased me into wakefulness.

A hard gasp jumped me back into consciousness, the dream fading from view but not from my other senses. The cloudy night sky did nothing to convince my nose there wasn't smoke in the air, the cracking of ice beneath Nyx's feet sounding far too reminiscent of fire crackling and popping. Sucking in sharp gasps of cold air did little to calm my heart as my hands went to my stomach, cold fingers searching to make sure the dream had left no permanent marks.

A quick set of steps brought Nyx to my side, her voice a soft hush amongst the calm night, words I couldn't quite register seeking to soothe me as my mind tried to catch up with itself. Her hands quickly snatched my own, nails threatening to cut my skin as I dug helplessly in search of what I knew shouldn't be there, but the sensation of something slicing through my body and protruding forth still too fresh for my mind to fully grasp that it was not real.

"Lykos, it is past, it is past, shhh, shhhh, it's okay."

Tears came unbidden and remained unheeded until with one hand gripping both of mine, Nyx used the other to wipe the beads of moisture from my cheeks. As my eyes met hers, I found myself once again lost in vibrant purple hues, the care and concern radiating from them something new and yet infuriatingly familiar. My mind flashed back to the image of her covered from head to toe in blood, her face satisfied with the carnage around her, certainly a mirror image of my dream self. There had never been much conflict in my heart about what was human nature and the justice that must be served to the cruel amongst us, but the images left me unsettled.

Panic threatened to return, my hands shaking as the tears burned my eyes once more. Nyx easily picked my body up and drew me into her lap, her cloak wrapping around us both as her hand cradled my head against her chest. Despite an initial struggle, during which I discovered that she was far stronger than I was, I found myself easily falling into the crevice of her neck, the scent of sandalwood and cinnamon filling my nose, drowning out the dreamscape of fire and destruction.

The sobs embarrassed me more than anything else, but she didn't do more than hold me, the pressure of her arms comforting rather than possessive. Relaxing into the embrace my breathing slowly evened out. When I finally calmed she loosened her hold, her eyes boring into me without judgment, though my cheeks burned red.

"What did you see?"

Her question seemed a bit invasive to my privacy, but given she'd just held me while I sobbed, I supposed it wasn't an absurd thing to be asking. Sighing, I drew my hands up to my eyes and pressed them back into their sockets. The realization of how silly I'd just acted hit me like a slap to the face. What was I, five? Angry at myself, a rather exaggerated groan fell from my lips, just as embarrassed at my reaction as I was of the dream itself now that I realized what she was asking me to describe.

"We were in a burning village. Something struck me in my stomach and I woke up."

Her raised brow proved that she wasn't buying that it was as simple as all that, but she was kind enough not to call me out on it. She nodded slightly, then her expression turned into a frown as she traced the spot on my stomach where I had been clawing, my shirt still pushed up enough that she could see the marks. When she spoke, her tone was a riddle mixed with a mystery but what she described was a mirror image of what I had seen.

"What was later written into history as 'The Decimation of Crowfields'. We had tracked them for months, our ravens were being disoriented with air magic so our information was constantly outdated. It was pure luck that we found them, though the bards painted it as if it was a clever stunt to herd them all into one place. The pain in your stomach was a lance. The coward waited, and watched his entire army get decimated, just to get an opportunity to strike you down. He died painfully and for nothing. You actually survived that wound."

I stared at her in bafflement. How the hell did she know all that, and did she really expect me to believe a word she was saying? It was absurd! I was only twenty six and I knew without a doubt that I had not participated in some 'Decimation' as she said. Yet, hadn't it felt like a memory? Hadn't it felt as if another life had been mine, one that had been lived alongside this gargoyle as something far more intimate than the mere acquaintances we now were. She laughed and offered me a smirk.

"Yes I know, you think I'm crazy. You always do..." Here she paused and ran her hand through her hair. "Listen

Lykos, believe me or not, the truth is that you, my dear Vixen, are far more complex than you know. Your dreams are memories, as I'm sure you have guessed by now. Just as your magic awakens me from sleep, my own calls out and triggers your memories. They will come in dreams first, to preserve your sanity. Then, when you open your mind to it, they will flow more easily. Until that happens, I will fill in as many blanks as I can."

The word 'Vixen' rolled off her tongue again, irony no longer sustaining the dismissal I'd given it before now. She knew, not just that I was a creature of magic but *what* creature.

What was it she said? 'Too high even from four legs.'

Suddenly I felt like a child, my teeth nibbling at my lip as I contemplated the now infantile ignorance that consumed me. There had been a time I'd have considered myself quite mature and experienced, yet that mirage had faded on the horizon, leaving behind a desert of sand that left my mouth dry and my mind numb. Nyx had surfaced like a raincloud, my mind trusting her like an old friend yet she was a stranger to me, more likely to let the wind sweep her away than to linger long enough to shade me or quench my indescribable thirst.

Magic was a strange creature, but could it really be true? Had I merely forgotten?

"There is no such event in the histories I have read." Surely she was mistaken. She had the wrong fox and this was some magic trickery.

"No, your history books probably wouldn't remember it, it was about three hundred and fifty years before the Scourge."

"It wha-"

I shook my head, denying the idea. There was no way, yet my palms began to sweat as my anxiety pitched forward. There was truth here, my soul felt it but I didn't want to accept it.

"Your soul has seen many lives you have yet to remember my Vixen. Just as I have slept centuries away, so has your soul been absent from the world for those periods. You are a catalyst, reborn when the Fates foresee impending loss on too great a scale to be allowed."

She sat calmly. I, however, did not. Confusion mixed with anger to create an explosive combination.

"What the ever loving fuck? What in Hades' domain does that mean? Seriously Nyx, you expect me to believe this ridiculous madness? I believe in reincarnation, sure, but the notion that I am some important, what did you say, 'catalyst'? That Is beyond insane. I know magic can do some crazy shit, but this is...It's...Well, it's crazy!"

She merely shrugged, infuriating me further.

"I've yet to see anything the Gods have put into action that resembled something close to what one might deem 'sane'. Though I must say the term is quite relative. I daresay Nemesis is less reckless than most though."

She was so calm it pissed me off enough to shove away from her, having quite forgotten I still sat so close. Rising to my feet I began to pace, amusement fluttering across her face as she watched me, though when I glared she had the courtesy to hide it for a second. To and fro I paced, mind reeling with far too much for me to sort through in a mere day. With no other solution readily available I simply decided to do what I always did when my brain couldn't quite wrap around something; I said fuck it and tucked it away for later. That would definitely work.

"Let's just get off this damned trail and out of the snow."

Huffing in a fit suitable to a five year old's tantrum, I slung my roll into my bag and strapped it to my back, barely giving her enough time to get to her feet to follow. She left me in silence, only reaching out to steady me when my temper made my feet reckless and I might have otherwise fallen. By the time we made it down the icy wind had cut through my core and chilled my temper enough for me to be a bit more civil. However, my mood did not improve enough to welcome the sight of Camilla, who would undoubtedly have far more questions than I felt capable of answering.

"Thank goodness you made it down, that blizzard is going to hit sooner than expected, we need to get back as soon as-"

Her words faded as she finally looked past me and caught sight of Nyx, who smirked with amusement at Camilla's dropped jaw.

"Who is that?"

Sighing I decided to be as blunt as Nyx had been with me.

"This is Nyx, a gargoyle I apparently woke up when I crashed into her bedroom. She wants to go back to the village, says the Amazons have a pact to offer her shelter."

"A wha- you know what? You can explain on the way, I don't want to freeze my ass off out here. She can double up with you on Prince, he is far more likely to be willing than my boy."

In my irritation I hadn't even noticed Prince standing a few feet behind her, his ears tilted forward as his nostrils flared attentively. My mood eased a bit at the familiar brown eyes and painted pelt, a smile crossing my lips as he nickered a soft hello.

Well, you certainly have been busy haven't you? How long has it been since the world knew a living gargoyle I wonder?

"I'm sure she'd be willing to answer any questions you have, Prince, but I am not in the mood to play translator."

My voice was but a whisper, Nyx crooking her brow curiously as she approached Prince, her hand extended to offer her scent to him first.

She smells good, like a weird Cinnamomum verum tree.

"Well I'm glad you like how she smells cause you're going to have to carry us both."

He tossed his head and pranced in place, every bit the teenager he was, bursting with confidence and pride.

Pshah like that's hard work!

I shook my head at him and sighed to myself, knowing all too well exactly what she smelled like and the sensation it caused any time I caught a whiff. I mounted and helped Nyx to hop up behind me, giving Prince a moment to adjust to the weight before setting off.

CHAPTER FIVE
A DIP IN THE DEEP END

The following days were spent at a steady and quick clip as we rode against the wind and snow flurries. It was harsh, but we didn't dare to let up, early blizzards were always far more ferocious than their late season kin. Every resting hour left me mentally exhausted as Nyx's words came to life. It was as if they were just as magical as the beast from which they came. There was not a moment when my eyes closed that images did not play across the backs of my eyelids. The things I saw never quite fit into what I knew about the world around me, yet always there were things that felt so familiar it was like living every moment with déjà vu.

Flashes began to come even as I sat awake. At any moment a memory would slide across my mind, feeding me information I should not have known and more often than not kept to myself. I couldn't bring myself to put the information out there, too afraid Nyx would confirm it as reality. At least so long as no one else knew, I could pretend it was all just crazy dreams.

Nyx's ever present warmth against my back was a comfort I tried in vain to ignore. Thankfully, our sitting arrangements made a conversation a bit awkward, as I could not easily turn to see her, so I let Camilla carry the conversation, as she was prone to do anyways. The Amazon seemed happy enough with the added company, peppering Nyx with questions which she seemed more than patient enough to indulge.

Camilla claimed to be baffled at the idea of finding a gargoyle, but it didn't faze her in the least. The Amazons had a long held respect for magic and its creatures just as they still respected the Gods and Goddesses, so she was not altogether ignorant of the existence of them, though she'd never met one.

That she was far more adaptable than I was obvious, her flirty nature allowing her to ease into any social situation with limited awkwardness and maximum charm. Beyond my frustration with wrapping my mind around everything, I was also plagued with an unjustifiable streak of jealousy which made me even worse company. Over the course of our trek back to the Amazon village a growl rose in my chest every time Camilla's eyes took in the scantily clad Gargoyle. Between that and the snow, we could not get back quickly enough.

Shortly upon returning to the village we were ushered into the Council's hut. Queen Iris entered and bid us to sit before taking her usual seat at the opposite end of the table. Her calculating eyes took us in while only two other members joined us; Freya the scarred warrior and Rhea the Seer. It was the latter who seemed most enthusiastic to see us. The older woman was smiling from ear to ear as she stared at Nyx.

"Well, what a course of events! Sent for flowers only to bring back a gargoyle. Do all your expeditions end like this Lykos? If so, I might need to send you out for herbs more often."

Her humor did not strike me as amusing, more often than not I had found disaster at the peak of my wanderings and exhaustion rattled my bones. "Tempt the Fates too much and I might bring poison back instead."

The old woman cackled, nodding in agreement. "Oh you have no idea, darling child, how much you already tempt them."

Camilla grinned, though she tried to hide it. Nyx's gaze flittered over the warrior, a respectful nod given, but on Rhea she lingered. The old woman quirked a brow at her and although it seemed insane to think it, there was a hesitation there, as if they recognized one another. When the Queen addressed her, Nyx's focus switched.

"Tell us then, Nyx, what Queen bartered for your protection."

Nyx gave a bow, respect in her mannerisms though there was a shift of challenge in the way her voice lilted.

"I was happy to give Queen Althea the offer of my protection should she ever need it, however It was her daughter who gave the promise of welcome should I find myself in need."

There was a look of surprise across the faces of everyone in attendance. Even Camilla's gaze was serious and astounded.

"So it's true then, the daughter of Nemesis does indeed grace us with her presence?"

Freya's words were loud in the quiet of the room but not unfriendly, though my hackles raised in response. Nyx's hand brushed against my own, a quick and subtle movement that hushed and unnerved me.

"We shall uphold the honor of our foremothers. This is your home for as long as you find yourself in need. Lykos, you have been more than successful and are welcome as one of our own." The Queen offered a warm smile that was mirrored by Rhea and Freya in turn. There was gratitude in my heart and what might have been described as warm fuzzy feelings, but there was also a tumultuous amount of other feelings screaming and shouting loud enough to drown out the good ones.

The whole ordeal was quite tiresome, though I felt the smile that pulled my lips as I forced my response. "Thank you, my Queen."

From there we were made to recount the events which had led to discovering Nyx, though she adeptly skipped over all the more intimate details of our unfathomable connection. Rhea's eyes seemed to search for the truth that we left out, but neither of us offered up anything more than the dry facts. When they were well enough satisfied by our recount and my yawning had become too noticeable, I was dismissed. Nyx caught my eye when I paused, nodding slightly before returning her attention to the Queen who waited for me to leave. With nothing more to add I left, unsure of what to do with myself. The decision wasn't left in the air too long however, for Camilla had waited for me around the corner of the hut and tugged me along.

"Come on! We HAVE to tell Serah! Oh my Goddess Xalia is going to flip her shit if they let a *gargoyle* stay!"

My hackles rose at her tone, triggered, though there was no singular reason why.

"Her name is Nyx."

Camilla didn't hear or didn't care, she just tugged me along behind her. She was charming when she wanted to be but I found myself annoyed by her antics. To be fair, my irritation was less about her and almost entirely related to the thoughts bouncing around in my head. After a moment I dug my heels in and she paused long enough to scowl back at me.

"Come on Lykos!"

"You go ahead, I need to lie down."

She sighed and shrugged, too excited to let it halt her for long. Most assuredly the whole village would know about how I stumbled upon a gargoyle and brought her home before morning hit. That in itself was enough to send me to the confines of my own hut and wish for snow to keep me there for a few days, but I didn't go there directly.

I wandered through the village without really seeing where I was going, far more time passing than I could measure with my mind so distracted. There was too much information to digest, too many subtle gestures, shifts in tone and cast of gazes. The pounding in my temples bled into my eyes making the snow flurries that drifted by blur. The icy wind had picked back up, rattling the bare branches and tugging at my clothes, searching for a way past the fur edges.

The snow had already begun to accumulate, a few inches sitting lightly upon the ground, the earth beneath frozen and hard. Many of the huts had pulled their shuttered windows closed, trying to block out as much cold as possible. Heavy fur pelts would be draped across the walls in an effort to keep the warmth inside. That my own hut lacked even a banked fire only made me shudder more against the chill seeping into my bones. I would not have relief any time soon.

With my head bowed against the wind I turned the corner to my hut only to plow straight into a shadow. Strong hands grabbed my shoulders to steady us both and as I looked up I found Nyx's face lighting up as she took me in. For a moment I felt a surge of warmth that shot through my core all the way to my toe and fingertips, my own face undoubtedly mirroring her own.

There was something about her presence that soothed the aches in my soul and that, perhaps, was the most disturbing thing of all. Thankfully the cold had pushed everyone indoors so no one noticed the way my own hands had instinctively grasped Nyx's waist in turn. Feeling the tightening of her stomach beneath my hands I suddenly jerked back and without a word turned and disappeared into the depths of my hut. The sound of her voice calling my name did nothing to halt my fleeing, my scarlet face was just too much to bear.

Throwing myself onto my bed I buried my head beneath the blankets and tried in vain to block out the orchestra playing rapidly in my mind. Restless, I rose time and time again, pacing until my knees ached and then curling into a tight ball in an attempt to drift off. The blizzard finally came, so I was left to my own devices, a whole day slipping away until finally I collapsed, too numb to argue with myself.

Sleep finally stole me but with it came dreams that were somehow part reality, just not of the current one I lived in. Confusion muddled my brain but there was perfect clarity in the options I faced. A subtle voice, perhaps my own, drew me forth from sleep with a bit of gentle coaxing.

You can either accept the truth as it is and move forward, or deny it and stay suspended in the air, unable to move forward or go back. You are your only obstacle.

The numbing chill that ran along my spine at the truth of it correlated directly with the shivering that took my body as my consciousness came to. Awareness filled me as the cold swept chill bumps across my skin, even as buried as I was beneath blankets, I could not escape it. Cursing loudly and flailing about in an attempt to untangle my body I felt air beneath me only moments before gravity pulled me down to the ground, the smack of the floor surely leaving a bruise behind.

Still shivering I shuffled my way to my fire, which was now nothing more than dying embers, the empty wood pile alongside it almost as depressing as the realization that I would have to leave my hut to get more. Overwhelmed and frustrated, there was no holding back the tears that fell down my face as I settled across the floor, curling up into a tight ball and letting myself feel all the selfish self-pity that could be conjured until a dreamless sleep took me away from it all once more.

Pounding on my door stirred me, the room like ice and the fire completely done, the heat long stolen even from the stone beneath it. I stumbled as I tried to gather the blankets around me, the tapping on my door was ceaseless, and when I finally made it to my door I yanked it open far more aggressively than was warranted. A snarl fell from my lips as a pile of snow fell into the doorway, my eyes narrowing upon a youth who instantly looked like she regretted taking this particular errand. There was no wiping the glare from my vision, my lips curled in annoyance.

"What?!"

She stepped back a few feet, her hands shaking with sudden nervousness.

"O-Onya has requested your help at the stables ma'am, and Councilor Rhea has asked that you join her after dinner."

A groan filled my lungs, exhaling hard as I pressed my hands to my face. "Let Rhea know I will be there, I'll head over to the stables as soon as I'm dressed."

She hesitated just long enough for me to realize there was more. How popular could I possibly become in two days? "Is there more?"

"I-is it true? Did you really bring a gargoyle back with you?"

My brows flatlined as I glared at the young girl then promptly shut the door in her face. There was no sense in even responding. Camilla had run her mouth to plenty and although the snows had surely kept the proof of her tale from the village, it wouldn't be long before Nyx was at the center of every conversation. That she was tied directly to me would not go unaddressed. Growling to myself I pulled a heavy set of boots and a thick winter cloak on over my normal attire, tying the cords snug so that the warm fur lining felt like my own coat if I closed my eyes and breathed just right. Oh the layers of shit I needed to wade through to get my mind back clear, but where to even begin?

There had never been love in me for snow until I'd raced across it on four legs and leapt high in the air, burying myself chest deep in soft piles searching for critters hiding beneath it. The cold air only taunted me, reminding me of a time when I had run free as the fox I yearned to embrace once more. She stirred again, Nyx's magic calling and coaxing in a manner that sent fire through my soul and tempted me in every way imaginable. The cost would be far too high if I ever indulged. I had finally found a place to call home, I couldn't risk it, no matter how much it killed a part of me to stifle the wildest piece.

The wind had died down now that the storm had passed, so getting to the stables was not nearly as unpleasant as I had prepared for. Women moved around me with haste, far too much work to be done in these cold temperatures to linger long.

Thank goodness for that.

That they had no time to stop and question me was a small blessing from the Mother, though it took no time at all for Onya to spot me and wave me over to where she was. There was a mischievous glint in her eye as she looked me over, waiting until I was almost to her before flinging a bale of hay at my chest. The air left me as it slammed against my torso, my arms wrapping around it just in time to save it from hitting the ground.

"You look like shit Lykos. What have you been doing, shut up in your hut the past two days, climbing the walls?"

"Oh cause you look like a crown princess eh?" I tossed the hay bale over the fence, watching as it broke apart and scattered on a patch of ground that had been cleared of snow for the horses.

"Bet your ass I do. Look at these beautiful accents!" She motioned to the pieces of hay sticking out in every direction from her hair and I couldn't help but laugh at her antics. Victorious she grinned and tossed another bale at me, pointing to the neighboring paddock where another bare spot had been made.

"If you knew half of the bullshit running through my mind you'd need more than a few days alone to get your head wrapped around it too." I tossed the hay over the fence with a huff.

She smirked back at me as we continued down the line of fencework, a rolling cart aiding her in carrying the hay bales.

"I think you underestimate my intellect and my acceptance of just how crazy shit gets when magic is involved."

Crooking my brow and cocking my head conveyed my confusion so she laughed and gestured out toward the pastures and the village as a whole.

"Not everyone accepts that the Centaur bred horses have magic in them, or that there are still magical creatures left in the world. However, when something - someone, like Nyx pops up, it's quite hard to ignore the proof isn't it? Yet if they knew what to look for, they'd have had their proof this whole time the second you arrived."

Shock froze my movements even as Onya laughed, her hand covering her mouth in an apology, but her peals of laughter broke through.

"Geeze Lykos don't look so shocked! I cannot take you seriously with your face looking like that!"

You can accept the truth and move forward or be stuck suspended.

Shaking my head I stooped down and gathered a ball of snow in my hands, standing and throwing in one smooth motion that sent the icy ball smacking into her chest, busting apart and spraying her face. Surprise, outrage, then absolute delight filled her as she took in her chest covered in snow.

"Oh you're dead!" Her words held joy and such a lightness that there was no need to ask her what she thought I was because she didn't care. She had known from the start and yet she had been nothing but a kind friend. The thought made me smile, no motive behind her words beyond acknowledging what was inside me and how crazy that would seem to others. They might all be wild with excitement about Nyx, but for her it was just another day amongst magical things.

A snowball splattered against my face, then another one came from behind, Serah's carefree smile vicious as she popped back around a corner. It was two against one and the world dissolved away from complex questions and unimaginable truths into the simplicity of a snowball fight and the pleasure of friendly company.

By the time we collapsed into a heap by the haystacks, thoroughly exhilarated and soaked through with snow, the sun was high and the rest of the Amazons had trickled back up to the main village to eat. Serah had once again brought down a picnic's worth of food, so we sat in a circle munching on dried meats and bread, the fresh snow sufficing enough to quench our thirst.

"So Lykos, tell us the real version yea? We know you're too clever to have given Camilla the *real* details." Serah's lips curled into a knowing look as she caught my gaze. "Before you choose to lie to my face, you should know I've met her - Nyx. Talk about breathtaking and her eyes light up like you hung the moon and stars when she hears your name."

From anyone else the words would have caused me to bristle, but these two women had become my closest friends, even in such a short window of time. They had never pushed for more than I was willing to give, Onya's words only an hour prior still warmed my soul, knowing that they resonated just as truthfully with Serah. The healer had given every opportunity for my truth to be spoken whenever I might be ready to do so. Taking a deep breath I settled a score in my own heart; trust had to start somewhere.

"Surely you, like Onya, have gathered that the pull I have felt my entire life, the dreams and such I've spoken of is attached to magic?" She nodded but said no words, as if she knew any interruption might change my mind.

"It was her. When I got there I thought it was the flower, but then the ceiling gave way and I fell. It's unfathomable, insane really, but there is this connection to her that utterly consumes every ounce of my senses. She says we are connected, that we have lived past lives together...but surely that's impossible! But...the dreams...they feel like memories and when I told her one, she knew it...I feel like I'm going crazy, but everything in my soul screams that she is familiar in ways I'd be embarrassed to put into words."

The words raced out of me, leaving me winded and breathing fast. Onya's hand gripped my arm, an anchor amongst the sea which threatened to carry me off. Serah frowned for a moment, contemplating, then offered me a small smile.

"Our histories hint at crazier things happening during the time when the Gods dwelled here. Perhaps they would have the answers you need. I know Rhea has been trying to reach Nemesis for ages. Gwen often tells me the things she hears and she has hinted very recently that the key to speaking with the Goddess was close at hand. I thought that was you, but now I believe they meant Nyx."

Onya nodded in agreement, her free hand idly playing with the ends of her braided hair.

"I had wondered at the strangeness in your task. Seems an awful weird coincidence the flower you had to find was right where the one thing they have been needing happened to be sleeping."

Serah tilted her head even as I looked at Onya with skepticism, the truth perfectly clear the moment the words left her lips.

"They know." The rest I could not manage to utter, for even to these two women who were my closest of friends, the damning words felt like a betrayal to all I had been taught growing up.

Do not tell them what you are. Deny it my love, or else they will hunt you down and kill you in your sleep. They will hang your fur upon their walls well before you even grow into its full strength and size.

My mother's words rang through my head even as an adult, a secret kept so that her daughter might live, even if exile was the cost. What loneliness she had dealt with, yet always she claimed Nemesis was with her, a presence held close to her breast every night. Had there been truth in those words uttered when her life was near an end? Even now there was no way to know, unless Serah was right. The council must have known what I was and where Nyx rested. They had used me to wake Nyx and now they would seek to speak to the Goddesses through her somehow.

"Rhea has requested I join her tonight. Perhaps I can find some answers."

The topic seemed to drop as a calm silence embraced us, until that coy smile flickered back onto Onya's face as she shared a look with Serah.

"Soooo.... Do you *like* her?"

I shook my head. "I swear you two are like teenagers when you're together!" Laughing, I sprayed them with a shower of snow as I swiped my hand across a crate whose top was still laden with the frosty stuff.

Shrieking in defense and pure amusement the game resumed until Serah was hailed by a youth saying Gwenn needed her help. With plenty of work left to do, Onya and I settled into our tasks, comfortable silence warming the air between us. My mind soared in twenty directions as I contemplated how to broach the subject with Rhea. It was hard to swallow being used, but had I not done the same thing? The Amazons had been nothing more than a ticket to freedom when I had first ran to them. Surely helping them in return was hardly too much to ask in exchange for welcome amongst their ranks.

"You need a bath! Get out of here and hit the hot springs. You should be able to bathe in peace, most of the women wait until after supper so they don't have to go back out with wet hair." Onya shoved me towards the barn exit with a playful wave of her hand in front of her nose.

"Oh, so you want me to catch a cold and die eh?" She threw a horse apple at me in response. Feeling much lighter than I had since the whole mess with the damned gargoyle had started, I set off to grab fresh clothes from my hut and made my way to the hot springs. Their knowing what I was, at least to some small degree, relieved some of the guilt I had carried.

Onya proved to be right. The sound of my footfalls echoed in the cavernous rooms of the hot springs, the air practically stifling in comparison to the freezing cold outside. Wishing to be left quite alone, I tread the paths until I found a smaller pool in the crevice of a bend. At first I had thought it was a dead end, but the dark shadows could not fool my keen eyes for long and so I followed the warm path until it finally brought me to a deeper pool surrounded by stalagmites.

The minerals in the water were a bit stronger here, but the water was also much warmer for it. Stripping my layers off and piling them atop a broken chunk of stone I stepped to the water's edge before a slight movement on the far end of the pool caught my attention. The shadows drew together into a solid form, the lack of light doing nothing to hinder the details of her form from me once I properly focused upon them. The air caught in my chest as Nyx's body raised up out of the water, her eyes wide with surprise as the water trickled away from her.

There was no tearing my gaze away once it found those violet hues, though the temptation to take in the peaks bouncing at the water's surface grew strong as the muscles along her shoulders stayed in my field of vision. The hard lines mimicked her sculpture form, the tone of her skin shifting like the minerals hidden in rock. The inky blackness of her hair melted into the long shadows, the purple blue tinge that reminded me instantly of a raven's wing breaking the illusion. Her lips curled into a tentative smile and silently I cursed myself, standing bare ass naked awkwardly staring down at her.

"I-I'm sorry I didn't know anyone else was here." *Liar.* My mind focused on my aimless wandering, the soft throbbing deep in my soul tugging me along until I had found exactly what I didn't know I'd been searching for. She might have felt the same pull, but she said nothing of it, which only frustrated me further.

"No need to apologize, though perhaps you'd feel more comfortable if you actually got in? Although you are breathtaking to gaze upon, I don't imagine you are standing there for my pleasure."

Her words brought scarlet to my face, the heat pulsing there but it was far too late to cover up now. Daring to be as brazen as she, I merely slipped into the water, the warmth like magic to my skin. Forever sore muscles relaxed into the heat, the minerals soaking into my skin, soothing the rough edges and softening the hard calluses. Dipping beneath the surface, the heat relaxed the tension between my eyes, their lids squinting open, the clear waters hiding nothing below the surface. Embarrassed at my own devices I blundered up to the surface once more, the hard lines of Nyx's body etched into my mind. Trying to be smooth and failing, I breathed in water as I surfaced with wet hair covering my nose. Spluttering as my hands tried to salvage my dignity, I pushed my wavy locks away from my face.

The small cavern echoed, the musical sound of Nyx's muffled giggles my only reward for looking like a complete idiot. Squinting up at her I couldn't help but share a smile as she held a hand up, trying in vain to recover from her amusement, which only escalated as she looked at me, her giggles turning into peals of laughter.

"Oh dear, it has been so long since I saw you so ungraceful. I hate to laugh, but it is the most precious thing." Her words were soft, reminiscent of a time I could not fathom. She leaned back against the far edge, the pool too small for her to fully stretch out without her legs reaching me, so she tucked them beneath her. There was so much that felt familiar yet so far away from the reality I knew and had lived.

"I swear between you, Onya, and Serah I am going to have a complex bigger than this mountain." She cocked her head at that, thoughts going somewhere I could not follow.

"I believe I had the pleasure of meeting Serah. Sweet woman, touched with healing no?"

I nodded with a grin. There was not a single person who did not find affection for Serah once they met her, she was too likable. That she could sense the healing magic in the Amazon made me smile. How long had it been since I was able to speak freely of such things? Surely not since my mother had passed.

"Yes, I smell it on her too, though I don't think she has recognized it yet."

"She may not have, but Rhea certainly has. That woman loves to meddle."

Cocking my head I was rewarded with another melodious laugh from Nyx.

"I had forgotten how much of your human gestures mock your fox mannerisms...Rhea has a long history of meddling, it's why my mother likes her so much. She is as magical, just not in the same sense, as you and I. It is troubling that my mother is not speaking to her."

Nyx's brows furrowed in a cute way that caused her nose to wrinkle, her eyes suddenly shifting a darker hue, the scent of magic stirring in the air then disappearing as she relaxed again.

"So Serah was right. They used me to find you so that they can speak with Nemesis?"

Unconsciously I leaned forward, my voice a whisper although we were alone.

"Seems that way, though they are mistaken to think so, as I have told them."

"What do you mean?"

"As much as my mother and I share love, it is you who has the stronger connection to her. Rhea has asked me to go to an altar that still stands south of the village. I believe she will now ask you to come along as well." She paused for a moment, scrubbing her hands together before dipping them back below the water. "As much as I would simply enjoy your company, it would also be the best way for you to get the answers you are struggling to find. Mother knows everything."

The pieces fell together, Rhea's request now making sense. Nodding in agreement was all I felt capable of. Speaking of a Goddess I had always imagined as a vague distance idea, as if she were going to appear in the flesh at my request, was mind boggling. As if sensing my unease, Nyx grabbed a bar of soap and motioned to me.

"Turn around, I'll wash your hair while you mull things over."

Unable to think of a valid reason to dismiss the offer I simply turned in place, listening as the water sloshed against her when she stood up so that she could reach me. The soapy suds smelled lightly of eucalyptus leaves, the scent relaxing as it tickled my nose. The first touch of her hands came tentatively, my body tensing immediately, then just as quickly relaxing back into the gentle massaging of her fingers. Her adept hands seemed to know every inch of my head as she caught the tight spots and massaged the tension down the back of my neck and skull. Losing myself in the sensation, a soft moan of pleasure escaped my lips, my whole body bracing against the cringe that radiated from my mind. She ignored it, moving away from my head and scrubbing the longer lengths until they too were covered with soap.

When she stepped back and gave my shoulder a tap, I dunked my head. I sorely missed the touch of her hands as I rinsed the soap out, the soft scratching of her long nails soothed an itch I hadn't realized was there. When I resurfaced she had stepped out of the water, destroying any offer I might have made to do the same for her. She offered me an almost sad smile, the edges tilting in a way that left me dissatisfied, knowing I was the cause of it.

"Things will get clearer with time, you just have to be willing to believe what your mind and soul already know. Let your fox guide you, she remembers more than your human self does."

With that she wrapped herself in a length of cloth and left, leaving me baffled and sorely disappointed with her departure, though not with the actual image of her hips swaying as she left. By the time I finished mulling things over, sprawled out across the hot floor, clean locks dried and shining, there was just enough time for me to grab a bite to eat before heading off to Rhea's hut.

The meal hut was buzzing, warmth radiating from the packed bodies of Amazons as well as the fires still blazing in the kitchen. Grabbing a bowl of rice and rabbit stew, I made my way across the room to where Onya waved me over, a seat next to her always opening up when I needed it. As I sat down she leaned close, giving a sniff and smiling.

"Hmmm…I know for a fact that isn't the scented soap you traded me for."

Growling I shoved her face away with a gentle push, ignoring her antics as I tried to eat my meal. Camilla however was one to listen to everyone, so she didn't miss the jibe and latched on.

"Ooo, who have you been bathing with Lykos?!" She curled her lips into a smile that didn't quite reach her eyes, reinforcing the jealous note to her voice. Rolling my eyes I spooned another mouthful of rice to my lips, the savory flavor causing my stomach to growl with satisfaction.

"Like it is any of your business." Xalia's voice rose from a few seats down, her gaze catching my own. A silent nod of thanks was given before she turned back to her meal, Serah squeezing her arm as she smiled at her. Onya poked my ribs with her elbow, a hush of interest trickling through the Amazons before it dispersed back into the regular jumble of conversation. With a nod she directed my gaze to the disturbance, grinning mischievously as she waved at Nyx from across the room. The gargoyle approached with her own bowl of stew, surprise then a smile covering her face when she saw me sitting alongside Onya.

I didn't get a chance to protest.

Onya's demeanor rarely allowed for her commands to be ignored and with a glare that spoke volumes the two women who sat in front of me shuffled over, allowing Nyx to join us at the table. The woman was radiant; her freshly washed hair shined like a polished stone, vibrant purple eyes stark against the cool tones of her flesh, chiseled features not lacking a feminine touch even for their sharpness. Around the table many stared, but on finding her no more unique in appearance than the next, their interest faded. My eyes however could not stand to lose her image, at least not until Onya stepped on my foot.

Shaking my head I finally tore my eyes away, a smile tugging Nyx's lips up so that her sharp fangs slipped past. Camilla, ever incapable of being subtle, gasped and leaned in to get a better look. Satisfaction came when Nyx allowed her to lean in then playfully snapped in her direction, causing Camilla to jerk backwards and trip over the bench, falling flat on her back. Xalia's voice echoed louder than the rest of us as we chuckled at Camilla's expense. For all her faults Camilla laughed right along with us.

"Alright alright, I set myself up for that one!" She grinned sheepishly, trying to catch my eye with a crooked brow. Ignoring her, I finished up my bowl as quickly as possible, trying desperately to ignore the conversation happening between Nyx and Onya.

"So Nyx, do you turn into some crazy stone creature or is the term gargoyle relative?"

She smirked, patient as always. "I don't get grotesque if that's what you mean. I have wings, but I typically tuck them away until they are needed. I only turn to stone when I intend to sleep through the years or I suffer an otherwise fatal injury."

"Why would you want to sleep that long?"

She cast a sidelong glance to me before turning her gaze back to Onya. "I have found that sleep and time are the only things that heal a broken heart."

Onya didn't miss the look that passed over to me, but she chose to ignore it, sparing me further scrutiny. Finishing the last of my stew I sat torn between the pull to stay near Nyx and the real need to hide from the attention. Camilla made my mind up when she asked the next question, having once again leaned across the table to grab something.

"Is that Eucalyptus scent Nyx?"

A nervous clench held my stomach, making the food there unsettle. Nyx had missed that bit of conversation so she paid no heed to my sudden rigidity, though Onya bumped my shoulder to try and ease me out of it.

"I couldn't tell you Camilla. It is a pleasant scent, but I'm afraid many of the plants here are not entirely what I am used to."

"I'm certain it must be." Camilla's eyes turned to me, a pout in every bit of her features, though I was given no chance to sour her mood before Xalia joined the conversation.

"Nyx, if you are interested, the scouts would be happy to share their knowledge. It will also get you out of the village a bit if you need a breather from all these vultures."

Serah popped Xalia's arm even as she chuckled. Onya looked confused as to whether or not she was included in that comment, and Camilla was thoroughly put out as Nyx and I laughed in turn.

"I am NOT a vulture!"

Xalila ignored Camilla's pouted protest even as I poked fun in turn. "Scavengers squawk first Camilla."

She threw a piece of her roll at me but I easily caught it and tossed it into my mouth, some of the tension finally breaking away from my body.

"Well if I am, can I pick your bones first?" She raised her brows provocatively, her interest sincere even if the words were joking.

"Not a chance." I said instantly.

To my horror, she leaned forward and gestured to Nyx with an open palm.

"How about you good looking? I'm sure it's been a while. You need someone to start a fire for ya?"

Nyx smirked, but a growl rose from deep in my throat, the noise hushed against the commotion of the food hut but not missed by Onya or the stable hand at my other side. Nyx cast a glance at me, possibly catching it as well. I felt my jealousy rising, surprising myself with the strength in which it crowded into my mind.

"I assure you Camilla, I am perfectly capable of starting my own fire, but thank you for the compliment. I'm sure there are plenty of ladies happy to offer you their kindling."

Onya squeezed my arm, the growl in my throat ebbing down to an inaudible tone, but my hands had unconsciously gripped the table and were currently leaving fingernail prints.

"Lykos, didn't you need to do something before you met up with Rhea?"

Bless that beautiful horse handler. Nodding, I recovered myself, releasing the table and making my excuses even under Nyx's scrutiny from across the table. As soon as I shut the door I darted off into the cold air, desperately needing to clear my head. Where had that even come from? Was it truly me? Was it the dreams? Either way there was no denying the attraction I felt toward Nyx, though there had been very few times I had ever felt jealousy.

Though, to be fair I hardly ever had competition. Lykos, you gotta get yourself together.

The thoughts ran circles in my head, my footsteps taking me around the village's perimeter until I finally felt like I had a grasp of myself again. The fox stirred, my magic rebuilding and the fire Nyx struck within me pulling her ever closer to the surface. Soon I'd be able to shift again, though I'd have to find an excuse to get away to do so. Still, at least there was that small positive to the whirlwind of things flying at me. For now, I needed to see what answers Rhea could provide.

CHAPTER SIX
GROWING PAINS

Rhea's home was no larger than my own, her hut built with all the essentials, but that was where all similarities ended. My walls had remained bare, but hers were lavished in oddities. The shelves held trinkets, foreign clothes were strewn about as well as fur blankets and there were pieces of artwork hung here and there. The largest wall was decorated with a large stretch of sewn skins, their stitches so small and precise that you had to truly search for them. Upon the skin a rather talented artist had depicted fantastic scenes in the style of the great city's stained windows, the pictures separated by frames that were accented with actual flakes of gold.

The bottom left corner hosted a unicorn and a young maiden overlooking a hunt, their expressions pained. The opposite corner showed a great golden eagle fighting with a massive serpent over what appeared to be some kind of egg with intricate swirls and vibrant hues marring its irregular shape. In the bottom right a Gryphon looked up at the stars, a litter of cubs dead at its feet, a fire blazing high in the background amongst the roofs of a city. The last corner displayed a mother and child shying away from a human shadow, a fireplace in the background shedding light only on their fear. In the middle were two women, Goddesses I recognized. Nemesis and Artemis stood, their forearms braced together, hands both covered in blood and determination on their faces while tears trailed down their cheeks.

I found myself lost among the images until Rhea touched my shoulder causing me to jump in place. For a woman who looked frail, her grip was surprisingly strong, a glimmer of mischief in her eyes as she chuckled at my jolt.

"Beautiful isn't it?"

Her voice was just as strong as her grip though it was no more than a whisper.

"Not many remember this story, never mind the inevitable results of such a pact as was made that day. Nemesis and Artemis binding their vows with blood. No woman, beast, or child would ever find themselves without aid if an Amazon or creature of Nemesis could be found."

Her words made my head cock to the side with curiosity but she merely gave me a wink. "Perhaps another day I will tell you the whole story. Tonight I would like to discuss more recent events. I believe your other half will be joining us soon."

She drew me toward the table just as a knock came upon the door. Nyx entered moments later, her cheeks red as if she had been laughing. Her eyes were their normal vibrant hue, but her skin seemed more alive, like a piece of gold shimmering in the light, a stark contrast to her long locks which I might compare to the obsidian pitch used in war games. She donned a diagonal wrap and long shorts beneath her fur cloak, her strong biceps appropriately looking as if they had been chiseled out of stone as she took the latter off.

Nyx offered a smile that showed off her sharpened canines, looking more feral than ever even though I had seen her no less than an hour prior. To Rhea she offered a lingering hug, their eyes meeting for long enough that I shifted in my seat with discomfort. They broke apart looking like long lost friends. Of course, according to what Nyx had said, they may have been.

A sigh fell from my lips and I couldn't help but plant my palms in my eye sockets. My head throbbed with a migraine that I hadn't noticed slipping in but refused to leave. The blur of images from my ever persistent dreams and memories suddenly made me dizzy amidst all the magical scent.

"Here child, the tea will help calm your mind and sooth your ache. It will also help your magic realign, which will be necessary if what Nyx says is true."

I let out a sigh.

"I wish it would realign my life instead."

My words were undoubtedly laced with bitterness, but neither of my companions chose to comment. Instead they sat at the table with me and waited for me to finish the tea which

I obligingly sipped. The taste was a bit bitter but I could sense a hint of honey used to sweeten it. When she was satisfied that I had drunk enough, Rhea ran her wrinkled hands through her long silver hair with a grim smile turning her lips at an awkward angle.

"I'm afraid the news I have is not very pleasant, but first let me say this; although you may find Nyx's information to be both overwhelming and unbelievable, I can vouch for the truth in it. You do not have to hide yourself, I have known long before you came into our territory what you are Lykos. It's why I sent you into the mountains to find Nyx."

She folded her hands in front of her, looking directly at me with her somehow all seeing eyes, perhaps to gauge my expression. I resented the manipulation, but so much of my life had been out of my control thus far, what was a bit more? It could have simply been the tea, but I felt calmer, the chaos inside seeming to take a seat as background noise. That I had most of that information already may well have swayed the extent of my reaction as well. That and the acceptance I had already received from Serah and Onya.

"Always glad to know my *fate* is in your hands Rhea. Though it took you long enough." Nyx smirked as she spoke.

The two shared a moment of amusement that I didn't grasp, as if some joke had been made but I wasn't savvy to it.

"Everything happens *precisely* when it should. I have perfect timing."

Nyx practically snorted in response, her eyes rolling in what could have been seen as disrespectful, but Rhea only winked at her. It occurred to me that I was still missing quite a few pieces to the puzzle that was their dynamic. It would just give me a new headache trying to decipher it, so I pushed it off for later. Instead I focused on the reason for us even being here at all.

"That news is a bit annoying but hardly unpleasant, so tell us what is." Patience had never been my strong suit and somehow seeing Nyx's face light up for someone else had rubbed me in the same way too tight undergarments did.

Rhea scowled for a moment, but finally relented.

"The Mad King has been an issue ever since he was put into the position and that is not a coincidence. There is someone manipulating him with magic. The problem is we can't figure out who or what. The Gods have slipped away, refusing to interfere, but someone with their blood or a strong magical ability is causing mayhem."

The soft echo of magic shifted across my mind.

"The last time he interrogated me, it was like he was talking to someone else and there was always a faint scent of magic - not his own, but definitely affecting him."

Rhea nodded "Many of our spies have said the same; that he rambles like someone is in the room right next to him. One has said that any sign of a hawk sends the man trembling, which may be his own fear or a clue as to who haunts him. We have lost our connection to Artemis, the only hope we have at gaining answers is Nemesis. She has always been willing to aid the Amazons, but we cannot reach her."

"The connections are so thin now... It is worrisome." Nyx's eyes shone with concern, her brow furrowing in a cute way.

"We need to know who is pulling the King's strings. He will only believe you are dead for so long and his men are becoming restless. He will either give them something to do or they will find it themselves."

"We will go." The words slipped from my lips before I thought to examine them. The hatred burning in my gut for the Mad King and all that he represented scorched my lungs, fire breathing into my chest and casting a red hue to my vision. Months of torture didn't disappear from one's memory easily, no matter how much else cluttered in with it.

Even in my small village word of the King's destruction had been vast, heavily detailed, and soaked with fear. The brute would destroy everything if given a chance and for whom? Some puppet master too scared to walk out onto the field? He imported slaves to keep him protected, then paid them in freedoms of grotesque nature: pillaging, raping, and killing. Any village that resisted his rule fell victim.

A growl rose in my throat as my vision cleared and Rhea smiled at me as if she had been waiting for this moment. Perhaps she had. My annoyance did not just dwell with the unknown, the Amazon council had withheld and manipulated in their own turn.

"There are too many questions that need answering and I'm tired of sitting around idle and useless." Rhea gave a small nod of her head, perhaps sensing my irritation.

"The altar to Nemesis is not far, just a few hours on foot. We can leave in the morning." Nyx murmured.

"I'll see you then." Giving a nod to Rhea I left, heading back to my hut so that I could try to sort out my thoughts before potentially facing a Goddess.

The idea alone sounded insane, yet there was no doubting that it had been done in the past. There were hundreds of accounts even in my small village's history. As I laid in bed, too restless to sleep, I could not help but think of my mother. As a child I had believed her with all my heart, yet the realities of the world had hit me hard and my faith had wavered.

If only she could see me now, heading to an altar with a gargoyle to chat with her Goddess momma.

"She'd know what to make of all of this." I whispered the words to my pillow, the heartache still hard to handle. There were so many layers to peel away, numbing my mind with exhaustion any time I tried to make sense of it. Mother had always said I was different, my shapeshifting just one sliver of all that made me special, in ways that would one day make sense. How often had she told me to reach within and follow the threads of my magic to the truth? There were never clear answers then, just as there were none now. Nyx swore my dreams were true memories and hadn't I too always felt they were far too real to be mere imaginings?

How could I swallow that down? It was one thing to believe it and pass it off as craziness, but for someone to verify it? Not just someone, but a gargoyle whose face had appeared in at least a hundred of those dreams. There was madness in me, yet every ounce of my gut believed her, despite desperately trying to convince myself otherwise. Survival had always demanded that I brush off the truth when others thought they held a thread of it. To try and embrace it now felt wrong on so many levels, although it was all that I had yearned for. The opportunity to run free amongst other people was presenting itself, surely I ought to have been ecstatic. Instead, fear wrapped its hands around my throat whispering of false hopes and wolves in sheep's clothing.

My heart yearned to trust, my brain screamed caution, and my soul raged against anything and everything that might take me away. Not from the Amazons, although I had found friends among them. No, it was Nyx which my soul pulled toward it like iron to lodestone. Honesty with myself did no good as I rebelled against the truth.

Everything about the woman was attractive. She had all the attributes I had consciously sought out in a partner, and with her my magic wasn't pulling me away in another direction; instead it drew me to her, content. That was perhaps the most terrifying part - that I might actually be capable of falling for her. With all other women I had known it would only be a matter of time before it ended. My soul yearned for a deeper connection that they simply could not provide. With Nyx the stirring within was nothing I had ever felt before except in my dreams. That meant I could very well fall for her and had on numerous occasions, if she was to be believed.

Falling however, meant I could also crash and break.

I tried to reason my way out of it, to find some other logical explanation, but there was no logic to be found where magic was concerned. Still I tried to find it, though the irony was not lost on me.

Oh yes, I can turn into a giant fox but Elysian Fields forbid I accept that my soul's magic might drag me across the continent to find a gargoyle who I knew in a previous life.

There was no taking myself seriously after that and a spiel of giggles interrupted my thought process until they turned to tears of frustration and eventually exhausted me into an uneasy sleep.

The next morning we set out on foot, a somewhat uncomfortable silence settling between Nyx and I as a storm brewed within me. The weather had warmed, though my fur trimmed cloak was still necessary until the sun rose to its peak. The snow still clung to the earth, painting it in shades of gray that blended together, though most of the village had been cleared well enough for foot traffic. The path we took was not a frequently traveled one however, so we trudged through high snowfall, trying to keep the cold debris from falling into our boots. Nyx tried to start conversations but I only gave short replies, trying with no success to shake the annoyed mood following me.

The trail was barren, the trees resembling bones as they shook and rattled in the wind, no foliage left behind in the cruelty of the blizzard. The boulders that framed the path lay hidden beneath several feet of snow so that all one saw was slopes of white. The world seemed to stand frozen in time, no footprints to be seen except behind us, all the mountain creatures hidden away in their dens.

Nyx's attire now included a hide wrap to keep the chill at bay, it had been dyed a deep red and somehow seemed more vibrant on her than hanging up. She also wore plain boots which looked comical on her, if only because it had apparently been a long time since she had donned footwear and so lifted her legs too high. The grumbling she'd let slip from her lips only made the entire scene all the more charming despite me wanting to be sour towards her.

After a half hour of silence, she finally stopped and turned to face me looking far more tired than I had noticed earlier.

"Lykos, please just say whatever is on your mind. This sulking silence is really starting to wear on me. I had hoped we might actually get a chance to talk without any eyes on us."

Guilt filled my gut, for she had done absolutely nothing to earn my ire. With a sigh I kicked the snow, only it wasn't just snow. The impact jarred my leg and sent a curse from my lips as my big toe throbbed, the snow falling down the path of my foot to reveal a spot of rock. Hopping up and down with my foot in my hand my balance escaped me and my unharmed foot left the earth below, sending me backwards into what thankfully was nothing but snow.

Nyx ran to where I was, the worry in her face melting into amusement as she looked down at me, hands on her hips, lips pressed together tight to hold back the laugh fighting to be free. Sprawled across the ground with my arms and legs spread out in surrender I couldn't even bring myself to be embarrassed.

"Themis works swiftly. Suppose that was my punishment for acting like a child and holding a grudge that you don't deserve."

She remained standing over me, waiting for a better explanation, those purple eyes practically glowing as the snow reflected the sunlight onto her.

"Nothing should make sense Nyx, but it does. The dreams, memories, and you. They all make sense with what you have told me. Mother always said it was the past trying to speak to me, but I didn't think she meant it literally. Now I'm here with the Amazons, by some miracle I still can't wrap my head around, and you're here and everyone is okay with it all? My best friends knew I wasn't a normal person but they treated me like I was, the council not only knew but counted on it and you...You have been welcomed with open arms as if you have only been gone for a trip and just returned. It shouldn't make sense, yet nothing has felt more certain and real than you, and this, and FUCK I sound crazy."

Breathing in deep to catch my breath from the rant I'd just let explode onto Nyx, I sat up, ashamed to have unloaded it all on her. She knelt down, her hand reaching out cautiously, fingers cold as ice but gentle as they touched my chin and lifted my downcast head.

"You have to ask questions to get answers, Lykos. There is a lot of information to take in here, most of it illogical to anyone who hasn't lived and breathed magic. I will answer any question you have that I can, but you must ask them. No one is going to offer it unbidden for fear of just this." She gestured to me sprawled out on the snow having a tantrum.

"Come, get out of the snow, moving will warm you back up." She moved her fingers from where they had stayed against my chin, the skin there warm from the touch. Grasping the offered hand I let her help me back to my feet, my toe still throbbing but unbroken. She smiled warmly, the familiar heat rising to my cheeks even as electricity seemed to shoot through me. Reluctantly I let go of her hand, constantly torn between whether my attraction was genuine or mere memory. Silence enveloped us as we began to walk again, this time far more comfortable as I gathered my thoughts before finally addressing her.

"What is your relationship with Rhea? You two act like you know one another."

Nyx nodded, her gaze turned to the sky as she watched a bird fly by. "Rhea is just as immortal as myself, just as immortal as you may one day be. She has known us both in almost every life we have lived. More often than not she orchestrates our reunions."

My feet stuttered in step, but I managed to recover well enough to stay alongside Nyx who looked like she'd merely stated the snow was white.

" Wait, what? Immortal? Please...explain."

She smirked. "Rhea was not her original name. She was once a Fate before the spindle was broken and the mortals took their fate into their own hands. When the Gods started to disappear, she stayed behind to help keep balance."

"Suppose it'd be too easy if she had all her powers intact huh?"

Nyx laughed, hand reaching up to brush hair away from her face, the inky locks fluttering in the breeze. "Life wouldn't be fun if it was easy."

She shrugged when I scoffed. "I don't believe that for a second."

There was no doubt that my life had never been easy and for that reason I had grown to be strong, but who could say I wouldn't have been so with a few more breaks? There was always something to be done, somewhere to be and although I hated to be idle for long, having a choice in whether I could or not was a luxury that would have been enjoyed. The life of a royal did not suit me, the fox within far too wild to be caged even by invisible fences, but some perks would have been nice.

Every day spent near Nyx stirred my other half more, my skin itching beneath the surface as the change beckoned for me to answer her call. There was no difference between my human form and the fox within, but separating the idea kept me balanced and in control. That alone was probably the only thing that had kept me safe all these years.

Rhea's scent was filled with magic, so although it was shocking, the proof had always been in the air around her. Aged magic was far more potent than anything new. Besides, what was one more thing among the ever increasing pile of things I could barely wrap my head around. Lying next to that in the pile was this idea that I could become immortal.

"What did you mean? As immortal as I may one day be?"

The taller woman paused for me to catch up to her, my wandering mind having slowed my gait so that she walked in the lead.

"That question would be best saved for after you have spoken with Nemesis." My brow crooked, eyes narrowing in defiance, so much so that she shrugged and continued.

"You reincarnate because your soul cannot be captured and taken to the Underworld, so it is reborn instead. That however, was not what was intended. You were meant to be immortal and we have been trying to sort out why you are not, at least in the traditional sense."

Laughter fell from my lips unbidden at the absurdity of it all. Immortal? Me?! Surely I could not be so special. Shapeshifters had existed before, most born as a product of the Gods' loose morals regarding sex with beasts. They had been hunted to extinction as far as any of us were aware, the closest to it being the Centaurs who had made themselves invaluable.

A shapeshifter such as I was rare, yes, but not unheard of. There were many bedtime stories told of shapeshifters, passed down through the ages and dramatized to keep kids in line. What could possibly make me so different?

There was only one way to find out.

My laughter ceased as we came to the end of the trail, the snow disappearing as the path shifted from snow covered earth to smooth sandstone. There must have been a hot spring beneath what had once been a small temple, likely placed there for that exact reason. The start of the cleared sandstone trail was marked with two statues on either side, the features of the women's faces were eroded with time, but their outside arms were extended in welcome. The bases had taken damage but otherwise the women were intact, a rarity amongst any remaining places of worship.

Following the path led us to a long abandoned area for gathering, in the center was a raised dais used by priestess' to deliver messages from the Gods. The platform had collapsed in, the wood it had been built from weakened by the elements until the weight of the world had snapped it. Behind that lay the entrance to the temple which had been sealed shut with stone and clay. There was nothing fancy or special about the structure aside from its size. Twice the berth of a normal hut, the building resembled a horseshoe, cradling the open area in its arms and shielding the believers from the harsh mountain winds.

"Here."

Nyx's words drew my attention from the barred door to a small gap in the structure's exterior that I might not have noticed, had she not pointed it out. The crevice had been built intentionally, so that donations and prayers might be given even when the temple itself was closed. A few feet in, another dais had been laid into the flesh of the building and a mural had been painted onto the smoothed rock surface above it. The Goddess Nemesis looked down upon the supplicant with a warm smile, a night sky behind her and balancing scales set in her hands.

Nyx followed me in, the taller woman smiled as she peered up at the image, the resemblance uncanny. Her flowing, inky black locks were mirrored in the portrait, as well as the sharpness of her cheekbones and pointed chin. There was a similarity in the eyes as well, though the colors were nowhere close to one another.

"The likeness is true then?"

She nodded, looking at me from the corner of her eye for a brief moment before turning back to the image of her mother. "Though last I had seen her, there was less joy in her eyes and her cheeks had hallowed a bit."

There was no imagining that this could have taken away from the Goddess' beauty any more than I thought it would Nyx's. There was something graceful in every move she made, the aura around her calming, tempting me to fall into its orbit. Perhaps that was what was more frustrating than anything else about her; how perfect she seemed. Still, I questioned how much of my opinion was swayed by the draw of her magic? Even if we had lived past lives together, I did not recall them beyond memories tied to dreams. What stock could I put into that? How could I rid myself of my doubt?

Focusing my mind back to the task at hand I examined the dais, a small bowl laid into the stone, a sharp piece of carved obsidian set beside it, the stain of blood evident in the brown tinge at its tip.

"Why is it always blood?"

Nyx smirked and shrugged. "Most have nothing else to offer. What better offering is there than the essence of life itself? Just be glad it is not the cream of pleasure like the Gods of Lust and Love once demanded."

I shook my head, believing her simply messing with me. When I looked at her with a crooked brow the devious smirk on her lips confirmed it. I growled softly as I gave her shoulder a shove. "You are a menace!"

She grinned and held her hands up in defense as she walked backwards to the entrance. She sat with her back to me, looking as if she were going to meditate. There was only one thing to do.

A sigh left my lips as I lifted the piece of obsidian and pressed it to the tip of my thumb. The bead of blood did not shimmer or shine, the light within the passageway dull and just barely penetrating the shadows enough to highlight the mural above. There was really no reason anyone ever needed to slash huge cuts across their skin, but some simply favored the dramatics involved.

Instead of letting the drop fall into the bowl, I reached up from my tiptoes and pressed the dot onto the mural, in one of the scales held in Nemesis' hands. Setting myself back down I waited, though I didn't quite know what for. For a moment I wondered where that impulse had come from. No one had done these types of rituals in my lifetime. There were stories, of course, but none I could trace back to ritual etiquette. Instinct told me it was something I had known for far longer, something I had witnessed but could not have possibly done so in this lifetime. Oh the questions I had.

A silence settled around me, one that I did not register immediately as unnatural. The heavy scent of magic crept in, even as the shadows grew deeper and darker. A growl rose from my throat as the hairs on the back of my neck sprung up. The walls suddenly disappeared, shadows swallowing me up so that when I turned around there was no sign of the entrance or Nyx beyond.

In the darkness a presence moved, the sound reminiscent of the skittering of leaves across the hard earth in fall, or their rattling high in the treetops when disturbed by a hard breeze in spring. The air grew cold, then almost uncomfortably warm before settling into something that was perfect. From the depths where the mural should have hung and no wall now stood, a whispering voice that sounded like a lullaby resonated out.

"Do not be afraid Lykos, I have known you long before the time you walked the earth in any true form. Let me show you, my dearest creature."

There was nowhere for me to run, the endless darkness around me as solid as any wall though it held no texture as it pressed against me, holding me in place even as I tried to step back and away. A hand reached out, a living shadow that held barely a wisp of solidity to it, fingers spread out with tips glowing a warm amber that matched a glow now emanating from my chest. The intangible digits slipped past my skin and reached deep into my soul, the magic within bursting with life as her other hand cradled my head, drawing it to her own. Her head was a black void with no real solid details, just sharp curves contoured out by the likeness she'd sprung from.

My mouth opened to release a scream but instead of sound my consciousness slipped out. Shapeless at first, I drifted away from my body, looking down upon a scene that did not reflect what I had just lived. My human form sat on the earth, head bowed into my hands as if deep in meditation. The image remained for only a moment before it flickered and faded, all sense of smell and taste dispersing as I floated through a stream of pure magic, the tide pulling me along with no care of my wishes. I was not alone.

Nemesis grasped my hand, pulling me along, her face now clear as day and an almost exact mirror to Nyx. Although they looked similar, Nemesis stood shorter than her daughter and was more daintily built where Nyx was thick with muscle. Her smile was just as warm, looking upon me as if she had known me my entire life. Her hair seemed to be made of shadow, one moment waving behind in liquid movements, the next becoming intangible threads weaving through the tapestry of the unnamable essence we soared through.

"This was never what I had planned for you, especially once you connected so deeply with my daughter. You are my greatest creation Lykos, moving through time acting as a catalyst for change. There must be balance in all things and justice for those killed before their time. You have fulfilled your purpose despite the difficulties of your reincarnation. I only hope that this will be the last time you need to do so."

Her gaze looked forward as if seeing something beyond the darkness that surrounded us.

"I don't understand."

"You will soon, child. Let me first show you how you were created, I believe that has always been the best place to start."

The world jerked and twitched, opening up to let us slip through a crack in the shadows, popping back out into a world I did not recognize as my own.

"It is a memory." Nemesis answered my unspoken question, bidding me to follow as she walked toward the edge of a cliff overlooking a vast valley filled with flora. She paused when we were close enough to see a replica of her standing there, her head turned up to the sky. I watched the second Nemesis with a sense of awe, the magic around her so potent that it had manifested outside her body in the form of shadowy wisps that swirled about her as she worked. Her voice seemed younger, or perhaps merely less mature and tired.

In the sky the constellations came to life, their vague outlines becoming vibrant glowing entities of white and gold. A hound chased a fox across the deep blue expanse, the nimble creature easily leaping starry rocks and trees, just barely escaping the chomping jaws of the dog who became increasingly frustrated. The fox leapt high across the stars and over the moon, then ran back to its place, shaking its fur before melting back into the vague shape of the constellation it had sprang from.

The residue which shook free of the star fox's body fell down to the earth. Golden stardust, shimmering with magic, scattered across the valley and where it fell the earth flourished. Flowers suddenly burst forth in bright oranges and reds, trees fruited heavily, and a sick fawn lying still beside its mother suddenly healed, standing and crying out with vibrant life. The Nemesis of memory reached out and grabbed the biggest chunk, letting the shadowy wisps rise and reshape it, a mirror image of the star fox now sitting in her palms.

"The stardust of the Camdean Vixen, a fox who could never be captured. I took inspiration from the fox legends from the Eastern World and shaped you into a Kitsune." The present Nemesis explained, but suddenly the whole picture ran through my mind, singing truth to my glowing soul.

"You created me, to fulfill your purpose."

"Yes, though you became so much more with time. I created you so that the task would not fall to my daughter, though she took it up alongside you all the same." Her tone held only a whisper of annoyance.

The small fox suddenly sprang to life as memory Nemesis brought it to her lips and gently blew upon it, magic in every aspect of her being. The fox ran back and forth between her palms, testing its legs, its overly large tail troublesome at first. Finally Nemesis beckoned it still in one hand and then reached out to her stream of magic with the other. In my core I could feel a thrumming of energy, pulsing with excitement, as if matching the call of the memory we watched.

"Magic is energy in its purest form, able to change and adapt to anything. Those of us who channel it are dubbed immortal Gods. Energy is the essence of life, so I simply combined the two, bidding the stardust and magic merge into a form that could switch between both worlds. The Vixen's gift prevents Hades from keeping your soul, though it takes time to find you again and draw you back. My magic should have made you immortal."

Right before my eyes I watched the flow of magic enter the fox, the beast growing too large for the hands and leaping down, growing by the second until I stared at my other half. The stardust it was born from still glittered upon the strands of fur, gold and red melding together, accented by the black edges left by Nemesis' magical touch. The tail was too large, shimmering with magical potential, the beast -no I- waved it back and forth, a portion of it splitting off until there were nine segments. My mirror kitsune self gave a satisfied nod as she looked back at them. Nemesis smiled at the beast, a hand reaching out to caress the muzzle that lovingly pressed back.

"I have given you life and ask that you help serve my purpose. Your magic is a piece of me freely given, but your soul has and always will be your own."

The memory Nemesis said these words to the Kitsune who bowed her head, her body shifting into the glowing star of a soul. The soul was cradled gently by Nemesis as she walked toward us, the memory disappearing back into the void, leaving me feeling like my chest would explode as emotion overwhelmed me. The memories came back, though they were old and blurred at the edges. I remembered the feeling, the warmth of love and magic melting into one sensation that filled every pore on my body and shaped me into a new one.

"What does that mean?" I could only whisper, my chest too tight to breathe deep.

"Every life starts somewhere and eventually the oldest stars disappear from the sky. When I created you your soul was brand new. You have always had the free will to walk away from my purpose for you."

There was no use lying to myself, though I was tempted to do just that. Everything she said and everything I saw felt true. Wild and incredible, but the soft hum of my own soul only confirmed it. There had always been an awareness that came with being able to shapeshift. The magic that coursed through my veins and fed my soul reached into the earth's essence and grounded me to its invisible structure like any of Gaia's creatures. The flow felt depthless, spilling out across my skin until it changed shape and became something more. The fox within was no separate beast, instead it was my soul's truest form, a reflection of a life I was just a piece of; the Camdean Vixen.

Controlling my breathing I tried to wrap my head around it, finding it much easier than I would have expected, though that was far from saying it was easy. Nyx's words came back to me, nothing less than truth having come from her lips. A catalyst, marking the start of change whether directly or indirectly. Vixen. She had truly known me through all those years, all those lifetimes. Looking up at Nemesis, she offered me a knowing smile.

"It's always easier when you know the beginning. Makes everything in between seem a little bit less insane doesn't it?"

She smirked when I frowned at her. "Hardly."

"Our time is limited, ask what you will Lykos."

"You created me for Nyx?"

"No, she chose you all on her own. I created you so that Nyx would not have to be my champion. I had no intention for the two of you to ever meet. My dear Medusa however, thought it would be grand to choose that moment to meddle in my plans. You and Nyx were inseparable from the time you met."

"She feels familiar, in my dreams we are always close, but I can't make heads or tails of it."

"It will sort itself out with time. Just trust your instincts and your heart."

Nodding I tried to skim over everything in my head to pinpoint what I needed to ask while I still had the time. Something about the events of my life seemed a bit off at points. Nyx had said her mother loved to meddle, I wondered just how much she had meddled in my current life. There were far more pressing matters though, so I settled for something useful.

"Why does Artemis remain silent?"

"She has the same struggles as us all. The Amazons are her people, but they are not of her blood anymore. She loves them dearly and watches over them, but she cannot speak to them as she used to."

"Nyx said that your magical bond to me is stronger than the blood she shares with you. So why then do the Gods not simply create something magical as you did?"

"Magic is not simple and we didn't know ahead of time that humans would discard us so easily. The Fates could not foresee the future clearly without their spinning wheel and threads. They only get glimpses, too vague to be of use. That is why they must live among the people in order to keep balance now. We had no warning we would lose our connection to our people, so even those who do possess the ability, didn't think to create something to tether them to your world. It was assumed we would always hold sway and be able to do what we always had."

"Sounds like you were too cocky."

"Oh yes. Pride has been our most harmful attribute I'm afraid. Make sure that it does not become yours."

"It is hard to fathom that all I have seen in my dreams and all that trickles into my consciousness could be real and true. Even your presence with me now is hard to swallow. How do I trust what I feel to be real?"

"Sometimes things do not fall into the box of what people think is possible, but that does not make them any less so. You are living, breathing, proof of that. Do not restrict your mind to the ideals of people who could watch you change and still deny it ever happened in their next breath. Do not dwell in a box that is too small for all that you are."

Her words struck me to the core. The whole reason my mother had moved us out of the main village was so that I would not have to be caged by what they considered 'normal'. She had wanted me to run wild and free and be everything that I was. Perhaps that was not so different from this. I was the villagers in my own mind, building a cage with expectations that were only realistic for someone else. Why should I live by the example of someone completely different than myself in every way possible? I smiled softly, knowing she was right, even if it might take me a while to wholly accept it.

As we once again flowed through the stream of magic, or what I guessed to be magic, I turned my head to face Nemesis, the lithe woman easily twirling to do the same. Aware that our time may be ending soon, it occurred to me to address the actual reason we had been sent. She became focused on me, as if she sensed the change of subject coming.

"The Amazons need your help."

"Ah yes, I suppose the pleasantries of memory lane must give way to more urgent matters. This Mad King problem. I'm afraid he is the reason for your reincarnation. Well, not him directly. Tereus has escaped his prison and has been manipulating the Kings for the past decade. Tereus, as you may soon remember, is a disgusting brute whose cruelty is matched only by his pride. He thinks himself worthy of Godhood and has recently come across what he believes is a means to get it."

She paused here while I rubbed my temples, a headache surely imminent from the rush of so much information trying to be processed at once. At least this information would lead to something more tangible.

"So if you are all still watching, why didn't the gods just put him back into whatever prison he escaped from?"

She grimaced as she uttered her words with a frustrated sigh.

"By then we could not interfere directly. The prayers were what allowed us to manifest or speak with the mortal realm. We now exist on a separate plane, unable to truly cross over. Tereus has only recently acquired a mortal form and his father only uses his connection to him to pass warnings. Most of the Gods no longer have blood to bind them to the mortal realm, even for my mother and I, Nyx barely tethers us enough to be able to speak. The few who do have a connection do not want to anger Aries. He is protective of his son."

"So we are on our own dealing with this mess."

"If you seek me out, I will find you and aid in any way I can. Though my reach is limited, I have always looked over you, and so in turn my daughter as well."

The implied meaning was not lost on me, the familiarity and comfort of Nyx's presence not so much a mystery now as it was before. It was a slow step in accepting that the dreams had once been reality. I could see in the distance the building and Nyx's form sitting guard. There was one last thing I wanted to know before I returned.

"My mother she-" The question soured on my tongue. The ramblings, the certainty in my mother's eyes, surely it must have been true. Did I not speak with Nemesis just as clearly as any other person? I looked to Nemesis for reassurance, hoping the things the village had whispered were as untrue as I believed. She gave me a gentle smile, her hand reaching out to rest upon my shoulder, a light squeeze given.

"Oh, your mother was not crazy, child. She was one hell of a woman and would have lost her life in one of the Amazon's skirmishes had I not bid her to live and serve another purpose instead. She accepted happily and often prayed to thank me for the greatest gift she had ever received. You are your mother's pride and joy. She is at peace in the Elysian Fields with her sisters."

Had I been in a mortal form my tears would have blinded my eyes as my heart swelled. A sorrow I had not quite buried or dealt with rose and bubbled out of my chest as a sob. Nemesis said nothing more on the subject, merely smiled as she pulled me in for a sidelong hug.

"You must go now. Tereus is no fool, he will not believe you are dead. He knows you will have found Nyx by now and will do what he can to draw you out into the open. You must be ready for him when he does. He must be stopped, Lykos. If he achieves Godhood, there will be no end to the cruelty and death. He will burn this continent to the ground. Be careful Lykos and know you are not alone. " She paused before adding. " Please, give my love to my daughter."

The darkness ebbed like ocean waves, then like a jolt of lightning splitting the earth and turning sand to glass, a blinding light filled the void as my soul was jerked back into my body. Tears flowed from my eyes, my heart full and broken all at once as my mortal body tried to keep up with the sudden rush of emotions I could now properly feel. Sobs racked my body, chest restricting so hard that I had to gasp for air. Nyx's arms were suddenly around me, her voice soft and calm, whispering that everything was okay as I rocked back and forth in her embrace.

Overwhelmed and overstimulated I didn't even bother to fight her grip, instead I turned toward her and let the comfort of her presence and the steady beat of her heart lull me back to something resembling calm. Soft shushing came from her lips as she held my head lightly, body surely getting stiff kneeling the way she was. When I finally caught my breath she released me, letting me get back to my feet. Shaking myself much in the manner the Camdean Vixen had, I found myself somehow feeling more myself than I ever had.

"Are you okay?"

"Yes, your mother just spoke of mine and well, honestly, I fell apart ."

Nyx smirked, gesturing towards my disheveled state. "Well at least I managed to glue you back together."

I couldn't help but crack a smile despite the craziness that surely lay ahead of me.

"Come, let us warm up and digest things a bit before we head back." She offered me a hand to help rise.

Giving a nod in agreement, I followed Nyx out into the gathering area and then to a sheltered alcove where a fire circle had been built into the ground. Thanks to the warm stone beneath us, the fallen limbs here were relatively dry and the gargoyle was able to get a small fire going to add to the heat that sifted through my butt, which I had promptly plopped down upon the earth.

What felt like hours with Nemesis had been no more than half of one. The sun had barely moved in the sky, the glittering snow on the outskirts of the temple's sandstone making me shiver with anticipation. There was so much to take in and even more to swallow as truth. An impending sense of trouble resting just beyond the horizon set my nerves on edge. The name Tereus did not ring a bell, though I was beginning to get used to being out of the common knowledge loop.

The dreams had continued, but more often the information was slipping into my mind unnoticed until I spoke on it, but I was still lacking compared to those around me. Bitterness rose on my tongue but I swallowed it back down, refusing to be cold towards those who had accepted what I was without hesitation. I could dislike their means, acknowledge that their intentions were selfish, but I would not discount their openness and the freedom I still had.

Nyx waved a hand in front of my face as she sat beside me next to the fire. Focusing back on the present I filled her in on everything I had seen and heard. She smiled gently, eyes set on something in the distance.

"Well, that's something at least." She said nothing more, staring into the fire while I stared at her. There were subtle differences between her and her mother, but there was no denying they shared blood.

Nyx's hair had more of a blue tinge to it, the inky blackness appearing to have no body until the light hit it just right. A gray tinge gave her pale flesh a unique tone, the cut of her muscles adding to the illusion that she had been sculpted from stone. There was a sharpness to her body that didn't reach those violet eyes. A softness lived within them and I found it truly amazing she had never lost that, even through all the nightmares she had seen. She stirred as I watched, her jaw clenching as she snapped her fingers together.

"That's it! Tereus is the one mama sent her Snakes after!"

"Her what?"

"Oh, so Medusa has been known to grant a select few women the ability to shapeshift. There aren't many people who know about them, they like to stay hidden."

Well that was certainly interesting information.

"So why did she send these 'Snakes' after him?" I cocked my head curiously.

"Tereus seduced his wife's sister, then cut out her tongue so she wouldn't tell his wife what had happened. He then tried to kill them both with an axe. The gods took pity and turned them all into birds, but Tereus is a son of Ares. His father released him and he took to abusing women out of spite for his exile. Neither of my moms liked that, but before her Snakes could do the job, he disappeared, said to have been entombed in an artifact by his father to save his life. Mama says they must have been close for Ares to interfere, but that was hundreds of years ago."

"Here I was thinking I was special and apparently there are snake shapeshifters hiding out in the world and Gods turning people into birds too, huh?"

Nyx smiled, a hand reaching out to squeeze my knee.

"You will always be special Lykos."

A blush ran hot across my cheeks even after the hand was quickly withdrawn as Nyx reconsidered her familiarity. Although I could not decipher what about my feelings was runoff from the dreams and what was from the present, they were one in the same. There was an intensity to it that I was certain came from the past, but the blush and warmth I felt in her presence, the way her voice sounded like music, and the way lightning danced across my body when she touched me was certainly all in the present.

"So what do we do now?" I tried to divert her attention, those sharp eyes always taking measure of me.

"We let the Queen know and let her council figure out their next move. "She shrugged her shoulders and poked at the small fire with a stick.

That sounded far too simple.

"Really?"

She laughed gently, her focus turning back to me.

"Yes Lykos. Despite how history is often written, there is no quick solution. Patience is sometimes your greatest ally. He will make a move and when he does, hopefully we will be ready to meet it."

Her cool ease was impressive, though I supposed if I could remember all the lives I'd lived and the wars I had apparently been a part of, I might have a cool head upon my shoulders too. Even as we sat there my fingers tapped upon my leg as I let all the information run loops in my head.

"Patience is still a work in progress I see." She laughed more heartily now, shaking her head as she rose to her feet. "Oh how some things simply do not change."

When we had warmed up we used the snow to put out the fire and trekked back to the Amazon village. A comfortable silence fell between us, even though my mind burned with questions. I just couldn't bring myself to ask them just yet.

When we returned to the council, it was just as simple as Nyx had said; we gave our report and then it was left for the Queen and council to decide what to do. For now that was nothing, or at least nothing they would share.

CHAPTER SEVEN
GARGOYLES KNOW BEST

The rhythm of life became more natural after that. The struggle of accepting my dreams as past reality became a bit easier, though no less disturbing. Thankfully winter brought about just as much work as any other season when it came to the horses, so I quite frequently escaped the world around me with them. Prince was especially sympathetic to my struggles and often read my emotions well enough to know when I needed a joy ride. He also called me out on my bullshit, which was less amusing but very much necessary.

You're a right selfish child, you realize?

Prince's words in my head were like a warm hug by your best friend after not having seen them for a while. Despite that there was no shortage of snark when it came to anything he had to say, making him what I'd imagine was quite close to having an older brother. His words were emphasized with a pinning of his ears, his lips pulled back from his teeth as he reached forward and pulled at the fabric of my coat. Reflexively my hand snaked out to lightly pop his nose, making him arch his neck in surprise, a shower of snow flying at me as he pawed the ground, flicking the mucky mixture.

"Ugh GROSS Prince!"

He snorted at me, prancing out of reach as I made a grab for his mane. He trotted with high steps that were not natural for his breed, clearly boasting.

"Fine, fine! Yes, I've realized I'm being a horse's ass, now will you stop being one? I'm trying to figure it all out."

Awe it's so cute when you pout.

A few weeks had passed since I'd visited the altar to Nemesis and I had done my absolute best to avoid being alone with Nyx. I simply couldn't settle on whether or not my feelings were genuine. If they were, that made all the things in my dream possible - for better or for worse. If they weren't, then I'd be misleading a woman who was wholeheartedly into me.

I didn't trust myself not to act without thinking, so I did what I did best; I avoided the problem as often as possible.

For whatever reason, Nyx didn't let it break her stride. It caused me guilt as well as a wicked sense of satisfaction to see that it hurt her, but didn't stop her from trying to bridge that gap between us. I wanted her attention and affection and I wanted to matter to her as much as she did to me, I just couldn't bring myself to show her just yet. Not until I was sure.

I turned away from Prince and leaned up against the fence, the rest of his herd stood around the hay pile watching us with interest, waiting for the inevitable. They were all horses at the core, no matter how much magic ran through their blood, so curiosity often got the best of them -Prince especially. Watching him through a space between my arm and side, I waited for my opportunity. His nose flared tentatively, concern in his deep brown eyes and the way he carefully lipped at the air trying to scent my intentions, worried he'd truly hurt my feelings. As soon as I felt the velvet of his nose brush against my back, I went for it.

Turning on the spot I darted along his neck to his shoulder, left hand reaching up to grab his white mane as I pushed off the ground and swung myself around to his back. He was already in motion. Neck arching, his front feet left the ground just as my legs wrapped around his middle, a squeal of surprise and delight following. His tail flagged as he kicked out his back legs, a fart ripping through the air as he bucked me a few strides before taking off. I kept my hands wrapped in his mane to keep me steady.

"That a boy, Prince!"

A wild yell fell from my lips as the rest of the herd suddenly broke from their gathering, kicks and rears marking their excitement. My heart filled and leapt alongside them. Only one thing in the world compared to this. The small herd ran alongside us, one or two reaching out to playfully nip Prince and I as we went from one side of the pasture to the other and back. Leaning forward I watched Prince's red ears swivel back, anticipating a question.

"Will you still run with me when I shift?"

His laughter rang in my head, full of joy.

How else will we find out if you can actually keep up?

There was a swelling inside my core, warmth creeping out to warm my skin even against the frigid cold of our galloping pace. Surely if a creature whose very nature would scream for him to stay far away could welcome my company, nothing was impossible. The Amazons who knew had accepted me and Nyx had spent lifetimes at my side. Perhaps the world was not as cruel and the future not as hopeless as I had convinced myself. Surely I could exist in both forms safely. Why was I so terrified of my memories from the past being true?

The answer was in the blood dripping from every lifetime, covering the ground, my hands, and just as frequently Nyx. Fear would drown out all the good experienced in those glimpses if I didn't start at least *trying* to swim with the current. Avoiding the things which scared me at my core would not save anyone from hurt, it would only limit my experiences upon this world.

Losing myself to the sound of horse hooves pounding out scattered rhythms across the still frozen landscape, I didn't even notice Onya waiting for me at the gate until Prince suddenly veered that way. The sudden shift of his body sent me off balance, my eyes having been closed as I felt the muscles beneath me in all their power. As I gripped his neck and went to curse him, I finally saw her waving at me. Still astride sideways, he came to an abrupt stop, lowering his head almost to the ground so that the momentum threw me over his head right into a pile of snow.

"That was fucking cold, Prince!" I burst forth from the snowbank I had been thrown into and tried to grab his head, but he had already pivoted and taken off. His laughter echoed in my head alongside the whinny he let out. He rejoined the rest of the herd who all nickered their own amusement. They were so frisky and riled up that they took off again.

Onya giggled as she opened the gate for me, brushing some of the powder from my coat as I shook my body to get it out of the crevices it had burrowed into. The snow had been inconsistent but it was sticking and piling up.

"Well, I hope whatever you wanted was important enough to warrant a blow to my dignity." I glared, though there was no heat behind my look.

She grinned, her hand pressed against her lips to stifle her giggles as we walked back toward the barn, which was much warmer thanks to a metal stove that was used to keep the older horses warm and less achy.

"The council has agreed to go forward with our last trade with the Centaurs before winter makes it easier for our borders to be breached. When the river freezes further South, our patrols have to double, which means we will be short-handed in the village. So, it's now or wait until Spring. We head out shortly, so I wanted to make sure I got to say bye and ask if you'd help the girls stay on top of the herds. We are taking the yearling bachelor stallions, so the group is mostly horse hands and Xalia."

"How long will you be gone?" I couldn't help the tinge of disappointment. Onya had become my best friend, followed closely by Serah. There hadn't been a day I had spent without Onya since I'd been sent on my trial task. Spending time amongst the horses would help, but it would be weird without her there every morning.

"Shouldn't be longer than a week if the horses behave themselves. You know how yearling stallions can be. Even with geldings as mounts, they are bound to get full of themselves."

Surprising us both, I reached out and pulled her into a hug, the warmth between us platonic but precious. There had been few people who had stuck around after finding out what I was, and even fewer who I wanted to stick around. She hugged me back then laughed.

"Don't worry, I'll be back soon enough to help you avoid being alone with Nyx and how much you actually like her. Or, and stay with me here because it's just a thought, you could just enjoy being alone with her? I swear it's exhausting watching you run from how you feel some days."

Playfully I pushed her away, the long braids of deep mahogany shaking as she laughed.

"I'll take care of the horses, just make sure you get back safely. Otherwise I might have to replace you with Camilla!"

She scoffed. "You wouldn't dare!"

"Better not make us find out huh?" I shrugged my shoulders high for emphasis.

We laughed even as she shook her head and waved goodbye. She headed out towards the front field where the older horses had been switched out with the bachelor herd. Watching her walk away sent a sharp sense of dread through my gut, though I couldn't decide if it was for her safety or because I was being left behind and would have to deal with my issues alone.

As it turned out, there was no need to worry about my issues being dealt with. Onya had not exaggerated; now with only half the normal staff, there was more than enough work to keep me busy throughout the day and sometimes even past dinner. Nyx had taken up Xalia's offer and was studying with the Scouts so we often passed each other but one of us was always too exhausted to linger long. I hated to admit it, but I found myself missing her in the quiet moments between tasks and began to regret the distance I'd tried to force between us.

Thankfully I was not left to my own devices as Serah often sought me out over the next few days. She made sure that I ate and visited with one of the pregnant mares she hoped would produce a speckled baby to match her. She wasn't shy about admitting she missed and was worried about Xalia. I simply reassured her that Onya had the horses well under hand and Xalia knew what she was doing.

I didn't start to share her worry until the sixth day had passed.

Barely any light broke through in the sky as I shuffled through the snow, a winterland of cold misery all around. The steady mountain breeze was chilling and rattled the trees noisily, but the echo of a whinny upon the air caught my ear. Shaking my head I simply huffed a few clouds of air before continuing my trudge through the snow. The horses had a habit of raising a fuss when feeding was too slow for their liking.

A second whinny echoed off the mountainside, this one sounding far more panicked. The hairs along my skin stood up as a sudden gut wrenching chill spread from my core to my fingertips. The sound was coming from the wrong direction. A series of shouts carried on the wind from the direction of the village entrance.

Something is wrong.

Pivoting in place I took off towards the noise, only for the source to come running right toward me. My heart seized for a moment, lodging itself in my throat before pulsing back into place. One of the yearling stallions, a beautiful cremello with a mane and tail whiter than seafoam, barreled toward the stables. His legs were stained brown from mud, his chest was splattered rust red from dried blood and his stride was marred with a limp.

I stood frozen in place until he was no more than a few feet from me. When he was close enough that the huts would prevent him from dodging, I stretched my arms out. His eyes were wild with fear but quickly zoned in on me, nostrils flaring heavily. The poor beast must have run non-stop and I feared for his lungs just as much as his wounded body.

He might have run right through me, but suddenly Nyx was at my side and her wings bursting from her back, their span enough to make the beast slam his back legs to the earth, practically sitting as he struggled to stop on the melting snow. The heaving beast might have tried to turn and run again but by then the shouts had drawn a crowd and a couple of women came forward to grab the halter still secured around his head, a broken length dangingly from the end.

"The rope was cut!" The woman who grabbed him announced.

The confirmation didn't make the earth any more solid beneath my feet. Onya had often said that in an event where aid was needed, the Amazons stripped the quickest or the least likely to be spotted of the horses and sent it home. A horse without a rider was all the sign the Amazons needed to know there was distress.

Nyx drew her wings back in, folding them against her back but not yet letting them slip beneath the skin, the clothing she'd worn now ripped to accommodate the appendages. She reached out a hand and gripped my arm, her eyes soft and concerned. The worry did not cease but the comfort of her presence eased the tingling in my hands and feet.

Gwenn was called for, the beast in poor shape to say the least, and alongside her came Serah whose face paled to match the beast's hair.

"Xalia was with them." She spoke the words and then paused, as if waiting for someone to deny it and tell her the woman she loved was perfectly fine.

"Onya too." My voice tightened as my stomach dropped.

My own fear would do nothing to ease Serah's, our eyes meeting in terror of what this might mean for our friends. Nyx's grip tightened for a second, steering me away from the gathering crowd even as Gwenn had someone do the same for Serah.

"Breathe Lykos. Whatever this means we will deal with it. That could just as well be the blood of an enemy, some communication method Xalia and the warriors know. "

Her words made sense but my body refused to let them calm me. The fox within was chomping on the bit now, my human form finally healthy enough to accommodate the change. She could surely sense it, for she pinched the bridge of her nose as if she wanted to sneeze, just as I did when encountering a strong dose of magic.

"Breathe through it, this isn't the time." Her words were a soft warning, cutting through the fog of fear blinding my vision. She was right, this was not the time or place to let my fox loose.

One deep breath, then two. She steered me towards the council hut alongside the rest of the group, half a dozen women had already run out to alert the Queen and council. There was hardly any time that passed before the crowd parted for the most important women of the village. Before she stepped through the door Queen Iris paused, addressing everyone.

"Do not stand out here to freeze. There is plenty of work yet to be done and your lingering will not hasten the discussion or decisions made within. An announcement will be made to everyone as soon as we convene. Go and do not make me repeat myself."

For emphasis, Freya paused alongside the Queen, her spear held in hand and the threat obvious; anyone who disobeyed would be going through drills for as long as their limbs were working. Having already been subjected to the exercises, I followed along with the rest and hastily dispersed. Nyx remained at my side, her face far off it seemed, the hard lines much like stone.

"Thank you." The words fell from my lips in a much softer whisper than I had intended.

"For what?" Her brow rose as she looked down at me, eyes a stark contrast against the hair that framed her face.

"You always seem to be there right when I need something to ground me... Your timing is impeccable."

She shook her head in denial. "Hardly, but any time I can help I am glad. Just try to breathe through it. Time will pass more slowly if you don't stay busy."

"Nyx, I have a horrible feeling about this." She met my gaze but said nothing for a while.

"As do I, but we must wait for the Queen. There are Scouts on patrol, I'm sure there will be quick action. I'll send for you when there is news." She finally whispered, her hand reaching out to hold mine as she noticed their nervous shaking.

The wait was far longer than I would have anticipated. I found myself finished with the morning chores, pacing the barn with nervous energy, relying on Nyx's promise to come get me if there was any news. There might have been a worn path in the stone had Prince's nicker not broken my stride. Another urgent nicker and I ran out to meet him as he cantered down the fence line with his head high, tail flagging behind him as he snorted nervously, the sound much like a loud purr.

Lykos!

His voice was filled with worry, his muzzle pressing to my chest as soon as he stopped in front of me, his head reaching over the top of the fence. The other horses had not followed him, which made me worry all the more.

"Prince. What have you heard?"

Nothing more than you know, the poor brute was so scared he remembers very little, just that someone cut his line, turned him toward home and smacked him hard enough to leave a welt. This isn't good."

"No it's not." There was nothing more I could say, the truth was that there were any number of possibilities as to why they might send a horse back for help, but my gut said it was the worst case scenario.

Your gargoyle is looking for you, that's why I came. They brought the stallion to us to try and calm him enough for Gwenn to treat his wounds. The healer rather coyly asked me to fetch you. Guess everyone knows I'm your favorite.

Any other time his statement might have caused me to smile, but there was only one reason Nyx would send for me. She had news.

"Did Gwenn say where?"

She told me to get you to Rhea's.

"Does she know you can talk to me?"

Perhaps. She spoke as if to the wind, so I'd guess she has spoken to Rhea.

"I'd suspect the healers are far more open minded than most. Stay close, if they ride out, we will not be left behind."

He reared in response, his forelegs pawing the air as if ready for a battle. Smirking despite the sense of dread in my gut, I took off to Rhea's hut.

"We received word of the Mad King's movement a few days ago. He is sending groups of his brutes to the villages outlying the Amazon and Centaur borders. Those are more closely allied to us than to their King and are poorly defended. There was hope that our women would be back before they got there, but as you can guess, we no longer believe that is the case."

Rhea sighed deeply, resigned.

"The council knows who and what you are. I would trust your judgment on when to reveal your nature to the tribe, but I could not risk an incident with those in your company. With that consideration those in the rescue party are now aware and accepting. You and Nyx will be welcomed additions. "

I had spent the last few months living free due to their generosity. There was no question in her statement, nor was there much choice. I could hardly begrudge the lack of choice when I had no intentions of staying behind anyway; if only for Onya's sake. That others knew my nature bothered me less than I might have imagined it would. The Amazons had proven completely accepting of Nyx, so why should I feel alarmed? Afterall, a big fluffy fox was hardly more intimidating than a woman who came to life from stone and had bat wings right?

The only worry I held now was for those who were in danger.

"Presumptuous to think I'm willing." Nyx commented with a smirk.

"Foolish to think she isn't. I know you Nyx, where she goes you will follow, it's why I argued for you to join them."

Rhea retorted, her brow raising in challenge as she nodded towards me.

"When do we leave?" I avoided Nyx's gaze, not at all interested in her opinion at the moment, which earned me a genuine smile from Rhea. She gave Nyx a grin, having obviously won that round of banter, though I couldn't say why I was so certain that was all it had been.

"Be ready at Dawn. Prince is already being prepped for you and we've got a mare set aside for you as well Nyx."

"I don't need a horse, I can fly."

I placed a hand on my forehead and sighed, words tumbling from my lips with information I shouldn't have known. "You're afraid of heights Nyx, don't be a stubborn fool, take the damn horse."

As I looked up into her eyes I immediately shrunk down in my seat, realization filling me with a sense of wonder and dread. Her violet eyes were wide with surprise but her lips had parted into the biggest grin I'd ever seen. Rhea kept quiet but I could feel amusement radiating from her, she had a glimmer in her eye.

How the fuck did I know that? Panic threatened to overwhelm me as my own mind felt like a mystery I couldn't solve, knowledge I shouldn't have had settling into my subconscious when I wasn't paying attention. The dreams and flickers of memory were more tangible, something that could be grasped on some level, but these slivers that crept in unnoticed scared me more than anything else. When had the trust between my subconscious and conscious self been so horribly broken apart?

"I'm sorry, I've got to go."

I couldn't handle the hopeful light that flickered in Nyx's eyes. Anger rose alongside my embarrassment, so before she could say anything - or perhaps before my own rude comment slipped up in venomous defense of something as stupid as pride - I pushed myself from the table. Pausing only long enough to give a respectful nod to the old Seer, I darted to the entrance, taking off at a run once I'd cleared the doorway. I made it to the edge of the training area before my lungs burned from the frigid air and forced me to pause.

Overwhelmed with worry, confusion, anger and an infuriating affection I wasn't sure was true or remembered, the chaos in my head pounded against my temples threatening to burst free. Muscles in my body tensed as the fox paced just under the surface, just waiting to be released for the first time in what felt like ages. Without the whole village aware, now was certainly not the time or place for that, so I did the only thing I could do to keep myself from screaming; I turned to the nearest solid object and took a swing.

The solid wood of a post groaned beneath my fist, the skin across my knuckles tearing upon the second impact. On the third strike the wood splintered and the follow up sent the top of the cross tie post to the earth. Pain pulsed down my forearm, blood trickling along the back of my hand and dripping from my wrist, a large splinter having slid right through the soft skin on top. The rapid pulse of my blood coursing through my body throbbed in my ears, tears of frustration were barely held back as I breathed deeply. No one nearby dared approach or reprimand my tantrum, at least none of the Amazons.

A shadow fell across the earth as the soft crunch of snow announced someone's approach. The folded wings gave her away, the pointed tips obvious in the shadow's form.

"You really should watch that temper of yours."

Nyx's words were barely a whisper but they were so close I could practically feel them. Too frustrated to care that she had done nothing to deserve it, I turned to swing at her but was surprised when her hand shot up to grab it. Fresh pain shot through my hand as her long nails curled into my skin, piercing the already broken flesh.

For an instant her eyes dilated, her nostrils flaring as the scent of blood wafted up from my torn hand, a hunger I couldn't comprehend flickering across her face and just as quickly disappearing. Her face softened into an expression of concern as I jerked my hand back, still bitter at everything broiling up inside myself. The residual effects of months of torture and isolation were rearing its ugly face.

"No one asked for your opinion." Childish, I knew, but so what?

My life had gone from crazy to insane and no matter how much I accepted the truth of what I saw and heard, there was still a small voice whispering that it wasn't possible. The sound was so small and so weak, yet it was enough for the seed of doubt to dig its roots in and poison the soil of my mind.

Just as soon as things started to feel normal something happened to remind me nothing about my life was normal.

The Mad King and his puppeteer weren't too far away to hurt me again. Everything could be taken away.

"Oh don't you worry, I never need to be asked, I happily give my opinion out whenever the mood strikes me." She offered a toothy grin.

Although I wanted to smirk, to enjoy the humor and the smile on her lips, that whisper of doubt and fear tugged me back down into confusion. So instead, I shrouded my face in a scowl and scoffed.

"Whatever." Months of pushing down everything and something as simple as remembering had set me off. What was wrong with me?!

Walking toward the woods, hoping to clear my mind there, I found myself being followed.

"I don't want your company." The lie fell from my lips as easily as a breath.

The problem was I longed for her company. I just couldn't accept that it was truly my own desire, not some weird side effect of the pull between our magic. That very desire to be close to her and the memories of being ripped away tangled into a mesh of trauma that had my nerves shot.

"Maybe not, but we don't always get what we *want*. Sometimes we merely get what we need. It's been a very stressful morning."

Shouting at her would do no good so I tried to swallow my words. She was particularly stubborn, and despite myself, I was glad she followed. Although thinking about my feelings toward her overloaded my senses, her presence calmed my nerves and grounded me. The conflicting feelings made me want to hate her just as much as it made me like her. Thus, round and around I went.

The inconsistency of my own mind was exhausting. The chaos in my mind continued boiling up with every step she took towards me until there was no choice but to swallow it down or explode. I finally chose the latter.

"Do you have to be so fucking annoying?" I finally yelled, turning to face her as we entered a copse of trees far enough from the main part of the village not to be overheard. The leaves had long since died and returned to the earth, but the trees grew close enough together to offer some seclusion.

"No, but since you're going to have a tantrum I figured I might as well amuse myself while making sure you don't do something dangerous."

Something in the back of my head said she was baiting me, but that was the exact voice causing my conflict of emotions.

With skin itching as the beast within scratched at the surface, my legs carried me in a pacing motion, seething growls falling from my lips unbidden. She kept pushing, smart ass comments continuing though the exact words became lost to me. My vision began to blur, a growl vibrating heavily in my throat as I said something that must have been nasty but I couldn't pin it down in my memory.

Before I knew what was happening, my feet stumbled as my body was shoved backwards. Or had I tripped? It didn't matter, it was all that I needed. I snapped and lunged.

"Fine then, if you're going to lash out, do it! Better me than one of your Amazon sisters." She might have shouted but I barely grasped her words.

My lunge was clumsy and her fist collided with the side of my face, causing my body to pivot. Using the momentum to kick a leg up I made contact with her arm as she lifted it to block. Fortunately she was far more clear minded than I was, my vision doubling and shifting hue. She caught my leg with her other hand easily and pulled my balance from me. As I crashed to the ground I felt her weight upon my hips, the pressure sending me thrashing, viciously and desperately trying to buck her off.

She struggled to grab hold of me, taking several punches to the face and torso as I flailed before she secured my wrists to the ground. Bucking and kicking my legs up and out beneath her, my energy and rage began to sizzle out. Her violet eyes tried to catch my gaze as I turned my head back and forth while I struggled, her words lost to deaf ears. When she finally managed to catch my gaze there were unshed tears glistening in the purple depths.

As my anger ebbed, my mind cleared and the soreness in my throat subsided as a defiant scream ceased from my throat. The fading of my own voice allowed my ears to tune into the rise and fall of her own, the soft tone cradling me like a lullaby, silencing my protests and calming my body.

Nyx leaned forward, repeating my name like it was a prayer she had spoken every day of her life but with no less feeling than the first time she'd done it.

"Lykos, please my Vixen, come back to me. It's okay, you've just gotten overwhelmed. Everything will be okay, just breathe."

A deep breath caused me to choke as sobs burst from my chest. Immediately she released my wrists and pulled me to her. Instinctively I resisted and punched her chest, though admittedly it was with no more gusto than a weak slap. She pressed my face to her chest making soft shushing sounds, rocking me like I was the most fragile thing she'd ever held. Perhaps in that moment I was just that, my mind shattered into a million pieces as I tried to shuffle it back together and make a clear image of the reflection there.

"Stop fighting it Lykos. You can't do this alone, it's too much. You can't just bottle this up, if you do you will lose control and hurt yourself or someone else. Let me help."

Her words echoed my own thoughts but I didn't know how to stop bottling things up. How could I just accept this invasion? These memories that were my own and yet weren't? How could I accept that the one thing that had been pulling me my entire life was right here in front of me. It terrified me beyond reason and possibly for reasons I didn't remember yet. I wanted to run and never stop, but I clung to her shirt instead, letting her arms support my tired body.

This was the danger of magic and emotion. If you ignored either they would explode, if you ignored both you would implode. The threat that lay before me, the one that threatened my friends and newfound family, that was merely the tipping point.

I was so tired of fighting both myself and the world, but I wasn't sure how to stop or what would happen when I did.

My own purpose upon this earth was apparently someone else's. Would this latest version of myself fit into the mold of what Nemesis had created long ago? Was that even who I wanted to be? Sure the idea of sitting idle was no more appealing than a porcupine to the face, but what was the alternative? Seeking out and fulfilling a purpose I barely understood?

Who was I? What was I beyond a woman who could shapeshift into a kitsune? Was there anything more on this earth for me beyond what a Goddess had decreed? Nemesis herself had said I'd become so much more, but what was *more*.

"What- who was I Nyx?"

I hated the way my voice quivered, but she only looked at me with compassion as she smiled, surely she had done this all before.

"You have been and still are a great many amazing and beautiful things, Lykos. You are a creature made from stardust, a woman made by experience, and someone with far more strength than she knows." There was a pause as she considered me, perhaps reading skepticism in my face.

"You're a catalyst, yes, but you are so much more. Don't let yourself forget that. You are many things, but you are still you; a strong survivor with more compassion in her heart than anyone would believe, with love as depthless as the ocean, and a complete goofball when given the space to be comfortable. Once you accept that who you were only adds to who you are now, rather than diminishes it, the memories will settle, your magic will calm, and you will be able to navigate this insanity."

"You make it sound so easy."

"Nothing about this is easy, but you are far more capable of handling it than you think, and I am here for you. Whether you choose to lean upon me or not, I'm not going anywhere."

I sighed, both annoyed and relieved. I believed her. Perhaps not about everything, but that she would be there I had no doubt. It was written in every inch of her expression and actions. I didn't know for sure what we had been in my previous lives, though obviously lovers in more than one, nor did I know if we would be as close in this one, but her presence in it was undeniable.

I had avoided asking if we had always been together, afraid of the answer. Was there more? Did I want to know if there was?

"Feeling better now that you've gotten to lash out a bit?"

Nyx spoke softly, her hand gently brushing a few strands of hair from my face as I resisted the urge to lean into the caress. She made it so hard to resist her.

"Yes." I replied with a wince, hating to admit to myself that my tantrum could have easily gone very badly had she not stepped in to control it.

The emotional frustration would not have been bad on its own, but It was dangerous to suppress a magic such as mine in normal circumstances, let alone stressful ones. There had been no choice; keeping that part of me hidden or ending up at the mercy of a merciless King. Now that I was free and healthy, I'd need to find a safe time to change and soon.

"Alright then, you need to pack and then get some rest...I have a feeling this trip isn't going to be nearly as smooth as they hope. This is likely a ploy to draw you out."

Her tone was a simple one, but it made me worry about what the next few days would bring. The king's men knew better than to strike on Amazon lands, but what would happen when we crossed over? What had already happened to our sisters? The Amazon nation would not be ready for that kind of bloodshed, nor would they forgive it. With the disappearance of the Gods long ago, there were few things keeping the balance these days, but something told me they were about to tip over.

Perhaps that was what was meant to happen. Hadn't Nemesis and Nyx said as much? There had to be a catalyst, something to set the scales back enough to allow them to reset. Could I even step up to the challenge beyond survival? That had been all I'd managed when captured, would I prove stronger without the cage? There were too many unknown variables, too much uncertainty every way I turned.

The next morning everyone gathered by the stables, a nervous energy buzzing in the air like bees around a honeycomb. The group was a small one; enough to assist but not so large as to draw unwelcome attention. Serah was amongst them, her worry showing only in the way her hands gripped her mare's reins a bit more tensely than was necessary. Camilla was also along, her usefulness with a bow was questionable but there was no doubt she knew how to handle the sword at her hip. The rest of the women I was not overly familiar with, but knew from their usual proximity to Xalia.

Prince was waiting patiently, already saddled though I had instructed no need for a bridle. He whickered as I arrived, the excitement surrounding him practically tangible. At his side was one of his favorite mares, a gorgeous buckskin with a broad white stripe down her forehead that trailed off sideways to frame her left nostril. She was a particularly animated beast, whom I had been told had a desert bred mother; which explained both her spunk and her considerably smaller build. The combination made her one of the quickest, which was why they had picked her out.

I see you finally found some common ground.

With Prince I felt no need to swallow my pride when I admitted he soothed my soul. His presence in my mind was warm like summer sunshine; a soft whisper of touch like the tickle of grass. Horses had been a comfort long before I had lost my mind and witnessed past lives play out in my dreams.

His words were of course referring to Nyx who had fallen into step beside me. He had undoubtedly heard gossip of my outburst the day before. The younger Amazons absolutely loved to talk, which was great when you wanted news to travel fast, but awful when you didn't. There was no reason to fault them for their intrigue, though I'd be sure to scold the next ones I caught doing it.

Glancing sidelong at Nyx I felt a warmth rise within. I hated to admit how natural it felt to want to step just a bit closer so that our arms would brush. Resisting the urge, my arms curled up and around Prince's neck, his chin pressing against my back to mirror a hug.

"I suppose you could say that."

My words were whispered but I saw Nyx's brow quirk and she seemed to take stock of her own mount. She offered her hand to the mare whose nostrils flared tentatively, ears flickering forward in interest as her lips searched the gargoyle's open palm for a treat.

"You always have had a way with animals, but I can smell a difference. I don't suppose this is a normal mare they have given me is it?"

Winking, I dared her to find out the hard way, swinging up into my saddle without comment. Despite the impending situation, laughter rose in my chest, barely escaping my lips in a soft snicker as I watched her lean forward and explain herself to the mare. Admittedly the mare seemed to appreciate the consideration as she bobbed her head up and down in agreement before Nyx lightly pulled herself into the saddle. We were the last to arrive, so once we had settled ourselves in our saddles we quickly fell into step behind the rest of the Amazons.

"Alright, let's go make sure our sisters get home safe. We will angle north once we cross the river and check the

Ftocho's village. If they had troubles they may have taken shelter there. If they are not there we will head west and cut through the Skoteino' Forest and cross the river to A'logo to speak with the Centaurs. Enjoy the easy pace, once we hit soft earth we leave our dust in the wind."

Camilla's role as a leader seemed strange after having seen her rambunctious flirting persona. Thankfully she took her duties seriously, her face much more controlled as she led the group forward at a steady walk, the icy paths too risky to take fast until our elevation dropped. The rest of the women followed in line, except Serah who waited a moment to ride alongside Prince and me.

"I'm glad you and Nyx are coming along. There is nothing about this that feels like it's going to be okay." Her voice shook slightly as she spoke, far more worry on her face than she had let show before.

"Of course I came. Even if I wasn't an Amazon, I would not leave Xalia and Onya to the mercy of the King's men. They are both strong capable women, there is hope we will merely be walking them home."

She wanted to believe me, the look in her eyes said it as much as the hand which reached out to grasp the one I stretched to toward her. Squeezing gently I tried to convey confidence, though we both knew it was a lie. The splash of blood on the cremello horse was undoubtedly just as fresh in her mind as my own.

"Whatever comes, we will face it together."

Serah offered me a sad smile before she moved ahead to join the others, Nyx and myself bringing up the rear. Knowing that Xalia was more than just a friend to Serah, I pushed my own dilemmas down and forced myself to focus. If she could walk with her head high, I could swallow my insecurities and do the same.

Perfectly content to have distance from the rest, Prince happily obliged when I signaled for him to stay back. I wasn't sure it was as much a favor for me as it was to keep his mare away from the geldings in the group. Magical or not, he was still every bit a horse.

Nyx drifted off into her own world as we traveled, her eyes taking in everything around her as if she was seeing it for the first time. As I glanced back, my heart warmed and marveled at the awe that settled on her features when a flock of birds flew overhead. I wasn't sure their name, but they were native to this side of the continent. Their bright underbellies were painted in shades of iridescent blues and purples, a stark contrast to the overcast of gray clouds blotting out the sun. When she caught me looking she offered me a shy but toothy grin that triggered a sudden flash of memory.

The rolling hills expanded out all around me, lush grass of deep emerald splotched with patches of clovers and long stretches of wildflowers reaching up past my ankles. There was a valley in the distance, the river that cut down the middle a glittering strip of blinding light as the sun's rays shone down unhindered. A rustle to my side drew my attention and a warm breath tickled the side of my face before the soft press of lips registered against my cheek. A familiar voice whispered 'Make a wish' as delicate fingers held up a dandelion. Bright violet eyes shone as an innocent and shy smile caused my heart to seize in my chest. When our fingers grazed, as I grabbed the dandelion, I felt a flame shoot through my body as her melodic voice carried in laughter. I closed my eyes and made a silent wish - a prayer. Hand in hand she lifted me to my feet and we took off through the fields.

The memory enveloped me, just as fresh and detailed as if it had been yesterday, causing a smile to pull my lips. From that simple glimpse of the past settled a stream of knowledge that felt far less foreign than the other images that had tracked me down in my sleep. It was from before Nyx had become a gargoyle, her teeth not nearly as sharp, her eyes more innocent and less critical; lifetimes ago in quite a literal sense. Feeling my shift, Prince paused with concern and Nyx guided her mare up beside him, her hand tentatively reaching out to brush my arm. Her voice was every bit as melodic as the younger voice that had resonated in my mind.

"Lykos, are you okay?"

I offered her a nervous smile, afraid she might see the thoughts crashing around my brain even as I kept the words I wanted to say from spilling off my lips. I nodded instead, and although she looked skeptical she pulled her hand back with a slight smile and let her horse carry her past me. With a heavy sigh Prince went after her, unhappy to be too far behind.

There was still a lingering doubt that what was felt in my memories could truly transcend lives and reincarnation, but that such things could be felt so innocently before gave me hope. Even if what I felt now was just residual, it meant that once upon a time my heart and soul had been capable of it all. If that were true, perhaps my life didn't have to feel so hopeless and lonely. Maybe, just maybe, I could find solace in another without always feeling that pull in a different direction.

I could do this. The doubt could linger, but I had to make a choice and cowardice did not suit me.

Chapter Eight
Not Quite Right

"Something is wrong." The words fell from my lips and were met with nods.

There was an ominous feeling in the air as we crossed the river into the King's territory. The shift set everyone on edge. With bows at the ready we carried on in silence, every break of a twig sending our eyes scanning the area. Despite the steady uneasiness, nothing hindered our arrival to the first grouping of homes that were part of the widespread village of farmers.

A gasp rippled through our small group as we rounded the edge of the forest that acted as a natural defensive measure against erosion for the farmed fields. The wind suddenly shifted and brought the scent of burnt wood and decaying flesh to my sensitive nose as Prince trotted forward to investigate. What had been an unsettled feeling in my gut suddenly twisted and almost made me want to lose my breakfast.

Beside me, a blank expression fell over Nyx like a shadow across the earth. Her eye color shifted from a bright violet to a deep magenta as her own nostrils flared. The horses shied at the smell but gave no other signs of distress as we moved forward to investigate. They walked on, trusting us to keep them safe. Prince pawed the earth, his voice a whisper in my head.

Let the earth heal quickly and the souls of the dead rest easy.

An eerie silence filled the clearing where once a total of eight homes had stood proudly against the green backdrop of the farms. The frames were now barely recognizable as such, the scent of accelerant making the smoke tangy, causing several of the women to cough.

"Whomever did this wanted to assure a speedy disintegration, there is a chemical in the smoke."

Camilla acknowledged my words with a nod, her voice failing her as she stood looking at the ruined buildings and the carnage left behind.

Sliding off Prince, I began to cautiously walk amongst the rubble. The scattered remnants were of no notable worth, except in the eyes of those who had lived here. The taint of death and decay was, oddly, not amongst the burnt and collapsed homes. Tasting the air for a direction to follow I made my way past two buildings that had not fallen in just yet, spotting a large barn down a hill that stood completely intact.

"The barn." Those were the only words I could utter as dread filled my body more and more as I descended down the slope.

The doors were sitting ajar and even the bright red of the chipping paint could do nothing to hide the splash of crimson that clung to the surface. Two bodies were slumped on the ground, the first's stomach had been ripped open and his entrails lay upon the earth spilling out of hands that had attempted to hold them inside. My skin went numb, a familiarity I didn't like creeping into my consciousness, making me want to itch.

Approaching the second body, any hope that there may be life in the man disappeared instantly. At a distance it had been easy to imagine it was his head which held the door aloft, but the brutality that lay at my feet proved otherwise. From the rough pattern of flesh and bone jutting out from his shoulders, whomever had detached the man's head had not used anything close to what I'd call sharp.

Gasps behind me alerted me to the other's presence, but there was no point looking back, their expressions would no doubt be flashes of horror, fear, and anger. There were eight homes and only two bodies. Fear of what would be found coiled within even as I accepted that there was no other choice but to look and know for sure. Taking a deep breath and carefully wedging open the door, I slipped past the bodies and into the barn.

A trail of blood from the head of the second man marked the path of whoever had carried and then haphazardly tossed it aside. Blood was not an unpleasant scent to a predator, but the fear preceding death held a gut-wrenching taint. The stench of it billowed forth like a tidal wave as I edged around a stack of hay bales, the massacre beyond stopping me in my tracks. Frozen in place I covered my mouth and nose to try and quell both the smell and the urge to puke up what meager offerings I had to the earth beneath my feet.

"Goddess give me strength."

There were three stalls on the right hand side, the horses were absent but the stalls were not empty. As my legs once again cooperated, I tried hard not to get lost in the details as I walked past, but it was horribly hard to look away. A young man perhaps a few years younger than I lay tied up, certainly beaten to death. His face had swollen so that his features were unrecognizable, the flesh a deep sickly purple. What shaggy hair hadn't been ripped from his skull was plastered to his forehead with blood and sweat. His clothes had been shredded from the strikes of a whip, and from the way his pants had been pulled down to his ankles, I suspected that was not the end or beginning of his torture. Cringing from the image, paired with the haunting scent, and ignoring the tears that were welling up in my eyes, I carefully moved forward.

The next stall broke something within me. Two lifeless women occupied the second stall, their bodies thrown over and tied to saddles. Blood streaked their inner thighs, bruises and lacerations marring their naked bodies. Death came in the form of slashes across their throats, the blood let to soak into the hay bedding. Their hands were woven together, desperately clinging to each other in those last minutes of life. Their faces had turned to each other so that they might witness the other's torment in a way that tore the last of my guards from me.

I couldn't go any further. Running outside, blind to the puddles of blood that my shoes tread through, I fell to my knees, promptly giving all that I had back to the earth. Disgust filled me and every inch of my body felt dirty and grimy. A deep sadness welled within, grasped by a beast that had slept too long and twisted into something far more dangerous. Anger simmered beneath my sorrow for the lives taken too soon, too grossly. There was a call deep in my core as if Nemesis herself whispered her outrage. Perhaps she was doing just that.

"Not here Lykos. Wait until we find the bastards who did this, then let her free."

Nyx had come to me, her hand reaching out to caress my back. It was her steadying touch that made me realize that I had begun to shake and a savage growl had started to rumble from deep in my chest. Her touch grounded me.

Looking up into her dark eyes there was no doubt that she meant it. Her words were not a hollow promise of vengeance but a declaration of intent to get retribution for the souls we were too late to save. There was a moment of surprise for myself, but somehow it felt as if a missing piece had finally clicked; this was my purpose, and I wanted to fulfill it.

Accepting the waterskin she handed me, shock, then gratitude filled me when I felt liquor burn my tongue. Swishing it around my mouth, to kill the taste of bile, I resisted the urge to spit it out and instead swallowed it.

Once my body had calmed I went with Nyx back over to where the Amazons had gathered. Serah had tear marks and her eyes were red from crying, but her face was stern, ready to do whatever was needed. Camilla's face was full of sorrow and anger as she addressed us.

"From what I remember, the adults living here are all accounted for, three children are missing as well as the livestock. We need to check the other homes, they aren't far from here. Maybe there will be survivors."

Camilla's words quivered, though I couldn't say if it was fear or anger. None of us missed the implication that the other homes would have been similarly hit, or the way her eyes glistened with tears she was trying not to shed. She was met with no arguments from her sisters, though one of the younger warriors did dare to whisper.

"They need to be put to rest first.."

There was only a second of hesitation, perhaps a moment of calculation, before Camilla agreed. With no time to waste, we set to work on giving them all just a single group pyre.

I was spared the task of helping move the bodies from the barn, Serah and myself constructed the base of the pyre with wood from a broken fence, using old hay as bedding. Nyx brought the remaining bodies in from the fields. She said nothing about where they had been, though it became very apparent when I saw them that what had appeared from a distance to be scarecrows on our ride in, had not been figures of straw.

We used a few remaining timbers from amongst the fallen homes to make sure the wind didn't kill the flame, then laid a thick sheet of hay on top of the bodies. We covered everything except the faces, which were given coins upon their eyes to pay the ferryman. The coins were a practice that had fallen away with the absence of the Gods' presence upon our small continent, but the Amazons had apparently held on to the tradition.

When the fire was struck, we all stood and kept guard, making sure the journey of their souls was not interrupted. Staring into the billowing smoke, I could feel Nyx's presence at my back even before her hand fell upon my shoulder. Her nearness felt more and more like a warm embrace. It was also the only thing that made me certain what I saw was not a figment of my imagination.

From the wafting smoke a vision of a featureless woman stepped forth. The swirling smoke shifted around what seemed to be negative space, the darkness it billowed around taking on a solid form that seemed to never settle. There were no fine details. Instead, as I watched, the darkness only seemed to shrink and extend, a loose figure but one that was enchanting. Almost like spilled ink one second, then seeming hard as stone, the woman drifted toward me, her lips becoming sharp and clear, curling into what was almost a smile. The form of her figure reminded me of Nemesis and the way her magic worked through the tendrils of shadow that wrapped around her, but this woman was far more busty, the features that appeared much more chiseled.

Filled with awe and wonder I quickly glanced around to see the other's reactions, certain they would be just as bewildered as I. Somehow, no one else seemed to see her. In fact, everyone seemed to have been frozen in time. Their eyes did not blink, their chests did not rise and fall, their bodies remained so still that they might be a painting hung upon the wall. The trees shifted in the wind, the flames danced as they ate the flesh and hay fed to them, yet no human moved.

Only Nyx and I seemed free of whatever spell had come upon the rest.

As the billowing woman stopped before us Nyx promptly bowed her head, violet eyes diverted to the earth in what I presumed was respect. The woman's voice was just as wispy as the smoke, which gave just enough contrast to the never ending darkness to form her shape.

"Dear ones, I'm afraid this is only the beginning, Tereus has set his plans in motion. Avenge the fallen but proceed with caution and remember this; you are always strongest together. The same magic that flows through one can flow through the other. Do not hesitate, this time your own fates are at stake. All your journeys' ends have led you here. We are trying to get what information we can, but it may not be much help. Stay alert, he will likely try to draw you to him."

A tendril of smoke reached out past me, turning into a very solid hand that gently stroked Nyx's face. A look of love and adoration was somehow apparent in the visage despite the softness of the features. The gargoyle leaned into the touch, her hand reaching up to clasp what became solid matter beneath her fingers. The figure turned her head to me as she withdrew her hand.

"Do not fear the love in your heart Lykos, it has always been your greatest ally. Trust it and doors you didn't know existed will open."

Her words resonated as if the darkness shrouding her was a vast endless space for it to echo. Doubt filtered into my mind, but just as quickly became smothered by the warm sensation of Nyx's hand returning to my shoulder.

Then the earth seemed to breathe in deep after a long pause and she was gone, the smoke that had outlined her dark form rising and disappearing into the wind. Time caught up with the rest of the Amazons, a rush of energy vibrating the air as they breathed and mourned once more, their bodies once again fidgeting as if nothing had happened.

Bewildered, I craned my neck around to eye Nyx, my head cocking in confusion. She smirked, leaning toward my ear to whisper so that no one could overhear.

"That, Lykos, was my namesake. The very Goddess of Night."

That she too knew me was not so much surprising as intimidating. There had been a fondness in her voice, but her features had been far too vague to be certain. There were plenty of questions that rose from what I had witnessed. I wasn't sure there was really going to be an appropriate time or place to speak of what I had seen anytime soon, but now was definitely not it.

The ride to the next grouping of homes was done in complete silence with everyone on edge. There were only a couple hours of riding in between the settlements, but it felt longer. The smell of smoke lingered, leaving a horrible taste in my mouth. As we moved closer, there was no missing the metallic twinge that I tasted in the air. Although the others could not smell as well as I could, I saw their faces tighten as they registered the shift. Their instincts were attuned to the balance of nature, which had been horribly skewed. Any hope of survivors that we had garnered from the lack of bodies on the way was quickly torn from us in a single glance.

The horses paused, their snorts a protest to the tainted air that we asked them to walk into. In the distance we could see that the buildings all still stood, but there was an eerie silence that created dread for what would be hidden within their walls. Dismounting, we left the horses hidden amongst the woods running alongside the trail.

Camilla pointed from me to the fields and with a nod my lithe form edged between the tight growths of wheat. The sound of the wind flowing through the tall stalks sent an ominous chill down my spine, their golden forms swaying in unison, creating a natural blur in my line of sight. There was barely a need to crouch, my short stature putting me just above their tips as I weaved through. The field stopped on the far end of the village, creating the edge of the trail leading north towards the King's castle.

Carefully slipping out of the field, my eyes quickly found the hoofprints of well over a dozen horses and rivets from a cart's wheels heading out. Bringing my fingers to my lips I sounded off the teetering all clear whistle. It was answered by three others. As I scanned the village I caught a glimpse of Nyx. She sauntered almost casually through the streets, stepping over bodies and around broken carts and rubble, unphased if not unmoved.

The smell of death lay heavy all around, but a twinge of fresher blood tickled my sensitive nose, causing me to raise my head to get a better whiff. As she came nearer Nyx's gaze caught my own and she cocked her head in question. Shrugging with a grimace I took off toward the source, tracking it down just as the hounds had done only months before, with my own scent.

A horrid sense of foreboding filled me as I circled around a blacksmith's work hut, the furnace still glowing an angry orange. Brain matter and blood lay splattered across everything. The burly blacksmith's skull had been cracked open with his own tools. A horse shoe had even been tossed onto a piece of metal that protruded from his head, like it was all just a game.

Despite the gruesome scene, it wasn't the fresh scent I tasted on the air and so I continued past it toward the stables. One of the warriors raised her arms, trying to warn me against proceeding, but it was too late. There was no unseeing what lay ahead.

There would be no solace for the images burned into my memory. The horses had been herded into the coral and from there I didn't want to know what kind of torturous things they had done in order to get the results that lay before my eyes. Tears ran freely down my face, my heart bleeding for the innocent beasts with an intensity it had not felt for the humans. These beautiful creatures, who had done nothing except exist, might have simply been set free but were instead led to this torturous end.

There had been foals in the herd, their broken bodies barely recognizable. There was no way to tell if they had been killed before being trampled from panic and confinement, or during. The horses had obviously been run until they had forced themselves through the wooden panel; a mare lay impaled by a broken plank, her eyes frozen wide in horror. The others hadn't made it far. Trip lines had been set up, causing the horses to fall in ways that made it so they weren't able to catch themselves, their broken necks bent in unnatural ways. The ones who hadn't died there were left with no other option except a path of barbed wire and then they were finished off. Who knew what other horrors had occurred between that time. The screams of their herd dying undoubtedly drove them into blind panic.

Still, the scent I followed was not that of the horses, though it was with a horse that I finally found the source. Trying to push away the tears and the images that would haunt even my waking hours, I followed a trail of drag marks and blood. Turning the far corner of the barn I found a woman no older than myself, her body laying over the neck of a dead mare, her hands wrapped around the beast's head, all the while blood trickled from her broken body, chest rising with what tiny bit of life remained in her.

"SERAH!"

My shout brought the woman at a run, relief upon her face when she took in the woman, though she quickly grimaced it away. There was no doubt she had feared one of her own found, the guilt of it pulling her lips into a frown. Squeezing her hand gently before I pulled her along, we approached the girl carefully. There was hardly any reason to be wary, all the fight had left her. Sky blue eyes looked up into mine as she pulled in a ragged breath. Serah leaned forward to take stock of all the woman's ailments. Her eyes were shining, tears held back as her empathetic heart bled for the woman she knew she could not save.

"There is too much damage, her lung has been pierced along with who knows how many other things."

The woman grabbed Serah's hand weakly, though the healer grasped it firmly in turn.

"If you want to help me, just end this. Everything hurts. Everyone and everything I love is dead." She glanced at the horse she laid over and her face twisted in pain with every movement. Her words were barely a whisper, broken up with shallow gasps of air. "I'm dying, just make it quick...please."

Glancing over to Serah a silent question passed between us. Her nod confirmed once more what had already been said. Her request was the least we could do, but I knew Serah didn't have the heart to kill anything beyond self-defense. To be fair, I wasn't sure I did either, but there was no way I would willingly choose to place the burden upon her shoulders. Pulling a knife from my boot, its sharp edge gleaming even in this dull light, I turned my attention back to the girl.

"Close your eyes, think of a happy memory and go there."

The knife in my hand shook, nerves spiking in fear that I might prolong the woman's suffering rather than ending it. Serah pointed to where I would need to pierce the skin, but I could not risk it. Instead I returned the blade to my boot, motioning for Serah to move.

"Stay in that happy place, it'll end soon."

The woman didn't stiffen or flinch when my hands gently stroked her hair even as Serah started up a soft humming meant to distract the woman from the sounds of my body shifting into position. Slipping a hand beneath her head, I grasped her skull just as my canid self might latch on with powerful jaws, channeling a bit of magic to make sure I had enough strength and grip. Just as quickly as a predator would thrash its head, so moved my hands, twisting the head so that the neck snapped with an awful crack. A chill ran along my spine.

Death came instantly.

Serah's face was streaked with tears as she offered a hug I didn't return. A growl fell from my lips as anger rolled through me, heat pouring into my veins as my magic stirred.

"Let the first life I take be in mercy. Lend me strength so that I need give no more. Daughter of Nemesis guard my soul and wipe it clean when I am done avenging these evil deeds."

The words fell from my lips unbidden, as if I had spoken them many times before. Even if my memory could not serve me well enough to show me, the echoes of a reply danced where I could not quite grasp. Whose words had they been? Were they my own or something I had heard and repeated back, like a child who hears their parent's recitations so often they begin to say them as if the words had always been their own. I wasn't sure, but I felt the fire behind them igniting something far more dangerous.

"In this life and the next I shall never falter."

Nyx's voice sang a reply in my ears, but when I turned it was still only Serah and I standing over the dead. The echoes of this memory did not scare me the way the others had. Perhaps it was the realization of what must be done, the outrage for what had already taken place, and the earth shattering anticipation of enjoying every moment of it. Those all factored into my mind's acceptance of those words uttered long ago. Surely they would still be true. I hoped they were. There was no telling if the Amazons would ever look at me the same when I got done with those responsible for this carnage.

Pulling back, Serah looked at me with a mix of awareness and fear but didn't shy away when I grabbed her hand and pulled her away with me. Instead she squeezed tight, shaken by the day's events just as we all were, but still trusting me just as she always had.

The area with the horses was the most gruesome of the scenes we stumbled upon in that grouping of houses. The people had been killed a lot quicker, perhaps because they were mostly older men and women. It was almost as if they had rushed through but then got bored and gone after the horses as an afterthought.

Camilla stood there puzzling over it when Serah's voice rose up, sorrow and anger mingling together in her tone, her hand still clasping my own for comfort.

"Why even bother to stick around once they'd killed the people? There is no way they had these horses all penned in the barn. They were rounded up from the pasture."

Camilla shook her head at a loss.

"The horses took time and the blood there is fresher than the humans, but they left the rest of the livestock."

It was Nyx who proposed a reason. "They were waiting for something, or someone. Perhaps they want us to catch up to them." Her words were calm and matter of fact. Her experience made her seem cold, though I could see the depths of her eyes swimming with emotion.

Camilla scoffed. "That's the dumbest thing I've ever heard! Why would they want that?"

She sighed and placed a hand to her eyes as if she were absolutely exhausted. Surely this was the worst thing she had ever seen and certainly the most difficult situation to have to lead in.

Nyx was about to reply, words falling off her lips even as I raised a hand to stop her, dread filling my gut as the pieces fell in place. These methods had been used before, but this hadn't been for us.

"It was a trap. The smoke in the first village, they knew it would draw attention. The Amazons do not ignore signals of distress."

Serah's hand tightened, her breath drawn in with a gasp as she too connected the dots and realized it had been our friends who the trap had been set for.

"Xalia." Her voice was a whisper but she suddenly looked to where the horses were. None of us had looked too closely at the scene. She swallowed hard and let go of my hand, taking off towards the butchered beasts.

There was only so much I could take, so I let Camilla be the one to follow closely behind. They had seen the group off and would know better than I which horses had been used. When they returned they looked sick, but Serah seemed a little relieved.

"There are two that could be ours, but Xalia's stallion is definitely not amongst them. If they were caught here, some of them got away."

That they might have simply taken the better looking horses need not be spoken. We were all dreading the thought that our sisters might have been captured by such nasty brutes.

One of the junior warriors looked grim and cast worried looks over toward us as she helped the others set coins to the dead's eyes. She was scared and would undoubtedly have nightmares for months after this. There was no time to wait and although the ceremony had to be finished, hope that everyone would make it home safely was quickly waning.

"Camilla. Nyx and I can scout ahead while you see to the dead. There is no reason for all of us to be at risk. We can see how much of a head start they have and if we catch up with them we can bring back news as to whether we need to signal for backup before proceeding."

Nyx's gaze found my own, her lip curling at the corner in the smallest of smirks. It took me a moment to realize I'd just volunteered her to my side. It had come as natural as breathing.

Camilla arched a brow and shook her head. "We won't be much longer, best to stay together until we know what we are dealing with."

There wasn't anything to be done for the horses. There would be too much wasted energy in trying to pull their bodies without the aid of an ox or two. Many of them were of the thicker draft breeds, as was usual for working farms. Still, there was so much time being lost and we were no closer to knowing if our sisters were alive or dead somewhere. Camilla was nervous, afraid to make the wrong choices. In this, at least, I was not.

The two amazons moved towards the pyres, but Serah held back a few strides so that Camilla could not see her motioning towards the stream. Her kind eyes held her heart in them, beckoning me to go. Xalia meant the world to her, but she didn't have the place or experience to defy Camilla. I had no qualms with either, though in truth this lifetime left me inexperienced by comparison. Still, I had to do something. Once they were busy helping with the pyre platform I slipped away and back to where the horses were waiting by the nearby stream.

Taking a moment to splash my face with the cool waters I waited until I heard footsteps stop close by, acknowledging my shadow.

"I'm fine Nyx."

She gave a gentle laugh. "None of us are fine Lykos, but that is not why I followed you. I know you can handle yourself well enough."

I arched an eyebrow as I spoke, challenge in my voice. "Well enough?"

She approached me and a hand moved slowly toward my face, pushing a loose wet strand of hair back behind my ear. It took everything in my power not to flinch back or jerk, the only reaction that might prevent me from leaning forward.

"Yes, Vixen. Although you have the soul of a warrior, your heart never becomes cold. In this lifetime you have not yet been bloodied. I fear that will change sooner than later and I won't have you facing that alone. If we are going, we need to go now."

The anger seething through my body made my skin itch like a bad rash. There had been too many innocents slain. My hands started to shake but Nyx took them into her own, silently offering her strength, if only I would accept.

Those bright violet eyes consumed me. There was a warmth to their depths that I fell into instantly, the harsh tug that I had followed all the way to the Amazon's land now a soft hum. The beast beneath my surface calmed and the itch faded from my mind but I could not look away. I stepped forward. She blinked but the spell wasn't broken.

Lifetimes of memories had spotted my dreams and my days and although there were some where the gargoyle didn't dwell, her presence was always there. The magnitude of what she had meant to me, even more so what I had meant to her, sat on my chest like a boulder. What did this all mean? The trail ended with a question mark followed by more and so I let myself refocus on something a bit more tangible.

All the memories and events equated to at least one truth.

I could choose.

Nemesis had said so, my own heart told me the same and the only thing making me hesitate was fear, not lack of desire. All I had to do was choose to accept that my feelings were valid, that my emotions were real even if they were influenced by the past. Afterall, everyone's feelings were, even those with only one lifetime's worth of experience.

I had invoked Nemesis' daughter to cleanse me and heard the memory of Nyx's voice swearing to always be there to do so. How then could I deny her presence alongside me? There was hardly a choice in it, she'd follow either way. Nyx had not always been a gargoyle, just as her words had promised to always be there, so her actions had followed suit to make certain of it. Quietly puzzle pieces were falling into place, but the bigger picture was too complex and missing too many parts to know what it would become.

We said nothing.

Prince silently walked over with Sprite, Nyx only letting go of my hands when I finally pulled them from her and mounted the painted stallion.

Camilla was waiting for us.

I saw the concern and doubt in her eyes and had no patience for it. I was not a child and certainly not as fragile as she seemed to believe me to be. It was apparent she didn't trust us with this task but I tried not to take that personally. She was doing her duty and looking out for her people which would include me now, but I was not the same as them. I was something far different than any of them had seen and more than I could even fully grasp yet.

"Let me be very clear on this Camilla; I am not asking your permission. I am not one of your scouts. The council sent me with you for a reason and this is it. We will rejoin you as soon as we can. This is undoubtedly just a small group of a bigger problem and we need to know if they have our sisters or if we need to be searching for them elsewhere."

She was just as surprised as I was with myself, but it felt right, as if I'd finally found my feet and had realized I could run forward instead of crawling backwards. Nyx's presence was, as always, at my back and I could hear her amusement as she muffled a snicker.

Nyx must have made some kind of face or movement, because all of a sudden Camilla huffed when she glanced behind me and threw her hands up. There was some kind of tension there that I had been oblivious to before now. I was too self-absorbed to have noticed their interactions beyond those which involved myself directly.

Camilla's words were strong but quiet, not wishing to rouse the others, though disappointment and annoyance vibrated strongly across her voice.

"Fine, but don't let this she-demon lead you to your doom! Get back here immediately and report what you find, don't be reckless and stupid."

She immediately turned on her heel and went back to the fire which had now been started. Serah had followed her over and now looked up to me with firm determination and pride. If the situation had not been so serious I was certain she'd have cracked a smile at Camilla's outburst.

"If you find them, bring them back no matter who you have to go through to do it. Make every last one pay if you can. Above all else, stay safe Lykos, we won't be far behind."

For all that I knew these women to be caring and compassionate I often forgot they were also trained warriors. Words failed me as I looked deep into her eyes, so I settled for nodding instead, my determination settling hard in my stomach just as I felt the magic burning beneath my skin, ready to come out and play.

We turned our mounts in the opposite direction, veering as far away as possible from the massacred horses as we went. Although they were not of their own herd, there was no reason for our intelligent mounts to have to see it firsthand.

Even from behind, the sneer in Nyx's words was evident, her voice was low but the quiet allowed it to easily find my ears.

"I wonder if she will have enough courage to apologize for that remark when she finds out it's YOU dragging ME along for the ride."

Her words were just enough to break me out of my mind, burying the brutal images and the nagging worry, even if only for a moment. A smirk pulled at my lips as I turned in my saddle, brows arched at her.

"Funny, I don't see any drag marks"

She smirked and gave me a wink. "The view of your behind, I mean *from* behind is just too lovely to pass up is all. Plus, there are rocks."

Shaking my head I turned back in my saddle and took hold of Prince's mane.

"Alright Prince let's play catch up."

With that we set our pace, pushing our mounts as hard as we dared to make up for the lost time. Thankfully, Prince seemed to be exhilarated by the chance to run flat out and the buckskin mare, Sprite was certainly in her element. She ran with her head and the dock of her tail held high so that her mane and tail trailed out like a banner.

Despite the impending confrontation, or perhaps because of it, Nyx looked absolutely enthralled atop the mare.

Her long hair flowed out behind her and her eyes were closed against the breeze. It occurred to me then that she had slept away in a dark prison that would have sealed her away forever if not for me. I wondered if she followed me into this from some feeling of debt rather than a desire to do so. After all the lives she had followed me through, it was hard to imagine love endured enough for that to be her only reason. It was almost absurd, but I would be putting her at risk and so had to ask.

"Nyx?"

A tilt of her head and a humming sound was my acknowledgement.

"You know you are not obligated to come with me? You don't have to do this if you don't want to, especially not for me."

She eased back on Sprite's reins, the eager mare snorting with impatience but obliging all the same. Prince's ears had swiveled around to catch the conversation and so he followed suit without prompting, his head bobbing up and down as he communicated something I didn't understand to the mare. I turned my gaze back to the woman at my side and found her gaze severe, yet enchanting. Once again her eyes held me sway and I was unable to look away, though their intensity made me want to.

"You may not remember it all yet, but let me reassure you; I have never done anything against my own will and conscience. Everything, and please Lykos remember this even with the hard memories, *everything* I have done has been my choice and no one else's. I would not change a single thing in any of the many life spans I have lived and I would not wish to live them with anyone else in the world, even if it is as nothing more than friends."

Her words were far more deep than I had anticipated, the conversation taking a twisting dive into waters that were far too familiar. The ever revolving questions of my own feelings in relation to Nyx, what that could mean, and what it would change made me anxious.

I couldn't find my tongue as I stared into her violet eyes, such fierce sincerity resided there. That, and something else I had a sense of but could not have named before the memories in dreams. The heat of attraction stirred within me, the fire licking at my insides having nothing to do with my magic. Every bit of this came from something much simpler. My breathing hitched and I swallowed hard until she finally released me from her gaze and let her mount move on. Prince's words echoed in my mind.

"You humans have such weird mating rituals."

"Wha-what?! Prince uh no that's not-

"Oh... Hmm perhaps it's just that you are too young to see the signs then? Though from how red your cheeks are I'd thought you got the message. Well, no worries she seems like a patient one, she will wait until you come of age."

I shook my head and ran my hands across my face as Prince moved on, humiliation humbling me to silence.

There was a lot I needed to sort out when this was over.

Chapter Nine
Harder than it Looks

The next day we got our first sign of the enemy. A freshly broken camp and a trail that split, with heavy tracks going down both. We stood there debating for a moment as Nyx examined the indentions, apparently having been a tracker long ago.

"Well, it looks like the left side travels a bit more lightly, a mess of horses but nothing that might be carrying their loot or prisoners. The right side has a cart and a smaller number of horses with it. I'd have said it might be a different group, but there are blood droplets with the carriage tracks."

I gave her a firm nod. "Right it is then. Rescuing any survivors is the priority."

She didn't have to speak her agreement, she merely set off with me.

Traveling down the dirt path we encountered a thick fog that refused to leave the boughs of the forest surrounding us. The chill of winter drove all the tree dwellers and birds to their dens and so although our vision was impaired, our hearing was clear. The lack of birdsong or telltale scrambling of squirrels allowed the creaking of cart wheels to ring in our ears long before they might hear our hoofbeats.

Grinning at our good luck we eased our mounts off the road and left them, their intelligence making the task easier. Other mounts might have thrown a fit or whinnied in protest at being left, but Prince and Sprite stood quietly, carefully allowing their stillness to make them invisible to a quick eye.

The damp air muffled our steps, allowing us to move quickly along the side of the trail until the fog gave way enough to see them ahead. The wagon smelled of death and was loaded down with goods, but there seemed to be no survivors amongst the cargo that we could see or smell. The cart was an old one, likely taken from one of the villages, built for hauling between short distances in good weather. The lack of cover upon it was another stroke of luck. We wouldn't risk being taken by surprise.

We followed along behind the cart, keeping low until we could confirm they were the men we were seeking. It didn't take long. Their gruff voices carried the gruesome details of their most recent conquests with the tones of a brag. Disgust filled me with the urge to vomit as the image of the two women who died only after being brutalized flickered across my mind. Anger swallowed anything else I might have felt.

My first target walked alongside the cart with no worries in the world, his pace leisurely, his gaze ever facing forward. His overconfidence made it easy to sneak up behind him and sweep a leg around the front of his own. He yelped and cursed as he landed hard on his front, my foot having caught him at the ankle, dragging it back with me so that he could not recover himself.

There was no hesitation.

Pulling the knife from my boot I lunged onto him. With a speed and skill that was more instinct than anything else I set a knee into his back, gripped the hair at the back of his head and pulled the knife's sharp edge across his neck. The knife slid in far deeper than was really necessary, but I wanted to make sure he felt more than just the simple slice of skin and arteries.

The scent surrounded me, metallic and hot but it was no different from a fresh kill. Meat, blood, bones - that was all it was. The spray of blood dotted the earth, crimson glistening like morning dew. Its shimmer drove me forward.

Without wasting any time I headed toward the next man. His voice carried as he laughed about his carnage, too loud in his boasting to hear the first man's cries. A thick patch of fog hid my presence as I walked right behind him. Keeping low I slipped into position.

A sharp cry of pain rang out followed by the snap of a bone as Nyx took out a man on the other side of the cart. Too late the man I hunted drew his weapon.

I emerged from the heavy mists, my bloodied knife slashing the tendons of both ankles before I darted out of reach of his sword. His scream of pain continued as he fell to his knees. The cart stopped but I did not.

A solid kick to the head made the man keel over, though he did manage to flip to his back, his sword held up to try and defend himself. A cruel smile pulled at my lips as I walked over to him, his arms swinging the blade haphazardly. There was an unfocused sway to it and it took only a moment for me to get the pattern and dive in between it. A knee to his nether region loosed his hold quickly enough, as he looked up at me his lips trembled, showing his cowardice. He was no longer willing to die a warrior's death but instead pleaded for mercy.

"Please, please I'll give you anything you want!" He muttered, hands held aloft as I stood over him.

"You've taken something that cannot be given back. Nemesis will have you now."

His eyes grew wide and the scream of pain that came from his lips as I raised a booted foot and slammed it down on his manhood was like none I had ever heard. As I twisted my foot there was a satisfying 'pop' as the testicles flattened. His voice died off as he passed out and just as I had the one before I let his throat water the earth. No time to spare, the driver ran at me, his cry of anger piercing.

My words taunted the driver even as I carefully ducked beneath the swing of his blade.

"Tell me, do you cowards know how to face an enemy that can fight back?"

His reach was longer than my own, but I could smell the fear that wafted from him. He had charged forward when he thought I was too distracted to notice. Grabbing the recently deceased man's sword from the earth I parried with him.

Two steps back then two to the right. Feigning strain, I let him think he was the one maneuvering us, his fear dissipating with every stride forward. I could see his sneer spread as his confidence grew, forgetting the cries of pain from his partners in crime. Raising my sword to meet his swings I retaliated with careless swipes, dancing to a tune he could not hear. He moved forward and I withdrew, luring him away from the cart which he had wisely kept to his back at the start. The dance lasted barely a minute, the sound of metal upon metal ringing out perhaps a dozen times before Nyx struck.

Slipping behind him she reached around and grabbed the sides of his head the moment he made a strike from overhead. The jerking motion of her arms was almost too fast to even notice but the second his neck snapped his entire body collapsed on itself, the sword falling back against his face, slicing it as both fell to the ground.

"Well, that was a bit too easy wasn't it?" Looking around it certainly felt like they should have put up a better fight, but then again they were cowards who picked on the weak. My expectations may have been too generous.

Nyx looked a bit worried but nodded in agreement. She checked out the back of the wagon, but there were only a couple of dead pigs.

"I fear this may have been a diversion to give them time enough to hand off any prisoners before we caught up with them. The only reason they'd have to suspect us coming would be if they ran across our missing Amazons and expected a rescue. It may have been the reason they attacked them to begin with."

As I helped her unstrap the cart horse a horrible feeling crept into my gut.

"You think they attacked the trade group to lure more Amazons out? To lure *me* back out?"

Nyx sighed and shook her head. She didn't have the answers, she barely even knew where she was and who ruled where, but I still found myself looking to her for reassurance. She set the horse free with a quick slap to its rump and we made our way back towards our own mounts.

"It's possible Lykos...Mother said he would not believe you dead, and he knows where you ended up. He may have even been counting on it."

"What do you mean?" The heat of the blood on my hands began to cool, making my hands numb and causing my body to shiver.

"From what the Queen has told me, the Mad King has been trying to push the Amazons into breaking the treaty for a long time. He has wanted their mountain territory for quite a while. It may very well have been to retrieve me, in order to get to you." She grimaced, as if the words pained her.

"He asked me about a partner in the last interrogation. He seemed to think it was the key to making me shift - awakening the magic was how they put it, though I've got no clue what he meant." Sighing, I turned to her, the expression she wore intense. No, passionate.

"Yes you do. At least now you do. You have dreamt it, felt it. You know exactly what he meant. I doubt his plans will work, but he is no idiot. Having me would have saved him a lot of time and energy, especially if I'd been closer. Lykos, you always find me, and if he knows I have awoken, our friends are in grave danger."

Worry caused my jaw to clench, praying to the Goddess that Onya and Xalia were alright. The rest I would have to deal with later, with a large vat of liquor.

"We have to find them."

Riding hard with sparse breaks, we finally caught up to the larger band. We left our mounts in the woods and skirted around the side of their camp, hiding amongst the shadows until darkness fell. A mixed bunch of what appeared to be soldiers but acted like barbarians wandered throughout the makeshift camp, their rowdy temperaments were evident in how they moved and the sporadic fights that broke out amongst them. Nyx scoffed, her eyes rolling to the back of her head. As she moved to get a better view she leaned in from behind me to speak, her warm breath tickling my neck and sending a shiver down my spine.

"Brutes the lot of them. I'd bet they are former slaves, probably raised in the arenas across the Great Sea; Rhea tells me the sport has survived. It would explain their cruel streak. The arenas change you." Her voice wavered at the end and I silently wondered what she was seeing as her vision seemed to lose focus for just a moment.

I didn't comment, merely nodded, my gaze flickering from one group to the other. Their numbers included both men and women whose bodies were splattered with blood and gore that they wore like a prize. I didn't see any prisoners, so if any were truly missing from the villages they had ravaged then they'd been passed on already, as we had feared.

We sat in the shadows, waiting, trying to learn what we could with the opportunity we were given. Nyx insisted there were too many for us to risk attacking straight out, and despite the evidence littered across their wardrobes, we had to make sure they were truly guilty.

As ale passed between them their boasting became loud and obnoxious, leaving no room to doubt these were our murderers.

"Winslow! Where did you learn that trick with the horses?"

The booming voice belonged to a man whose face was barely discernible from all the facial hair he had let take over and remained unmanaged. His muscles bulged out from his thick frame, easily standing at Nyx's height. He would be a formidable foe even half-drunk as he was. The man he was speaking to was far less impressive, his slender frame no less muscled but his posture was squirrely at best, his dark eyes beady. I felt my lip curl instinctively, disgust running through me as he lit up at the attention and credit given to him.

"Learned it from the wildlings back home. They use it against invading armies out in the deserts. Hard to spot the traps when the sun is so bright! Almost died when the masters sent me out there after some nameless artifact."

"Slithered your way back somehow though didn't you?" This new voice was a woman whose face did nothing to hide the disgust she felt for the man in front of her. There was no warmth in her icy blue eyes, and although she didn't stand much taller than me, the rest of the group seemed to purposely leave as much space as possible between themselves and her.

Nyx growled softly beside me, a sound that put me on edge, the image of a big cat stalking from the shadows doing little justice to the impression it left behind.

"There is a very subtle magic being used here. Her image is false. Look closely, you will see the way the edges blur and shift when she moves too quickly."

Refocusing on the woman I tried to see what Nyx could, but my night vision was not as keen. Instead, I focused on the scents which came to us on a soft breeze. Ever so faint was the tingle of magic, blocking not only her true face, but also her scent. Whoever this woman was, she was taking no chances of being tracked down for her crimes, if she had committed any beyond horrible company. Unlike the rest she was pristinely clean, no stains or marks upon her body or clothes.

The conversation had continued without my attention, but it was drawn back when the subject shifted.

"What're we going to do with those Amazons once we catch em? Think we can have some fun before we take em back to the king?"

My gut clenched, fingernails digging into my palms as I held my breath, hope mingling with fear for the women who had managed to avoid capture.

"Absolutely not!" The woman glared at the man who had sheepishly asked.

"The Amazons are to be untainted, the King plans to sell them back to their Queen. He wants cooperation, not all out war. That will come later when he is granted more power. Now, you lot, get moving! The last scout said there were signs they may have backtracked to try and throw us off. Go cut off the route to the Centaurs, they will expect us to assume they are only taking the woods, but the cart trails will be easiest to move along."

A group that hadn't been drinking grumbled, eyes looking longingly at the ale barrel as they trudged off towards their horses and left.

There was no way of knowing if we would ever be able to catch them this vulnerable again, let alone in such a small gathering. This small party was not the sum of the ravagers. From the sound of it, there were other groups out looking. My body tensed as I counted, surely we could take them and save ourselves a lot of trouble.

Nyx quirked her brow at me and then shook her head, pulling me back and away from the camp towards our mounts.

"We won't get another chance like this Nyx! We can't just pass it up!"

Her violet eyes met mine and my body cringed back, wishing to wither away from her severe gaze. Forcing myself to stand taller I kept her gaze and swallowed the way my heart hurt at the disapproval in her eyes. This was absurd and I was tired of running away. Nyx's gaze shifted, something told me she was miles away to a time I didn't remember yet, seeing something that made her body shiver.

"It's not worth the risk, we don't know when the other groups will return, or what other magic the woman has up her sleeves. We need to go back and get the others, find the missing Amazons and get to safety."

Anger rose inside and although I kept my voice low in case they had people patrolling, I felt the venom. We were still moving away from the group but I didn't want to lose any advantage we'd have because I couldn't control my temper.

"Why? Just because you are afraid of what one woman could do?! We can do this Nyx, we have faced worse in the past!"

"It is not the same, we have only just found each other again." She kept walking even as my steps paused.

"All those people are dead, they need to be avenged! Nemesis demands it!"

At the mention of the Goddess, Nyx's calm persona fell away. Her wings burst from her back as she rounded on me, anger and fear distorting her face.

"Do NOT lecture me on what my mother demands, Lykos! She is not the one who suffers when your soul departs this world just to fulfill her purpose! I can't -"

I lost the words of anger that threatened to lash out as her face filled with turmoil, her last sentence left unspoken, though I felt the missing words in my core. She stood strong in her conviction but I could see the emotion in her eyes. She was fighting for control, perhaps she had been the whole time. Pride made me want to argue, but as I let my anger simmer it dawned on me that although we were strong enough, we truly were not in any kind of position to rush into battle together.

There was still too much between us that I had not allowed to be addressed and she couldn't hide. She was right. We had worked as a team with the smaller group but we were hardly in sync. We were nowhere near the dancing partners we had been in the scenes that had played out in my dreams. There had been a level of intimacy then that didn't exist now. Our movements had been like practiced choreography, every touch a message, every look holding words that had been spoken wordlessly hundreds of times in lover's exploration. This life found us reborn again, starting fresh with clumsy steps that didn't quite match. We wouldn't win, not like this, not right now.

With an angry sigh that was turned more inward than out, I mounted Prince and turned him back the way we had come, Nyx following quickly behind.

Nothing more was said, neither myself or Nyx making any attempts to conjure a conversation. She seemed lost in her own world, eyes avoiding mine whenever I looked back. Selfishly I longed for the silence to be broken, unable to stand the dissonance now between us, but too proud to do it myself.

My mind was buzzing and my soul wrenched against its purpose, though truly there was time enough to do it the smart way. If we could regroup with our missing Amazons we would be plenty strong enough to send them to their graves. My haste might have felt justified, for the larger group would pose the biggest threat to the Amazons if they were captured, but with no one to keep them in check, might not the smaller groups do as they pleased? Suddenly all the consequences of my actions became clear to my narrowly focused vision. Shame filled me, I was nothing more than a pup playing with the big dogs in a game of chase, too prideful to see the wisdom handed to me in a reprimand.

Prince felt my sulk, bumping me lightly, nickering softly.

"Don't worry Lykos, it will all be well again."

I couldn't say I believed him fully, but I certainly hoped so.

We went around our asses to get to our elbows just to ensure we were not being followed, and so when we returned to the rendezvous point just outside the massacred village it was early in the morning. A thick fog had once again settled, so that it was only the sharp whistle that fell from my lips that saved us from an arrow as our group slipped out of the trees like ghosts.

Camilla looked rather smug after we reported our findings. The beautiful face contorted into something I no longer found attractive, though she did try to hide it. Serah was disappointed, having hoped to have had the situation taken care of sooner rather than later, her fear of what may have happened to Xalia and the other Amazons evident. There was at least hope in knowing that they had gotten away, so that was something to keep spirits lifted as much as was possible.

The discussions were long and more than once I felt Nyx's hand on my shoulder, silently calming me before I lost my patience. Shame from my previous actions humbled me enough to listen properly afterwards. Serah noticed and offered a half nod to Nyx, sharing an odd camaraderie with the gargoyle I had not previously noticed in their interactions.

It was a few hours after sunrise when Camilla finally agreed to go back to where we had found the group. They would not engage, they would merely track so that the trail did not go cold before the reinforcements she'd sent for could catch up. I had wanted to rage against it, but I had been outvoted and the look in Nyx's eyes reminded me of what my haste might have cost us.

The argument was made that there was no better tracker in the group than a fox and our healer could not be risked, so Serah and myself would wait here. The reinforcements would need guidance.

My own impatience tugged at my temper. The fluffing of my pride to get what Camilla wanted was insulting, but the worst part was her argument was also completely true and relevant. I could track as a fox, but I also had the magical pull that drew me to Nyx in the first place. It had dissipated into a soft pulse when we had been reunited but I had no doubt I could tap back into it if we were parted.

Nyx didn't need to sleep, she claimed, so they set out immediately. There was a pause before they left. Words ran through my mind but none seemed to be the right ones. Even the wrong ones might have been better than nothing, but as I stood looking up at her, I couldn't bring my voice to breach the seal of my lips. Nyx offered me a small smirk, a knowing look in her eyes as she turned Sprite around to face away from me, her body turning to keep me in her sight.

"Do not fret Lykos, my body is not easily broken and I will protect the others."

They set off, leaving me feeling like I had somehow been betrayed by being left behind.

The day passed with no sleep, my body restless as we waited for anyone, anything. Serah was less annoyed at being left behind, but that did not mean she was not put out as well.

"Xalia has trained me. I'm not helpless! My talents for healing should be a reason to take me, not set me aside. Yes! I know we will also protect their rear in case any reinforcements come this way, but it is SO FRUSTRATING. Something is wrong Lykos...I can feel it in my bones. They shouldn't have gone, not without us."

There was something about healers that convinced me they were the most attuned to the earth and its balance. Afterall, it was they who brought people back from the brink, and who knew how precariously the scales held. It was for that reason alone I'd have paid heed to what she said, never mind that my own heart mirrored her distress.

"I tried Serah."

"I know, I know. But, the warriors with us are too unseasoned, apparently Xalia took the only bloodied ones left in the village. The skirmishes in the southern Tribes have borrowed all the weathered fighters. Though, it does give me hope to know our missing Amazons are in trained hands."

She grimaced and shook her head and said the rudest thing I'd ever heard come from her lips. "Still, Camilla doesn't know her ass from her head sometimes..."

I smirked as she flung her hand over her mouth, realizing she had said that out loud rather than merely thought it.

"Well I'll be damned Serah. I didn't know you had it in you."

She looked close to tears from embarrassment but laughter erupted shortly after between the two of us. It was a nervous thing at first that rose and then fell in volume. As it dwindled it became a chuckle that would have turned to tears had we been less strong. We locked eyes and knew there was nothing we could do but let it out, stuck as we were between laughter and tears. Too much had happened in a short time with no chance to truly process it. Now the people we cared for were at risk and we had to sit amongst the shelter of wilted trees and wait. That was by far the hardest task. Waiting.

Our dread turned into premonition the next day. The sound of hooves announced the arrival of our Amazons, but as we ran toward the sound of their hoofbeats and whistle I immediately knew something had gone horribly wrong. There was a clenching in my gut as the scent of fear and blood beat them to me. It was too soon. Surely the fates had not worked so quickly? So efficiently.

Despite the worrisome smells, at first sight the fear was overrun with a jolt of excitement and hope. It wasn't just our small group but also part of the missing women from the trade.

The horses were nervous, their energy high from a run that was started by a chase. The women looked rough and blood was splattered here and there across pelts and clothes. Serah cried out as she ran past me, the woman barely making it in time to soften the landing as Xalia fell from a horse that was not her black stallion. The smell of magic drifted into my nostrils, burning as if it were in opposition of my own. A woman I barely recognized dismounted and locked eyes with me. I met her halfway, catching her as her legs gave out. Camilla dismounted and helped me move the woman off the trail.

"They were cut off on the normal trail and ambushed. Xalia said that they split off into two groups, but that woman you saw, she was able to find them no matter how well they hid. Said she was using some kind of magic to do it. Xalia's pretty sure the other group got away though. Onya took them towards the Centaur lands."

The information offered a momentary rush of relief that drained back out as a thrumming grew in my core. Like a stressed heartbeat, the rhythm was erratic, my own heart leaping up to match it as Sprite trotted forward, a whicker of sympathy uttered as she met my gaze. She could not speak to me as Prince did, but the words weren't necessary.

"Camilla! Where is Nyx?"

"They took her. The woman and her brutes. Nyx traded herself to save us and the other Amazo- Lykos wait!"

There was no hearing her from those first uttered words. There was no thought on my part beyond acknowledging where Nyx would be and that I would not leave her there for another moment. Camilla reached out and grabbed my arm, my momentum causing me to spin as she jerked me back. There was no calm in my voice, only desperation as I snapped at her.

"Don't you fucking dare!"

Ripping my arm from her grip I watched her wither beneath my gaze. Her eyes were wide with fear, the snap of my teeth coming from a distorted muzzle that produced the words with a horrid scream-like growl. Snorting I turned and took off, feeling the magic burst out as I finally let my soul fly forward, rage and fear tearing through me in blinding red streaks. I stumbled as the wave of nausea hit me. It had been a long time since I let the magic run free and in that moment I let it consume me.

The itch beneath my skin festered into a moment of deep seated tingling as my skin became malleable, the muscles beneath stretching and shifting around the bones that thickened and elongated. Nails became claws that protruded past fingers and toes, whose calluses became rough pads that cushioned paws designed to pull the earth and push it behind. Pain blasted through my body as if it had captured a bolt of lightning. All at once my spine stretched, skull contorting to satisfy the shape necessary for my long snout and rows of sharp teeth.

My human skeleton had shifted to that of an enormous fox, the sleek red fur sprouting from my skin in one smooth motion, as if a hand had passed along it, leaving behind a coat in its wake. The tail that erupted from the dock sprouting from my rear waved in the air, the black tip splitting off so that nine thick plumes trailed like a wave behind me. Two blinks and one leap into the air and no longer was I a human running, instead the kitsune that had paced beneath the surface broke free in joyous bounds.

I was a creature of the night sky, chasing the only thing on this earth that had ever resonated within my soul the way my mother had told me love would.

Stupid ass selfless gargoyle better survive long enough to be rescued or so help me I'll drag her statue ass back by the damn hair!

The earth tasted fresh, the scents flowing through me like a spirit with a name and history I could only snag a piece of. The protrusion of snout now formed perfectly, cream against a lighter red with black lines that framed my fox mouth. Taking in a deep breath a wave of smells filtered through my mind. All the horses and Amazons that had passed this way, as well as the small prey animals who'd fled from their motion, were filtered into a pile unheeded. The unique scent of cinnamon and magic was the only thing I searched for.

The taint of the mystery woman's magic was like a beacon, practically visible in iridescent as its marker screamed danger to all of my senses. It blinded me and made everything horribly sharp all at once, giving me an instant headache that I pushed away. There was only one strand I needed to follow, the only one that pulled my core and smelled like sweetbread. The taint of the cloaked woman was just background noise.

Pulling from within, channeling the image of Nemesis' dark magic seeping into my tails, I let the magic creep through my pores until the red of my fur disappeared beneath a haze of shadow that instantly silenced the noise of my trek and masked my scent in a void. The elements suddenly became hushed and my mind singular as I disappeared into the forest edge's shadow.

I'm going to tear that bitch apart limb from limb.

Miles passed beneath my rough paws before I caught a fresh trail of Nyx's scent. It mingled with the magic of the strange woman, leading off a path we had not taken yet. I was running into a trap, of that I had no doubt, but there was nothing in my heart or soul that faltered when I closed my eyes and saw violet eyes and a soft smirk on the back of my lids. At that moment I knew that there was no arguing with myself anymore. Present and past had merged, I just needed to make it to the future with her alongside me.

Doubling my pace it took no time to close the gap, the sounds of their camp increasing until I slinked along the edge, settling in to wait. Hunkering down between two fallen trees and allowing the shadows to hide me, I prayed softly for Nemesis to aid me, though it may have been the Goddess Nyx who answered my need.

"Your daughter is in danger, hide my presence until I can use the night to strike."

The tickle of magic around me was all the answer I received, but it was enough. Trusting the Goddess to her silent word, I let myself rest. I wanted to barge in, but I'd be useless to Nyx if I could not keep stamina in a fight. When the sun began to sink, a feeling much like the stinging of ants bit at my feet, though no bugs could be seen. Ears flat I peeked over the trees, eyes easily cutting through the dusk light to catch the rotation of the guards before night took them from my immediate vision.

When darkness fell I made my move, slipping through the shadows with ease as they milled about their camp. The mystery woman was not amongst them, but a good fifty head of men and women were gathered. Their smaller parties had kept their word, as was part of Nyx's bargain, and no longer hunted for the other Amazons. As much of a relief that was, I was now severely outnumbered. Flexing my paws in the earth, my muscles tensed and then relaxed. Drawing myself inward I touched the magic that was bound with my soul, welcoming memory into my limbs and subconscious, willing them to guide me unseen. Warmth radiated from my core, magic shimmering upon the ends of my fur, beckoning the dark magic to once again hide my glossy coat.

The numbers didn't matter, I'd rip them to shreds.

Roaming the outskirts, out of the way of the guards and always traveling equidistance between them, I scanned the camp until I finally laid my eyes on Nyx. My stomach went cold, then the fire inside blazed. Tied up in the center of their camp she hung limp, either unconscious or pretending to be. She had lacerations all over her arms and legs and had been set upon a Y shaped platform with her wings spread out and pierced to the wood. Her hands were bound behind her back and her feet rested on a rock that had more sharp edges than smooth, her blood dying it scarlet.

My heart broke and my fox raged. They were all going to die if I had my way. For now I crept towards the far side, picking up my pace as I began my hunt.

The patrol in front of me walked along, blind to my presence, for the darkness swallowed me whole. The sound of a rock underfoot didn't give him enough warning as I plucked him from the earth, my fangs clamping hard to his throat before even a squeak of surprise could escape. The warm taste of copper ignited something within. Like the black powder across the sea, the blood sparked an explosion that set off colors behind my eyelids that became all-consuming in that moment. The killer within awoke as my own dark magic was fed with the most powerful magical conduit on earth; blood.

Three more necks snapped beneath my jaws before anyone noticed, and by then it was too late. The first shout triggered chaos amongst them and like the fiend I was born to be, I danced to the sound of screams. The men nearest me gave war cries that turned to panicked shouts as they caught sight of just what they were facing. I tackled one, long claws slicing through his leather armor like it was nothing more than parchment. My jaws cut off another's scream just as the shadows engulfed me once more.

Instinct drove my body as I tore through flesh and left the wreckage behind. Curses followed me as men and women alike bled out. I made it halfway through the encampment with a trail of blood marking my path before the mystery woman finally made her appearance. She smiled as she stood beside Nyx, her words dripping with menace.

"Ahh yes, there's the one I've been waiting for. You seem quite yourself these days Lykos."

I snarled in reply but she merely smiled a sickly sweet smile that seemed familiar, though I did not recognize the face it belonged to.

"I'm sorry it came to this darling Lykos. It could have been easier but you chose the hard path. Shame I've been told I can't kill her *yet*. Still, if an accident were to happen, who could blame me?"

She giggled as she held a blade to Nyx's neck and in a movement almost too quick for me to follow she sliced a line into her flesh. As I lunged forward she disappeared just as quickly as she had shown up, a puff of purple smoke all that remained. Fully alerted to my presence, a sea of bodies now stood between myself and Nyx, the momentary distraction allowing them to circle me.

I had to get to Nyx.

Lashing out with tooth and claw I grabbed onto any piece of flesh I could, thrashing my head and ripping limbs off. Sickening shrieks of pain coincided with the distinct squelch of flesh tearing.

The world shifted and I lost my capacity to think. It was all red; my vision, the smell, and the taste upon my tongue. It was all streaked scarlet and tasted like life and death. Ignoring the pain of slices and stabs I tore through them and cleared a path to Nyx. There was a rush of relief as she held onto consciousness, the cut not so deep as to cause her to die just yet.

They struck from all sides, my tails lashing out just as often as my claws as I fended them off the platform I now protected. The shadows that swirled around me stretched out with a life of their own, choking anyone who breathed the tendrils in. The magic might have been my own, or it may have been Nyx's mother or grandmother using their connection to me to manipulate the world. Either way, I was grateful for the aid, the tendrils giving me enough berth to focus on Nyx for a moment.

Pulling the nails from her wings first, I worked to release her from her post. Tooth and claw sliced through the ropes holding her, my body positioned so that when Nyx's bindings released her, she fell gracelessly onto my back. I curled a tail around her to steady her balance and a tendril followed suit, engulfing and protecting her body as I lunged forward once more.

There was no sense of up or down, though the crowd around me was thinning as bodies piled up. When I finally registered anything beyond the flesh I snatched, it wasn't the screams of my victims but the sound of hooves that caused my heart to leap.

The sudden surge of hoofbeats filled my ears and distracted me just long enough to give the men surrounding me a moment to time their attack. A slice above my right eye spilled blood, blinding me on that side. Turning my head to try and find the cause I received a hard blow to the skull with a hammer. The world went fuzzy and then black, the sound of

Prince's voice in my head the last thing that registered before darkness took me.

"*Hold on Lykos, Serah is coming!*"

Chapter Ten
Three Heroes and Two Pains in my Ass

When I awoke my nostrils were filled with the mingling scents of magic and horseflesh. To say it was a potent combination would have been a severe understatement. I had shifted back into my human form, and now lay draped in a heavy fur cloak that hid my exposed body. Grogginess blurred my vision and skewed my equilibrium for a minute, focus coming and going on a whim. My body ached, a throbbing in my head traveling into my eyes and down my neck, the muscles there too tight. Blood had dried upon my skin in lieu of the fur that had been drenched with it. I could feel bandages around the worst of my wounds and suddenly a jolt of panic filled me as the world caught up. I went to jerk up but a hand steadied me, the voice was gruff but kind.

"Peace Lykos, Peace. You and your lady are fine. We got all your Amazon sisters as well, but you took a bad hit to the head. You need to rest."

"All of them?"

The words came unbidden, croaking out as if I had spent hours screaming.

He smiled as he removed his hand, trusting me to stay put now that I'd been reassured.

"Yep, all of them. The ones sent to trade with us as well as your lot."

Knowing we were all safe eased my mind, allowing my body to relax enough for my senses to calm and focus, letting me register my immediate surroundings a bit more clearly. His words were true, I spotted Nyx just behind me, her body wrapped as well. Her sleep was as peaceful as one could hope for, the rise and fall of her chest as smooth as the bandage covering the line across her throat. Peering out over the back of the cart I could see others with wounded Amazons resting within. To our left I spotted Serah, who cradled Xalia's head in her lap, her eyes never leaving her. I didn't see Onya, but trusted the man at his word.

Sighing with relief I gave him a grateful nod, sidling backwards until Nyx's body was close enough to feel my heat. She mumbled something as her nostrils flared at my scent and scooted herself against my backside, her arm pulling me in tight against her chest. The man who sat opposite us gave an amused smile before politely averting his gaze. I nestled back, a deep breath released as I realized we really were safe, at least for now.

The road was smooth, but the sound of hooves was not coming merely from the horses pulling the cart. As I took a better look at the party we now moved with I realized that the heavy dose of magic in the air was due to the two variants of Centaur we traveled with. The man in the cart with us had the typical features of a Centaur, his hair was grown long and braided to keep it neat; both that which grew on his head and the long goatee on his face. His eyes were the typical deep brown of the species, though blue eyes could also occur in one or both eyes as well. He wore a leather vest over his linen shirt and his breeches had been dyed a deep blue. This was a way to tell his particular trade, though I couldn't have said what trade was signified by what color.

The most notable of course were the Centaurs who had chosen to live in their hybrid form. From the waist up they were the typical image of any person, but that was where the similarities ended. Their forelegs stood in the place of human legs, the bodice of a horse providing them with all the perks of four legs as well as spare parts. With two of everything, Centaurs were a lot harder to fatally wound, making them excellent warriors, despite their peaceful natures. They believed in the balance of life just as my mother had raised me to.

You didn't kill what you couldn't eat or use. You only took life to provide life, you always remained humble and thanked the earth for its provisions.

I tried to take in more of my surroundings to garner how the hell we had managed to get so lucky, but exhaustion quickly pulled my eyelids closed. With Nyx's arm wrapped around my middle I let sleep take me.

It was well into the day when the rattle of the cart woke me again. The path we were traveling was sloping down, making the cart jar a bit against its structure. Two centaurs now walked along the sides of the horses making sure they didn't receive the pressure of it. It was easy to see how they kept themselves so well built as they took hold of the corners of the cart and slowed its descent.

I felt disgusting, tired, and sore but the crisp scent of grass filtered into my senses and stirred excitement. The centaur lands were close to where I had once called home. I let my gaze take in the rolling sea of rye grass that would soon shoot up to be harvested as hay. It was endless, or so one would think. Even with my keen eyesight it blurred into nothing at a point and hurt my head from the strain of trying to separate the hues.

A noise from behind me caught my attention and I felt my breath hitch the moment violet eyes captured mine. A soft, almost vulnerable, look flickered across her face before a smirk shifted it to her more mischievous default look.

"You must have been sleeping pretty hard for all that snoring you were doing."

Her words were playful but I growled softly in protest, knowing for a fact that I certainly did NOT snore, ever! She only grinned when I grabbed an apple that rolled into me and tossed it at her head. The movement caused pain across my back that I ignored, her response was to deftly catch it and take a juicy bite.

A bit of fire raced through me as I watched a drop of juice slide down her chin and along her jawline. An impulse to lick it clean off made me almost choke on the air I breathed in. She finally wiped it away and grinned with a knowing look that made me shy from her gaze. We'd almost died and my body was still succeeding in betraying me. With a scowl, I turned away completely, giving her my back like I would few others and continued to take in my surroundings, though the rumble of my stomach made me regret not taking a bite of it myself.

I had feared I might have been too late.

Prince's voice was a soothing hum of warmth inside my mind as he lifted his head over the cart's edge to nuzzle my neck, tickling me with his whiskers.

You stink, but I'm glad to see you both are whole at least!

"How on earth did you manage this Prince?" I decided to ignore the insult to my scent knowing it was true.

Quite by the skin of my teeth I'd say, though not without help.

His laughter made me smile as I rubbed his head and ears gently before he made a more serious reply. Nyx's obnoxious bites making my stomach groan.

When you took off after Nyx I knew there would be trouble. Serah and the others couldn't follow your trail right away with the wounded, so I went searching for Onya. As suspected, she had headed to the centaurs and gotten reinforcements, her own mount easily shouted the message ahead of her, so that the centaurs met her halfway. I happened to cross paths with her on their way back to where the ambush had happened and led her to you.

"Thank goodness you did, though your arrival did distract me long enough to get a blow to the head."

We all play a different part in someone else's story. In yours I'm the distraction that cost you the winning blow, in mine I'm the noble steed that saved his princess from the clutches of death. You know, it's all relative. Let us just be glad this one turned out well.

Shaking my head I couldn't help but laugh. Prince bobbed his head out of the cart, whickering to Sprite and another magical horse as he trotted off. When I sat back against the side of the cart I set a glare on Nyx. It wasn't the time, but now that I knew she was safe I could let out the frustrations that had fed my fears the entire time I had raced to save her.

"What in Hades were you thinking?"

Nyx's glare met my own but she was exhausted and finally just sighed.

"It doesn't matter now. I knew she wouldn't want to and couldn't kill me, but the Amazons were expendable. I couldn't stand by and let them be harmed when I knew my risk was significantly less. She took the trade since I was the better bait to get you to show your true form and confirm you were alive."

She reached out her hand, extending half the apple, which I begrudgingly took, my stomach still rumbling from the smell of it.

"For the record, I'm glad you came. I honestly wasn't sure that you would."

There was no way to eloquently put the feelings that drove me, none were enough to encompass it, but she had to know. There was no denying it now. Yet to look into those eyes and admit that my fondness for her had grown as the days passed, that memories had settled and warmed me with such ferocity that it scared and exhilarated me as no one ever had, that seemed an impossible feat. Biting my lip I met her eyes, trying to will all the things in my head and heart into the simple words that passed my lips.

"I had to."

She said nothing in response and silence settled between us as I ate the rest of the apple, the taste of her saliva in the first few bites taking my mind to places it shouldn't be. She smiled softly as she watched me, making my heart flutter, and when I had finished the apple she leaned against me, her head on my shoulder as she shut her eyes once more to rest.

The village was made up of cottages built to house both variations of centaur. The ones designed for the standard humans stood on stone foundations that raised them enough that the doorways and windows opened up at the level of the average half horse to make communication easier. The cottages obviously designed for the half horses were more like small barns. Stalls were converted into bedrooms for families, with lofts for their human counterparts where necessary. The combinations showed a large range of familial dynamics which could be observed. The regular horses were kept apart, though their stables were no less well built or unique in design, having to accommodate the height of half horse centaurs as well.

Centaurs were unique, each human among them having been given the choice to retain their half-horse body or live out their lives as humans. The choice was made once puberty hit, which was later in life than most species, occurring around twenty. Until that point a centaur could switch between forms on full moon nights when magic flowed more easily. Any other time the change was too drastic to be done and once puberty hit the flow of magic ceased and change was no longer possible. Many people forgot this when they heard the word 'centaur' thinking only of the half horses which were understandably far more remarkable.

When the carts finally slowed to a stop in front of the first large stable, a familiar voice rang out, causing me to bolt up from my seat to get a better look. The image that met me made me want to laugh aloud, though I thought better of the perceivably rude reaction. Riding astride a gorgeous centaur woman sat Onya, one arm waving wildly while the other lay in a sling. The woman she literally rode wore a welcoming smile, her olive skin making her one blue eye stand out strongly. Her pelt was painted, white forelegs melding into dark palomino splashes with a large spot over her butt. The one eye that was blue marked had a paler spot around the eye, just as you might see in a horse with such coloring. Her arms were behind her, gripping Onya's legs so the enthusiastic woman didn't fall.

"Thank goodness you all made it!"

Her words were for everyone, but as I waved she gained an even brighter smile that matched my own.

"Lykos! I knew you'd come!"

The woman carried Onya over to the cart, neither of us paying much heed as we leaned forward to hug each other. The warmth of her skin was a comfort, the pulse beneath the only thing that mattered in that moment. She had become my best friend and the thought of finding her anything but well had wounded me almost as much as Nyx's capture. There was no solace to the 'what if's' so I didn't let myself go down that road, instead I simply hugged back as hard as her wounded arm would allow.

"Tell ya what, I may not have the benefits of quick healing, but at least I look and smell better than you."

Snorting indignantly I looked down and took a sniff. I was caked in dry blood and smelled of metallic sweat and dirt. Nyx snickered as my nose wrinkled up, my glare doing nothing to dissuade her amusement.

"Don't worry, now that everyone is safe, we can get cleaned up and rest. Everything else can wait a few days, nothing will make sense right now anyways. The centaurs will work on gathering information while everyone recoups."

There was too much to say and a lack of energy with which to do it, so the option of waiting and resting was well received. Those who hadn't been wounded had fought hard to keep their companions safe and so were thoroughly exhausted. We were all unloaded from the carts and led to our temporary lodges. Many of the women doubled up and stayed with centaurs but Nyx and I were led to one of the few empty homes that had been prepped for our arrival.

The man who had ridden alongside us was the same person who escorted us to the home. Assured that we would be unbothered and protected, he led us in, showing us where all the necessary supplies were. After that he bid us good rest and reminded us that the bath water was fresh and hot.

"Nothing cures ailments like a warm soak. Take advantage while you can, and don't feel the need to hurry out. We won't be offended if you take a few days to yourself. We will send someone when we have more information to go on."

"Thank you."

The words weren't enough but it was all I had at the moment. What could you really say beyond 'Thanks for saving my ass'? He grinned, his dark features kind and warm in every good sense of the words. He waved and then left, shutting the door behind him.

Nyx was in need of a bath just as badly as I was, but didn't heal quite as quickly as I did. She had wasted no time in examining the steaming tub, the cloak that had been given to her discarded on the floor, but that was as far as she had gotten. She stood staring at the bandages, wincing as she tested her flexibility and found only pain awaiting as she tried to find the tucked end.

When I approached her a sigh fell from her lips; whether in relief or resignation I wasn't sure. I stood in front of her and lightly tapped her with a finger. She closed her eyes and obligingly lifted her arms so I could remove the wrapping on her torso. Doing my best not to let my touch linger against her skin, far too aware of how it sent heat through my core, I managed to get what she had been bandaged with off her. My gaze never fell lower than her shoulders but I couldn't help but take in the beauty that was her strange skin, which at once looked like flesh and stone. She sighed again when my hands slid down her arm to grip her elbow, though no sound of pain followed. She used her free arm to reach down and relieve herself of the undergarment which had thankfully been left intact. Once she'd stepped free of them I steadied her while she settled down into the hot water. When I tried to leave however, her hand caught my wrist, her grip causing my feet to pause.

"It's big enough for two...and the water will chill quickly."

Her voice was barely a whisper but there was something so desperate lying beneath the tones that I couldn't deny her. Plus, she wasn't wrong.

Against my better judgment or merely in a moment of indulgence, I removed my borrowed cloak and slid into the depths of the water. I couldn't deny myself the moan of pleasure as the hot water engulfed me, the closeness of our limbs barely noticeable against the bliss of heated water. My tight muscles started to relax until I eventually became aware of our touching limbs. My stomach grew taut but neither of us acknowledged it, each afraid to shift and make the other uncomfortable. The silence between us was usually comfortable, but the tension that had begun building was now thick enough to need cutting with an axe.

Finally I relented, my knees had begun to ache from my crunched up position and I had to stretch out. As I tried to shift my legs my skin, which had been stuck against the smooth tub, slid loose unexpectedly. My legs quickly followed suit sending my head beneath the water and my limbs flailing in the air beside Nyx. Rather ungracefully, I pulled myself back up only to hear a muffled giggle. Blinking back the water from my face as I got my ass back under me, I sputtered out bath water that had managed to get down my nose.

Glaring between coughs, I watched as Nyx's violet eyes tried not to meet mine. Failing to completely stifle her giggles she covered her mouth with her hand, the other keeping a solid grip on the tub. When violet finally met cerulean and she took my soggy glare in, she lost all control and peals of musical laughter rang clear in the empty cabin.

I wanted to be insulted but couldn't bring myself to grasp the emotion. I stared in awe at the gargoyle sitting before me, now holding her ribs because it hurt to laugh but she was unable to contain her humor. What else could I do? A giggle slipped from my lips and that only made her laughter come harder. The pain of tight muscles and hearty laughter caused tears to stream down our faces. The light mood only lasted for a moment before there was a shift and I realized her laughter had stopped but the tears still flowed as she turned her face away from me.

Hesitation held my body still even as my heart swelled and tried to reach out from its cage within my chest. It yearned to comfort and soothe her. Hatred for my own second guessing surged through my body. Hadn't I sorted this out?

Why was I still acting like it mattered whether or not my feelings were truly of this life or part of the ones I'd dreamt back into reality. Past and present were each a piece of the other, cause and reaction, an evolution of feelings was inevitably based upon the events of the past. Surely this was no different. The feelings were genuine, far deeper than anything I had known. Why run from them simply because they were mirrored from lives lived before?

The answer was quite simple; I was afraid. Afraid of the pain I'd heard and felt in those echoes of memory, both hers and my own. I was scared to pay the price of loving someone so fully, to give her a piece of my soul knowing it could be dropped and shattered like fresh baked clay. Shame filled me as I saw my own cowardice compared to her bravery. Through everything, had she not stayed true? Had she not pushed through the pain for the hope of 'someday'.

After a moment Nyx had calmed herself and when she finally raised her gaze my chest seized. The look in them told a story that had not changed once for her and it was the push I finally needed. Lifting my hands up to cup her face, I let the pads of my thumbs wipe away the tears. Her breath caught. If I continued, there was no taking it back without cruelty attached. No excuses, no impulsiveness. No, this had to be a lucid decision; a conscious choice.

Leaning forward I closed the gap between us and paused. I was poised so close a piece of dry skin from her lip grazed mine in a moment of questioning silence.

Permission granted.

My lips pressed against hers just as light as a feather and my chest seized, breathing paused by a jolt of excitement. Slowly our lips met again only this time a bit more confidently. I released the breath I had held, her own tickling my face as I breathed her in.

Was it mere minutes or hours? Losing myself in the curves of her lips and the taste of her tongue, time became an illusion I refused to give life to. Our motions were smooth, nothing awkward in even the soft grasp of a neck or arm. It was as if we had rehearsed it over and over. We parted long enough to breathe deep from the lungs of the other and then crashed back together, moans of pleasure becoming soft murmurs as we finally settled back.

In that moment we had stepped back into something we had always been, but it needed to be rediscovered slowly.

Kisses were more than enough for now. This was just the start of bridging a gap that had been narrowing since long before I had found her in the mountains.

I felt a yawn pull at my jaw and couldn't help letting it contort my face, turning my head just in time to avoid Nyx's finger trying to hook into my mouth. Laughing, I snapped at the offending digit as she retracted it, using her knees to keep me at bay.

"Perhaps it would be a good idea to actually get clean and then get some rest."

Nodding was all I could manage as I gazed into her eyes, filled to the brim with affection that spanned lifetimes. She smiled shyly, breaking the stare as she grabbed the bars of soap that had been laid out for our use. She handed me a sliver and we both averted our heads, pretending we weren't watching each other from the corners. By the time the water was soapy and my skin and hair smooth, exhaustion had begun to pull on my body, eyelids feeling heavy.

Rising up out of the cooling water a blush rushed over me as the gargoyle's gaze did not even attempt to divert this time. She gave a predatory grin and a wink when I shook my head and rolled my eyes, trying not to focus on the attention. Wrapping a drying cloth around my body I held the other out to her, trying not to get distracted by the nearness of her bare body as she stepped out. Leaning in she placed a soft kiss on my cheek before grasping the cloth and wrapping it around herself.

They had brought our saddlebags in ahead of us and we were finally able to put on fresh and clean linens. Since her wounds would ache longer than my own, I took the couch so that she could stretch out across the bed. She might have welcomed me alongside her in the bed, but it was all still too new. Too precious. I couldn't risk spooking myself with too much too quickly. The worry was perhaps for nothing though, as soon as my head hit the pillow, sleep stole me.

CHAPTER ELEVEN
I Want a Unicorn

The shadows swirled around my body, braiding into my tails and giving my form a haunting background against the bright blue full moon. I felt excited though I couldn't grasp the reason why. A shifting in the corner of my eye made me turn to face a broad figure as it emerged from the space between two large oak trees. I could feel the earth shifting between my paws as excitement made it hard for me to sit still. I'd finally done it. I had accomplished something grand, something important. The puzzle piece was there, I just didn't see it yet. The man smiled but his good nature did not flow into his eyes. Even so, I was hardly concerned. Afterall, I was done with all this, now Nyx and I would be free to live our lives. Perhaps that was where the excitement was brimming from, causing my paws to tap back and forth and my tails to sway impatiently. Whatever I had achieved would set us free.

"Well, that took less time than I had expected. You have done a great job, perhaps there is a way I can convince you to add on a few years, yes? After all, there must be more that you desire beyond the everlasting life of your lover."

I scoffed and shook my head.

"Not a chance, Hades. I've done my part. I've paid for Nyx's immortality and I'm ready to start our life together."

The man smiled cruelly as he walked toward me. I felt my hackles raise up and my lips pulled back from my teeth as the God in front of me chuckled. He was no close friend, but he was the only one who could do what I needed done.

"That's a shame...almost as much as what must happen now to fulfill it. Sorry kids, debts owed and all. Just know I'm rooting for you."

There was no time to react, his hand shot out and pierced my flesh like a hot blade. The wound did not bleed, the veins and arteries cauterized as the cut was made. The smell of magic was too strong to be my own. Something had gone awry. The pain barely registered as the hand that pierced my skin now pushed in and disappeared. Immediately I knew this wound would be fatal, the look in his eyes said it all. I hadn't known I'd have to leave her so soon. This wasn't how it was supposed to go. Something had changed, but I wouldn't live long enough to figure it out.

"Nyx." The words fell from my lips and her presence suddenly registered beside me, worry on her precious and young face, not a hint of gargoyle there yet. I had promised we'd face the world together, but she would have to wait and I didn't know how long.

"I'm here, don't worry." She spoke with a shaking voice. She had been so hesitant to agree and now it was too late to back out, but this was not at all the way we had planned.

"I love you darling." The words fell from my lips as shock numbed my body, my kitsune form melting away, leaving me naked and exposed.

Her smile was warm, but confused. She didn't understand yet.

"I love you Lykos. Forever and beyond, it'll be okay."

Hades twisted his hand and jerked, tearing back through my flash, his appendage sliding out from my chest holding a floating wisp that was a piece of my soul. Faster than any of us could react he shoved his hand into Nyx's chest, her gasp of surprise followed with a cry of pain. His hand reappeared empty.

"I'm sorry Nyx...I didn't know it would be like this."

Hades laughed and blew a blue dust at Nyx's chest, the scent was something I had never encountered in all my years, but he had said it would seal a piece of my soul to hers, preventing it from being kept in the underworld. The Camdean Vixen could not be caught, only chased.

"That's my cue. I won't lie and say this isn't a little bit satisfying, all things considered. Still, good luck in your next lives ladies. You're going to need it when he comes for you."

Nyx's eyes grew wide as things began to add up. Her eyes filled with tears and she screamed as the hole in my chest showed no signs of trying to heal.

"Lykos! No not yet! Please don't go!"

My heart broke to leave her, even knowing we would not be parted forever, not now. A piece of me was sealed to her soul, Hades had at least kept his word in regard to that, I could feel the faint throb of it. Would it be enough? I could not risk it.

"We will find each other my love. No matter where I am reborn, I swear to Nemesis, I will find you."

As I fell to my knees, blood finally began pouring down my chest and I barely caught myself on my arms, the puddle beneath me spreading quickly. My magic could not touch the wound. The bastard had used stronger magic to ward the wound from healing. Nyx's face pressed against my own, kisses and tears plastered on every piece of skin she could find, but I focused on my own blood.

"Nemesis. I swear it with blood, make it true. Guide me when my memory fails."

Collapsing to the earth, I listened as Nyx desperately murmured things I couldn't comprehend. The world was growing darker, but I wasn't ready to go. The cold of stone touched my face as Nyx sat over me, her tears flowing freely. A smile touched my lips as I recognized the pendant dangling from her throat.

"You wore it." I murmured. She replied but I couldn't hear her, though her hand grabbed the stone and cradled it as if it were the most precious thing in the world. The gift I had given her when we had taken vows the night she'd agreed to a piece of my soul. The shape of my kitsune form suspended in air, carved from the most gorgeous of flecked gems and warded against damage. The brilliant blues and purples had been melded together naturally, the light reflecting off its surface. The last of my energy faded away.

The last thing I saw was a shift in the shadows, a figure who had witnessed it all but dared not to step forward - perhaps had arrived too late. Tendrils of shadow drew forward as the world disappeared.

Jolting awake, I shivered as a cold sweat left my body damp. Nyx was gently shaking me, worry filling her face as she sat over me, much as she had in the dream. My name fell from her lips, a desperate plea to break me away from the nightmare that had pulled me under. Her voice soothed me, my heart calming even as my hand gripped my chest, the skin smooth beneath the shirt. As I sat up Nyx wrapped her arms around my shoulders, my heartbeat was calming but it still pounded out its beat in my ears. Sucking in a deep breath my lungs seemed to sigh in relief, my whole body shook with another hard shiver, but I was whole and safe.

Anger rose shortly after as the dream processed, a snarl crawling up from deep in my chest.

"Damn you Hades!" I cried out, the memory fresh and the pain tangible.

"What did you see?" Nyx's eyes had narrowed at the man's name, her own growl rising to her lips, its tone far more grating than my own, much like the rasp of a big cat.

"He killed me, he wasn't supposed to, but he did. Something about a debt owed? He took a piece of my soul and put it in you, but I wasn't supposed to die."

Nyx looked surprised for only a moment.

"You traveled back quite a while tonight."

"Tell me."

She gave me a sad smile, no joy reaching her eyes as she paused long enough to draw a deep breath. Tentatively I took the hand in her lap, pulling it to mine and holding it. She squeezed back, though I couldn't hold her gaze for long, the scream of heartbreak echoing in my mind as the dream memory settled.

"That was our first life together, the first time I lost you. Hades did indeed do as was agreed by the deal you had struck with him, and it obviously worked. He disappeared immediately afterwards, but my mother was there. She said she had feared Hades had been gotten to. She knew you would live, so she waited, not wishing for Hades to know that she had witnessed his betrayal."

"So that was Nemesis in the shadows."

"Yes, and rest assured I was so angry and heartbroken that I did not speak to her for a long time afterwards. I still don't believe that she could not have helped that night. Though, true to her word, since he did not know she had witnessed it, she was able to get more information. It was Ares who had called in the favor on behalf of Tereus, but we never knew why. That is the part they have been trying to figure out, but many of the Gods will not help for fear of Ares, especially with the depletion of followers causing their powers to diminish."

"Well, the assumption would be that he feared the Fates would reincarnate me to go after him."

"As we all thought and what came to be, but momma Medusa does not believe it is so simple. She has been searching, even in this lifetime, for the answers. My grandmother whispered to me while I was captive, passed out as it were. Medusa has found something, once she knows what it is she will reach out again."

The information was of little comfort, considering it had taken how many years to get a clue? Some game had been in play for quite a while and that I was some revolving piece in it was beyond frustrating. There was something missing, some key that I could not find in order to unlock the door with the answer behind it. If only my memories were not so random and scattered. I knew how to bake a bread I'd never even heard of in this lifetime, but couldn't grasp the threads that wove together to form the memory I'd relived.

"What did you do after I died?"

Nyx used her free hand to push her inky black locks behind her shoulders, cringing a bit as she answered.

"Well I wallowed in self-pity for a few months. I found Rhea and pleaded for your return, but you had already served your purpose in that lifetime, the Blood Feud had ended, so they would do nothing. Rhea was bound then to the wheel, so she was a bit less compassionate back then."

The trickling of information pulled at my memory, a bloody war had raged between brothers over a wife and I had been the turning point. Part of the deal with Hades had been for me to round up the souls I reaped and deliver them to the River Styx. The job was usually his wife's, whom he saw only six months of the year and wanted more time with. Easy enough gig for a Kitsune whose soul could not be lost by crossing the waters.

"What did you do then?"

Unconsciously I had begun to play with her fingers until they interlocked with my own. Something in the action was so innocent, yet it filled me with warmth and finally shook off the rest of the bad vibes clinging from the dream.

"I tried to live as you would want me to, but a few years passed and my ache never ceased. We had been together for forty years, though we looked no older than twenty. I couldn't stand it anymore. I went home to Momma."

"You became a gargoyle."

"Not immediately. Medusa is not one to give her power away to just anyone, even her own daughter. Eventually though, she did. Mother was furious, but when I slept I dreamt of you and found peace in waiting."

There was no way to fathom what that must have felt like, though having lost my mother I knew a taste. That it was only the first time in a series of lives and events made my heart ache for her and for the memories I could not yet grasp.

"How many times have you had to watch me die Nyx?"

The question spilled from my lips before I could think better of it. Surprise hit her only briefly before the sorrow overtook her features. Leaning against her as I was, I could feel her heartbeat jump as she bit her lip, taking a deep breath to steady herself. I regretted asking, but it was too late to take it back. Her words held the weight of all the memories she had of my deaths.

"Too many times."

Her eyes closed and I reached up with my free hand to caress her cheek, her head leaning in and kissing my palm.

"We have been trying to figure out how to attain your true immortality for well over a couple centuries, Lykos, and we have both lived far longer than that. To be honest though, what's worse is when I'm not there and I know you have died alone."

Her words struck me to the core, the amount of love and adoration pouring out from her in that moment filled me to the brim, my eyes watering as my heart threatened to explode from the sheer magnitude of feeling. There was an echo of pain within me, something I could not feel fully for the memory was not whole, but it hurt like an old wound refusing to disappear. The ache pulled at me, tried to tear me apart even as I whispered words I knew did not cover it all.

"I am so sorry Nyx.... I cannot even fathom everything I have put you through."

She made a soft shushing noise and drew my face up so that she could take my lips to hers. The velvety smooth surface ignited fire down to my core. I gasped, making her kiss me a little deeper before she broke apart just enough to hold my gaze, refusing to let it go so that I could see she meant every word that followed.

"Never regret bringing me with you. I told you I have chosen, and I will always choose to live these lives at your side. No matter how short some have been. I love you Lykos, now and forever. I know this is a heavy sentiment when you have only known me for a few months and only have pieces of your past lives, but it is no less true. One day there will be no death, no more goodbyes. We were so very close last time, perhaps Tereus will lead us to the final missing piece."

Her words were dispersed between softer pecks, each one preceded with a whisper of a pause, just long enough for me to pull away if I wished. Every bit of it filled me with a warmth I hadn't known since I was a child consumed by a mother's love. This was what it felt like to feel completely adored in every possible way. This woman had endured so much just to be with me, and stayed at my side even when I was covered in the blood of my enemies. I stared into her eyes and found my heart soaring to have heard the words that lingered in the air like tangible figures, musical notes dancing across the sky.

Our connection seemed like a tangled piece of string, a mess at first glance but no matter how crazy the path got, one end still led to the other. Until this moment, I felt I had lost or been born without something needed to love fully or successfully. Now it seemed I was not so loveless after all.

Tears streaked my face and exhaustion pulled at my body. The last few days had been a wild river ride of emotion. There hardly seemed to be enough hours in the night to try and process it all. Surely another attempt at sleep was the solution.

"Perhaps so. Though there is nothing to be done for now."

I couldn't bring myself to say anything more, afraid of the flood of emotion that might escape from my tongue. Instead I simply snuggled against her chest, letting her wrap her arms around me, her own eyes drooping with the need to sleep. I didn't know everything we had experienced together, but the pain of leaving her was still fresh, like an open wound festering as the dream clung to my mind. What must it be like for her to recall each and every loss? It was too much to fathom. We had to figure out the missing piece, immortality was the only answer to how I could keep from breaking her heart again.

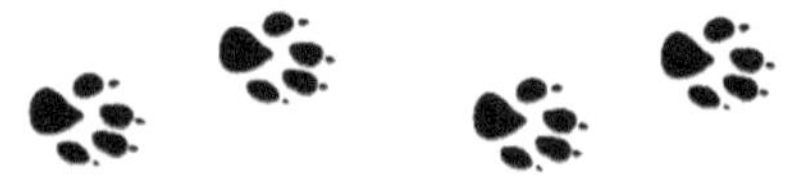

I awoke snuggled in Nyx's arms. She'd managed to slip behind me, her arms wrapped around me like a cage, keeping me from tumbling off the edge. Sometime in the night I had wiggled around so that I now faced her. Keeping my eyes closed I pulled in a deep breath, falling into the scent of cinnamon always around her. I couldn't figure out why that was what surrounded her. Was it the particular taste of her magic or the natural oils that mingled on her skin? Even as a child cinnamon had been my favorite. Perhaps, that was how ingrained she was in my subconscious.

With my face buried in her chest I slowly became aware of the heat running through my body as I grew more conscious of the rise and fall of her breast against my cheek. My arms were, thankfully, trapped between us or else I might have awoken to my hands betraying me. As it were, our positioning made it quite difficult to try and slip away without disturbing her. Just as I was about to execute a poorly thought out plan I felt the huff of her gentle laughter atop my head.

"I'm not asleep Lykos, if you want to get up go ahead."

With that she lifted her arm, smirking as I looked up at her. I was certain my face had turned scarlet, wondering in horror if she had noticed my mild arousal in the stiffening of my body. It sounded like the whole hut was resonating with the sound of my heart beating against my ribs, surely that would give me away. Jolting away like the spooked rabbit I was, I wrapped my cloak around my body and went out to relieve myself. Nyx was merciful and acted like she hadn't noticed anything, but I didn't miss the smirk on her lips when I returned.

I ignored her look and instead went straight to business. "We need to sort out our next step. That woman obviously knew who we were, so Tereus must have been the one shielding her identity. Perhaps he has jumped from the king to some other-.......FUCK."

Nyx's eyebrow raised in question as she moved from the couch to the table, grabbing an apple and cutting it into slices, half of which she set aside for me.

"Leola...The King's daughter. That has to be who that woman was, it's the only thing that makes sense. Though I still don't know what she wanted from me, she did say something about awakening the magic in her, but it's not like my magic works that way."

Sighing with frustration, I snatched up a slice as I paced. My body was still sore but the surge of magic my shifting caused made me more restless than anything.

"Huh. Well, Tereus has definitely been busy. That or she has seriously done her homework. Individually we are not capable of such, but it is a not so well known fact that when we reunite a ripple effect is caused and dormant magic is awakened. Rumor has it that we are the reason unicorns existed."

Her words were casual, as if it were no more interesting a fact than the weather or what was for breakfast. I on the other hand floundered and stuttered in step.

"We what?! Unicorns?! Are you serious?"

Everything else flooded out of my mind as the image of a unicorn hanging from Rhea's hut wall flashed across my mind. Nyx, ever amused at my bafflement, giggled and nodded.

"As I said, there is no proof the beasts would not have been born anyways, but as the Fates have it written, upon our reunion a burst of magic rippled across the continent and a herd of pregnant mares absorbed it. Fetuses are full of magical potential, and so their little bodies took in the magic and the first unicorns and Pegasus were born."

"Pegasus too!? Please tell me that we had some. Of all the things I don't remember this is very near the top of 'MUST REMEMBER'!"

My enthusiasm sent Nyx into a peal of laughter, but my seriousness beckoned an answer which she obliged with a quick response.

"Yes, of course we did. They were gifts from the owners of the herds who made quite a hefty profit raising the beasts. They were favored by the Gods and Goddesses and so very few mortals possessed them, making them a very significant symbol of power."

With my mind reeling at the idea I popped another slice of apple into my mouth, chewing slowly as I tried to dig the memories out, though to no avail.

Nyx, still affording a snicker or two at my expense, finished her own slices off and excused herself to the outhouse.

The morning passed slowly, my muscles twitching with the desire to move again, surged with energy now that my body had healed, but still itching with residual magic from shifting. Nyx, who seemed to have no qualms sitting still for long periods of time, finally shooed me off, my pacing pulling an annoyed growl from her lips.

"Seriously Lykos, I cannot handle the tapping of your feet on the floor any longer. I need another day to heal, but you do not. Go find something to occupy yourself with until the centaurs have news. I can't reach out to my mother with your constant pacing distracting me."

Snorting with abject offense, but withering beneath her hard gaze, I ducked my head and slipped out the door with coat in hand. Shrugging into the coat, though the weather was actually quite pleasant here, I debated where to go. The answer found me instead.

Onya was walking up the sloping path when we locked eyes, a smile on her lips as she waved with her good arm. Meeting her halfway I caught her in a sideways hug, the smell of horseflesh and hay potent but not unpleasant.

"Were you looking for me Onya?" The question brought a smile to her face.

"No, I just felt like walking all the way up here to have to turn around and go back."

Rolling my eyes I bumped into her hip, causing her to stumble sideways, a light laugh echoing into the morning.

"Come down to the stables with me, Prince has been anxious to check up on you and I'd like to hear what happened on your end while I was dealing with the chaos on my side."

The prospect of the stables was exactly what I needed along with Onya's company. I readily agreed.

"I'll tell you everything, but have you seen Serah and Xalia? Are they okay?"

Her smile wavered for a moment, though she nodded reassurance.

"They are both fine, though Xalia is going to be down for a bit. She took an arrow to the shoulder and chest, then got a slice to the thigh. Nothing vital was hit, but the muscles aren't going to heal quickly."

Guilt trickled through me, having not cared enough in the moment to even see that her wounds were so grave.

"Though, to be fair, she will recover much more quickly than most since Serah finally tapped into her healing gift. Took a lot of energy out of her, but they are both doing well."

"Well, at least some good came out of her getting her ass handed to her."

"Don't let her hear you say that. Her pride has taken a bit of a hit. To be honest, she is the only reason we even got out of that pinch with as few wounds as we did."

"What happened to your arm?"

"Damn panicked stallions. One caught an arrow in its shoulder and reared up thrashing like a fool and caught me. Clean break, so no worries."

As we walked I filled her in on all that had happened on my end, most of which the other Amazons had told her. The only new information I gave was what had happened when I found out Nyx had traded herself. It was something I had purposely avoided discussing with the gargoyle herself, though I knew the conversation needed to occur eventually.

"Whoa! So you like, seriously do like her huh?"

We had stopped just outside of one of the barns so that we would not be interrupted with greetings. The sun shone brightly overhead, the warmth of it spreading across my exposed skin, my coat pushed back so that I could soak it in. With my eyes closed I had cast my face skyward, only looking back to her when she poked my side.

"Yes, yes, I suppose there is no denying it. The thought of her being in danger just overrode every other sense inside me. I've been struggling with whether my feelings were genuine or just the magic between us. At that moment though, it didn't matter. All that mattered was her."

Onya's face softened, understanding etched into the furrows as she nodded.

"That is love my dear Lykos. When it comes down to it, in those moments, all the issues we cause with overthinking and worrying about what others might think, fades away and shows us the undeniable truth. Don't forget that feeling, it will guide you when your mind and heart don't agree."

I was a creature who had been reborn countless times, and yet I felt like a child. I smiled because it was all I could do. She was right, even though I was terrified to admit it. The truth was set out clear as day, my feelings just as raw and exposed as a flesh wound. I had lived my entire life chasing something I didn't know the name of, then when I found it and she had a name, I was too scared to grasp it only because I let my mind complicate it.

"When did you get so relationship savvy?"

"I've always been, people just don't ask me because I keep my love life private."

Taking the opportunity to turn to a lighter subject, if only for a moment, I bumped her again and smirked.

"That pretty Centaur?"

Her blush gave her away and so I made a huge dramatic gesture to tease her.

"Oh what shall we ever do!? Think of all the Amazon hearts that would be crushed to know that Onya is not only off the market, but she has scored a woman five times more attractive than she!?"

Onya smacked my arm with false indignation, then shoved me sideways so that I almost fell into a pile of muck. Laughing she put her head to the sky, nose held high.

"Don't be bitter and jealous. We all know you will pine for the loss that is this ass."

She emphasized her words with a heavy overdramatized sway of her hips, round buttocks bouncing beneath her deerskin leg wraps. Playfully I pushed her with my foot, though only hard enough to make her step stutter, since she only had one arm to catch herself with.

"Almost as much as that strong sense of humility."

She rolled her eyes and grinned as we continued on. Prince's voice rose alongside a long whinny as we finally made it to stable.

You two move like cows. Slow and loud.

Onya's furrowed brows and scowl confirmed she did in fact hear his words as well. She'd done a great job hiding it, but I'd suspected as much.

"Here I was thinking you couldn't hear him."

"Can't give away all my secrets now can I?"

She gestured to him with a turn of her head, our time together letting me know exactly what she had in mind. The beast was full of himself as per usual, might as well have some fun with it.

"Cows huh?" Onya's words sounded indignant.

"Says the horse who looks like one. Why don't you show us what speed looks like then?" I retorted with a snicker.

He gave an insulted huff and whipped his tail around to slap me as I slipped through the fence. Ducking the appendage, I quickly leapt to his back before he could say anything more. Onya laughed as he shook his head, a foreleg pawing the air before he pivoted.

Careful what you ask for pup!

Rising to the occasion, he darted out of his open paddock and gave a few bumps and kicks. The momentum sent me forward onto his neck before he evened out his stride. I laughed with him, feeling joy despite the craziness of our circumstances. Onya's hoots only encouraged the powerful beast beneath me as he slid into the far corner, sat back, pivoted and bolted forward once more.

At least for that moment I could just enjoy being alive and free with the fresh air in my face, wavy locks tangling in a banner behind me. There was very little that compared to his smooth gait. I could feel his muscles bunching beneath me as I let my body roll in rhythm to his own. The feeling of it all was the closest thing to flying I had ever experienced.

The comparison brought a flood of sensations as a memory flashed through my mind like a jolt. Sometime in my second life with Nyx.

"You can't be serious! Lykos I can't!"

Nyx's face seemed so young, her wild violet eyes the size of saucers as she looked out over the edge of the small cliff we stood upon. I could feel her innocence as well as I could smell her fear.

"Of course you can Nyx! You've got wings and have had them for a lifetime without learning to fly! You need to learn to use them!"

"Says the fox! I'd happily trade my wings for your tails Lykos! You know I'm afraid of heights!"

She visibly shook, her large leathery wings hanging behind her as she wrapped her arms around herself much in the manner of a youth, though she looked like an adult. I reached out and placed a hand against her cheek, the skin there cool from the spring breeze.

"You can do this, I believe in you."

I looked deep into her eyes and willed every bit of courage I had to her and could see her smile start as she took a deep breath. Taking her into my arms, a sigh escaped my lips as I breathed in her scent; always, always the same sweet smell.

"Fine but if I crash you're coming with me to soften the landing!"

Her words were tinged with humor and she had a devilish glint in her eye that almost masked the fear there. She slipped around behind me and before I could even react she grabbed me tight and fell backwards off the cliff - taking me with her.

A yelp that turned into a scream of surprise and fear fell from my lips. As we twisted she snapped open her wings and I found myself gliding over the valley, screaming cut off with pure awe.

The first few minutes were rough and more than once I felt us lurch forward and became a little nauseous, but once she had the hang of it I found myself grinning from ear to ear, hooting and hollering with amazement as the world passed below. She still shook, I could feel it in her arms, but the smile that met me when I looked up at her was filled with such love that I knew she would not falter, at least not while we were airborne.

The landing was more of a crash, though she curled herself around me to soften the impact. We hit the ground in a roll and when our momentum dispersed we lay splayed out beneath the sunshine giggling like children. When we finally stopped, our hands searched out the other's and entwined.

"I couldn't have done this without you."

"Well of course not, I'm the one with wings."

"You know what I mean." I scoffed, tossing a handful of grass at her before murmuring "I love you Nyx."

Nyx turned to look at me, a smile on her lips as she nodded and whispered the words back. It wasn't a secret between us, yet when she spoke the words, no matter how often, I felt my heart swell to the brim. This is what would keep me going, I knew it then with such fierce certainty that all other thoughts disappeared and as the images slipped away I was left with more than just a memory of the feeling.

Once we had taken a full turn around his field, Prince very politely reared straight up, my legs unable to find a grip so that I slid right down his back and off his rump, which I smacked with just enough force to make a noise. He tossed his head with laughter as I crawled back out of his fence.

Don't be mad cause I'm faster than you.

"Keep eating all that extra feed and you won't be. Your hips have gotten so full I couldn't even grip them to stay on."

Onya laughed while Prince turned his rump to us and trotted off, tail flagging as he pranced, just as light footed as ever.

"Alright let's go find Serah and see if there has been any news. We sent out runners to check our information chain, they should have gotten back by now."

With that we left the empty barn, its horses all turned out so that there would be less work. The afternoon brought no news, but catching up on all that happened helped us to process it a bit more.

When I finally returned to the cottage with supper for Nyx and I, the moon was fully visible in the night sky and the weight on my shoulders seemed a little lighter.

We sat at the table to eat the freshly cooked rabbits I'd procured from one of Onya's friends. The meat was well seasoned and a nice change from the dried stuff we had eaten on the trails. Once it had been cleared Nyx broke the silence.

Her smile was enough to tell me she had spoken with her grandmother rather than her mother. There was a lot of history there I was not savvy to and perhaps I never had been, but her namesake seemed the favored family member. Though as she spoke the margin of error increased, for perhaps it was her second mother who held her fondness more. Either way, Nyx's day of meditation proved to be far more productive than my own.

"Momma found it! Her snakes discovered the cage Tereus had been imprisoned in. The harpies had stood guard over it for ages, but since they were all killed, it allowed the mortals to find it. It was the cage and tether that kept Tereus' soul bound to the hawk, but once released he was free to latch onto something -someone else."

"Suppose Ares probably had something to do with that."

"Most definitely. Along with the empty cage, her snakes found one of the ancient scrolls with the Fate's prophecies on it. That alone would not be interesting, their words were written down and passed along so many times that often the messages were completely wrong. What *was* interesting was the letter that had been left behind, from Ares to Tereus."

"What's interesting about that? Surely that is no surprise to anyone."

"No it is not, but what he wrote to Tereus is. Ares did not want his son to die, but he did not want him to become a true immortal and steal his place either. Which he would have done. Many worshippers favored Tereus over Ares, who never joined his men on the ground. Ares does not like competition, ironically."

"What does that have to do with us?"

"Ares told him that the Camdean Vixen is the only thing that has ever been created that could not be caught, so to become truly immortal he must steal the soul of the creature born of it. Chasing after you has kept Tereus at bay for hundreds of years. It took him off the battlefields and put Ares back in favor. The father essentially sent his child on a wild goose chase so he couldn't steal his throne."

"That's all well and good, but how is this good news Nyx? How is this life any different from the previous ones? If he has been trying to kill me and probably succeeded a few times before, what's different?"

"This time he has a plan but it isn't going to work, the prophecy he was given was never intended for him. It doesn't make him less dangerous, but it certainly makes his schemes far less worrisome knowing ultimately he will fail in his goal. We just have to find and kill him, permanently."

"Why does everything you say sound so simple and easy, and every word out my own mouth makes the world seem like it is about to implode?"

She smirked. "Perhaps I'm simply better with my tongue?"

Surprise made me stutter as my face went red, her laughter worth the embarrassment, despite my mortification. When did I become so shy?

"Anyways, I've spoken to the centaurs, they received word back from their spies within the castle. The King and his daughter have been spotted going to and from the nearby caverns. They have supplied a map but could do no more as the spy may have been compromised, so he has returned home. Now we need only go and confront the problem at hand. The Amazons will be given aid to secure their path home, just in case the 'soldiers' are still around. Though I doubt there were many left alive by the time the centaurs got there."

She gave me a smile that held more confidence than I felt, but I could not argue that the whirlwind of my teeth and claws had brutalized their numbers. What was one man with a bit of magic? Surely he would pose no great threat, why else had he not simply come for me outright? Hadn't he played the puppet master rather than face me head on when I had been imprisoned? What kept him hiding away? Was it fear or this so-called 'prophecy' that he was going off of?

The ridiculousness of it all was enough to make my head ache with the effort to sort it out. What else was there to do? Sit around and endanger more people through waiting?

Certainly not.

So it was settled that we would simply cut the head off the snake. Without the puppeteer surely the rest would fall apart. We would be heading to an alcove just outside the castle's walls. What was marked as a destroyed temple on the map the Centaurs provided. The caverns seemed to connect there creating a large area that might have been used for gatherings once upon a time. The terrain would be rocky, so as the night progressed and we discussed our plan, it was settled that we would leave the horses behind.

"I would rather not risk Prince or any others, especially if we are walking into a trap." I said as I tapped my fingers on the table.

"Agreed. Besides, you have notoriously claimed to be faster than any beast of burden."

I shook my head with a grin. "Perhaps not with a stone maiden astride."

"Hey! I'm not that heavy!" She tossed one of the shirts that we had recycled into bandages at me.

As the night deepened and we finished packing our bags, Nyx settled into the bed.

"Best take advantage of the comforts of a bed and bath. Seems it'll be a while before we get the luxury again."

The bath was easy, cleaning the dust and dirt away with a strip of cloth and the soapy water from Nyx's bathing. The hard part was approaching the bed with her scantily clad body warming the blankets. She lifted the blanket, her arms open to me if I so chose. Casting a glance to the couch which had made my body stiff, there was no real choice but to indulge my own desires.

I was still unsure of my footing around her, but when I let her draw me down against her there was nothing but warmth and comfort. Resting my head against her breast the slow beat of her heart thrummed in my ear, a sigh of contentment escaping her as I nuzzled in even closer. Her familiar scent filled my nose, a hint of something else along with soap stirring my senses in a way that caused my entire body to respond. Looking up into those violet eyes, the smile on her lips did not quite meet her eyes and somehow I knew my own looked the same.

We had almost lost each other after only just finding the ground we stood upon once more and the danger would be no less in the coming days. My heart skipped a beat, chest tightening with a wave of fear I refused to let drown me. There was so much love between us, crossing the years. I could not ignore it. I couldn't brush this next step in our journey off as just another day wandering in the woods. I didn't want to lose her, I couldn't, not now- not again.

The sentiment was the same, reflected in her watery gaze. As much as we both wanted to play tough, there was something far more powerful in being vulnerable. We might not get another chance. Although I hoped my actions had spoken my feelings just as efficiently, I let my lips utter the words my heart had been dying to echo back to her.

"I love you Nyx." My pulse skyrocketed, anxiety spiking now that I could not take the words back. There I lay, feeling as silly and nervous as a teenager waiting for their crush to say they liked them back, with a woman who had left no room to doubt her feelings.

"My sweet Vixen, I love you more than words will ever convey."

She smiled sweetly, her words something between a whisper and giggle.

The words drew us together and what started out as the most gentle of kisses deepened, tears falling down the gargoyle's cheeks as she repeated those three precious words against my lips. My heart swelled to hear them, relief and exhilaration causing my body to shake.

Lips never parting, we breathed the other in. Her arms pressed me close until the rhythm of our lips began to spread and a gasp fell from her as my leg slipped between her own, caressing her core. The sound brought back memories of wild nights and long mornings, in sensation more than vivid images, subconsciously I knew her body.

The exploration was slow starting, my touch just as shy as she was patient, though the look in her eyes showed a hunger I longed to satisfy. Bolstered by the soft sounds of her desire and the response of her body to my own, I became more bold.

As my body arched up and then rolled back down I let my kisses move from her lips to her neck, the slightly salty taste tingling along my sensitive tongue. I was desperate to convey all I had kept bottled up. Her moans became louder, encouraging me as I kissed my way to her bare shoulders, soft nips replacing the tender kisses as she began to buck up against my thigh.

The fire had been raging for so long that it did not take long for her to explode. When the friction became too much she cried out, her body crashing against mine with fervor as she rode the wave of her climax. My lips captured hers once again. swallowing her moans and feeding my soul with her pleasured cries. I slowed my movements, but didn't cease them.

My own desires were pushed down, desperate to show my newfound devotion in every way possible. Sliding my hand down the length of her torso, agile fingers easily slid beneath the band of the shorts she slept in. A moan of pleasure escaped us both when my fingers met slick moisture in the folds of her lips.

Before I could continue with a second round of pleasure, Nyx got a different idea. Her pupils had gotten wide and I couldn't help but yelp in surprise when she suddenly snatched me up and flipped me over. Constantly forgetting her own strength exceeded my own, my jaw hung open with awe as I stared up at her beautiful face. I gasped as she pinned my hands above my head, my once innocent lover hovering above me with hunger and love in her eyes. She smirked as I gave a playful growl, my body arching up beneath her, not quite close enough to get contact.

She teased me with soft kisses, tasting my lips with tender nips and swipes of her tongue. She pulled just out of reach so that I could not be completely satisfied by the contact. It didn't take long for a whine to replace my growl, my lips pouting out to solidify my need. With a look that clearly showed she was satisfied with my submission, she slowly lowered herself between my legs. The whole of her body pressed against my own, allowing pressure in all the places I needed it.

"By the Goddess I have missed you."

She whispered the words into my ear, her heart pouring out into every syllable. Our movements were far from silent, our desperate pleas structureless sounds as we tried to express what words could not convey.

I moaned softly as she kissed the pulse points of my neck, a memory of a previous life's pleasure making a chill run along my spine in anticipation. She paused, her hand slipping along my body as she caught my lips for a kiss that lingered then moved to the other side of my neck. As her fingers slid against my clit I arched up, her palm applying steady pressure just as her teeth grazed my neck.

The moment she curled her fingers inside, she bit me, though it did not pierce the skin. The hot rush that flooded my body with pleasure overloaded my senses. My vision shifted to red then back to a vibrant color scheme that seemed way too bright for how late in the night it was. Time slowed and I couldn't tell if it had been mere seconds or minutes or hours. My body moved of its own accord as I was filled to the brim. Then, like a dam without repair, I burst over.

I might have screamed or merely cried silently into the night. My mind blacked out until the shudders of pleasure subsided and her lips met mine, the taste of her tongue heavy with an essence of magic that made me think of earth and fallen leaves. Pheromones scented the air, a heavy perfume of desire that could have easily pulled us into another romp had this moment not been so special and important.

This bond, this love between us, it had to be approached with care. Anything too zealous and it might be scared away for fear of capture. This wild thing needed to know it was not bound, nor restricted by its own existence.

If I had been honest, I'd have said it was just my own fear, but there was no need to explain myself. Nyx was perfectly content with whatever I was comfortable giving. Though surely, it must have been hard to be so patient when she knew every moment of love that had existed between us. There was no end to the gratitude I felt for her steady presence, though I didn't let the words slip from my lips. I was too afraid of breaking the spell that had pulled us under.

Nyx pulled me back into her arms, our panting breaths seemed to take forever to slow. With soft murmurs of love we collapsed into each other. Sleep overtook my exhausted mind and body, but it was with a smile and filled with happiness that I let the dreams pull me under.

When morning came I found myself curled into a tight ball, the edge of the blanket that had been wrapped around me tickling my face until I slapped myself awake. The jolt made me lurch and growl, laughter echoing out from a short distance away.

"Some things never change." Nyx's voice was melodious and filled with humor and contentment. I blinked bleary eyed until she came into focus and I could see the love beaming down at me from her soft smile.

"Others just get better with time." I responded.

She grinned, the recognition in her eyes making me smile. Every night more memories came back and thankfully the latest bunch had been only pleasant things.

"Hard to find wine older than I am." She said it with a smirk and I couldn't bring myself to argue that I was just as old. Afterall, she had never left this plane, whereas I went wherever a soul like mine went while it waited. Limbo didn't quite seem accurate.

I stretched and found myself a bit of breakfast before we gathered our gear and set off to get water and say our farewells. As much as I would have loved to spend more time amongst the centaur's village, I was ready to finish this madness. There would be time to enjoy life's small treasures once Tereus was dealt with.

There was an awkwardness between us, as if she were waiting to see if I had truly bridged the gap of my own insecurities. Knowing that it would be cruel to keep her wondering, though a streak of mischief had me tempted to play coy, I slid my hand into hers as we walked down the short path to the well. Our time together could be short, who knew what we were walking into, I did not want to waste whatever time we had second guessing myself anymore.

She smiled at me as she awkwardly filled her water bladder with one hand, eventually succeeding in doing so as I watched her struggle.

"Stubborn." I muttered when she refused to ask for my help.

"Skilled." She replied as she corked the top with one hand.

Our farewells had to be quick, winter would not hold off for anyone and the Amazons were also preparing to leave. The worst of the wounded had been seen to well enough to make it back to Gwen's skilled hands. The able bodied were rested and the centaurs would see to it they got to the borders without harassment, which made all the difference. The backup Camilla had sent for would be waiting at the river to help with the crossing, relieving the centaurs of their guard duty.

Serah shook her head at my worried look.

"Don't fret Lykos. I am just not used to magic like you. I'm afraid I may have over exerted myself making sure Xalia didn't die on me."

Xalia was up, but barely moving, she'd be traveling back in a small cart pulled by one of the centaurs who would be accompanying them home. I smirked to myself, betting I knew which centaur that would be.

"Just remember to take care of yourself too, Serah. Rest is the best cure for magic exhaustion." She gave me a long hug before returning to Xalia, who offered the slightest of nods.

Sure as anything, Onya's eyes were bright and her smile too big to resist, even on the precipice of danger. She wrapped me in a tight hug, the female centaur I had witnessed her riding just days ago allowing herself to be strapped in for the journey. Onya's gaze followed my own and she shook her head.

"Not one smart ass comment from you Lykos! Just make sure you and your gargoyle get your asses back home in one piece alright? Then we can carry on giving each other shit about our impeccable taste in women, yea?"

Laughing, I gave her an extra squeeze.

"Don't you worry, I would never miss the chance to bond with someone over how much of a pain in the ass you are."

She slapped my arm and smiled, taking me at my word and heading back over to help with the straps to the cart. The centaur woman waved, but just when I might have asked what her name was, since Onya had conveniently not mentioned it, I thought better of it. Let it be one more thing that carried me through the next few days and brought me home to the Amazon lands in one piece.

Nyx's hand caressed my shoulder, a silent sign that we needed to go. The centaurs did not bother to stop their day, the world's battles had come and gone and they remained. The everyday responsibilities could not be neglected if life were to continue. It was understandable and I envied them for the option. How different life might have been if I could have disappeared into the monotony of a normal life.

Different, but also dreadfully empty.

Once we had walked to the edge of the fields Nyx took our bags and tied them together so that they stayed attached but also created one large loop with an extra strip of leather. The distance would be too great to take on foot, so I would be taking us.

Letting the magic spill out from my soul, the change took over. The pain was blinding for a moment, but slipped away just as quickly. The snapping and readjustment of bones caused Nyx to wince, too fast to be followed by any less keen eyes. Fur sprouted from my skin as my nails became claws, tail splitting into smaller appendages and ears shifting to the top of my head while growing pointed. The shimmer of magic fell away as shadowy wisps climbed up my legs, staining the golden-red black as it melded with my fur. Snorting out the heady taste of magic I lowered my long snout to scoop up the bags, shaking my body so that they shimmied down my neck to lay across my shoulders.

Nyx wasted no time climbing up my back and settling herself just behind my withers. The feel of her hands against my skin as she luxuriated in the softness of my coat sent a shiver down my spine that turned into an itch. Feeling my skin twitch she gave a scratch that made me want to tap the earth with satisfaction. I resisted for dignity's sake. Once she finished scratching she used the bags to help hold herself in place as I took off, the pressure of her legs only mildly uncomfortable.

As we traveled we only paused long enough for me to take a quick nap and hunt down a meal. We had packed as little as possible, leaving out food for the sake of weight. When I rested I remained in my Kitsune form, Nemesis' magic coiling around us to keep our presence hidden from the outside world.

We arrived at the location circled on the map a few days later, purposely timing it so that we would slip in after sunset, watching for signs of a trap from afar. When a familiar face finally showed up, I was overwhelmed with conflicting emotions.

Leola.

I had no proof that this was the same woman from the fight, but who else would have known? I had not had the time to truly contemplate all that had happened within the King's castle. Or rather, I had the time but simply chose not to. Yet there stood the woman who had claimed to want me to love her in a way that wasn't possible and beside me was the reason.

There was more underlying the situation but it did make me wonder.

Would spite have truly pushed Leola over the edge? Or had she been playing me from the start? Was the blood of all those innocents also on my hands? Had I selfishly set the course for destruction unknowingly? Had I been too oblivious or selfish to notice I was leading a woman into heartbreak, as it had seemed then? Surely the crazed look in her eyes had been a hunger for power, not desire.

"Are you okay?"

Nyx's concern was soft, but her quirked brow held something I could not quite decipher. I had refused to speak of my capture, preferring not to revisit the lowest time of my life.

I simply nodded and tried to swallow my guilt. The past was not going to be changed and the future may not even occur. I could not afford to get distracted. We had no idea what Tereus was capable of no matter how many nights we had spent trying to guess.

"That's Leola, the King's daughter."

The lithe young woman approached the mouth of the temple, her eyes casting about cautiously. Her green gaze was distinguishable, even at a distance, against her pale blonde locks and porcelain skin. She drew something away that had been tucked behind a large piece of rubble. Something shiny, though I could not quite make out what. She peered back around and then disappeared inside the temple's archway.

"Guess that's our cue to go see what she's got up her sleeves."

Nyx's nonchalance unnerved me, her tone seemingly uncaring. Surely I was imagining it, but anxiety was a very good liar.

I grabbed her hand before she could move past me. She turned back and smiled as I reached up to kiss her. A soft purring hum rose from her chest as we lingered in the kiss, her tongue tasting my lips before her hands slipped around to pull me in harder. I gasped when she finally pulled back.

With a grin I nipped her lip and nodded, the reassurance in it exactly what I had silently been asking for.

"Alright, I'm ready."

I smirked as Nyx's chest practically puffed out, her head held a little higher. She knew me better than I knew myself, but the reassurance of it seemed to benefit her as well.

We approached where the hidden object had been, the alcove too small to have held much. Without anything really to go on there, we slipped into the temple, steps muffled by sand which had been blowing in for centuries. The temple had been carved into the mountain, but there were several parts which had collapsed in on itself. This at least narrowed our choices since we could not see very far ahead for the numerous turns and bends.

The deep shadows did nothing to heed our vision, but the footing grew more dangerous as the path became littered with rubble. The pathways were not wide, just big enough for two people, allowing a flow in and out but nothing that might invite trouble. The earth moved underfoot, despite appearing solid, and every sound either echoed up to the tall ceiling or died abruptly when it hit a dead end. Somewhere there was a trickle of water, but it was hard to source.

A strange but almost familiar scent carried on the air, but I could not pinpoint it.

"Do you smell that?" I asked as I lifted my head towards the sky, trying to remember.

"All I smell is dust and wet dog." She offered me a toothy smirk with the latter of the statement. I merely rolled my eyes. I didn't smell *that* bad wet.

When the path finally split into two viable options, we did as well. Nyx pointed left toward a spot in the hallway where moisture had allowed a footprint to preserve, then tossed her head off to the right. I went after Leola hoping that my gargoyle would not find any surprises down the other corridor.

As I traversed the narrow pathway there was no sound beyond the soft howling whisper of the wind trying to find its way. The sound of trickling water cut off as I rounded a curve towards a faint light. Pepper flakes were sprinkled across the sand, the scent like sharp needles to my nose. Someone was definitely feeling spiteful.

Despite that, I was able to catch the scent of the young woman who awaited in the room ahead. Careful to tap my feet down as I entered, so as not to startle her, I walked into the next cavern. Surprise filtered across Leola's face when she spotted me, but something about it felt false. The gasp sounded practiced and that crazed glint was once again in her eyes. She was waiting on the other side of the chamber, a jeweled knife held at the ready. If she wasn't expecting me, the cruel smile that curled her lips showed she was not disappointed.

The room we stood in was obviously a place for sacrifices. The divots in the ground were designed so that spilled blood was channeled into a bowl-sized impression under an altar. That knowledge was not at all reassuring as she kept her stance, recognition doing nothing to ease her guard. I held up my hands, my words somehow managing not to echo in the large chamber though they sounded loud to my own ears.

"It's just me Leola, I'm not going to hurt you."

She laughed and nodded, her smile bright and so misplaced against her otherwise dark expression. What on earth had she been through in the months since I had left? I would probably never know and now was certainly not the time to contemplate it. They often said magic would corrupt a soul that was not born to wield it. Perhaps this was the truth after all.

"Oh Lykos, I wish I could say the same."

Her words finished just as a high pitched ringing suddenly hit my ears. A snarl of pain ripped from my lips just as a scream joined the ringing in the distance. My heart leapt into my throat. Nyx was in trouble.

Pivoting hard on the balls of my feet I darted back towards the path I'd just walked, only to be slammed backwards. A hot wall of air preceded the explosion of rubble that spewed forth as the hallway collapsed on itself. A large chunk flew at me, the impact splitting the skin of my forehead and sending me backwards into the hard ground.

The world spun.

The air around me became clouded with dirt and rock particles, the smell of fire heavy. In that moment it came to me; the familiar scent. It was black powder, used to cut through rock and bring even the grandest of towers crashing to the earth.

Leola's footsteps barely registered, though her figure looming above me was clear enough - even with spotted vision.

"It didn't have to be this way, you know. If you hadn't been so selfish, this all might have turned out different. All you had to do was share your magic with me. Instead, here we are."

She scoffed. "Maybe Tereus will let me keep your pelt for my floor."

Leola's voice carried through the dust and debris but the ringing in my ears overwhelmed me. I couldn't tell if she was still talking to me or someone else. Her words continued as her hands touched my face, but I couldn't tell what she was doing as my vision doubled. I tried to make sense of it all but coughs suddenly took me and caused my head to spin further.

Darkness slipped away, the light making my head pound as my eyes blinked open. Pain throbbed through my body, reminding me of where I was and what had just happened. A jolt of fear shook me to the core, my hazy mind clearing rapidly. How much time had passed? Where was Nyx? Was she okay?

I carefully tried to rise but was met with pressure at my hands and wrists. The jingle of metal drew my eyes to the source, a growl of annoyance following. Metal cuffs rubbed my skin, the loops on their sides attached to chains that were anchored to the middle of the floor. Had they been there before? It didn't matter. Once again I was caught like a rabbit in a cage.

You were too careless!

Scolding myself would do no good, but it helped clear the fog in my mind enough to register a voice from above.

"Lykos..."

Relief flooded me, though it lasted only long enough for me to look around the room and not find the source. Listening for her voice to come again, the only other sound in the room hit me. A soft dripping, steady and distinct.

Like that blasted water.

Fear swept me up and cradled me close as I looked up and felt my insides fall out of place, twisting hard. My gasp filled the room and I cried out with unintelligible words as I lunged against the chains holding me to the ground. The pain that threaded into my flesh as the metal cut into me, and the pressure that threatened to pull my arms out of socket, was nothing compared to seeing my love hanging from the ceiling.

She was bruised and had lacerations that oozed. Undoubtedly the explosion had subdued her long enough for them to get their hands on her. The worst of it was revealed when she tried to raise her arm towards me. The motion turned her just enough for me to see the whole picture.

The anguish on her face broke my heart more than her bloody backside. She spoke through the pain, her words painting a gruesome scene in my mind.

"They took my wings...."

A pulley system had been set up and hooks had been lodged into her back where her wings had once protruded. It was from those wounds that blood freely flowed down her legs and to the earth below. The crimson liquid collected in a sacrificial bowl as it trickled between the raised edges in the ground.

There was no easy way to take a gargoyle's wings. Only magic could do it. Old magic and an ancient knife with a jeweled handle that only Hades would have known the location of.

What had we walked into? Whose chess pieces had we been this whole time? Was Hades' debt so deep that he had surrendered that information to Ares as well, or had the son of the God of War simply gotten lucky?

Sure, they would grow back, they could be recovered, but the message was quite clear and intimate. Tereus knew exactly who and what we were and the weaknesses that went along with that. Cupping my hand so that blood trickled into it from the slice I'd received from the cuffs, I whispered a prayer to Nemesis.

"Nemesis guide us, we may be in over our heads."

A whisper of a reply echoed softly in my mind.

"What is eternal life
But a double-sided Knife
A deal struck with blood started this
Only undone by clever artifice
One strike through two souls bound
Simultaneous death must then be found
Death cannot capture what can never be caught
With the uncatchable caged shall endless life be bought
With the Catalyst's demise
An immortal will arise."

The poem meant nothing to me, but Nyx must have heard her mother's words as well, for she mumbled out words that made more sense.

"The prophecy."

What good that did us was beyond me. The Fates were notorious for speaking in riddles. Their words were often too misconstrued to ever be reliably transferred to the people the prophecies belonged to. Besides, it was likely a complete fake planted by Aries to keep his son hunting me for eternity.

Frustration and anger filled my core, muscles flexing against my bindings. I could feel the fox boiling with rage beneath my skin, my vision flickering between fox-sight as my body tried to shift. My control was steadily wavering, but I knew that this was what he wanted. He had to be here somewhere, just waiting.

Where are you, you bastard?

The question was answered moments later when great peals of laughter broke loose. They were maniacal in nature, seeming to be everywhere at once. The dark glee twisted into savage cackling that reverberated off the walls, creating a horrid cacophony of sound.

A snarl fell from my lips, the sound vibrating my rib cage, the notes savage in a way that a normal fox could not produce. From above I heard a hiss coming from Nyx. As my magic gathered and built up within my body I could feel her own magic stirring in response.

The piece of my soul vibrated at a different frequency within her own, calling out a response to the echoes of its original owner. She could feel the pulse of my magic, the pull having always been mutual. A look of resolve shifted her features as I locked eyes with her. I watched as she pushed the pain aside, clenching her jaw and giving the slightest of nods. We were not out for the count just yet.

"Only cowards hide in the shadows playing puppeteer. Why don't you show your face Tereus."

His laughter continued as the sickly sound of his voice became more uniform and from across the room his form appeared out of thin air, magic shimmering around him. At first I saw the Mad King's face, but it was slowly being consumed, the magic seeping in through the pores, changing him. The man within had undoubtedly been gone for months, the possession of his body complete in this moment. There was nothing left of the Mad King as Tereus walked forward in what was once his body.

His eyes were wide, or perhaps just seemed so since he had no eyebrows. His facial features were shallow and hallowed out, his nose long and hooked like the bird he had once been. There was something severely unnatural about the way he walked, as if he had no control over where his lower extremities went before they hit the ground. There had been side effects to his possession it seemed. Some part of the Mad King had tried to fight back.

The gaudy robes worn by the late King had been replaced with magenta robes trimmed in black. A great hawk was embroidered on its right side and on the left were a nightingale and swallow set in cages. The cruelty in the imagery was enough to make me cringe.

"Oh you wound me so." His laughter was still raucous, the words spat out in between his bursts of amusement causing him to gasp in air between every few words.

"As if I have not been called far worse through the years. Rest assured this is the last lifetime I will be mocked. Soon, thanks to you three *lovely* ladies, I will have everything I need to take my place in the world as its rightful ruler and God. "

He approached Nyx, caressing her leg in a manner that made me want to vomit as much as it made me want to tear his throat out. Tereus just barely moved out the way quickly enough when she tried to strike him with the other, the pain of the movement showing in her features.

The count of three didn't pass me over and as if summoned, there stood Leola, her sweet green eyes filled with the same crazed look her father wore. Was it possible she was partially possessed as well? Could the son of a God be so powerful? I didn't know, but it no longer mattered.

She was covered from head to toe in blood, as if it had sprayed up at her. Her tongue darted out to lick her lips as she caught my eyes.

She took her wings.

The knife was still in her hand and when she saw me glance at it, Leola just grinned.

"We could have had it all you know. We could have ruled side by side. None would have dared defy us. If you had JUST shifted! I could have taken just a little foxy blood and it'd have been so much easier. None of this would have had to happen."

"You're insane! Do you honestly think he is going to keep you around? He will use you up just as he did your father." The words were practically a hiss as they squeezed out from behind my clenched teeth.

"He is going to make me a God, and then I am going to kill you." She grinned wickedly, her tongue taking another swipe of the blood on her face.

I snarled as I continued to track Tereus. He had begun to play a game of hide and seek, disappearing and reappearing with a snap of his fingers. He moved away from Nyx's body, over to Leola and then back to where he had first appeared. Leola was closest to me, but Tereus was the bigger threat. Why she would want my blood, specifically kitsune blood, was beyond me. There were very few creatures whose magic could be passed that way, and Nemesis' was not one of them. If it had been, Nyx would have had no reason to be changed by Medusa.

His next words caused my hair to stand on edge, while Leola giggled.

"Well, this hardly seems fair. Two against one. Why don't we make it a bit more interesting shall we? I'll even give you a fair chance to fight back. Though I do hope your dear gargoyle knows how to fly..." His laughter spilled out, the sort of sound a child's nightmares might be made of and creepy enough to give adults chills.

With another snap of his fingers the chains holding Nyx suddenly tightened, scaling her up to the high ceiling before a shift of his hand caused them to release completely.

I lunged forward, the transformation happening in the blink of an eye as Nyx plummeted towards the earth. The chains around my wrists and ankles burst free as hands and feet became paws, my body twisting in the air even as it changed shape. My tailbone burst forth, elongating as the heavy fur split into individual lengths, muscle and sinew shifting and growing in milliseconds as the fluffy appendages flared out to catch and cradle Nyx just before she hit the ground.

My body slid through her blood, the impact nothing compared to the way my heart hammered against its cage. A worried whine crept from my muzzle as I nosed my own tails, searching her out. A shaking hand reached out to reassure me she was okay, my tongue darting out to caress her palm, relief rushing over me in waves.

Tereus was overjoyed.

"Oh goodie!!! Who'd have thought we just needed the right gargoyle to drop from the ceiling? Oh that's right, I did! Now you idiot girl - drink it now."

He rambled on but his words faded into the background as I stared at Nyx.

A few moments later I was forced to refocus, jumping in surprise as Leola suddenly screeched in pain. The bowl of Nyx's blood fell from her hands with a clatter, her lips crimson from where she'd drank it. The pain turned into laughter as her body contorted, her muscles growing as the gorgon magic in Nyx's blood affected her.

"It worked! Tereus, you were right. It really worked! Now for some kitsune blood to complete it." Her eyes glowed a faint purple as she lunged forward.

Nyx found her feet before I could, her blood making my footing a bit harder to recover as I caught my breath from the impact. Leola lunged to strike at me while I was still prone across the floor, but Nyx was there to meet her blade. The gargoyle's strength had waned but not enough for Leola to overpower her. With Nyx's blood in her system she was just able to hold her own.

Nyx's hand hardened as the blade came down upon it, the magic within the artifact unable to penetrate the solid flesh. Within a blink of an eye Nyx used her other hand to hit the inside of her elbow, causing Leola's arm to fold in. She pressed the arm against Leola's chest as she moved behind her, still holding it so that Leola could not strike with the weapon.

"Foolish girl. Do you think it'd be so easy? Tereus has sentenced you to death."

Leola laughed, her free arm jerking backwards to elbow Nyx in the stomach. The gargoyle groaned and folded over as the strike hit bruised flesh. Leola turned and followed it with a kick that Nyx barely caught in time. The blows kept coming, pushing Nyx back as she played defense. Then, there was a shift.

Leola paused in stride, confusion contorting her face as she looked down at her legs. Her scream of fear was ear piercing as she began clawing at her flesh. The magic in Nyx's blood moved like venom through her system, changing and then destroying her from the inside out. Just as Medusa's gaze turned those who meant her harm to stone, so too would her blood.

"Tereus! Help!" Her cries were ignored, his haunting laughter rising from the shadows and bouncing back and forth.

"To think, all I needed was a couple of pawns to bark some orders and lead you right back here. Nothing better to feed my magic into than a desperate man and a woman scorned and bitter. A bit power hungry and delusional doesn't hurt either. Oh she was so easy to convince. Drink their blood and become immortal. As if I'd have needed her help if it were that simple." He laughed as she screamed at him, begging for help.

"Idiot girl. Whose magic do you think could create a creature of stone? Only a Gorgon with a gaze that can do the same." Nyx's words were cold, hatred laced in every word. She casually walked around the panicked Leola, whose fingers were now bloody as she tried to stop the stone spreading up her body.

"Medusa does not bestow her gifts on any but those who can handle her venom. Those who would do her no harm. Did you truly believe my magic would be any different?"

There was no hesitation when she used her free hand to grip Leola's head by the hair, lowering her mouth to her neck. The bite was deep, Leola's thrashing limited by her stone lower half. A squelching noise accompanied my gargoyle's snarl as she ripped the side of Leola's throat out.

It happened so fast I could hardly follow, my feet finally gaining traction enough for me to stand just as a fresh spurt of blood splattered across the side of my face. I might have felt sorrow for the life corrupted and lost if not for the shock of it all and the attempts on Nyx's life.

As I watched, Nyx drank deep from the spurting wound until the gurgling that started out as a scream ceased. It was not enough to regrow her wings but it was enough to seal the gaping wounds in her back and give her a rush of adrenaline. It would be enough to keep her going.

"Well, that was abrupt." I muttered as Nyx put a fist through Leola's now stone form, the pieces shattering upon the floor.

Nyx's glare was enough for me to understand she'd have prolonged it if she could have. My beautiful, deadly creature was not cruel or cold by nature, but years of enduring pain and hardships had certainly created a demon that could give exactly what she got.

My words made Tereus pause, his eyes glowing a strange green as his smile split his cheeks and showed more teeth than he ever should have had. The strangeness of it was alarming but somehow fitting.

"On that we agree. Still, she played her part well. After all, if she hadn't threatened Nyx and your precious Amazons, would you have really risked coming here to find me? Together nonetheless! My work was done for me just in time for me to regain my footing in this world. Soon I will reclaim my father's title and make sure the Gods are once again feared here, then the rest of the world."

He snapped his fingers again and disappeared, the sound of footsteps tapping out a clear cadence as a hidden door opened up allowing a batch of his army into the space around us. Their weapons glinted in the dull lighting, the sconces on the wall flickering as the air rushed in with them. Their eyes held the same hint of madness, their sins heavy and so their lives no longer their own, even if their actions were. They would find Nemesis unforgiving. Their weapons had been enchanted; the scent of magic potent, tickling my nose and causing me to sneeze.

"Kill them."

The command came from everywhere, eager calls echoing out from the mouth of every soldier, each obedient of their own will, their twisted smiles savage.

A laugh fell from lips like honey as Nyx placed a hand on my shoulder, with fresh blood she looked significantly better. A smirk tilted her lips as she spoke, her words soft and for me only.

"Shall we dance my love? Careful of the magic on their blades, it smells nasty."

Panting a fox's grin, my tongue lolled out with laughter as Nemesis' magic flowed from within. It was not enough to spill out of my tails and consume my body in darkness, but just enough to make my tongue hungry for the taste of retribution.

Thinking us distracted Tereus's men decided to strike. Larger and so seemingly more formidable, the group tried to use their numbers to their advantage, moving to surround and cut me off from Nyx. Wary of the magic upon their weapons I was forced to stay on the defensive, though that did not stop me from directing their movements as I snapped and whipped my tails at them.

Even as I guarded Nyx's back she revealed why she had never been helpless even before she was a gargoyle. Like a dancer she spun and pivoted, quick enough to avoid their attacks and strong enough to send them stumbling backwards when she managed to land a punch or kick. She was far more agile in the limited space than I as she used my tails as a springboard, leaping back and using the momentum of my push to overpower her enemies. The movements were a reflex, a dance we had done time and time again.

Watching her with my head turned, I baited a particularly bold soldier into thinking I was unaware of his approach. The snap of his arm reverberated across the cavern as I swung my head around and chomped down. Unfortunately I had no time to finish him before the others lunged forward, causing me to have to pivot, half of my tails lashing out and throwing them backwards as a squelch and horrified scream came from the man whose arm I had just ripped off in the process. I proceeded to snap and take limbs where I could until that sickening laughter came back and the sound of an arrow flying caught my ears.

There was no time to call a warning, so I plowed through two of the men in my way, turning and leaping over Nyx, knocking the woman she was fighting to the ground as a glowing green arrow caught my shoulder, skidding painfully off the bone.

The laughter continued as the game changed. The magic in the arrow disrupted my own, nausea turning my stomach as my kitsune form was forced back, my body reverting painfully to its human shape far more quickly than was natural.

The arrow hadn't stuck, so it wouldn't last long but it didn't need to. Tereus' men were savage but they were not dumb and they had known the strategy. The second wave had waited for this moment and now came rushing in.

Winded and momentarily crippled from the forced change, my saving grace was the deadly beauty at my side. Nyx became a whirlwind of movement around me, the clash of metal on metal ringing in my ears as I collected myself up off the ground. A punch landed against my ribs as soon as I turned and caused a yelp of pain and surprise to escape my lips. The action spiked the levels of magic flowing inside my blood, adrenaline releasing with the pain, numbing the sensation and letting me shake off the side effects of my change.

A scoff fell from my lips as the soldier paled when I caught his follow-up fist. They thought me weaker in my human form and I was happy to prove them wrong. The fox could just as easily ride beneath my human skin, her strength my own because we were one and the same. Twisting my arm so that his turned I used the other to block his other hand, bringing my knee into his gut so that he doubled over. Grabbing the shoulder of the arm I still controlled I brought my knee up again, this time forcing his elbow unnaturally skyward, his shout of pain answered with a scream at my back.

The slosh of blood hitting the ground, alongside the noise, meant the stone guardian at my back was doing just fine. Blood would only fuel the beast within us both and so we continued to dance. Several times we pressed back to back, twisting and turning to meet the attacks of the soldiers facing the opposite person. A silent language existed between us as Nyx rolled across my back to kick a female soldier in the face just as I twisted around to bring the sword I had stolen up and through the chest of the man who had tried to follow her. In this fashion our movements flowed, the soldiers dwindling despite their best efforts to attack together. They used good methods and dirty ones, landing more than a few blows successfully, but were ultimately unable to keep track of both of us.

Tereus laughed as I stood in a pool of blood, his loyal servants strewn across the floor of the cavern, the dull light casting an eerie reflection. I could feel Nyx come up behind me, her presence like a warm beacon of comfort. Glancing back at her, I watched as her fangs protruded past her lips in a snarl, her body coated in blood, a bit dripping down her face. I wasn't sure if it was hers or one of her victim's, though it hardly mattered. I felt her strength pulsing in the air as if it were a tangible thing, like the calm ebb of ocean waves upon the shore. The moment might have been morbidly precious if not for the obnoxious laughter coming from Tereus. I couldn't guess what he found so funny about the situation and I didn't get a chance to ask. His laughter was replaced by a maniacal grin and with the flick of his wrist he once again became nothing in my vision.

"Where the fuck did he go?"

My question was answered when an arrow flew past my head, a step back pushing me into Nyx who had ducked sideways to avoid a second and third one that had come at her from the other side of the room. We darted back and forth, trying to get to the source, but every attempt to move away from one another was met with an onslaught of arrows that pushed us back to back again. Too late, I realized exactly what he was doing.

The last one wasn't visible to the naked eye and only materialized upon impact. My mouth opened but the yelp of pain didn't manifest, the sound catching in my throat just as a cut off groan came from Nyx. I couldn't tell whose blood was warming and wetting my back but the arrow that lodged within us had ripped jagged edges on its way in, the shaft barbed and glowing with magic as our blood soaked its end. The same magic that had cut off my shifting, now prevented me from healing my wounds.

Nyx snarled and with a hard push against me, jerked herself free. Immediately I turned to face her even with the arrow still poking out both my front and back. To be fair, the thing was closer to a javelin than an actual arrow, as it had to be to go into us both. Nyx's face hinted at pain, but freely expressed her worry and sorrow. She reached out toward me but was already beginning to turn to stone even as I felt my own energy leaving me, my life spilling quite profusely onto the floor. Manic laughter chattered around us but my eyes never left that bright violet gaze.

"No, no he can't win! We can't lose! I can't lose you."

Tereus snickered from behind.

Anger rolled through me in waves of heartbroken agony as I watched Nyx's skin hardening. My bloody hands caressed her face as tears flowed from both of us, the arrow preventing me from reaching her fully. Consumed by the woman in front of me, I didn't notice Tereus approaching until I felt a boot to my back, the arrow jerked from my body. I fell forward into Nyx's arms with an agonized scream. She caught me just as her arms solidified, her head turning down so that her lips pressed against the top of my head, her voice unable to rise as her lungs hardened.

Our blood poured out together and as I felt myself dying, the pumping of my blood becoming fainter and fainter in my own ears, I heard a whisper.

You are stronger together. You must look within to see.

I wasn't sure where the words came from. Did one of the Goddess' whisper the words or was some haunted memory the source?

As I felt my life slipping away I became acutely aware of my soul, particularly the piece resting within my stone gargoyle. It was enveloped in her own, a barrier firmly in place, cradled with love though it yearned to move, to flow, to *live*. It no longer belonged to me, yet it had not merged with its new owner. It was this that had called to me, a piece of stardust trying to unite with its star. There was still a place for it in my soul, something it would reach for so long as it remained vacant. An idea formed as I once again heard the words.

You are stronger together. You must look within to see.

Reaching into my magic with the last bit of strength I had, I pulled myself further up to Nyx, whose eyes followed mine with a glazed tint. Her neck was unable to move, so I had to angle weirdly so that her lips could meet mine. As we kissed I whispered between them.

"We are one. I surrendered a piece of myself, but the link isn't complete."

She didn't have time to look confused for her face shifted to stone even as my own life dissipated.

CHAPTER TWELVE
WELL, THAT HURT - A LOT

In the silence of what should have been death, I felt her. There was no way to see and yet I knew she was there, her spirit smiled and thrummed with a piece of me. I felt her as she pressed close and although her voice didn't rise from any place in particular, I knew her thoughts. The memories between us had always been random or triggered by an event, but as the images were pulled from my mind, I knew this one had been selected very carefully.

I was nervous. Every bit of me shook with anxiety, the soft vibration uncontainable. As I looked down at my hands I cursed. Why was I always the source of embarrassment for myself? For all I tried to be tough, I knew I was weak when it came to her.

Every glance between us turned my legs into mush. I'd almost walked into a tree two days ago because I was so distracted by the way her eyes lit up when she laughed. The only thing that stood between us was my fear that she did not feel the same. She always seemed so calm and collected, surely I did not have the same effect on her as she did me. Still, I had to try.

Medusa answered the door when I knocked, a coy smirk turning her lips as she lifted a finger to her lips in a quiet 'shhh'. I smiled back and nodded, stepping around the corner of the house to wait. Nemesis did not quite approve of Nyx and I spending so much time together. Medusa tried to orchestrate it any chance she got.

A few minutes later, my trembling grew worse as I heard her soft steps coming towards me. As soon as she turned the corner and spotted me her face lit up. Mine must have done the same, for there seemed to be a heated glow between us.

"You came!" She muttered, voice soft so as not to draw any attention to us as we stood in the shadows of her hut.

"Of course I did. I'll always come when you call for me Nyx."

Her pale cheeks grew pink, eyelashes fluttering as she stepped forward and grabbed my hands.

"You're shaking!" She sounded surprised, but her face looked amused.

"Just chilly." I muttered, wincing at the fib.

"You are a horrible liar." Her lips pulled into a smile and my heart leapt wildly within my chest.

"You said you wanted to tell me something?" The nerves were getting to be too much and the longer I stood there the more I was tempted to do something stupid.

"Yes, but you have to close your eyes." She giggled lightly, the tone mischievous.

"Ugh. Okay, but if you hit me with something just remember your moms will know it was you. No one else gets close enough to do the job."

"Oh shush I'm not going to hit you." Her words didn't reassure me, but I closed my eyes all the same, fingers tugging at my shirt.

The soft crunch of her feet stepping across the earth made my hair stand on edge. The smell of cinnamon wafted in the air and intoxicated me with her scent. The soft shuffle of her sleeves against her skirt let me track her pace, the sound getting closer and closer. When she stopped I could feel her body heat, mere inches from my flesh. She was taller, so her warm breath tickled my forehead, the moisture clinging to my skin as if it were my own sweat.

"What are you-" My words were cut off by a finger upon my lips. She traced them gently, my lips parted slightly in mid-speech. My body was stiff, every muscle in my body burning to move, but my mind and body had gone numb, ignoring the twitches of anticipation.

Her finger disappeared but something softer took its place. Confused, I opened my eyes, gazing directly into hers. Surprise made me gasp but when she made to move away my body finally woke up and gave chase. Our lips pressed together once more, questioning at first, then more sure. I closed my eyes so that I could devour the sensation, her hand cupping my jaw and drawing me in deeper. I lost track of time, consumed in the wet softness of her lips and the gentle pressure against my face.

When she pulled back, I asked, breathless. "What was that?"

"What I needed to tell you."

I stared up at her, my face numb and my heart pumping so fast I felt light headed.

"I'm not complaining, but you could have just said you liked me." My words were a whispered attempt at snark, my amusement outweighed by pure awe.

"Sure, but it's more than that, isn't it? More than words can really cover." She shyly looked down at her feet, the first time I'd ever seen the young woman look anything close to demure.

"You're right. It's way more than that." I swallowed my fear and reached up on my tiptoes to bridge the gap between us once more. This time our kiss was less soft and no longer questioning. We sought a way to explain the connection we had through that kiss and every single one that followed.

"You have always had a piece of my soul Lykos. From the very first time we kissed." Nyx's voice echoed around me.

That is when I felt it inside me.

At first it was a small spark of warmth swallowed by the shadows which were my own soul, but then it grew into a bright light that left my essence feeling full and warm. The light faded to something more subtle and then everything became clear and complete. That nagging magical pull had not been the piece of my soul in her as I thought. Instead, it was the opposite; the piece of her own soul calling out, lost within mine, but leading me always back to her.

How long had I cradled this gift? When had it been placed there? Surely not when my own had been struck into her chest. Perhaps it had been a more subtle thing, accumulating from shared kisses, shattered hearts, and mourned lives. I could not account for when she slipped little pieces of her soul into my own. The fragments accumulated quietly and waited for my own to welcome it home. As soon as I accepted it was there, it began to settle, filling a hole I'd hallowed out for it. It had taken us dying together for me to feel it, for the prophecy to be complete.

The sensation was all consuming as her magic twisted and pulled until it had intertwined within my own. The warm light that was her sliver of soul then burrowed deep to the center of my core, as if it were its own living creature seeking protection. As soon as it settled an explosion of color burst out in front of me. When it faded I could see her, just as she had looked when we first committed our hearts and souls to one another. Her smile was sweet, innocent, and full of love for me. Our souls and their detached pieces began to hum loudly, much like a bee in the ear, until finally the vibrations synchronized and became a single smooth note.

The sensation of our lips touching flowed over me as life rushed through my body and pulled my soul back down into it.

Tereus's angry voice bellowed around me, echoing off the high cavern walls, but it was muffled by a thick barrier of smoke-like magic. Nemesis' shadow magic seeped out from us both, weaving together to form a barrier of protection.

My lips were still pressed against her own as Nyx became flesh again, her eyes hungry. Lightning danced across my lips as we parted, her soft smile turning into a wicked grin that seemed so out of place and yet perfect on her. The warmth that spread through my body was more than just the spark of her soul and the life rushing back into it.

"Well, that was new. Was it as good for you as it was for me?"

Her voice was a melody I could listen to forever, the notes carrying a mischievous lilt. No doubt I would hear about how oblivious I was later. That there would be a later was all that mattered in this moment. Smiling my own foxy grin I nodded as I motioned towards my chest.

"Made my heart skip a few beats, that's for sure."

The wounds at our hearts lay gaped open, the blood still fresh and shimmering but no longer flowing. Streams of shadow weaved between the wounds, consuming us. The night sky became tangible, channeled by magic and sprinkled with stardust that shimmered with raw intent. The weaving threads flowed from our spilled blood, entwining it, and then siphoning it back through us. Kitsune and Gargoyle magic melded into one.

As the magic flowed into me through the now healing wound, my shift began to take over.

My body contorted, reshaping into the familiar shape of a kitsune, but this time was different. Nyx's arms wrapped around my body as I began to shift, her body melding into my own as her own magic joined mine. She slipped into a gap created as my ribs grew and expanded, our magic stitching us together just as our souls had already done. My red fur sprouted then melted off my skin, pooling at my feet and hardening into obsidian claws. The once luxurious coat was now gone, leaving behind a skin of impenetrable stone.

My tails arched above me, thrashing out at the shadows until they had threaded together into thin braids that then twisted to form a deadly chain. Nyx's wings broke free of what was now our back, and grew to the point they sliced through the smokey barrier, causing it to slip away.

My vision was sharper, the darkest crevices now as clear as if a lantern shone upon them. My hearing was tuned in more clearly, the sound vibrations practically tangible now. The hard cast of my skin felt no heavier than a sheep skin shirt, so although I knew myself to be tougher by mere glance, I felt just as agile as before. The wings were new, moving of their own accord it seemed, much like my tails tended to do. I tried to ignore them for the moment, now was no time to figure out their nuances.

Tereus' curses were now louder and almost visible as his words echoed off the walls. His body blinked in and out of view, but my improved hearing let me track even the lightest of footsteps. His scrambling took him back towards the rear opening in the cavern. His confusion and anger mixed with desperation as he shouted.

"No! This is wrong I killed you both at the same time with one strike! Your soul should be broken! This... THIS isn't what was supposed to happen!"

Desperate to turn the tides he began slinging magicked arrows, swords and even a few rocks at the hybrid form we now occupied. Each time they hit they simply skidded off to the side, Nyx's stone flesh impenetrable.

Furless lips curled into a snarl as I spoke instead of growling. The intent was mine but the voice I used was Nyx's.

"You know, it's almost as if someone lied to you in order to get you to do their bidding. Tell me Tereus, who gave you the prophecy? Who said it was about you?"

He continued to send things flying at us and with each step I became even more hungry for his soul. This twisted and cruel man, who had harmed even the ones he had claimed to love, needed to die.

I leapt forth, sharp stone teeth slicing through the soft flesh of his shoulder as he turned to flee. His yelp of pain preceded an abrupt face plant into the earth, gravity aiding in the slicing of his muscle.

"Not so fast, we aren't done with you."

He magicked himself away just in time for my teeth to miss his neck a second time, dust making me sneeze as I inhaled earth. Frustrated, my growl resonated in my chest. Searching the area I finally laid eyes on him, further up the trail. He had nowhere to go and in his flustered state he'd only transported himself a few feet away.

"Your reign of terror ends here, with us, Tereus. Nemesis will make sure you suffer." Nyx's voice was a warm tremble in my throat, the words hers alone.

"What is suffering but fuel for power? I WILL take my father's throne, and when I do you will be sorry. Every last one of you. This body may die, but I am the Son of Aries. I will not give up so easily." He glared as he spoke, pulling himself up from the earth with his right arm - his left dangled loosely, the tendons and muscles shredded.

With nowhere to run as we stood on a ledge, a surge of satisfaction filled me as I watched him search for a way out. There was only one. He glanced behind him for only a moment, grinned at us, then turned and leapt from the cliff.

I leapt towards him, but my jaws snapped shut a few inches from his body, his cackling laugh mocking me as he fell.

Tereus' body crashed into the rocks below with a sickening splat. His soul leapt forth, once again in the shape of the hawk he'd been changed to long ago. The disembodied creature flew quickly towards the sky, then disappeared.

"Don't waste your time. He won't get far without a mortal body." A familiar disembodied voice made our ears flit back towards the cavern.

The air shifted as a shadow crawled across the ground, rising to take the vague shape of a woman whose face was lit with pride. The bowl of blood appeared in her hands and as she drank the woman slowly became more solid. Nemesis stood, shimmering as her shadows shifted back to the earth, her body just clear as we were.

Her facial features showed how much Nyx favored her, but her eyes were almost silver in hue, their blue tint faint. Her raven locks were shorter than my gargoyle's and her wings were not leathery but feathered. I could not remember a time I had seen them and from the shock that filtered through me, I assumed Nyx was equally at a loss.

Nemesis approached, her hand reaching out to caress our muzzle, and although I felt Nyx jerk back, I lowered our head. A mother's love engulfed us as the Goddess who had birthed Nyx and pulled my soul from the cosmos placed a kiss against the smooth stony flesh of our forehead. Pride and warmth seared through the anger and confusion of what had just happened, calming the beast within.

The sensation that followed was a strange one. Our flesh pulled apart, but there was no void left where she had been, no sensation at all that I had ever been more than I ever was. The change was a bit less painful, my bones contorting back to their usual shapes and sizes until I stood with Nyx pressed against my chest once again, her arms around me, her head curled over my shoulder. A shiver ran through my body as we parted, the cool air creating goosebumps across my blood splattered skin. Nyx was no better off, the hue of her flesh almost purple with the dried blood covering her.

Stepping back only enough to face each other, Nyx arched her eyebrow as she looked me up and down. Then, with a completely blank face, said "I think we've officially taken the sexy out of 'I wanna be inside you'."

All the tension that had built up and threatened to explode over the last few days fell apart as I burst out laughing. The chuckles started out easy then became loud and overbearing as I wheezed and held my stomach. All the emotions poured out until I cried from laughing so hard.

Nyx was not unaffected, her own humor-filled tears streaming as we finally recovered enough to face the Goddess who waited patiently for us to collect ourselves. Once we had, Nemesis spoke.

"My darlings, I am sorry. I wish it could have been easier, but we could not defy our laws. We could not directly interfere...Medusa and I, we did all we could...I'm just sorry it took us so long to find a way."

Nyx motioned towards her mother, or rather her mother's wings.

"How can we see you so clearly?"

"True immortality comes with perks, my darlings. You had to merge to complete the transformation. Now, both of you can see through the veil of different planes - and cross them."

"Wow...It's...Is it really over?" Nyx's words were filled with relief and awe, but also uncertainty.

"Yes daughter, it's over. Death can no longer part you."

Nyx squeezed my hand, her smile contagious even as tears accompanied it. Pulling her close I wrapped my arms tight around her as I felt the relief coming off her in waves. I surprised myself as I too sighed, tension I didn't know I'd held, releasing. My own mortality had never really been an issue for myself, though I had strived not to die. Until I had found Nyx, there was nothing truly to lose in death, no fear beyond not knowing what had lay ahead. That was over. I knew what I had lost and could leave behind.

Now, there was nothing to do but live. No more endless cycle of death and rebirth, of forgetting and remembering. We had broken the cycle for good, though what had happened when we died was still more than I could comprehend fully. The relief and adrenaline made me want to just fall apart right there, my body unable to contain it all.

"My love. It's over, no more leaving or forgetting."

I whispered the words into her ear, kissing her face all over until finally she could take it no more and once again there was laughter. It was that light innocent laughter of our first life together, when she wasn't a gargoyle and I wasn't a catalyst- we were just two women in love.

Somewhere amongst it all Nemesis had politely disappeared. I didn't question it. She would surely be back at some point to explain how we would be able to cross the planes and all that came with immortality. In the meantime, this moment was ours and ours alone. Exhausted, we stood on the cliff and held each other, our lips brushing as the stars shone down upon us.

"What should we do now?" I whispered as I gazed into her eyes.

"I've got a few ideas and they all involve a bed." She grinned sideways at me.

I laughed even as I agreed, our bodies pressing tight as I reached up and locked our lips together once again.

The moon glowed bright and full, its silver light glistening across the woods below, the battered body of Tereus' puppet forgotten. Our love had stretched over lifespans and drawn us together time and time again. Now, at long last, there would be no more goodbyes. No more forgetting. We could deal with everything else in the morning.

EPILOGUE
MAKING NEW FRIENDS

There was an eerie silence to the forest as all the birds and small creatures vacated the area. Their absence left only the sway of a slight breeze to ruffle the branches, but even that was scarcely enough to kill the uneasy feeling of apprehension one might be consumed with. The sun was rising but its light had not yet become more than an obscure glow of soft light below the horizon that gave no apparent shape to the shadows far below the tree line.

One might walk a mile and feel as if they had only traversed a foot for the way everything seemed the same. That was how it remained until, at last, the soft trickle of the creek caught the ear, calming nerves on edge. As the mist began to rise the moon's waning light revealed a grotesque scene spilled out beneath the thin canopies cast with a haunting silver sheen. The scent of death clung as closely as the mist, yet I walked through it unhindered by either.

As the creek fell away behind, the earth became littered with large puddles of thick liquid. An intriguing shimmer caught the surface and made the leaves and scattered debris glint unnaturally. The scent was enough to confirm it was not water, if the way it shimmered did not. The clearing was once an ideal picnic or camping area but now bodies lay twisted and thrown about.

The first bloody scene was that of entrails spilling out a set of slashes set upon the front of a man whose body had gotten hung up on a low lying branch. The blood dripped slowly to the earth below in a melodic cadence. Another man's skull was cracked open, the brain missing a savage chunk from impact upon the boulder it had been smacked against. The loose bits slid off the edge and lay in the hand which had splayed there.

Here and there more bodies littered the forest floor, faces wide eyed with horror or shut from a slower end. Many had their throats torn out, their voices removed before death could come for them. Others lay crumpled in ways that suggested their anatomy no longer kept its previous structure, death coming from the irregular turn of their heads or the deep wounds along important arteries. The latter was evident from the way the earth was stained with coagulated puddles of life. The savagery was not withheld from the few women in the group, though it did seem that there had been a bit of mercy in the rather macabre way they had been set up, as if to be witness to the devastation even in death.

A disgusted sneer twisted my face only when one of my bare feet slid on the soft earth and ended up in a small pool of blood, the coagulating substance creeping up grossly between my toes. A man whose legs were twisted weirdly beneath him continued to try to crawl forward, his choking words a warning as I approached, ignoring the horror surrounding me.

"R-run girl! The beast is here!" Oh how he remained oblivious, not knowing that his fate had been sealed weeks ago. Lifting a finger to my lips I offered a soft 'shhh'. There was much to be preferred in silence compared to the choking cries of guilty men reaping the rewards of their darkest sins.

He finally collapsed forward, his efforts wasted as his body failed him. The sound of the earth squishing beneath heavy feet brought my gaze back upright.

I could feel the vibrations in the air, could see what no others would; the souls of the dead lingered, awaiting transport. Awaiting me. There was no reason to rush, they could no longer escape their fates. Work could wait.

Forever there would be a reason for my feet to touch this earth, and never was that reason the task which had long ago been set into motion. Instead it was the creature to whom I had partnered. The love of my very expansive life.

The great beast strode forward, shadows swirling about its body to hide its true form. The sputtering man's skull held no resistance against the beast's large paw, the sound enough to make most people squirm, but I had seen far worse in my seemingly endless lifetime.

A grin pulled at my lips, my own sharpened canines a mirror of the larger set that settled between the now gaped jowls of a beast covered in blood and gore.

"We should get you washed up my lovely Vixen, don't want these new Gods thinking we are heathens."

The beautiful, blood splattered fox lowered her head to nuzzle my chest. The smell of blood was strong and metallic, but it could do nothing to shroud the distinct woody scent of my love. The foxy chirrups she made as I hugged her close made me giggle, a smile pulling at my lips as I led her away from the bloody mess.

The souls were our only witnesses and now, having lost their lives, they stood oblivious to the world. They were shamed into silence, the reality of their own losses and fortunes all-consuming so that they paid no heed to the world around them. They would remain anchored to the earth by their bodies until I severed the bonds and transported them to their afterlife.

For now, they would have to wait.

The river ran red as the water washed away the grime and gross debris. As Lykos shook off the excess I shielded myself from the cold drops with my wings. The shadows had slipped back to the earth, cast in normal fashion at her feet and leaving her coat an array of reds and oranges, contrasting sharply against cerulean blue eyes.

A hand sprouted forth from a paw as the magic in her shifted, her naked human form slowly reappearing. Streaks of blood remained, so I soothed soap along the stains, massaging muscles and scrubbing away the dirt. When finally the waters were clear, I faced my love and leaned in close, no longer able to resist.

The moment our lips met, the world dissolved. The softness of her lips entrapped me as the sweetness of her tongue crept in and devoured me. A soft plea for more was all it took for her to grant me all that I desired.

When the map of our bodies was once again well-worn and traced over, the sun was beginning to peak above the tree lines. It was time to go.

The bright wash of light cast a skewed perspective on the scene we returned to. Where the moonlight had created a certain degree of serenity to the massacre, the sun's harsh gaze made the scene chaotic and blinding, and soon the heat would make the smell insufferable.

The shadows which had shielded Lykos' true colors returned, but this time they stretched out and revealed a tear in the plane. The path ahead was clear. Hand in hand we walked through the ripple of magic, the souls of the damned humans trailing behind. They had been severed from their mortal forms, the threads of life gathered and held in my free hand like leashes.

It was still a strange sensation, gathering souls and taking them to the other side. This trip however, was unique. These people, whoever they had been, had pissed off a Goddess in the worst of ways. Enough so that they were our ticket to some vital information, stealing them from Odin's grasp and delivering them to her.

A thick grove of apples appeared, their hues varying as we traveled to their core. Lykos said very little, her ears pinned in annoyance. Understandably so. We had been awoken to a whole new world of existence and she was not a fan of change. The Greek Gods remained in Olympus, but their influence was gone. The Norse Gods were now in charge and hardly a fan of their predecessor's offspring. We had been anything but warmly welcomed. Tereus was certainly to blame for that, his newest reputation was just as bad as his previous, only this time he had active allies just as cruel as he was.

The sweet smell of apples fermenting upon the earth tickled my nose and tempted my stomach. Our midnight romp had made me quite ravenous, but I didn't dare poach even an apple on this Goddess' land.

As we approached the center, Freya walked out from behind her most prized tree. The lumbering beast was heavy with fruit, none of which seemed to have a flaw upon it. As I glanced around, none had fallen to the earth either.

Strange.

Almost as strange as the massive boar which walked like a puppy at Freya's heel.

"It's done. Here are the souls of those who stole from your people."

Lykos' tone left much to be desired, but considering our circumstances it could surely be forgiven.

"Hmm, I see you're the business part of the duo huh?" She spoke to Lykos then met my gaze with a coy smirk, her eyes roaming my body in a way that made my skin twitch and Lykos growl.

"You can imagine our tempers are not the best, considering how we were woken up and the news delivered to us shortly thereafter." Silently I prayed my words would garner enough sympathy for the Goddess to not take offense from any further brusqueness on Lykos' part. The fox didn't even show an ounce of humility as her lips twitched and the growl remained, her hand clenching my own as she barely tried to hold her temper.

"I suppose I'd act no better, to be fair. Though, I am impressed, I didn't expect such a quick turn around." She held out her hand as I offered up the threads of life, a look of disgust flickering across her face for a moment as she glanced past me. Her sneer could curdle dairy.

"I have a very special reward for these brutes, don't I Brutus?" The boar grunted in response.

"How do we find Loki?" Lykos' annoyance was etched into every syllable. A quick elbow to her ribs made her grunt and glare, but she seemed to get the message.

"Please." She added.

Freya seemed amused, her smile hard to read but seeming genuine enough.

"You'll need the Valkyrie's hound. Though I can't guarantee she's going to be eager to help you, of all people."

"What do you mean? Why wouldn't she?" The tone she'd used made my brow arch in question.

"Oh, you will see. Find the hound's handler, she can sway the hound and the hound can find anything you desire."

"How do we find her handler?" Lykos sighed, tired and grumpy.

"Just look for the biggest and bloodiest battle happening on Earth. Trust me, you will know her when you see her, she's got a literal mean streak." With that Freya laughed as if she had made a joke, waved and then her, the boar, and the souls disappeared, leaving us standing quietly in the orchard.

"This is going to be one hell of a headache." My words made Lykos smirk even as she nodded agreement.

"Just what we needed, a whole new set of powerful assholes and a brand new world to navigate." Lykos pressed her hands to her temples, imagining the impending headache, no doubt.

"I think we may have overslept my love." I laughed even as I reached out to brush a stray strand of hair away from

Lykos' face. Her eyes lit up at the affection, her cheek pressing into my hand as it lingered.

"You may be right, but at least we woke up together this time." She kissed the palm of my hand gently.

Her words struck a chord in my soul and made my eyes begin to water as I was overwhelmed with feeling. It was the first time I'd awoken to a Lykos who remembered me, and it was the most amazing feeling in the world.

Whatever this new world and new Gods threw at us, we'd face it together.

AUTHORS NOTE

Dear reader,

As a kid I dreamed of publishing a book but as an adult I thought there was no way I'd ever get to this point. It took two years of self-discipline and a lot of advice and encouragement from my amazing best friend, but here we are! This has truly been a dream come true.

Thank you so much for taking a chance on Catalyst! If you enjoyed my book, please take some time to leave a review. Reviews are one of the best ways to support authors and encourage them to keep writing!.

I have always loved writing and it means the world to be able to share that with others! Thank you so much for being a part of the journey. I hope you enjoyed this world and the characters within as much as I loved bringing them to life.

L. A. Rae

ABOUT THE AUTHOR

L. A. Rae's love of reading and writing started young, encouraged by her mother who has supported her every step of the way. When her head isn't in the clouds dreaming about future stories, she's most often found gardening, horseback riding, and making weird noises at her dog. She lives with an endless supply of dog glitter generously donated by her pack of corgis.

www.ingramcontent.com/pod-product-compliance
Lightning Source LLC
Chambersburg PA
CBHW061225310726
48971CB00007B/1948